TENTH MAN DOWN

The Border Reiver's Philosophy

I would have none think that I call them thieves

The freebooter ventures both life and limb,
Good wife, and bairn, and every other thing;
He must do so, or else must starve and die,
For all his livelihood comes of the enemie.

TENTH MAN DOWN

by

Chris Ryan

C

Century · London

First published by Century in 1999

First published in the United Kingdom in 1999 by
Century, 20 Vauxhall Bridge Road, London SW1V 2SA

Random House Australia (Pty) Limited
20 Alfred Street, Milsons Point, Sydney
New South Wales 2061, Australia

Random House New Zealand Limited
18 Poland Road, Glenfield
Auckland 10, New Zealand

Random House South Africa (Pty) Limited
Endulini, 11a Jubilee Road, Parktown 2193, South Africa

Random House UK Limited Reg. No. 954009

A CIP catalogue record for this book
is available from the British Library.

Papers used by Random House UK Limited are natural, recyclable products made from wood grown in sustainable forests. The manufacturing processes conform to the environmental regulations of the country of origin.

ISBN 0 7126 8081 0

Typeset by SX Composing DTP, Rayleigh, Essex
Printed in Great Britain by
Mackays of Chatham plc, Chatham, Kent

Brian

Able man, somewhat unruly, and very ill to tame.

By the same author
The One That Got Away

Novels
Stand By, Stand By
Zero Option
The Kremlin Device

ACKNOWLEDGEMENTS

I wish to give special thanks to all my family and friends for their patience and understanding. To my agent, Barbara Levy; also to Mark Booth, Liz Rowlinson, Katie White and Rachael Healey and all the team at Century.

GLOSSARY

Basha	Sleeping shelter
Bergen	Rucksack
BG	Bodyguard (noun or verb)
Blue-on-blue	Accidental strike on own forces
Bwangi	Hello
Casevac	Casualty evacuation
Choka	Piss off
Comms	Communications
CTR	Close target reconnaissance
DA	Defence attaché
DOP	Drop-off point
DPMs	Disruptive pattern material camouflage garments
DZ	Drop zone
ERV	Emergency rendezvous
ETA	Estimated time of arrival
Exvil	Exfiltration
Fiti	Sorcerer
Go-away bird	Grey lourie
GPS	Global positioning system, navigation aid
Gympi	General-purpose machine gun
Head-shed	Headquarters
ID	Identity, identify
Ima!	Stop!
Incoming	Incoming fire
Juju	Spell cast by witch doctor
Kremlin	SAS headquarters
LUP	Lying-up point
LZ	Landing zone
Magellan	Brand-name of GPS
MRE	Meals ready to eat
NBC	Nuclear, biological and chemical

ND	Negligent (accidental) discharge of weapon
Nshima	Maize meal
OP	Observation point
Pinkie	110 Land Rover adapted for SAS
PNGs	Passive night goggles
QRF	Quick-reaction force
RTU	Return to unit
Rupert	Officer
Satcom	Satellite telephone system
SEAL	Sea, Air and Land – American special forces unit
Shamouli	Parachute flare
Shreddies	Army-issue underpants
Sin'ganga	Witch doctor
SOP	Standard operating procedure
Stag	Sentry duty
U/S	Unserviceable
Zikomo	Thank you
319	VHF radio

WEAPONS

203	Combination 5.56 calibre automatic rifle (top barrel) and 40 mm grenade launcher below
.50	Heavy machine gun
AK47	Russian-made 7.62 calibre automatic rifle
Colt .45	American automatic pistol
Galil	Israeli-made 7.62 automatic rifle
Milan post	Vehicle-mounted missile launcher
RPG7	Russian-made rocket launcher

ONE

Typical Welsh autumn weather. The rain was just heavy enough to be annoying. If I kept the wipers going, even intermittently, they created smears, and whenever I switched them off, the windscreen soon became thickly beaded with water. Driving in those conditions was a pain. Tim was fidgeting about, twisting in his seat, punching the buttons on the stereo. Instead of looking out of the window and taking an interest in the mountains, he kept fiddling with the sound system, trying to get track five on his new Robbie Williams CD. There was something wrong with the player, which kept stalling, but he wouldn't let it alone, so we got endless jumping of tracks and burst after burst of disjointed screeching.

But although his restlessness was distracting, I wasn't letting it annoy me, because I knew it sprang from nerves. We hadn't met for nearly six months, and he wasn't at ease with me, any more than I was with him. Now I had the chance, I really wanted to get through to him, and I knew that if I talked too much I'd only make matters worse. So I told myself to stay cool, and concentrated on the road, now and then looking down sideways at his close-cropped blond head.

Because I saw him only after long intervals, whenever we did get together I was always surprised at how he'd changed. Now that he'd just turned ten, I realised how much of his mother he had in his looks: the same blue eyes and clean profile, with forehead, nose and jaw all straight and in good proportion. His hands and fingers were mine in miniature; they'd grown a lot, and looked pretty useful.

What was I doing, driving out into the Brecon Beacons with

some sandwiches I'd got from Marks & Sparks, which I aimed to eat on the summit of Pen-y-Fan, with this son I hardly knew? Even I wasn't sure. What I did know was that I was seriously ill. I knew that after this school holiday I might never see Tim again. But did I really imagine that, in one afternoon, I could influence the rest of his life? Did I really hope that he'd follow my example and go for an army career? I don't think so. Part of me wanted him to find an easier way of making a living. Perhaps he should try to become a doctor? A lawyer? A teacher? I couldn't wish him a road as hard as the one I'd travelled myself.

Looking back, I realise those vague ideas were at the back of my mind. At that moment, while I was still capable of climbing the hills, all I wanted was that Tim should see the country in which my SAS career had begun. In particular I wanted to introduce him to Pen-y-Fan, the mountain whose silhouette is supposed to be graven on every Special Forces man's heart. Whatever profession he might take up in the end, I wanted him to become an open-air person. I wanted to pass on to him my feeling for the hills. I wanted him to get some idea of what my service career had meant to me.

Above all, I wanted him to know what had happened in Kamanga. I suppose I was trying to justify my conduct there – but only a shrink could have explained why I wanted to pour everything out to a ten-year-old.

After a while I couldn't stand the racket from the stereo any longer, and said, 'Eh, give over with that. The player's messed up. And anyway, we're nearly there.'

Obediently Tim hit the off button and turned to look out of the window. I didn't sense any hostility in him: as I say, he was just covering his shyness until he got the measure of me. Back in my flat we'd already had stilted conversations about his school and his teachers. English was his best subject, he said: he liked writing, and had just done an essay on family life. I didn't fancy asking exactly what he'd said. An easier area was football: he was obviously showing promise as a striker, and as a fan he'd transferred his affections from Chelsea to Arsenal. He was tough on the subject of football hooligans, who he thought were the pits. We'd also had a run-down on his home computer, compared notes about the Internet and discussed digital TV, but we'd exhausted every subject quite quickly.

Now, suddenly, he turned his attention to our surroundings, and said indignantly, 'Hey, Dad, it's raining out there. We're not going to walk in this, are we? And boy, are these hills steep!'

I laughed, and said, 'You wait till we're on them! They'll be steeper than the ones at home.'

'Oh, sure!'

His voice had a Northern Irish twang all right, but what else could I expect? For six years now, since Kath's death, he'd lived with her parents in the well-to-do eastern suburbs of Belfast. His school was there, his mates were there. Northern Ireland was his environment.

'Pity about the cloud,' I said. 'But it's lifting. I think we're going to be lucky.'

A few minutes later we came down to the Storey Arms, once a pub, now an adventure centre, and pulled up in the car park opposite. I opened the back of the car, and we started to sort out our gear. Once we were in the open, the rain didn't seem so bad. It was only drizzle, really.

On that dull morning there were only three other vehicles on the hard standing, one of them a zebra-striped minibus with a party of hikers, girls and boys, disembarking from it. Tim must have seen me staring at it, because he said, 'What's the matter, Dad?'

'It's just those black and white stripes. They reminded me of something. When we get to the top, I'll tell you.' And to deflect his curiosity, I asked, 'Boots okay?'

'Sure and all.' He looked down at his new green-and-grey Goretex ankle-length trainers and turned his feet in and out to show them off.

'We're all set, then.' I locked the car and pocketed the key. 'Let's go.'

My small day-sack contained a minimum of kit: our picnic lunch, a water bottle, two waterproofs and a sweater for each of us, plus a spare pair of socks for Tim. The whole thing can't have weighed more than ten pounds, yet as soon as we started up the steep track alongside the wood, it began to feel full of lead. Jesus! I thought. Oh for the days when I used to *run* up here with a load of bricks in my Bergen.

For a while Tim didn't notice that I was labouring. He was excited by the climb and skipped on ahead. I liked the athletic way he moved, and laughed to myself when he turned round to shout and tell me to hurry up. But soon I was sweating and panting too much to see the funny side of anything, and I had to call a halt.

'Take it easy,' I called, sitting against a bank. 'Let's be like the tortoise, slow but sure.'

'Dad,' said Tim, looking up at me, 'how old are you?'

'Ninety-nine.' I pretended to be offended. 'And mind your own business.' Then I laughed, and said, 'No – I'm nearly forty.'

'That's not very old.'

'Old enough. Four times what you are.'

Still he was looking at me. 'But you look nearly as old as Gramp. Your hair's going grey.'

'Thanks! That's because I've had a hard life. Wait till we get a bit higher, and I'll tell you a few things about it.'

'Why's your face so yellow?'

'Must be the African sun.'

So began a strange but rewarding climb. Somehow I'd gained Tim's full attention and got him hanging on my words. So, every time we slowly climbed a few hundred feet, I'd call a halt and tell another story about SAS operations – in Libya, Colombia, the Gulf, Ulster. Without planning it, I found I was working backwards through my career, and when we reached the obelisk, about halfway to the summit, I'd got to the point of explaining about SAS selection courses, and how I'd been over this very route hundreds of times, first training for my own selection, then training others.

We sat down by the obelisk, which is a memorial to Tommy Jones, a boy who got lost in the mist trying to cross the hill from one farm to another, and never reached home.

'It was twenty-nine days before anyone knew what had

become of him,' I said. 'Then they found him curled up in this hollow, where the pillar is now.'

'Was he asleep?'

'No, no. He was dead. He'd died of exposure that first night. That's why you mustn't ever go into the hills without a compass.'

Tim listened intently as I told the story. Then, looking round, he asked, 'Why aren't there any trees up here?'

'It's too high, and too cold. The higher you go, the colder it gets. Also, there's hardly any soil.' I scuffed at the grass with the toe of my boot and showed him that rock lay just beneath the roots. Then on an impulse I asked, 'D'you remember your mum?'

He shook his head. 'Not really. Gran's got a picture of her, that's all.' After a pause, he said, 'Dad – why did she die?'

'I know *how* she died. She was killed by a terrorist bomb, out shopping in Belfast, in the city centre. But as to why – that's a difficult question.'

'Was it because you were in the army?'

'No, no. They wouldn't have known your mum was married to a soldier. She wasn't a target. The bomb went off prematurely. It was an own-goal. The bomber was killed, along with five innocent civilians.'

'Was it because we're Prots, then?'

'It was a bit to do with religion, yes. I'm afraid there's always going to be some people who hate other people, just because of what they believe in. The bomber was a Catholic, but he wasn't targeting your mother specially.'

To change the subject I waved around us, and said, 'You might not believe it, but I know every rock, every bend on this path. Every yard of it holds a memory for me. Right here, by this big slab, a guy sat on an adder and got bitten in the backside. Over there, a fellow called Richard came off his quad bike and broke his leg. Now, look at that!'

Across a valley a group of eight men had appeared, walking hard in single file up a ridge, silhouetted against the cloud. They were wearing DPMs, and from their fast pace and strained attitude – leaning forward to take the weight of their Bergens –

I could tell they were under pressure, hurrying to reach an RV inside the time limit.

'Just what I was telling you,' I said. 'Those guys are training for selection.'

'Where are they going?'

'They've probably got to get round a set course in a given time, calling at check-points as they go.'

The sight almost made me feel young again. Yet no amount of fresh air and fine scenery could banish the knowledge that I was in lousy shape – and not just short of breath, but afflicted by a deep, leaden heaviness all over my body, and a feeling that I wanted to throw up, even though there was nothing to get rid of. Already I'd twice thought I was going to have to call off our ascent, but somehow, each time, I'd got going again.

I looked down at Tim and saw he was thinking. I couldn't help comparing him with my own ten-year-old self. At his age I was constantly fighting to defend myself against school bullies. Most days they'd pick on someone, and provoke him so the fight took place on the way out of school, where all the other kids were lined up to watch. Tim never mentioned fights; besides Kath's looks, he'd evidently inherited her calm temperament, and that pleased me.

Presently, he asked, 'Dad – it's wrong to kill people, isn't it?'

'In peacetime, yes. But in war it's different. You sometimes have to kill the bad guys, to stop them killing you.'

'But people are still getting killed at home. There isn't a war on now.'

'Well, in a way there is. There was then, anyway.'

I felt his next question coming.

'How many people have you killed, Dad?'

'Not many at all.'

'How many, though?'

'I'd have to make a count. I've never tried to work it out. Often in a battle, if one of the enemy gets dropped, you can't tell who's done it. Guys go down, but there's so much noise and confusion you don't know where the bullets have come from. You haven't got time to worry. All you know is, it's going to be them or you. Let's go on a bit while I think.'

Still Tim was staring at me curiously. Then he asked, 'Are you a colonel, or what?'

'A colonel!' I laughed. 'Heavens no. A colonel's a rupert.'

'What's a rupert?'

'An officer. I'm a *warrant* officer, a sergeant-major. It's people like me who run the show.'

'What do ruperts do, then?'

'Make a lot of noise and sign forms.'

'I've got a friend called Rupert. Does that mean his father's a colonel?'

'Oh no. It's only an army word – a kind of slang. A rupert's any officer, from a second lieutenant to a general.'

Suddenly I spotted movement in the valley beneath us. Two RAF Tornados were heading almost straight for us. Their dappled camouflage made them hard to pick out against the variegated background. They'd slipped round a shoulder of the mountain in a tight turn, below our level, and were climbing hard in our direction.

'Look out!' I shouted. 'This is going to be noisy. Cover your ears!'

I was just in time. If we hadn't been prepared, the jets would have given us a bad fright. Even with hands clasped to our heads we were rocked by the thunder-clap of their engines as they roared past, with fire blazing from the tails as their re-heats blasted them upwards and over the ridge.

For a moment Tim was shaken, but he recovered immediately and said, 'That's what I want to do.'

'Be a pilot? Well, if you could hack it, at least you'd see some action. The fast-jet boys are always the ones who get deployed.'

We talked about the G-forces the pilots would be experiencing – how, if you pull five G, you can hardly lift your hands off your knees, your head weighs the equivalent of fifty pounds, and all your blood tries to run down to your feet, so that only the special suit you're wearing prevents you passing out.

By then the clouds were thinning and breaking, and I pointed out various landmarks as they came into sight. At last we skirted

Cribben and moved out on to the short, dry grass that sloped gently up to the summit. I almost said, 'Race you to the top,' but I knew I couldn't accelerate to save my life. Tim was ahead anyway, so I just called, 'On you go. I'll see you up there.'

Five minutes later we were sitting in bright sunshine on top of the mountain, where the trig stone used to stand, with a 360-degree panorama spread out below us. I felt a little flutter of elation at having reached the highest point and seeing all the familiar landmarks, even if it was for the last time.

'Chicken or BLT?' I said, breaking out the sandwiches.

'What's BLT?'

'Bacon, lettuce and tomato, with mayonnaise.'

'Chicken, please.'

'There you go.' I handed him the packet, along with a can of Coke. 'Get that down you, and I'll tell you about the witch doctor.'

'What's a witch doctor?'

'Someone who puts spells on you.'

'Why does he do it, though?'

'Well – for money. He's like a combination of doctor and magician. People pay him to cure them of diseases and suchlike.'

'What does he look like?'

'I expect they are all different. But the one we saw was tall and thin.'

'Like Rasputin?'

'Let's see.' I was thrown for a moment, because that was the name we'd given one of the Russian mercenaries we came across in Kamanga. Then I said, 'The mad monk, you mean?'

'In *Anastasia*.'

'Oh, *that* one. No, not like him. For one thing our witch doctor was black, and for another he didn't have a beard.'

The boy was staring at me, full of curiosity. 'Were you scared of him, Dad?'

'Not at first. I thought he was a phoney. But later, yes. I did get *very* scared, with all the things that happened. Come on, now, eat your lunch, and I'll tell you.'

TWO

Every day for the past couple of weeks the sun had grown slightly hotter, until at noon the temperature had started to hit the low nineties. But the nights were still quite chilly, and now once again, as full darkness closed in, the air was cooling quickly.

As if reacting to a command, several of the lads moved closer to the fire, all at the same moment, dragging their seats forward so that the steel ammunition boxes grated over the beaten earth. We'd made the fire in typical Kamangan fashion, with branches of dead mopane wood pointing inwards like the spokes of a cartwheel, so that all you had to do to stoke the blaze from time to time was to push a piece inwards towards the hub. Mopane, we'd soon discovered, was an ideal fuel. The sticks burned so steadily that they'd smoulder all night, but you could make them flare up again into a hot fire when you revived them in the morning.

Above us, the leaves of two big mahogany trees shivered as a breeze ran through them, and all around in the bush crickets were sounding off a continuous, zinging buzz. From the edge of the village, a hundred metres away, came bursts of laughter and chat as the locals brewed up supper, separated from us only by a grass stockade they'd built in a pathetic attempt to deter elephants from raiding their little stores of maize.

I looked round the circle of familiar faces. Including myself, there were eight of us, all with low-mow haircuts. One of the traditions in the Regiment is that nobody need have a squaddie's traditional short back-and-sides. Recently, it was true, one or two officious individuals had crept up through ranks and gone about fining people anything from £50 to £100 for looking unkempt. But that was exceptional. It was also ridiculous, because one of the SAS's skills has always been to blend in with the local population. Here in Africa there was no chance of that, and for this trip to a hot and bug-ridden country everyone had opted for crew-cuts, so the guys had a vaguely American appearance.

The glow of the flames was softening their complexions, even Whinger Watson's. The ruddy light seemed to iron some of the wrinkles out of his face; certainly it disguised the grey bristles in his Mexican-type moustache. Like me, he was heading for forty, and had that strained, heavily lined appearance which SAS guys tend to get from repeatedly pushing themselves to their physical limits, and also from the mental stress of working and playing hard; but now he looked ten years younger. He and I were so much the senior members of the party that we spent a lot of time together, and tended to compare notes about the younger guys, almost as if they were apprentices in our trade.

After a fortnight of African winter sun, everyone had started to acquire a serious tan. Everyone, that is, except Pete Jones, known to all as Genesis from his tireless reading of the Bible. He, poor bugger, with his gingery hair and freckled skin, had immediately started to burn: he'd had to wear a wide-brimmed hat and keep his sleeves rolled down to stop himself being sizzled. Also, he'd reacted violently to the bites of mozzies and tsetse flies. All of us had got bitten, but whereas the rest had developed nothing worse than itchy bumps, Genesis had come up in horrific-looking blisters full of yellow fluid, all along the insides of his forearms.

'How are the bites, Gen?' I asked.

'So-so,' he replied – from which I knew they must be itching horrendously, because he always played down any problem he had. Lately he'd started carrying on about how the Lord had inflicted Job with boils, and my enquiry set him off again.

'"Behold, happy is the man whom God correcteth,"' he went in his singsong Welsh lilt, shining a pencil torch into the pages of his little bible, with its battered cover of white leather, which he kept about his person twenty-four hours a day. '"Therefore despise not thou the chastening of the Almighty. For he maketh sore, and bindeth up; he woundeth and his hands make whole."'

'But what have you done to annoy the Big Boss?' I asked.

'Our sins are not to be accounted for,' he replied. But Pavarotti Price, our other Welshman, who was twice Genesis's size and famous for the fact that he had a Chinese-looking eye tattooed on either cheek of his arse, groaned, 'Ah, for fuck's sake! Give over.'

Genesis looked at him coolly over the top of his bible, then closed the book without remonstrating. That was typical of him: he had such a forgiving nature that he could rise above any number of obscenities, and never resorted to any himself. Sometimes one of the lads got seriously pissed off with his pious attitude, but everyone had to respect the guy for his integrity and professional skills. Now Pav, having bollocked him, gave him a friendly grin to show he meant no harm. He was amused by the fact that Genesis obviously felt at home in Kamanga, where the colonial missionary influence had left many of the men with biblical Christian names: David, James, Joseph, Philemon, Isaac.

Tilting the face of his watch towards the fire, Pav said, 'They're late.'

'Yep,' I went. 'Another air-lock in the fuel, I expect.'

At lunchtime the seven-ton Zyl truck had gone off on its weekly supply run to Chiwembe, the nearest town. Most of us had never been there, but Pav, who'd master-minded the first trip, described the place as 'the arsehole of Africa'. When somebody remarked that we were already in that location, Pav came back with, 'In that case, Chiwembe's a hundred and something ks up it.' Although it was only 120 km to the east, the dirt roads were so diabolical that the journey took over four hours each way. That day's drivers, Joseph and Sanford, were African, but two of our guys had gone with them to ride shotgun and make sure that no sell-offs took place on the way home. Even allowing an hour for loading, they should have been back by now: they'd left at midday, and already it was past eight.

Meals had been kept back for them, but the rest of us had already eaten: impala curry with rice – and very good, too. Like everyone else, the Kamangan soldiers preferred fresh meat to their rations, which were mostly canned, and they shot whatever they could. One of them had gunned down two antelopes with his AK47, and Stringer Simpson, our comms specialist, had helped him skin and butcher the animals, because before he joined the army he'd worked in a slaughterhouse and was an ace at handling meat. The local cooks also knew what they were at, especially when it came to spices. Pondani, the kitchen boss, had done two versions of the curry, billed as 'hot' and 'nuclear', and the nuclear version had been enough to blow your head off.

Round the fire, uncomfortably full, we chit-chatted about our task in Kamanga. At the briefing in Hereford everything had sounded simple and straightforward. Our role was to bolster the government army by training their select Alpha Commando, and we'd come out under the impression that they just wanted general instruction. But as soon as we reached camp, out in the bush, it became clear that Alpha was preparing for a particular operation: an attack on Gutu, a diamond mine in the south of the country captured by rebel forces the year before, and it was in planning this that they needed our help.

Equally clear was the fact that the officers expected us to accompany them into battle when the time came. This we'd been specifically forbidden to do: our orders were to act as advisers only, and not to get involved in any fighting. On paper, that was fine, but from previous operations Whinger and I knew all too well how the best of intentions go to ratshit in the field. It had happened in a big way during our time in Russia, a year before. There, too, we'd been told not to tangle with local villains, specifically the mafia, but circumstances had got the better of us, and we'd ended up fully engaged. Back in Hereford, we'd taken a token bollocking, but we got away with bending the rules because we were judged to have done far more good than harm.

This time, we hadn't made any firm decision. Whinger and I both liked the Alpha CO, Major Joss Mvula, and wanted to keep our options open. Joss was a lively, likeable guy, a bit younger than me, with crinkly black hair already receding from his forehead. He'd never been out of Kamanga, but he'd studied at the military academy in the capital, Mulongwe, and seemed well educated. He had quite a clear idea of world politics: he knew about the special relationship between Britain and America, and the tension between East and West during the Cold War. He'd seen for himself the mess the Russians had made of things when they were empire-building in Africa, and the speed with which they abandoned ship, leaving most of their equipment behind. He'd had enough communist ideology to last him a lifetime, so he was predisposed in our favour. Just as important, from our point of view, he had plenty of common sense and a reasonable grip over his men. Also, he saw the funny side of things, so he was good gas to work with.

As we waited for the truck, our talk turned to the training ambush due to go down next day. We'd already hammered out most details, both on our own and with Joss, but, as always, doubts niggled. We'd seen what happened when the Kamangans started firing live rounds: they got so over-excited they were liable to lose control. On a simple fire-and-movement exercise one guy had already gone completely hyper, screaming and shouting as he squirted off a whole twenty-round magazine, waving the weapon around in one hand like a pistol and spraying rounds through 360 degrees. Tomorrow night they were going to be firing live rounds in the dark.

During our first week we'd done what we could to steady the guys down, taking them through the various stages of range work. Then we'd started teaching them to move through the bush – individually, in pairs, finally in patrol groups. They'd learnt quite fast, and improved to the point where we'd made them do a dry attack on a dummy camp we'd built for the purpose – an exercise which went off better than we'd expected. But still I felt sure that in a real battle a lot of them would go ballistic.

The country was ideal for training. The land consisted of low hills covered in bush and forest, with rivers of pale sand winding through. We'd heard that in the rains, from November to March, these shallow channels filled up and became tributaries of the Nasangua, a big river to the south. But now, in July – the middle of the African winter – they were bone dry and easy to cross on foot, although dodgy for vehicles, which easily became bedded in the fine sand.

Before the civil war the area had been a game-park. The villages had been cleared out of it thirty years earlier, and there were no humans living in a block of at least five million acres. The Kamangans told us that, once we got outside the park, we'd find burnt-out villlages by the score, fields uncultivated, everything gone to waste; but in the country we'd seen so far, there had been no inhabitants anyway. This meant we could fire live ammunition in any direction we fancied without endangering anybody – a fantastic freedom from restrictions. In that environment it was hardly surprising that the Kamangans were trigger-happy. Whenever they had weapons loaded, they'd loose off at anything that moved, whether they themselves were on foot or riding in the backs of vehicles.

After two years of war, the park had gone to ruin. The village where we were camped had been just outside the boundary, beside the main gate. Somehow the grass huts had escaped destruction, but inside the park the tourist lodges had been burnt, and the tracks used for game drives had either grown over or been washed away by flash floods during the rains. Most of the animals had been shot out. The rhinos had gone first, killed for their horns, and hundreds of elephants had been poached for their ivory. Already we'd found gaunt hulks of elephant carcasses, eaten to the skeleton by vultures, hyenas, jackals and insects. Joss told us that normally the hyenas would have eaten the bones as well, or carried them away, but the war had produced such carnage that the scavengers couldn't keep pace with the supply of rotting bodies. Everywhere we found heaps of hyena droppings – so white, from all the calcium the animals ate, that they were known as 'missionaries' chalk' – and at night eerie howling sounded off from all points of the compass.

For the ambush exercise Whinger and I had recced a perfect

site, where a dirt road crossed one of the sand rivers. On the home side of the crossing the terrain was open, with scattered trees and shrubs growing from stony ground, but the far bank of the river – enemy territory – was cloaked with thick bush, and it was from there – according to the scenario we'd devised – that the terrorists would appear.

'The second lot of pop-up targets,' said Whinger. 'It might pay us to move them another hundred metres along the bank. That'd give the killer group a better arc.'

'Okay,' I agreed. 'We'll have time to take another look at it in the morning. What's that?'

I broke off as a hefty, low-pitched *hoo-hoo* sounded somewhere close above us, and I looked up to see a huge bird pass silently overhead, a fast-moving silhouette, black against the stars.

'Jesus!' exclaimed Chalky White. 'A bloody great owl.'

'Where?' Everyone started craning their necks around.

'It went thataway.' Chalky pointed towards the village.

Seconds later, from among the grass huts, there burst an eruption of noise: people yelling, pots and pans being hammered. We stood up to get a better view, and Pavarotti nipped across to the nearest pinkie, where he grabbed a spot-lamp, switched it on and swept the beam over the shiny, dark-green canopy of the mango trees which rose above the settlement.

'It must be a great eagle owl,' said Mart Stanning, our medic, who'd got talking about birds to one of the Alpha guys. 'The locals don't like them. They reckon the devil uses owls for transport, so it's bad news if one comes into the village. If it sits on the roof of a house, it means someone in that family's going to die before morning.'

'Cheerful lot, these buggers,' said Pavarotti. 'With that racket under it, I don't reckon the bird'll so much as touch down, let alone stay long enough to organise a funeral—'

The rest of his sentence was cut off by a hollow report, and we saw a spurt of flame shoot into the air.

'Christ!' exclaimed Danny Stewart. 'The head-man's let drive with that bloody old muzzle-loader he showed us. I hope it hasn't killed him.'

We'd seen the weapon a couple of days earlier – a fearsome, home-made contraption about six feet long, held together with rusty wire and leather thongs, which the owner displayed proudly, showing us how much powder he would load: two fingers' width for an antelope, three for a buffalo, four for an elephant. We reckoned any discharge would be a greater threat to him than to whatever he fired at, but clearly the gun was his pride and joy. At the same time, we couldn't help noticing that he'd lost his left thumb.

Danny – a compact little Yorkshireman with fine, sandy hair – had a funny habit of dropping his chin and rotating his head through half a circle, as if he were trying to peel his neck away from his collar, whenever he came up with a commentary on anything interesting that happened. Now he did just that as he said, 'It's quietened the buggers, anyway, the old gun.'

'Aye,' Pavarotti agreed. 'From the way the commotion's died down, I reckon the bird's got away. If they'd dropped it, they'd be screeching something horrible.'

We settled back round the fire and started talking about our tour. Looking at the faces again, I realised that Chalky had gone almost as dark as some of the Africans. It's standard practice for anyone with the surname White to be called Chalky, but with this one there was some point, because he had jet black hair and a swarthy complexion. What with his tan, and the fact he hadn't shaved for a couple of days, you could hardly see him in the firelight.

Stringer looked like the butcher's boy he'd been: rosy-cheeked, blue-eyed, big, powerful, a fitness freak. In the UK he spent hours in the gym, and here in the bush he was constantly skipping or doing press-ups or dips between two boxes set out a couple of feet apart. Also, he couldn't resist the long tendrils of creeper trailing from big trees in the forest; whenever he found some good ones, he was up them in a flash, earning derisive shouts of 'Fucking Tarzan!' He was also our best linguist, with reasonably fluent Arabic and Russian. Neither of those was any cop here, but he'd already picked up a useful amount of Nyanja, the language common to the various native tribes in the area.

Pavarotti, the biggest guy in the team, always fighting his weight, was pretty dark as well. His rubbery face – typically Welsh – seemed to have grown larger, its tan emphasising his heavy features and thick eyebrows. Apart from Whinger and myself, Pav was the oldest of the lads, at around thirty-one or thirty-two. Among many other hairy tasks, he'd taken part in our Kremlin job a year earlier, and his strength had saved the day when we were struggling to hoist a suitcase bomb into position in the tunnel under the Moscow river. That episode had finally cured his phobia about being caught in confined spaces.

As for Whinger, he and I had survived numerous dodgy situations together, in Belfast, Libya, Colombia and Grozny, not to mention England itself, and I'd come to rely on his coolness and efficiency, whatever the threat. We'd worked together for so long that I took his presence, and his bastard rhyming slang, for granted. The guys who knew him less well had been puzzled at first when he started talking about 'silveries', and I had to explain the derivation of the term: silver spoon – coon. The moment they got it, everyone took it up.

Aside from Whinger and Pav, the lads were all around the twenty-seven, twenty-eight mark, and although I'd never worked with any of them, I felt solidly confident about their capabilities. They were well tried and tested, and so far on this trip they'd been a hundred per cent. Mart Stanning, for instance, was an excellent operator. Slim and wiry, and so fair that people often mistook him for a Dane or a Dutchman, he stood out even among our own lads. Unlike Genesis, he tanned easily, and while the sun was bleaching his hair, it was darkening his skin, so that he looked as though he was wearing a straw-coloured cap. To the Africans he was a phenomenon, and they referred to him by a native name that meant 'Yellow Doctor'. They quickly saw that he was a good practitioner, and every morning he had to conduct a regular surgery, treating sores and septic wounds by the dozen, and doling out harmless aspirin for things like cancerous growths which he couldn't deal with.

The one guy I had reservations about was Andy Dean, who was away on the supply run. That May he'd got married to Penny, a farmer's daughter from Shropshire, and most of the team had been to his wedding near Ludlow. I'm afraid we behaved in typical SAS fashion, collaring a table in a corner of the big tent and getting stuck into the champagne without bothering to make polite conversation to the other guests. Then, before we left the UK, Andy had bought a cottage in Kilpeck, a village near Hereford. The house was more than a hundred years old, and tiny. It needed a hell of a lot doing to it to make it habitable, and I knew the mortgage payments were going to stretch him to the limit. Once or twice in Kamanga I'd found him looking preoccupied. His heart didn't seem to be in the job, and it was obvious financial worries were preying on his mind.

Except for myself, married and widowed, and Whinger, who'd been married for a couple of years, but then divorced, without any kids, Andy was the only one who'd got spliced, and with the dire record of the Regiment in this area, everyone was waiting to see how long it would last. Several of the others had woman problems, but nothing that wouldn't wait the six weeks until we were home again. Looking round the circle again, I reckoned we were a pretty typical SAS team: all fit, all well built, all fairly undemonstrative, all quick on our feet, both physically and mentally, all able to do each other's jobs, should the need arise.

Before we'd come out, Stringer had got quite excited about the trip, his first to Africa. He thought it was going to be a great adventure: the Dark Continent and all that. Now, by the fire, Whinger said cynically, 'Didn't I tell you? It's like I said. Where's the action? Here we are, miles from anywhere. No bar for a thousand miles. Bugger all entertainment. HIV wherever you look.'

'Come on!' said Pav. 'We're gonna have a ball!'

'Have your motor flown out, Pav,' Danny told him. 'Take it for a drive on the Chiwembe highway.'

'Thanks, mate. As long as you stump up for the repair bills.'

Just before we went to Russia, Pav had bought a second-hand XJ 120 Jaguar, flame red, and the wretched thing had become the love of his life. No matter that it had already put six points on his licence, at the slightest opportunity he was away down to Ross and the M50 for what he called a pipe-opener. The idea of driving it out here, on the dirt roads, made him groan.

'Whinger's right, up to a point,' said Mart, scratching at his blond scrub. 'That briefing I got at the med centre about not touching anybody wounded unless I'm wearing rubber gloves – they reckon one in three of the population are carrying the HIV virus.'

'Don't touch 'em, then,' said Pav. 'Just let 'em carry on.'

There was a pause, and then Stringer said, 'I reckon they're all right.'

'Who?' Pav demanded.

'The Alpha guys.'

'Listen,' I told him. 'They've been all right so far, but these people are volatile as hell. They can turn in a flash. When I was in Zaire in ninety-one, the whole population went fucking berserk. In Kinshasa, the capital, they started looting shops and houses like savages, trashing everything. They were even nicking amputated limbs from the skips at the back of the hospital.'

'What for?' Stringer looked a bit sick.

'To eat, of course.'

'Christ!'

There was another silence while everyone took that in. Then Chalky said, 'At least we can't spend any money. There's that.'

'You wait,' said Whinger. 'If we get that week of R and R they promised us at the end, and end up in Sun City, you'll spend everything you've got.'

Presently, through the bush in the opposite direction, we spotted headlights flaring and swinging in the distance as our supply truck came lurching back towards base. We got up, walking towards it, and within a minute it was pulling up on the open ground in front of our tents. The whole area was pretty dark, with no illumination except the flicker of cooking fires in the distance, but from the speed at which the lorry slid to a halt, I got the impression that something was wrong.

A cloud of dust rolled forward from behind it, boiling up into the headlights, and a figure I recognised as Andy jumped down off the tailboard.

'Eh, Andy,' I called. 'What's up?'

'Geordie!' he went, in a strange, tight voice. 'There's been an accident.'

'You all right?'

'Fine.'

'What about Phil?'

'He's Okay. It wasn't us. We ran into a group of kids.'

'Oh, Jesus! Anyone killed?'

'I don't think so. But two of them are quite bad. We brought them with us – in the back.'

Immediately I yelled for Mart.

'Right here, Geordie.' His voice came from close behind me.

'Hear what Andy said?'

'Sure.'

'Get your kit, then.'

An African came running with a hurricane lamp. Moths swirled round the light as he held it aloft. I saw Phil Foster in the back of the truck, holding something in his arms. A moment later he handed the bundle down to me – a child wrapped in a dark-coloured blanket. Instinctively, I started out towards our own tents, which were nearest to the spot. The child was warm, but limp and not moving. It felt pathetically light.

Mart had moved with commendable speed. Under the fly-leaf of his tent a hurricane lamp was burning, and he'd got some of the contents of his medical pack spread out. I laid my burden gently on the ground and opened up the blanket. Inside was a boy of maybe eight or nine, barefoot, clad in a dirty brown T-shirt and dark-blue shorts, powdered all over with pale dust. His eyes were shut, but his little chest was lifting and falling in very short, quick breaths. The sight of him immediately made me think of Tim.

'Gloves, Mart,' I said.

'It's all right,' he said. 'There's no blood. His skin's not broken.'

He started to check the boy over, feeling carefully for broken bones. Then another blanket came to rest beside me. This one held a girl, also barefoot, wearing a simple dark-blue shift. She looked younger than the boy, perhaps only six. Blood was shining on her right temple, and down her right arm. Her eyes were open, but they were wide with fear.

'You're okay,' I said gently. 'Take it easy.' I couldn't tell if she understood English, but I hoped soft words would soothe her.

Looking round, I found Phil crouching beside me. In the harsh lamplight the hollows in his long, lean face were full of shadows. 'What happened?' I asked.

'Joseph was driving. We were way out in the bush, well clear of the village. Already dark. Suddenly a load of kids jumped out of the grass into the road. I reckon they were after a lift.'

'These clothes.' I pointed to the dark blue and brown. 'They can't have shown up in the headlights. Arms and legs the same.'

Phil shook his head. 'I was standing with my head out the top of the wagon. I never saw a fucking thing. It wasn't Joseph's fault. He stamped hell out of the brakes. Nobody could have stopped any quicker.'

'Nothing broken,' Mart reported of the boy. 'But I don't like the look of him. His breathing's very shallow. He's had a bad bang on the head. There – feel that.'

Gingerly I ran my fingers through the soft, furry stubble on the boy's scalp. The skin seemed to be intact, but I could feel a large swelling high up over the left ear.

'Is there anything you can do?'

'Not much. Keep him wrapped up, that's all. He needs to go to hospital soonest.'

'Hospital!' I exclaimed. 'Some hope. What about the girl?'

Mart pulled on a pair of surgical gloves, took a swab and carefully wiped the blood off her forehead and arm. 'Only scratches,' he said. 'Limbs seem okay. Looks like she was knocked into some thorns. It's him we've got to worry about.'

Hearing voices behind us, I turned, to find we were surrounded by a crowd of maybe fifty Africans. Some of the men I recognised – members of Alpha, wrapped up in khaki cotton sweaters and tracksuit trousers – but the rest were strangers, people from the village. The lamplight glinted off white teeth and flashed on shiny black skin. As they pressed forward to see what was happening, their voices rose rapidly into an aggressive chorus. In the distance drums had started beating out some message.

I stood up, towering over most of the people, and made placatory gestures, moving my open hands gently up and down. 'Take it easy,' I said. 'We're only trying to help.'

Most of them already knew that Mart was our medic, and respected him, but now they sounded angry, as if the accident had been our fault, and they were accusing us of trying to kidnap the children.

'What are they saying?' I asked Godfrey, one of the Kamangan soldiers.

'You give boy bad spirits.'

'Bollocks. Hes was hit by the truck – got a blow on the head.' I was going to remonstrate more, but I knew the guy's English was poor. 'Where's Major Mvula? Get the major.'

'Major coming.'

He was, too. I looked through the crowd and saw Joss hurrying towards us, dressed in the sky-blue tracksuit which he wore in the evenings. As usual he was grinning, eager to help.

'Hey, Geordie,' he went. 'Mind if I join the party? What's all this?'

His face fell as I explained. 'The girl's okay, but the boy's pretty bad. We need a chopper, to get him to hospital.'

'Not a chance.' Joss used a phrase he'd picked up off me. 'Not tonight, anyway. We can get on the radio, but they won't fly at night. Can we send him by road?'

'How far is it?'

'Seven hours.'

'The journey'd kill him.'

Joss nodded. Behind him the hubbub was getting louder. He turned and shouted something to quieten it. As the clamour dropped, he began to explain about the accident in a loud voice, and for a few moments his words seemed to be swaying opinion. Then a new wave of yelling started up, and the crowd opened to let a small woman through. With a screech she rushed past me and dropped beside the boy, lifting him up. His stick-like arms and legs hung down as she cradled him in her arms.

'The mother,' said Joss.

Mart knelt beside her and tried the boy's pulse again. In his big, square hand the little black arm looked skinny as a bone.

'He's fading,' he announced. 'Not going to last long.'

The woman began screaming and shouting, repeating the word *sin'ganga, sin'ganga* again and again.

'What's she saying?'

'Take him to the doctor,' Joss translated.

'I didn't think there *was* a doctor.'

'It's the witch doctor she means.'

'Jesus, that *will* kill him. Tell her he's got a better chance if we just keep him quiet.'

Joss spoke forcefully to the woman, but she kept on with her shouts. The crowd backed her. Out in the darkness the drums were getting louder. I began feeling the sheer level of noise would finish the child off.

'Where is he, this doctor?' I yelled.

'Here, in the village.'

'How far?'

'Two minutes' walk. Three minutes.'

'What'll he do?'

Joss shrugged. 'How do I know? Consult the spirits for a remedy.'

I shot Mart a glance. 'What d'you reckon?'

'Better go. There's nothing I can do for the kid. As long as we handle him gently, a short carry won't hurt. This crowd could turn nasty any moment.'

'Right, then. You carry him. Phil and me'll come with you as escort.'

Joss put a hand on the mother's shoulder, restraining her, and said something to her while Mart took the boy from her. So we set off in an amazing procession, Mart leading, the mother wailing at his elbow, myself and Phil immediately behind with Joss, then half the village. Some of the people had oil lamps, and several were carrying torches of burning reed bundles. Any moment, I thought, these grass huts are going on fire, and the whole village will be up in smoke.

Above the hubbub, I shouted, 'Hadn't somebody better warn the guy we're coming?'

'He knows,' Joss called back. 'The drums have told him.'

As we advanced between huts huddled under mango trees, I liked the feel of things less and less. The crowd was so hostile that I was glad we had pistols on our belts. I was happy to have Phil with me, too. In the flickering light, with his close-cropped dark head and hollow cheeks, he looked quite dangerous. The impression wasn't misleading, either: he was the most hawkish member of the team, always keen to get out there and top somebody.

'Whatever happens,' I shouted to Mart, 'we're going in with the boy. I'm not leaving him alone with the witch doctor. I want to see what gives.'

In less than three minutes we were outside a big, circular hut with a thatched verandah running round it. The crowd dropped back and fell silent as we approached over beaten earth, leaving us alone outside the open doorway. The hut was pitch dark, but I was aware of movement and rustling noises inside, as if someone was making rapid preparations. Then a lamp flared, a curtain was drawn aside, and a voice said something in Nyanja.

'Go inside,' said Joss quietly. 'The mother must hold the child.'

Mart handed over his burden. I think he felt the same as I did: that we'd better do what we were told. Phil was more sceptical. Even though he said nothing, I could sense him seething with indignation just behind me. But when the woman stepped forward, we all followed.

The air inside was full of a powerful smell, half animal, half acrid human sweat. A single, primitive oil lamp flickered on the ground to our right. Towards the back of the hut there was a kind of cubicle, walled in with hanging black material, wide enough to accommodate two standing figures. The left-hand one was ordinary: a man dressed in normal, scruffy clothes, bare-headed, bare-footed, using both hands to hold a book open in front of his chest. It was the right-hand figure that made me catch my breath: a tall man, six foot at least, dressed in a blood-red robe that reached almost to the ground, with a zebra skin slung over his left shoulder and diagonally across his chest. On his head was a hat like a big muffin, also of zebra skin. His face was dead white, covered in paint or ash, so that his mouth and eye sockets showed up black on a pale background. In his left hand he was flicking what looked like an animal tail vertically up and down, and in his right he held a curved black horn.

'The tail is from giraffe, horn from buffalo,' Joss whispered in my ear.

I could see how scared the mother was from the way she cringed in front of the doctor, especially when he began to grunt and moan and whisk his giraffe tail with a faster, jerking motion. But the helper spoke sharply, obviously ordering her to come closer, and she moved forward a step, so that the boy in her arms was only a couple of feet from the hissing hair.

As the witch doctor's hand flew up and down, and shadows leapt about the grass roof like huge bats, the mask of a face began to twitch and gibber in a high-pitched, squeaky voice, letting out staccato bursts of sound that reminded me of machine-gun fire. I shot a sideways glance at Mart and saw his eyes switch from the doctor to his helper and back. Phil was still behind me.

Suddenly, the helper spoke, in a normal voice, and Joss translated for us: 'The spirits are talking.'

'What are they saying?'

Joss relayed the question, but all he got for a reply was an irritable shake of the head.

'Eh,' I muttered to Mart. 'The helper guy's a fraud. He's pretending to read from that book, but it's that dark he can't see a bloody word.'

'Fucking ridiculous!' muttered Phil, but Mart, who was closer to the acolyte, said, 'Fuck me, it's a bible.'

I stared at the tattered edges. Sure enough, one title page was hanging open towards us, and the flickering light was strong enough for me to make out, in big type, THE BOOK OF DANIEL.

The gibbering outbursts rose even higher. The witch doctor's eyes were tight shut. His head was rolling on his shoulders. Beads of sweat flew off his forehead. There was a touch of red about his lips. Blood? No, it was crimson froth. He was chewing something, leaves or roots or berries. Suddenly a shudder ran through his body and he stood stock still, holding the narrow end of the horn to his right temple. For a few seconds he remained motionless and silent. Then his lips moved and the twittering broke out again, this time in a steady stream.

The helper began to interpret.

'He says evil spirits have come into the boy,' Joss translated. 'The trouble is in his head . . . His brain is damaged . . . He has bad pressure in his head . . . He is very sick.'

I bit back the impulse to say, 'We know that,' and asked, 'What can he do about it? Can he give him anything?'

'Wait, there is something else.'

The *sin'ganga* rolled his head and gibbered, the acolyte interpreted, Joss translated. 'The boy will die. There is no medicine for this condition.'

There followed a pause of maybe half a minute, during which I found I was holding my breath. Then came the message. 'His spirit is leaving him now.'

The mother, who'd been standing still and quiet, gave a sudden hoarse cry and sank to the ground, decanting the child out of its blanket on to the earth at the witch doctor's feet.

What happened next, I'll never be sure. I saw Mart go down on his knees to recover the boy, but then something soft brushed across my shoulders and a sudden draught put out the lamp. In the darkness I felt an intense chill close in on me.

Behind me, Phil gave a sharp exclamation of 'Fucking hell!' I heard a movement, looked round, and found he'd disappeared.

'Phil!' I said sharply. 'Are you feeling anything?'

He didn't answer.

'Phil!' I went. 'Where are you?'

It was Mart who answered: 'He's back in the crowd.'

'Did you feel anything just then?'

'Cold,' said Mart. 'Freezing cold, horrible.'

'I got it too,' I told him. 'It was deadly. How about pulling out?'

'I'm okay.' Mart sounded solid. 'D'you want to?'

'No, I'm okay to stay.'

That was what I said. But in fact I was shuddering and felt sick, as if gripped by fever. What surprised me most was that Phil had quit. Phil, the least scared of all our people, the toughest, the most punchy.

Through those unnerving seconds the twittering had kept up unabated. Then I heard Mart exclaim, 'Shit! He's gone!'

'Who?'

'The kid. No pulse. Breathing's stopped. I'll try mouth-to-mouth.'

'No, for Christ's sake!' I told him. 'If the people see you doing that, they'll think you're killing him.'

'They think that anyway.'

'Try it,' I said. Then instantly I changed my mind and ordered, 'Cancel that. Leave him!'

The crowd outside seemed to sense what had happened. The tide of voices swelled again. I heard more drums going in the distance, and at our feet the woman began to wail. Joss called out something in Nyanja, and a man came through from the back of the hut carrying another lamp.

Light showed that neither the witch doctor nor his assistant had moved. Both held exactly the same posture: the giraffe tail was still thrashing the air; spirit messages were still arriving. The woman was on the deck, with Mart on his knees beside her. Apart from Phil having vanished into the crowd, nothing had changed. Certainly there was nobody close behind me who could have flicked a garment or shawl over my shoulders.

The back of my neck was crawling. What was it that put the

lamp out? What had produced that icy chill?

'He says, white men must leave Kamanga,' Joss translated.

'Tell him we had nothing to do with the accident,' I said. 'It was a Kamangan driving the truck.'

'He knows that. But he says white men bring evil to our country.'

'We're trying to help. The only reason we're here is that your government invited us.'

That information produced a long pause. The witch doctor transferred the buffalo horn to his left hand and clawed at the air with his right, fingers spread, drawing in handfuls of air towards his head, as if plucking at the spirits who were talking to him. Several times he turned his hand slowly and brought it back towards his face, palm-first. But in the end his message was the same: 'All white men must leave Kamanga.'

'What happens if they don't?' Mart demanded.

'They will die.'

'All of them?'

Another pause, then, 'Some.'

'How many?'

'To find this out, the *sin'ganga* needs to consult his bones.'

'Okay, then,' I agreed. 'Tell him to do it.'

Later, I wished to hell I'd never issued the challenge. But at the time, in the heightened atmosphere of that stinking hut, one question seemed to lead on from another so fast that there was no time to think of possible consequences. Before I could start worrying, the acolyte was ordering the woman out, shooing her backwards as if she were a sheep.

'She will have to pay for the consultation,' said Joss.

'It's all right,' I told him. 'I'll pay. How much is it?'

The answer came back, 'Four thousand *kwatchas*. One dollar US.'

'Okay. We'll see to that.'

The woman rolled her dead child in its blanket and disappeared into the crowd with her pathetic burden. Wailing broke out, but the anger seemed to have given way to grief. The people began to move off, back into the middle of the village, leaving us alone.

The witch doctor was coming out of his trance. Convulsive shudders ran through his body, and he gave a few loud gasps. Red froth still hung around his mouth, but at last he opened his eyes and looked about, as if trying to get his bearings.

The acolyte, who'd disappeared into the blackness behind him, came out again into the light without his bible, holding a small, pear-shaped bag made of leather, with a draw-string gathering the neck. The witch doctor handed over his horn and giraffe tail, took the bag, then abruptly sank down on his haunches, his knees cracking as they bent. Then he started sweeping the flat of his right hand across the earth floor in front of him. Once again the helper stood at his master's right shoulder.

A high-pitched humming started up, like the drone of bees. At first I thought it was coming from the helper, then I saw that the witch doctor had his lips pressed tight together as he produced the sound, which had a slight beat in it, so that it seemed to come and go. Shaking the bag, he tweaked the cord at the neck and shook out the contents. With a light, dry pattering about a dozen bones landed on the beaten earth. They were brown with age and use, and must have come from a small animal about the size of a hare.

After a few seconds' scrutiny, he said something, speaking now in a normal voice, surprisingly deep.

'Death,' Joss translated. 'He sees death.'

'Fucking roll on!' went Mart under his breath.

'We've had a death already,' I said.

'More now.'

'Who?'

'Wait.'

After a pause and more humming, the wrinkled old hands gathered the bones, shook them like dice and threw them again, harder than before, so that they clicked on each other and spread out over a wider area of earth. I saw that the man's right-hand index finger was missing.

This time the pattern seemed to give an immediate answer.

'Ten will die,' Joss translated.

'Ten what?'

'Ten white persons.'

'Men?'

'And women. Either.'

'Why ten?'

As the questions were relayed through our interpreter, the witch doctor never glanced in our direction, but kept his eyes down, fixed on the bones, his right hand, with its missing finger, stretched out downwards over them. There was a long silence before he gave his next answer.

'Because the boy was ten years old. One death for every year of his life.'

Mart, who'd been squatting still and silent beside me, suddenly asked, 'Why's he putting this spell on *us*?'

Joss answered that one off his own bat, without translating the question: 'The spell is not from the *sin'ganga*. He's only telling you about it. It is from a *fiti*, a sorcerer. Very bad man. The *sin'ganga* can feel the spell coming.'

'Where's this *fiti* then?'

Joss shrugged and gestured outwards into the darkness. 'He lives in the village, but now I think he is hiding in the bush.'

'How the hell can he put a spell on us if he hasn't seen us?'

'He has seen you. In the past few days he has watched you all. He is a powerful man, very dangerous.'

'Can't this guy make up a counter-spell?' Mart gestured at the witch doctor. 'Put something on the other bastard?'

I knew the question was meant to be sarcastic, but Joss took it seriously, translated it, and passed back the answer: 'He will give you medicine, to stop you being witched.'

'Medicine!' snorted Mart. 'Medicine against evil spells? For fuck's sake!'

I felt just as cynical, but I reckoned this was a game we had to play.

'Okay,' I said. 'I'll have some. How much will it cost?'

'Twenty thousand *kwatchas*. Five dollars.'

'All right, then.'

I reached into my shirt, going for my money belt, but Joss waved my hand down, and said, 'No need to pay now. He has to prepare medicine first. He will give it in the morning. Pay then.'

'Okay. But I'll pay for the woman, anyway.' I handed over a one-dollar bill, which the acolyte accepted.

I'd had enough of this mumbo-jumbo, so we pulled out. We left the witch doctor still squatting, still staring fixedly at his bones, and the acolyte sorting little heaps of wood and bark that lay about on the floor. As we pulled away, Phil materialised out of the darkness.

'What the fuck happened to *you*?' I asked.

'I dunno. Something horrendous.'

'Feeling of cold?'

'Like a tomb. I had to get the hell out.'

Back in camp we found that the crowd had dispersed, and there was no immediate threat. The mother of the dead boy had taken his body away. It turned out that the girl with the scratches wasn't related to him, and had been recovered by some of her own people.

Round the fire again, we broke out a bottle of rum and shot the shit while we had a good slug apiece – all, that is, except Genesis, who stuck to his normal Coke. I felt shaken.

'What do we reckon to *that*, then?' I asked the circle in general. I gave a quick run-down on what had happened, for the benefit of the guys who'd missed it.

'It all started with that fucking owl,' said Pavarotti.

'Did they kill it?' Chalky asked.

'Did they hell!' said Pav. 'I bet it just cleared off. It probably does a fly-past every night, just to wind the bastards up.'

'Surely,' said Genesis, 'the accident to the kids must have happened before the owl appeared?'

'I dunno,' I told him. 'I reckon the two were much the same time.'

'Maybe the old owl came to tell us about it,' Chalky suggested.

'Bollocks to the owl,' went Stringer. 'It's only a bloody bird, after all.'

'Those guys were both phoneys,' Mart declared.
'Who?' Genesis asked.
'The old witch doctor and his mate. The whole thing was just a performance. No disrespect, Gen, but that business with the bible really gave them away. The helper guy never turned a page or anything. Besides, it was far too fucking dark for him to read a word. The book was nothing but a prop. What could the Book of Daniel have to do with the injured kid? If you ask me, the entire show was a load of shite.'
'I don't know,' I said. 'It was and it wasn't. How did the guy know the kid was dying? He couldn't see him. He never even touched him. He never asked the mother any question. He just knew – at the exact moment, as well.'
'Lucky guess,' said Mart.
'Could have been,' I agreed. 'But his timing was spot on.'
'True.'
'Another thing,' I went on. 'Something touched me on the shoulders when the lamp went out. Something like a big bird, with soft wings.'
'The owl!' cried Stringer. 'To-whit to-bloody-whoo!'
'Piss off, Stringer,' I told him. 'You didn't feel it. You didn't get the cold, either. Phil got it, though, didn't you?'
'Yeah. And I don't fucking want it again.'
'Cold?' went Pav. 'What are you on about?'
'It was like I'd stepped into a freezer,' I said. 'I was shaking like I had malaria or something. It made Phil do a runner.'
'Philip Foster!' went Whinger in mock horror. 'Don't tell me you left your colleagues in the shit.'
'You'd have shat yourself,' Phil told him, 'if you'd felt what I was getting.'
'Geordie!' said Whinger, relentlessly. 'I can't believe you were bricking it as well.'
'I was,' I assured him. 'I was scared shitless, because I didn't know what was happening. Brrrrrh!' I shuddered again. 'Get that rum moving, for Christ's sake.'
We passed the bottle round again and sat gazing into the fire.
'I dunno,' said Mart. 'Joss was telling me yesterday that witch

doctors' medicines really work. These guys are herbalists. They get their stuff out of the bush: leaves and roots and bark and things. The point is, for the locals, these are the only drugs that exist. There's no hospital this side of Chiwembe – not even a clinic. The clinics that do exist don't have any drugs or trained staff. Joss reckons that without traditional medicine, very few of his mates would have made it to twenty-five.'

'Come on, Mart,' went Whinger. 'You can't swallow all that crap.'

'It works,' Mart insisted, stubbornly. 'That's all I'm saying. Maybe a lot of it's psychological. If you believe in it, you get better.'

'Yeah,' went Danny, 'or you can get witched.'

'Better not to believe in it,' said Genesis. 'If you don't let it get to you, it can't do you any harm.'

'That's right,' said Whinger. 'And for fuck's sake don't take any medicine the quack throws you. Don't give me any, either. Imagine calling up the CO in Hereford and saying, "Boss, I'm dying. I've been poisoned by a fucking witch doctor."'

Everyone laughed. I took a deep breath and got up to kick some pieces of wood towards the centre of the fire.

'One thing about it,' I said. 'There's only ten of us, and no white women in sight. If ten freak out, there won't be many left.'

'Nobody's going to freak out,' said Phil, confident and aggressive again, in spite of the fright he'd had. 'It's all in the mind.'

If we'd taken a vote on the genuineness of the witch doctor, I reckon it would have gone seven to three against, or possibly six to four. Phil and Mart and myself had all felt that peculiar cold, and Genesis, who was wavering, couldn't help being fascinated by the fact that the acolyte had wielded a bible.

When I told the guys to watch themselves particularly over the next few days, they gave me some peculiar looks, as if I was going soft in the head. But my own mind was far from easy. I lay looking up at the brilliant stars, thinking of the white powder, done up in a twist of dirty paper, a messenger had brought me. It was a long time before I could go to sleep.

THREE

The Kamangans had a form of reveille that I found spooky but attractive. At 0530 a single hand-drummer would start up, tapping out any rhythm he liked as he went on his round – and since a different man did it every morning, each day's summons was unique, sometimes quite short, sometimes carrying on for a couple of minutes, until everyone was fully awake.

Next morning, as always, we were up in the dark, but by the time we'd had breakfast in the grey light of dawn, and everyone had got themselves sorted, it was already eight o'clock and the sun was hot. Whinger and I had recced the ambush site and laid out half the pop-up targets the day before; now our task was to show the location to Joss and his section commanders so that they could work out their own plan.

The dry watercourse we'd chosen for the ambush had no name – it didn't feature on our maps – so for ease of reference we'd called it the Congo. The scenario of Exercise Mantrap was simple. Intelligence sources, it said, had revealed that terrorist forces were planning to come across the border with a shipment of arms: the party would use the earth road that ran roughly east to west along the far bank of our Congo. If the terrorists performed as predicted, they would cross in front of our guys from left to right. Alpha Force's brief was to intercept and eliminate them in a linear ambush.

We were planning a conventional ambush, with a killer group and and two cut-off parties, right and left, and a Bergen cache which would act as rear protection. At the point we'd selected, the sandy bed of the river was forty metres wide, and the track that ran along the bank was three or four feet above the level of the watercourse. Beyond it lay thick bush. From the home forces' lying-up position on the near side of the river, the range to the track would be barely a hundred metres – a perfect killing ground. On our side of the river the vegetation was relatively sparse, but the terrain was rough, broken up by banks and dry ditches, so there was plenty of cover for the Kamangans to conceal themselves.

Another feature that confirmed our choice of site was a small hill, no more than a mound, made up of enormous lumps of smooth black volcanic rock, with grass growing between, about fifty metres behind the centre of the killer group's position.

'Look at that!' exclaimed Whinger. 'What a treasure.'

I knew his rhyming slang well enough to realise he meant 'made to measure', and so it was. The mound would make us an ideal tactical headquarters and OP. From there we could oversee the whole of the exercise area; even better, we'd be able to move around a little without causing any disturbance. By crawling away along the grassy hollows among the rocks, we could withdraw on to the back of the hill without being seen, and kip down, one at a time. In deference to the fact that we were in southern Africa, we called the hill the Kopje.

In a line straight across country, the ambush location was no more than six or seven kilometres from camp, but because the direct route was severed by two deep gullies, the only way to drive there was along thirty kilometres of roundabout dirt tracks, and the trip took a good hour. Therefore I decreed that, once we'd finished our planning, the whole of Mantrap would be carried out on foot.

First, though, we needed to ferry out the remaining targets and set them in position, and we had so much kit that we needed to go by vehicle. Whinger, Genesis and I went in one of the pinkies, and the Kamangan O-group followed us in one of their Gaz trucks, bringing a selection of home-made claymore mines loaded with nails and ball-bearings. Joss had two of his junior ruperts and three sergeants with him, so they were quite a crowd. The ruperts looked very young – in their mid-twenties, I guessed – and very nervous. They had note-books and ball-point pens tucked into the breast pockets of their immaculately ironed bush shirts, and were trying to appear efficient, but I could see they felt they were very much on trial.

For most of the way we followed a track of sorts, but for the last few minutes, once we were beyond the second ravine, we struck off on a bearing through the bush, weaving between trees and jolting over hard, dry ground until the open stretch of river bank came into view. Towards the left-hand side of our theatre stood a single baobab tree, huge and old, with its great mop-head of branches looking like roots, as though it had grown upside-down. Its massive trunk, at least six feet across, acted as a natural goal-post on that side of the playing field.

'There you are, Joss,' I said as we walked forward. 'It's all yours.'

'Oh, wah!' he went. 'I like it. Great location! Enemy coming along the far bank, left to right, heh?'

'That's it.'

'Okay.'

Quickly I suggested how he might dispose his forces: killer group in front of the Kopje, the others, within certain limits, where he chose. He'd never set a full-scale ambush before, but he got the idea quickly, and his questions were sensible.

'Take the baobab as your left-hand marker,' I told him. 'The task of the left cut-off group's just what it sounds: to cut off anyone trying to escape to the left of the main killing area. Their arc of fire can be from the baobab outwards. The right cut-off group has the same task on the other side. Their marker's that side channel running away from us. Okay?

'Fine, fine.'

'So, while you're sorting your plan, us lot will go forward to set up these extra targets straight out in front of us, in the middle of the killing ground. That's where I want your guys to place their claymores when we've done. Back in a few minutes.'

With Whinger driving we lurched on as far as the edge of the river, then walked down the bank and out across the burning sand. We were carrying four figure-eleven targets and a crowbar with which to dig holes for their mounting posts. On the track at the far side we already had eight hinged targets laid out ready, flat on their backs, set so they'd come upright, facing the killer group, at a pull of the cords. Another three were fastened to the trunks of trees, so that a tug would swing them round into view.

Our task now was to place four static targets upright, edge-on to the firing party, so that they'd be virtually invisible at night; their purpose was to test the accuracy with which the Kamangans set their claymores, which would blast their contents horizontally into the killing zone. In a live ambush the claymores would be detonated by enemy walking into trip-wires, but for the purposes of the exercise, we'd set them off ourselves.

Genesis was first up the bank on the far side, and he'd hardly reached the road before he exclaimed, 'Eh – what's this?'

He stood staring down at the dusty surface. In a second Whinger was beside him, muttering, 'Firekin' 'ell!'

'What's the matter?' I called.

'Footprints.'

'Ours, probably.'

'Come off it. Our guys wear boots.'

The sandy dust all round the prostrate target was printed with the patterns of our boot-soles from the day before, but on top of them, superimposed since the previous evening, were the smooth indentations of bare human feet.

'Keep off,' I said. 'Don't spoil them. We'll get Jason to suss them out.'

Jason Phiri, one of Joss's sergeant-majors, had worked as a forest ranger in a game-park, and was an ace tracker. An incredibly thin man, with arms and legs like charcoal sticks, he was known to his mates as Mabonzo – Bony Person. He stood out from the rest of the Kamangans partly because of his shape, partly because of his colour: whereas the rest were various shades of brown and black, he was more grey, as if he'd been dusted with wood ash. Joss told me he was a Bididi, from the west of the country, on the fringes of the Kalahari desert, where his tribe were akin to the Bushmen. Although his English was limited, he was the friendliest of the Kamangans, always grinning, always in a sunny temper. At the same time, he was quiet and rather shy, reluctant to push himself forward, and had an annoying habit of not letting on that he knew something until it was too late for the knowledge to be of any use. Behind his good humour there was a sense of strain, as if he was being driven by some deep sorrow or anger, which was what made him so eager to please us.

Now I shouted back to Joss to bring him over.

'Hey, Jason,' I said, as he approached. 'What d'you make of this?'

He looked hard at the tracks, then crossed to the next target, five metres away.

'Here also.' He pointed down.

'How many people?'

'Five, six.'

'When were they here?'

'Late in the night. Four, five o'clock this morning.'

'What were they doing?'

Jason shrugged. 'Poaching, looking for food.'

'I thought there weren't any people in this area.'

'Officially, there aren't,' said Joss. 'But some guys are always wandering about. These are on the move from one place to another.'

'What weapons would they have?'

'AKs, probably, nicked during the war. But mainly they'll be setting snares for antelopes and stuff.'

'They'd better look lively if they come back tonight,' said Whinger. 'If they walk across here in the dark, they'll get a fucking surprise.'

Joss gave one of his high-pitched laughs, reminding me of the witch doctor's twittering. 'They won't be back. I bet these targets scared the shit out of them. Cardboard men lying flat on the ground? Oh, wah!' He rolled his eyes extravagantly. 'Witchcraft, you betcha. Somebody making a *juju*. They'll think some big *fiti* has been here.'

The discovery livened everyone up. Where had the barefoot guys gone? The idea that eyes might be watching us out of the bush was interesting, and as we fixed the targets for the claymores, we kept a sharp lookout. A grey lourie called persistently from tall trees in the middle distance: *go-wee, go-wee*. After every few calls it flew to another perch and started again, and when it was stationary, it was impossible to make out, especially when the heat haze built up and everything began to shimmer.

'He can see somebody,' Jason told me. 'He only call for humans.' But as far as we could tell, it was us, rather than anyone else, the lourie was barracking, telling us to go away.

We were coming back from the targets when Joss called us across to look at something – a tunnel about a foot in diameter, going down into the ground at an angle.

'Hey, man!' he said, as I stopped in front of it. 'Don't stand there. You might have an accident to your wedding gear.'

'What is it?'

'The hole was dug by an aardvark, an ant-bear. You know, with a long snout, like this?' With his hands he sketched a downward-pointing proboscis. 'He's the greatest excavator in creation. He digs himself a hole like this every night. But now, I think we've got a warthog in residence.'

'How can you tell?'

'There.' He pointed at a heap of round balls of dung, quite fresh-looking, a few feet away. 'The thing is, warty can't turn round in a hole like this, so he goes in backwards, and when he comes out, he comes like a—'

As he was still saying 'rocket' a subterranean rumble started up and with a terrific rush a bristling grey pig erupted into the open. Vicious curved tusks gleamed yellow-white on either side of its snout, and it made off at high speed, with its ridiculous tail straight up in the air.

'You see,' Joss giggled. 'A hundred kilos, jet-propelled. Get that amidships, and you wouldn't feel very well.'

By 1030 the sun was really hot and our party was glad to sit in the shade, not interfering, while the Kamangans set their claymores and ran the firing wires back. I reckoned they'd put the mines too far from the targets, and told them so, but I wanted them to learn from experience, so when they stood up for what they had done, I gave in and let things rest. Once that job was finished, we were ready to roll back to camp.

So far we'd given no indications on timing. All we'd told Joss was that the exercise would go down that night. At last light his guys would move forward on foot to a forming-up point, and then, in the dark, they'd go on to occupy the ambush position itself. All they'd know was that the arms shipment might come through any time within the twenty-six hours from 2200 that day to 2400 the next. What we didn't tell them was that we had no intention of cracking off the action during the first night. That would make things too easy. Instead, we planned to have them lie out all night and all the next day before we made anything happen.

Back in camp, we got a surprise. The British Embassy in Mulongwe had sent a message via Hereford saying that the President intended to visit our training establishment to watch Alpha Commando in action.

'The President!' I went. 'For fuck's sake! Who is he?'

'Haven't a clue,' said Stringer, who'd taken the radio message. 'It just said "The President".'

'He's called Bakunda,' said Genesis, who always did his homework. 'General Kabwe Bakunda.'

'Back under!' said Phil, derisively. 'Sure it's not Bakongo, or Banzongo, or Bonanza? What about Canaan Banana!'

'They put him away for getting his banana up the wrong end,' said Pav. 'Big joke!'

'Wrong,' went Mart. 'He did a runner over the border.'

'Yeah,' I said. 'But they went after him and nicked him.'

Genesis grinned, tolerantly, and said, 'Definitely Bakunda. And his nickname is Rhino.'

'Firekin 'ell!' groaned Whinger. 'That's all we need.'

'What does he want,' I asked, 'a bloody drill parade?'

'No, no,' said Stringer. 'He wants to see his guys working.'

'He'd better get a shift on, then. We're supposed to move south the day after tomorrow. When's he due?'

'They were talking about this afternoon or tomorrow.'

'This afternoon's no good. Tell them tomorrow. That's his best chance. How's he getting here, anyway? Not by road, surely?'

'No, chopper. Apparently he's got a Puma.'

'Well,' I said, 'bollocks to him. We're not going to make any special arrangements. If he comes, he can fucking walk out to the ambush site like everyone else. I'm not having him fly in. It would make the whole thing too phoney. Tell them tomorrow afternoon, Stringer, and get an ETA. Seventeen hundred would be best for us. Tell them he'll have to walk at least fifteen ks in the dark. And if he wants to see the ambush go down, he'd better plan to stay overnight.'

Stringer looked a bit uneasy at all my instructions. In his innocence he obviously thought everyone should go on their knees in front of the President, so I told him not to worry: just carry on.

I thought Joss might be fazed by the news, but on the contrary, he seemed quite chuffed. Although he'd never met Bakunda, he reckoned the guy was all right; apparently he'd been through Sandhurst, and had some genuine military experience. His rank was not entirely unearned.

'No sweat,' he said, cheerfully. 'Let Rhino join the party!'

'Why's he called Rhino?' Pav demanded. 'Anything to do with the thickness of his skin?'

'Could be,' Joss agreed. 'But it's more to do with his shape. His height and width are exactly the same – no difference at all.'

Joss gave his briefing at 1600 in the shade of an ebony grove. By then the power of the sun was declining, and under the big trees the air was pleasantly cool. The Kamangans sat round on the earth in their four patrols of eight, each with a couple of NCOs in command. The SAS team sat in a semi-circle behind Joss, keeping a low profile while he talked.

With the Africans grouped together like that, the variations in their uniform became obvious. The guys were all wearing DPMs of a sort, but there were differences in pattern and colour which showed the garments had come from different sources.

Some men wore berets, dark green or black, some had woolly balaclavas, some wide-brimmed bush hats; a few sported American pudding-basin helmets, a few more had long-peaked DPM caps, and others were bare-headed. Their weapons were more standardised: AK47s and Galils formed the main armament. In each patrol there were two RPGs and one gympi, and everyone, no matter what weapon he carried, wore bandoliers of 7.62mm ammunition slung both ways across the chest. One or two of the guys also had fearsome-looking machetes in scabbards attached to their belts. I'd seen them fanatically sharpening those knives for hours on end, until they could have shaved with them. Not that many of them did much shaving; the majority hardly seemed to grow any beard. Jason was a bugger for sharpening: he was at it day and night, as if doggedly preparing for some major carve-up.

We hadn't liked to enquire too much about the scars most of them had on their faces. We assumed they were tribal marks, but the only man we questioned – about the row of small vertical cuts he had under each eye – claimed that they were the result of some operation he'd had for vision defects when he was a child.

Most of these men were Kaswiris, the tribe that occupied the northern half of the country. The rebels were Afundis, their traditional enemies in the south. Even though we hadn't seen any fighting yet, we'd heard any number of stories about how each tribe hated the other's guts. It sounded just like the Hutus and Tutsis in Rwanda. Given the slightest excuse, either side would start a massacre.

These, I kept telling myself, are the absolute élite of the Kamangan army. Joss had told us some hair-raising stories about recruiting practices down south, how Afundi boys of twelve or thirteen were kidnapped from their villages, taken to a different area, beaten up and forced to become killers with threats of having their arms and legs cut off if they failed to perform. How many of these guys in front of us had been co-opted by such methods? How many believed that if they smeared themselves with palm nut-oil, it would make them bullet-proof? Some did, we knew, because Joss had described a fantastic scene in which one man, having anointed himself, volunteered to act as a target for an RPG.

'Jesus!' Phil had said, greatly excited by the idea. 'What happened?'

'He stood up on a wall, and somebody fire at him from about thirty metres,' Joss replied. 'The rocket killed him, of course. It blew him to pieces.'

'So how did his fellow believers explain that one?'

'Easy. They said he'd eaten food cooked by a woman, and that had destroyed the oil's magic powers.'

I kept thinking of that as Joss went carefully through his plan, first on a blackboard, then in the dust on the ground, using small pieces of wood as individual men. He explained how, when the ambush went down, the directing staff – that is, us, the SAS – would illuminate the area with parachute flares from a Shamouli hand-held launcher. Figure targets would spring into view for a few seconds, disappear, then come back up. He emphasised how quick and accurate the members of the killer group would have to be, and rammed home the need for discipline.

He did the job well, giving clear explanations, repeating himself just the right amount, answering questions. He talked in English, but now and then, if a man didn't seem to have understood something, he would break into rapid volleys of Nyanja. Although all the Kamangans spoke English, some of them had such peculiar intonation that it was often hard to tell what they were on about.

When he'd finished, he asked if I'd like to say a few words, so I got up and went forward beside him.

'*Zikomo*, Major,' I began. The local word for 'thank you' was an easy one, and several of our guys were already using it to each other. 'Just a couple of things,' I began, talking slowly. 'First, I repeat what Major Mvula just said about discipline. In any ambush, the most important thing is self-control. While you're waiting, no matter how uncomfortable you are, *you must keep still.* Even if a scorpion's attacking your bollocks, you don't move. You've all been in the bush. You know how movement catches the eye. If an animal keeps still, you don't see it. If it flaps one ear, you spot it. No matter how long you have to remain in position, I don't want to see anyone flap his ears.'

I paused, and saw one or two grins spread across the intent faces.

'The next thing is, water. Again, it's a matter of discipline. You must make your water last. Budget for the worst. Expect to be in position all tonight, all tomorrow and most of the next night. Drink as little as possible. Apart from anything else, the less you drink, the less you need to piss.

'The third thing is this. There's a chance that the exercise may turn into a live operation. As far as we know, the enemy forces are a good way to the south. But we don't have any up-to-date intelligence. It's possible that in the last couple of days one of the Afundi units has moved north. They may have a long-range patrol out – we don't know. They may be creeping up the very track you'll be watching. In other words, there's all the more reason to remain fully alert. If an enemy patrol does come into the killing zone, you want to make sure you drop every single one of them.

'All right, then? Do your best. We'll be watching you.'

With that, we were ready to move. We deliberately concealed the fact that the President was due to visit, as we thought it would distract the guys and spoil their concentration. The chances were that even if he did see the ambush go down, he'd arrive on the location and leave it in the dark, so that most of his subjects wouldn't realise he was there.

The move-up went without a hitch. The column set out on foot in single file at 1730 as the sun was going down behind the trees on the horizon, a vast, blood-red ball. In that latitude, south of the Equator, the light faded fast, and by the time the ambush party reached the site we'd chosen for the final holding area and Bergen cache, at 1910, it was fully dark. The place was easy to find, even at night, because a group of fifteen or twenty tall leadwood trees stood on their own in the middle of a sea of grass. You could see them from some distance off, no matter which way you approached.

The ambush parties left their Bergens neatly set out in formation in a glade among the trees, eight to a row, each touching the next, so that if they came back at night, every man should be able to identify his own by touch. In a last-minute check Joss made sure that everyone had full water bottles, and basic rations in his belt-kit.

We left Genesis in charge of the rear cut-off group. He had four men to maintain all-round defence on the Bergen cache and make sure nobody was trying to follow us up. There was also a Kamangan signaller to man the radio link with base. The rest of us went on. I'd detailed Pavarotti to master-mind the left cut-off group, Andy to take the right, and Phil to stick with the killer group. Whinger and I were going to lurk on the Kopje, keeping behind Joss in a kind of tactical headquarters from which we could control the exercise and react if anything went wrong. With us we had Mart, who'd brought his full medical kit in case a casualty needed immediate attention. That left Chalky, Stringer and Danny back in camp, listening out for messages from Mulongwe, and ready to receive the President, if he came.

Those of us controlling the exercise up front were in touch with each other through our covert radios, but the commanders of the various groups had only comms cords with which to send messages. Once they were in position, onc pull would mean 'Enemy in sight', two pulls, 'Fire!'

With only a sliver of crescent moon hanging in the sky, the night was very dark, and it was difficult to move quietly. When the eight-man left cut-off group headed out, they sounded like a herd of buffalo crashing through the scrub, and after a minute or so I went on the radio to Pav.

'Too much fucking noise,' I said softly. 'Tell them to slow down.'

'I have,' came the answer.

'Okay.'

The other groups were no better, and when we ourselves followed them up, I had to sympathise. In long, dry grass the going was bad enough, but in the frequent patches of mopane scrub, where the ground was littered with brittle dead leaves, it was impossible to avoid crackling and crunching. I kept telling myself that if we were in the war zone, we'd be making ourselves very vulnerable, advancing noisily in this fashion, without any forward vision.

Except for the background chorus of crickets, the night was dead quiet, with only the faintest easterly breeze, and from our vantage point on top of the Kopje Whinger, Mart and I heard a good deal of rustling and scraping as the groups settled into position. Then Pavarotti's voice came up in my earpiece: 'Left cut-off in.'

'Roger,' I answered. A couple of minutes later Phil reported the killer group in. Then came Andy, from away on the right.

'All stations, listen out,' I said.

I wondered what the silveries were thinking. Most of them were country lads, who'd come from villages of staw huts, without electricity, so presumably they were used to the dark. But for us Brits it was still an adventure to be out in the African night. Above us the stars were bright as diamonds, far brighter than they ever shine in the northern hemisphere. Diamonds, I thought: that's why we're here, to help win back the diamond mines for Bakunda. But why was Whitehall supporting him? What was the Brit government's interest in shoring up his regime? Nobody in Hereford had been too clear about that. Maybe, if the President did join us, he'd spill a few beans.

For the time being, there wasn't much light at ground level. Through binoculars I could pick out the smooth, grey trunk of the baobab, and occasional pale-looking strips where a few yards of the sandy track were in view. But apart from them, the bush was a ragged sea of black. Provided the guys kept still, no intruder could possibly guess that thirty-odd armed men were lying in wait.

Whinger, Mart and I had agreed to share stags – two hours on, four off. I took the first, comfortably settled in a cleft between two big boulders. The floor of the little gully was about two feet wide, and the front end of it looked straight out over the killing ground – a perfect vantage point.

My time was nearly up before anything happened. The odd mozzie came whining past, but I'd smeared on a good dose of repellent, and nothing bit me. Then, out of the silence away to our left, came a deep, booming call that made the hair on my neck stir. *Aoum! Aoum!*

I heard a rustle in the grass behind me, and there was Whinger, crawling up the gully. 'What the fuck was that?' he whispered.

'Lions.'

The call came again, closer.

'There.' I pointed. 'Jesus!' I breathed. 'This'll make the silveries' bollocks shrivel.'

We lay there listening. The call sounded a third time, closer still. Then suddenly, as if the lions had summoned it, the wind got up. One moment the air was still; the next, we felt a vigorous gust. Then a loud roar came sweeping towards us through the trees from the west. The noise grew so fast that at first I thought a train or an aircraft was approaching, even though reason told me that was impossible. Next I reckoned that heavy rain must be falling and about to swamp us.

It turned out to be none of those things, only this violent, freak wind, which hit us with a cold blast. It blew for no more than three or four minutes, but the noise was so loud that it drowned out the lions, and we couldn't tell if they were still moving our way. Then, quite quickly, the wind died, and silence returned.

The disturbance left me shuddering, not so much from cold as from the memory of the chill that had hit us at the witch doctor's.

'I bet the darkies are shitting themselves,' I whispered.

Whinger nodded. I don't think he was too happy himself. The sudden violence of the gust had been quite alarming. But before he could say anything, *brrrrrrppppp!* A burst of automatic fire ripped out from away to our right. In seconds every man in the right cut-off group was blasting off long bursts. Through the racket I heard Andy bellow 'Fucking *stop! Stop! Stop!*' And then in Nyanja, '*Ima!*'

With glasses I swept the river bank. The hail of rounds had kicked up dust in thick clouds. Apart from that, I could see nothing.

'Green One to Green Three,' I called on the covert radio. 'What the hell's going on?'

'Something moved to the right of the killer zone,' said Andy.

'Those lions?'

'Not big enough. Only one, anyway. I think it was a hyena.'

'Get your commander to give them a bollocking.'

'He's at it already.'

'Tell him to repeat: no firing until a Shamouli goes up.'

'Will do.'

'Make sure they all get properly stuck in. I'm resetting the ambush, as of now.'

After that little burst of excitement, everything went quiet, and the rest of the night passed without incident. Taking turns, Whinger and I got our heads down for good stretches; then, at 0515, just before first light, I left him and Mart on the Kopje and pulled back to find out what was happening about the presidential visit.

The Bergen cache was designed to be part of the exercise: the guys left in charge were supposed to challenge anyone who approached – so I was glad to find that one of them spotted me moving towards him through the half light of dawn. Correctly, he called out, 'Two.'

'Six,' I replied. 'Well done.'

I came in under the deep black shadow of the trees, found Genesis and said, 'Any word from base?'

'Nothing yet.'

'Let's get through, then.'

'Sure.'

He led me across to where the signaller had slung his aerials. The 319 set was on listening watch, and in a couple of minutes we got a response.

The presidential visit was on.

FOUR

Bakunda's chopper was due in to base camp at 1645. Our guys there could welcome him and bring him out to the cache on foot, but protocol demanded that I should go back to meet him there, give him a briefing, and escort him personally to the ambush location.

I spent a good deal of the day at the cache, chatting with Genesis in person and with Stringer over the Kamangan radio circuit.

'I don't know who he'll have with him,' I said. 'There's bound to be some aides and/or BGs. But the point is, we don't want a shower of hangers-on up front. Tell the guy only one other can go forward with him. Okay?'

I knew I was sounding edgy – the result of too little sleep – but Stringer got the message and didn't argue.

Once he'd told Mulongwe the score, and details were settled, I went forward again and sneaked up the back of the Kopje, taking Whinger and Mart a three-litre container of water to top up their bottles. I found them in good shape, comfortably ensconced in a tent of mozzie netting which they'd slung from some of the boulders.

'Cushy bastards!' I said softly. 'It's all right for you.'

'And you.' Whinger opened a flap of netting to admit me to the sanctum. 'I'm sorry for those poor sods out there. The tsetses are fucking horrendous. Pavarotti and Andy reckon they're being eaten alive.'

'I expect they are. I knocked off a good few on my way in. Look at the bastards on the netting, too.'

The big grey flies were dotted all over the outside of our

fragile canopy, crawling about, trying to get through, as they scented prey below.

'How are the guys doing?'

'Pretty well. There's been practically no disturbance. Discipline's good. The thing is, they've got a great cabaret to watch.'

'What's that?'

'You know that outbreak of firing? Somebody killed a hyena. Now every vulture in Kamanga's homing in on the body. Look through the gap in the rocks.'

I peered out through our observation channel and saw an amazing sight: on the far bank of the sand river a mass of feathered bodies was writhing and struggling, apparently all piled on top of each other in a heap. Binoculars revealed that the naked heads and necks of the vultures were shiny with blood and slime. As I watched, more heavy bodies came plummeting in to land on the outskirts of the group and hopped inwards to join the feast.

'Jesus!' I went. 'Nightmare birds.'

'Can't be much left of the hyena,' said Mart, matter-of-factly. 'They only found it about an hour ago. Just two of them at first. We saw them circling, way up. Then they dropped down, and all the rest came bombing in.'

'Sure it's only a hyena?' I asked. 'Not one of the poachers?'

'Nar,' went Mart. 'Before the birds arrived we could see it laid on its back with all four feet in the air, like a spotted dog, its stomach blown up like a balloon.'

'At least it means some of the silvery spoons can shoot,' said Whinger.

'Even you might have hit the poor bastard at that range,' I told him. 'Listen. The President's on his way. His Puma's due into camp at 1645. They asked if we couldn't clear an LZ for it to land nearer the ambush location, but I refused. I'm not having the exercise buggered up by some darkie rupert.'

'How are you going to get him here, then?' Whinger asked.

'Stringer'll bring him forward to the Bergen cache, which I've downgraded to a transit post. I'll go back, meet him, brief him and bring him on.'

'What time will we crack off the action?'

'No point in keeping everyone hanging about longer than we need. The guys will have had a belly-full of waiting by then. It's fully dark by 1800. If old Back-Under's here by 1830 or so, we'll go for 1900.'

As I waited with Genesis at the cache, I didn't know what to feel. On the one hand, it was irritating that Bakunda should muscle in on our exercise, and that I should have to make these special arrangements to deal with him. At the same time, it was flattering that he cared enough about our training task to come out and see some action. So in a way I was looking forward to his visit; after all, a president's a president, even if his country's third world and third rate.

The air was so still we thought we might hear the Puma coming into base camp, even though we were several kilometres away. In fact we never heard a thing, and, as dusk was falling, I'd begun to wonder whether there'd been a last-minute cancellation. Then we saw the party approaching across the low ground that fell away behind the grove. Stringer was in the lead, with five black guys following in single file. The one immediately behind him barely reached to his shoulder. *That* can't be him, I thought, but a moment later I realised it was.

I slipped forward and stationed myself behind a thick trunk at the edge of the grove. When Stringer was about four feet off, I called, 'Stringer – over here!' As he stopped, the last guy in the file reacted so violently that he rose clear of the ground.

I stepped out into the open, and said, 'Welcome to Mantrap.'

'Hi, Geordie!' Stringer grinned. 'Can I introduce the President, General Bakunda? Mr President, this is Sergeant-Major Geordie Sharp.'

'How d'you do, sir?' I stepped forward and shook hands.

'Pleased to meet you.'

In the last of the light, I couldn't see much except a big white smile, and touches of grey or silver in a clipped moustache. There was more grey in the sideburns that came down below a dark beret, and the broad face put me in mind of that monster from the distant past, Idi Amin. Bakunda hadn't got the height – he was knee-high to a pisspot – but he was pretty much the same width. I'd feared he might turn up in some Mickey Mouse uniform with rows of phony gongs across his chest. In fact he was wearing plain DPMs, without any insignia, and carrying no weapon except a pistol in a belt-holster. Slung round his neck was a pair of useful-looking binoculars.

'Good journey?' I ventured.

'No problem. We had a nice, smooth flight!' The accent was very much Sandhurst officer, not bush at all.

'Well, I can't offer you any hospitality, I'm afraid. But before we move off I'll brief you on what we've arranged. Then we'll head on to the location.'

I led the way to a patch of sand in which I'd scratched a map of the ambush, switched on a torch and introduced Genesis. As the President pulled off his beret, revealing short, tight curls of iron-grey hair, the light glinted off beads of perspiration on his forehead. At close quarters he smelt of lavender overlying acrid sweat.

'We're now in the Bergen cache, two ks from the location,' I explained. 'Those are your guys' packs, over there.' I flashed the beam on to them. 'They've left them here so that they can vacate the area at speed as soon as the ambush has gone down. They'll come back here, recover their kit, and disappear into the bush. That's all part of the exercise. Normally, this site would be a tactical one as well. That is, it would be under guard, and nobody would show a light like I'm doing now. But with your visit . . .'

Bakunda gave a high-pitched giggle. 'You mean, I've wrecked your plans! That's what they call me – the wrecker!'

'No, no. But just imagine this place as dark and quiet as everywhere else, with guys deployed in all-round defence. Anway, the plan is this.'

I took him quickly through the scenario, indicating the positions of the targets and the various groups, and telling him that I'd initiate proceedings by firing a flare. As I talked, I was eyeballing his followers. Two of them were really big young lads, well-built and athletic looking – bodyguards, for sure. The other two were older – some kind of staff officers, I guessed – and they looked hellishly uncomfortable.

'How long will you give them?' the boss asked.

'What – to shoot?'

'Yes.'

'The centre targets will be up for fifteen seconds, initially. Then a couple more exposures, but shorter. We've also got one target way out here, on the right, and one on the left, to simulate people doing runners. Then there are the claymore targets in the central killing ground.'

'Quite difficult for the chaps, having to react fast after so long a wait.'

'That's the whole point of the exercise: to get the feel of what a real ambush is like. Way back in the fifties, when our Regiment was in the jungle in Malaya, the guys sometimes maintained ambushes for five or six days on end.'

He nodded, looking impressed. 'And who's giving the orders?'

'I'll fire the Shamouli, but after that it's all Kamangans in command – Major Mvula and his subordinates. Our guys are only there as back-up.'

'Good, good.' Bakunda nodded again.

'There's only been one hiccup so far.' I told him about the hyena, and added, 'OK, then – if you're ready, we'll go. There's just one thing.'

'Yes?'

'I don't want all these people with us.' I gestured at the entourage. 'If it's all right by you, they can stay here, and us two will go on together.'

Bakunda glanced up quickly. 'Are you giving me orders?'

'No, sir.' I looked straight at him. 'I just said what I'd prefer. I thought it had been arranged over the radio, in any case.'

He sidestepped my remark and said, 'What's the objection to them coming?'

'There'd be too much noise. Don't get me wrong, but your

soldiers aren't totally reliable. We've seen that in training. We saw it again with the hyena. There's supposed to be no firing until a flare goes up – but somebody freaked on that animal. If they hear a party crashing through the bush, they could easily open up on us.'

'By Jove, they'd better not!' he said.

'If they did, it might be too late to worry. Besides, space in our OP's constricted. These other guys of yours wouldn't be able to see anything, even if they reached it safely.'

'Well . . .' Bakunda looked round at his men. 'I make it a rule: never move without my big fellers around me.'

'Listen,' I said. 'There's nobody going to touch you. Half your special force is lying in ambush out there. It's up to you.'

For a few seconds he stared at me – not that he could see much in the starlight. Then he suddenly gave me a playful punch on the shoulder and said, 'Hey! Your name's Sharp. You are sharp! I like it.' Turning away he said, 'All right, chaps. Wait for us here.'

In the starlight it wasn't easy to navigate accurately. I was walking on a bearing of 84 mils, and several times I recognised the lie of the land. But similar features kept recurring – open areas, patches of scrub, stands of trees, one after the other – and I needed the way-marks I'd memorised during my earlier trips.

About halfway to the location, lions started calling from the same quarter as the night before. I stopped to listen, not sure how my companion would react. I was amazed when he whispered, 'An old male.'

'How can you tell?'

'The depth of the voice.'

'You're a lion expert, then?'

'I wouldn't say that. But I grew up in the bush. When I was a boy, we saw lions every day.'

'Where was that?'

'Here, man, right here!' He gave his high-pitched giggle again and pointed behind us. 'I was born in a hut in Mbiya, the village where the camp is.'

'So that's why you opted to come out on this exercise?'

'Partly, yes. I wanted to see you fellows in action, but it's always nice to come home.'

The lions had gone quiet, and I started forward again, wondering how the hell a ragamuffin boy raised in one of those grass huts could have climbed to the top of the tree. This guy must have both brains and guts, I decided.

In a few more minutes we reached a single big rock which stood in the open about 200 metres short of the Kopje. I stopped beside it and gave the pressel on my radio two jabs.

'Green One?' Whinger's voice came low but clear in my earpiece.

'At the rock,' I told him. 'Our visitor's with me. Everything okay?'

'One ND.'

'I thought I heard something. Nobody injured, is there?'

'No, no.'

'When was it?'

'About an hour ago. Otherwise, no problem. Come on in.'

'Roger. With you in a couple of minutes.'

'What happened?' Bakunda asked.

'They had an ND – a negligent discharge. Somebody let off a round by mistake. Come on – let's get in there.'

Over that last stretch I moved with extreme care, partly to impress my companion, partly from a sense of self-preservation. When I warned him about the danger of getting fired at, I hadn't been bullshitting. I knew that by now the Kamangans must be well on edge, expecting action any moment: after the fiasco with the hyena, it wouldn't have surprised me if one of them loosed off at any noise he heard, and bugger the pre-set arcs of fire. The news of the ND only strengthened my suspicions.

As we crawled the last few yards up the ridge of the Kopje, I saw Whinger's head appear above a rock. I'd already told Bakunda who we'd be meeting, so I just whispered introductions and moved him up to the good vantage point, in the gully between two rocks. The starlight was bright enough for all the main features to show clearly.

'There you are,' I whispered. 'The River Congo. The killer group's straight down below us. Right-hand cut-off group over there, left-hand there. See the baobab? That's the divider between the arcs of fire on that side.'

'How do the groups communicate?' Bakunda whispered. 'Radios?' He gestured at my earpiece.

I shook my head. 'No. The guys are lying very close to each other – only three or four feet apart. The commander of each group has a comms cord. At this stage, one pull will mean "enemy coming in", two, "enemy on target".'

It took only a minute to show him our dispositions. Then I pulled back to make final checks with my own guys out front. When Phil, Andy and Pavarotti all reported satisfactorily, there seemed no point in waiting any longer, so I said, 'Green One to all stations. Action in figures two minutes from now. Wait out.'

I'd already got five shamoulis laid out on a flat patch of grass among the rocks. Now I pulled out the safety pins on their white cords, so that the brass triggers dropped down, ready for firing. I handed the first of them to Whinger, who stood it on the ground and held it at an angle, like a mortar.

'Green One. Thirty seconds . . .' My own heart was going faster than usual, even though I'd been through this many times before. 'Twenty . . . ten . . . five . . . stand by, stand by.'

I raised a thumb at Whinger. WHOOSH! went the rocket, racing up over the killing ground. The para-flare burst with a soft pop, and suddenly the whole area was bathed in harsh white light. Whinger waited a second, then, as soon as he saw the chute starting to float left-handed, put up another rocket to the right.

BRRRRRPPPP! A burst of automatic fire ripped out from below us. Tracer rounds skimmed away high over the bush ahead, way above any possible target on the ground.

'CUNT!' roared a voice which I recognised as Andy's. 'Wait for the fucking targets!'

'Ground targets,' I said quietly over the radio.

With a faint rattle in the distance, eight figure targets sprang into view. At the same moment Pav switched on the battery-powered ambush lights, flooding the scene with light.

From in front and below us a high African voice screamed out the order '*Rapid fire!*'

As one, the killer group opened up. After the night silence, the noise seemed phenomenal. I could hear the AK47s firing short bursts of three or four rounds, with the gympis putting in longer bursts among them. Somebody's rounds were going very low. Dust exploded in front of the targets and boiled up in the lights, obscuring the figures. Tracer showed that many rounds were flying way over the trees.

I counted to fifteen, then ordered, 'Ground targets down.'

The figures vanished, but the firing continued for several seconds. As soon as it ceased, I called, 'Tree targets up.'

This time the response was much slower. Whinger and I could see the new targets, which had swung into view round the trunks of trees, but through the dust haze nobody else spotted them. At last the Kamangan commander yelled out, '*Engage single targets!*' and another fusillade began.

Again we gave them fifteen seconds, then a pause with nothing in sight. Next I got Pav to bring up four of the ground targets for five or six seconds only, and in the middle of that barrage I got Andy to fire the claymores.

Ba-boom! With blinding flashes the two heavy explosions went off almost simultaneously. Seething dust blotted out the entire killing ground.

'Runner targets,' I ordered.

Up they went, single figures way out to right and left. The right-hand cut-off group opened up instantaneously, but the guys on the left were slow. I heard Pavarotti roar, 'Fucking *fire*!' but they only got five or six rounds off before their target vanished again.

The claymores had set fire to the bush beyond the killing ground. Red flames began to run along the ground and surge up into clumps of grass. Loud crackling noises reached us. I heard the commander of the killer group shout, 'Watch and shoot!'

'Ground targets up,' I ordered.

Now the figures were just visible through the swirling smoke, showing up as silhouettes against the flames behind them. Again there was rapid fire.

'Down! I called. Then, 'Runners again,'

This time Pavarotti's guys pulled themselves together and blazed away like lunatics. Finally I ordered, 'All targets down. Search parties out.'

I heard our guys pass on the instruction, and the Kamangan commanders repeat them. Then suddenly the bush was full of running figures as dark, camouflaged shapes sprinted forward to the river bank. Most of them were shouting and screaming with the release of tension. Pavarotti had doused the ambush lights, and the last of Whinger's Shamoulis was burning out some distance off to the left, so that the main illumination was a red glow from the fire.

'How was that?' I said, standing up behind the President.

'Fantastic! Splendid show! Some wild shooting, but who wouldn't? What are they doing now?'

'Clearing the area. In a real ambush, they'd be making certain there was no one left alive in the box. Now, we've told them to count the hits on the targets and get back in fast. As soon as—'

My words were cut short by a new burst of firing from our left. I heard Pavarotti yell '*Stop!*' but several more rounds cracked off, and to my consternation I saw tracer streak towards the killing ground. We already had guys out there. Something was badly wrong.

There was more yelling, another burst of rounds, tracer hurtling vertically into the sky. When the firing ceased, the commotion continued, with several voices shouting and the sound of a struggle.

'Pav,' I went on the radio, 'what the fuck was that?'

There was a pause before he answered, and when he did, he was panting. 'Little local difficulty,' he gasped. 'One of the bastards flipped.'

'Anybody hurt?'

'I wouldn't call it that. Let's say he lost his head.'

I swallowed an exclamation. Knowing Pav, I was pretty sure what he meant. All I said was, 'Can you handle it?'

'Yeah, yeah. I'll see you shortly.'

The extra shooting put the fear of God into the guys round the targets. The search parties came flying back, the cut-offs first, then the killer group, each commander calling out, 'Last man . . . *in*.' Then suddenly everybody had gone. We heard footsteps crashing away towards the north, and soon the only noise was the crackling of the flames beyond the river.

When the disturbance broke out, Bakunda had still been lying on the ground between the boulders, so that he hadn't appreciated the full extent of the fuck-up occurring out to his left. But now he was on his feet and asking, 'What happened over there?'

'Not sure,' I said non-committally. 'Sounded like somebody dropped his rifle and it started firing automatically. We'll hear when we get back.'

That seemed to satisfy him, and he asked, 'What next, then?'

'Your lads are already on their way back to the Bergen cache, fast as they can go. They'll grab their packs, and then our guys will beest them about fifteen ks to the east.'

'Beest?'

'Hustle them on. Your commanders have to navigate, find their way to an RV. Our guys just keep the pace up. The point is to simulate a fast evacuation from the ambush location. That's what we'd do in a live situation – get the hell out. Tonight we've arranged for a truck to go round and wait at the RV, to bring everyone back to camp.'

I was still struggling to get my mind round the dust-up in Pavarotti's group. From his laconic answer, I felt certain the silveries were going to arrive back at base one man deficient.

To take my mind off that worry, I said, 'How about a quick look at the targets?'

'Sure.'

The fire had already retreated from the killing ground as it ate into the bush beyond, and we needed our torches to get a clear look at the figure eights, most of which once again were flat on the deck. All the ground-mounted group in the centre had been well riddled, but the tree targets had taken only a couple of rounds apiece. The right-hand runner had one bullet through the shoulder, and the left-hand target was untouched. So, too, were the two edge-on figures, set for the claymores.

'Look at these,' I said. 'I *told* them they'd got their mines too far apart,' I said. 'This'll be a good lesson to them.'

'What about the fire?' Bakunda asked.

'Nothing we can do about it. But it'll burn out when it comes to the next sand river.'

The President didn't say much as we trekked back to camp. I thought he was maybe worried or annoyed by the lack of discipline his guys had shown. We passed straight through the Bergen cache, pausing only to pick up his escort of heavies. I was afraid we'd see one pack still sitting on the ground, but the whole lot had gone, and nothing was said.

Once we reached base, Bakunda became very matey. He started calling me 'Old Boy' and chattering away about his time at Sandhurst. He'd done two years there as an officer cadet, he told me: No. 1 Company in Victory College. He was quite disappointed when he found I hadn't been there too and couldn't swap reminiscences.

The cooks had prepared a special supper table for the presidential party, but he insisted that we all got together, so the tables were pushed up into one, and we ate in a single group – spiced meat balls, rice, tinned pineapple. The heavy bodyguards looked ill-at-ease using knives and forks; I reckoned it was normally fingers. Then, after the meal, Bakunda said to one of them, 'Hey, Basil, where's that beer?'

Out came cans of King Lion lager, brewed in Mulongwe, and soon we were swapping stories round our fire. Normally, I wouldn't have started drinking until the exercise was well and truly finished, but I knew that with Pavarotti and Genesis in charge the last phase of it was in good hands, and in any case I felt I had a duty to entertain our visitor. At first I was on edge, but when a radio call confirmed that the party had reached their transport and was on its way in, I was able to relax.

'In my day,' the President was saying, 'we didn't have

anything like the equipment you chaps have. Satellite communications, for instance – unheard of. Spy satellites – ditto. GPS – nothing like it existed. We had to find our own way around.'

'In my day'. That was one of his favourite phrases. It came out again and again. It was clear he'd enjoyed his time at Sandhurst, and he had nostalgic feelings about England. Apart from anything else, he'd managed to lay some white woman there during a passing-out dance. He'd got her into some attic room, and banged the back of his head on the sloping roof when he stood up after the performance. But at the same time he genuinely admired our modern equipment and methods.

By the time we were on our third round of beers the atmosphere had grown quite mellow. Chalky White was well away, trying out his few, newly acquired words of Nyanja on the President.

Bakunda himself was becoming indiscreet, and I felt the moment had come to ask a few pertinent questions. I turned to Whinger, and said quietly, 'Crack out a bottle of rum – see if we can get this guy going.' Then I turned back to our guest, and said, 'I don't want to seem rude, but can you explain why we're here?'

'Because I asked for you!' he exclaimed with his bark of a laugh. 'I asked Her Majesty's Government for assistance in fighting the Afundi rebels, and here you are!'

'Yeah, but HMG get a lot more requests than the SAS can fulfil. Again, no offence, but what's special about Kamanga?'

'My dear fellow, the well-being of our country is critical to the stability of the whole region. If we come apart at the seams, the rot will spread very fast. Zaire, Angola, Namibia, Botswana, Zambia, Malawi – every country will be in danger. They could go down like dominoes.'

He lit off into a political tirade, talking angrily, denouncing Marxists and revolutionaries in general. I couldn't help smiling at the thought of him, personally, coming apart at the seams. He looked as though he might do that at any moment, so tight was his tunic stretched over his stocky torso, and his out-of-date colonial expressions gave his speech a wonderful period flavour.

The only thing that broke his flow was Whinger looming up at his elbow and offering him a plastic cup, with the words, 'Try this, General.'

Bakunda sniffed it, and rolled his eyes theatrically. 'Rum! I thought rum was reserved for the British navy. Splicing the mainbrace, and all that.'

'It is,' Whinger agreed. 'But we get it too when we're on arduous duties.'

'You call this arduous?' Bakunda beamed round at us. 'I call it a holiday! A busman's holiday – when you do what you normally do, but for fun!'

'Cheers, anyway,' I said, raising the cup that Whinger had given me. 'Sod the rebels.'

'Agreed!' He took a mouthful, rolled his eyes again, grimaced, swallowed, smacked his lips, and said, 'Hey! This is the real McCoy!' Then he cleared his throat and went on: 'You want to know why you're here? I'll tell you. Uranium. Don't pass it on, but that's the secret.'

'Yeah?' I replied, deliberately casual. 'I know you've got uranium mines, but what about them?'

'I've had overtures,' he said darkly. 'People wanting to buy the stuff. People your government doesn't approve of. '

'Such as?'

'You can guess. That crazy fellow in Libya, for one. Another madman in Baghdad. Both have made serious offers.'

'I bet. But you aren't playing ball?'

'Of course not. How could I? If we moved an inch in that direction, we'd be hit by international sanctions. The UK, US – everybody would clamp down on us.'

'But I thought the uranium mines were in the north.' I pointed over my shoulder.

'That's right.'

'So what's the worry?'

'The Afundis. They're the worry. And in particular, Muende. Why don't you use your special skills to go and, say, take him out?'

'Who's Muende?'

'Gus Muende, the Afundi leader. He should damn well know better. But he's another lunatic. He's a friend of Gadaffi. I ask you! Worse than him, even. Last year he went to Tripoli and got practically a royal welcome.'

Bakunda was working himself up, talking louder and louder. He downed the rest of his rum in one swallow and waved the empty cup around.

'Treacherous bastard!' he cried.

'What's the matter with him?'

'You tell me! His mother was a Scottish voluntary worker in Kamanga in the sixties. She abandoned him when he was only five, and I helped him. I got him into the military academy at Mulongwe, then I got him sent to America. I got him his place at West Point. I got him his military education. Without me, he'd be nothing. This is his way of saying thank you.'

Whinger circled round to Bakunda's elbow and skilfully refilled his cup. The President took a big swig, and shouted, 'Get him! Make the sun shine through him! That's what you chaps need to do. That's what you're here for.'

'Wait a minute,' I said. 'Our brief is to train Alpha Commando, not to go assassinating people.'

'That's what HMG say. But what they'd like is for you to put Muende underground. Their fear is the same as mine: that he'll take over the whole of Kamanga. If that happens, God help us. God help *you*. Gadaffi and Saddam Hussein will get all the uranium they ask for. What about that, hey? How's that for a scenario?'

It was hardly for me to tell the President to take it easy, but that was what I felt like doing. The veins in his neck were bulging; beads of sweat were standing out on his forehead, even though the night air was cool. A change of subject seemed in order.

'These guys we're training,' I said, gesturing round about. 'I gather they're Kaswiris. Different from the Afundis, obviously.'

'Different! By George! Different language, different customs, different everything. We hate the Afundis' guts.'

'We – you – you're a Kaswiri?'

'Of course. What else?' He drew himself upright on his ammunition box and thrust out his chest. 'We Kaswiris know how to behave.'

'Don't get me wrong, Mr President, but discipline isn't the force's strongest point yet.'

'Are you criticising Alpha Commando?'

'Not at all.' I held up a hand in token appeasement. 'Just pointing out the need for good control. You saw how high some of them were firing – all that tracer into the stratosphere.'

'Okay, okay,' he went. Then he leaned his grizzled head closer to me, and said confidentially, 'As you know, some of these chaps are not long down from the trees. So of course they need training. That's why you're here!'

'What about Bididis?' I asked. 'Where do they come in?'

'Bididis?' He seemed surprised. 'They're okay. They don't cause trouble. Why?'

'There's one at least in the commando, and he seems a useful fellow.'

'Well, that's a turn-up.'

'Why?'

'Because we have jokes about the Bididis. Like you and the Irish. They're the thick men of Africa – not a brain in their heads.'

'How about this Muende?'

'Muende!' The President gave a snort. 'He's the Afundi of Afundis, the worst. The fundamental orifice of the Afundis. Ha ha!'

'What age is he?'

'Thirty? Thirty-two? I don't know. What does it matter?' He turned and scowled at me, his jokiness veering towards irritation. 'Why don't you do me a favour: get down there and put some bullets through him?'

It wasn't the moment for a serious argument about the extent of our commitment. Bakunda was too far gone for that. So I just said casually, 'Well, of course we'll do anything we can to help.'

'Good man!' Bakunda leant over to slap me on the shoulder, missed because his arm was so short, and nearly swung himself off his perch. 'In the morning, we'll settle details. But in any case you'll go as far as Gutu.'

It was more a statement than a question.

'The mine there,' I said, stalling. 'Is it that important to you?'

'Of course! Gutu means diamonds. Muende's smuggling the diamonds out over the border, into South Africa, Namibia, everywhere. He's getting so much revenue that his strength is increasing all the time. He's buying all the weapons he wants. Look here! Only yesterday we heard that he's brought in foreign mercenaries to fight for him.'

'Mercenaries?' said Whinger, sharply. 'Where from?'

'How do I know?' Bakunda waved his cup about, slopping rum. 'Somebody said America.'

'Americans!' I went. 'Jesus. If we don't watch out, we'll find ourselves fighting former SEALs.'

'Seals?' barked Bakunda. 'What are they? Fish, are they not? How can you be fighting fish?'

'US special forces – sea, army and land. Like the SAS. When American guys finish their service, they often take mercenary jobs.'

'Okay, okay,' said Bakunda. 'I was only trying to be funny.'

The conversation was interrupted by the sound of an engine: the truck coming back in.

'Excuse me a minute,' I said. 'I'll just check everyone's okay.'

I got up and moved off quickly, afraid that Bakunda would try to come with me. Luckily the troops were debussing some distance off, out of earshot, and I picked out the tall, bulky figure of Pavarotti. As soon as he'd squared things away with Joss, I drew him aside.

'Everything all right?'

'One silvery down.'

'I thought so. What happened?'

'This guy opened up on the search party as it went forward. Apparently he'd been feuding with one of the lads in it – tried to take him out as he ran towards the targets.'

'But he missed.'

'Yeah. His mates didn't miss *him*, though. One of them

snatched his AK47 off him, and another whacked him with a panga. One swing, head off, clunk.'

'Christ! What did the rest of them do?'

'Nothing. They left him where he dropped. I told them to bring the body in, but Manny, the group commander, just said, "Food for hyenas. Let's go."'

'These people!' I said. 'Like I was saying the other night: Kaswiris, Afundis – one lot are as bad as the other.'

'Yeah,' went Pav. 'They need watching. It wouldn't take much to make some of them turn on us. They got really pissed off with us for forcing them to lie out all day.'

'Nobody threatened you?' I said.

'No, but they came pretty close. I just think everyone ought to be aware they're pretty volatile. Maybe we'd better slack off a bit.'

'Screw that, Pav. We're here to train the bastards, not entertain them.'

I looked back to the fire and went on. 'Listen. We've been chatting up Bakunda. We've got him well pissed already. He's spouted quite a bit. Get some food down your neck and join us. But for fuck's sake don't mention this business. I don't think he realised what happened – or at least, if he did, he doesn't want to know.'

Whatever the President suspected, no further mention was made of the incident that evening. We continued to hammer the rum, and after a while Joss joined the party, along with Pavarotti, Andy and Genesis. I hadn't seen Joss drinking before, and now he began to worry me a bit. It may have been that alcohol started to bring out his true character, or it may have been that he was trying to impress the President, or both. In any case, he started saying that the time when Kamanga needed the services of the West was coming to an end.

'The whole of Africa's independent now,' he shouted. 'We're in charge of our own destiny.'

'But you still need blokes like us to help with your military training,' Phil told him.

'I wouldn't be too sure of that,' said Joss, louder than he need have. 'This could be the last assignment the SAS gets in Kamanga.'

'Now then,' said Bakunda, and he quickly followed up with some remark in his own language. Joss looked abashed and took a big gulp from his mug.

I shot a glance at Whinger and saw he was thinking what I was thinking. Time to change the subject.

I turned to Bakunda, and asked, 'Ever bought a ticket in our national lottery?'

'No!' he shouted merrily. 'How much can I win?'

'Millions,' I told him. 'Up to ten million, anyway.'

'Pounds or *kwatchas*?'

'Pounds, of course.'

Luckily, the conversation became totally frivolous. We began talking about what we'd do, back home, if we won the main prize. Whinger said he'd buy a pub, Pavarotti that he'd hire Concorde for a private trip round the world and have it stop off in Polynesia while he put in a couple of weeks' shagging. Genesis that he'd buy an island off the Welsh coast and set up a foundation for religious instruction. Chalky fancied buying a luxury yacht and cruising in the West Indies, and Danny reckoned he'd set himself up in business as an international arms dealer.

'And what about you, Geordie?' burped Bakunda. 'What would you do?'

'I'd hire one really good guy to go and take out Saddam, and another to sort Gadaffi.'

'Good!' Bakunda roared. 'I like it!'

'General,' said Phil, always a bit of a joker, 'what does *choka* mean?'

'*Choka!*' Bakunda raised his eyebrows. 'That's quite a rude word. Who said that?'

'I dunno,' said Phil innocently. 'I heard it somewhere.'

'Well, it means "piss off", to put it politely.'

'Thanks,' went Phil, who'd known that all along. 'It might be useful, sometimes. And General, can I ask why you're called Rhino?'

'Hey!' Bakunda stuck out a mock-accusing finger. 'Who told you that?'

'Can't remember.'

'Since we're all friends, I'll tell you. Partly it's this.' He held out his hands to indicate the width of his torso. 'Partly it's because when I was at Sandhurst, I took up rugby. I can see you smiling, but I did. I thought it was wonderful, how all these white wogs were murdering one another on the field. I reckoned that if I joined in I could maybe smash one or two of them. Nothing personal, you understand. Anyway, once I ran into someone – *poom!*' He smacked one fist into his other open palm to illustrate the impact. 'The opposing centre three-quarter. He went straight up in the air, and was laid out cold. When he came round, he said, "Christ! That was like being charged by a bloody rhino!"'

At around 2300 I decided I'd had enough. It was clear no serious discussion would take place until we held a wash-up on our own in the morning. I knew the President's aides had sorted out somewhere for him to sleep, so I had no compunction about making my excuses. Then, just as I was leaving the fire, a thought struck me.

'If you come from this village, General,' I said, 'you must know the witch doctor.'

'The *sin'ganga?*' Old Chilukole? Of course. What about him?'

It seemed too late to start on the saga of the dead boy, so I just asked, 'What d'you think of his spells?'

'Why, has he witched somebody?'

'Not that I know of, but I wondered if he can foretell the future. Doesn't he do something with bones?'

The President's manner changed. It was as if my question had let the wind out of him. His boisterous good humour vanished, and all at once he looked serious, even alarmed. 'Did he make a prophecy, some forecast?'

'No, no.' Suddenly feeling bad vibrations, I decided to turn the enquiry into a joke. 'I just thought he might tell us how to win the lottery.'

'Steer clear of him,' said Bakunda heavily. 'You never know

what trouble that old devil might stir up.'

I said nothing else, but secretly felt glad that I'd binned the dose formulated to ward off evil. I'd sent the witch doctor five dollars, as agreed, but next morning, instead of taking the medicine, I threw it into the fire, where it went off with a miniature explosion and a spurt of bright green flame.

FIVE

As our little convoy rolled south, Whinger and I had plenty of time to discuss the situation. The morning after the ambush, Bakunda had been up at dawn, none the worse for having put away half a bottle of rum on top of ten or fifteen beers. Far from sporting a hangover, he'd come out, cocked a leg, executed a couple of rhino-power farts, and gone off chatting and laughing with his officers, handing out *zikomos* and compliments all round.

The fact that one of the Kamangans had lost his head didn't seem to worry him in the least. He knew what had happened, all right; I had overheard him talking to Joss about the incident. But when I cornered Joss about it after breakfast, and suggested we should recover the body, the answer was, 'Forget it, Geordie. All our guys knew Chidombo had been witched by a *fiti*. Sooner or later he was going to die. Now he's dead, no one would touch his body even if we went looking for it. They think the spell might jump into them. Anyway, it's probably gone already.'

'Eaten by animals, you mean?'

Instead of answering straight, Joss gave me a peculiar look, half evasive, half angry. Then, after a pause, he said, 'Maybe the devil's got it.'

I wasn't sure what he meant. There was something odd about his manner. He didn't sound quite himself. But I sensed there was no point in arguing. The strange thing was that when Pavarotti had gone out with a recovery party to bring back the targets, he'd found no trace of a body. He, if anyone, knew exactly where the scuffle had taken place, and while the

Kamangans had collected the figure-eights, he'd gone straight to the spot. As he said, if hyenas had eaten Chidombo, he'd have found traces of blood and chips of crunched-up bone – probably the head, too, or at least the remains of it. In the event, there was nothing – not even any flies around the place. It was as if something had lifted the body whole and whisked it clean away.

As Pav had reported this back, I felt the hair on my neck creep. We'd been getting too many stories about the devil using owls and hyenas for transport, too much stuff about witching.

'Don't mention it at the wash-up,' I had warned Pav. 'If one of the Africans starts in about it, okay, but otherwise, let it go. I reckon they'll bin the whole episode and pretend it never happened.'

My hunch had soon proved right. At the debrief, which Bakunda attended, the incident was simply passed over. Joss bollocked men for other mistakes – firing at the hyena, the ND while I was away, somebody walking off his position to have a dump – but never mentioned what had been by far the worst incident of all. It, and poor old Chidombo, were wiped from the record.

'I don't like it,' I said to Whinger as we jolted along the sandy track. 'If they act like that during an exercise, what are they going to be like when they get into a real, live battle?'

'Fucking awful,' he replied, and he pin-pointed my own worry by adding, 'They're all right for a bit, but then the buggers go bananas. They seem to lose their reason.'

When I had spoken to Hereford over the satcom the previous evening, I'd been deliberately vague about our plans for the next few days. I certainly didn't tell them that I'd more or less promised the President we'd go as far as Gutu. But that, for better or worse, was what I'd done. I'd developed quite a liking for Rhino. His visit had ended happily and he'd gone off in his Puma highly chuffed, fancying Alpha Commando to win the civil war in a couple of weeks. In his estimation, the sun shone out of the backside of any member of the SAS.

'*Zikomo! Zikomo!*' he had called, waving graciously as he boarded his chopper. Chalky had given him a few *zikomos* in return, claiming that the word meant 'goodbye' as well as 'thanks'.

So here we were, driving towards the edge of the disputed zone, with the mine at Gutu our next major objective. All we knew about it was that its buildings stood on a bluff on the south bank of the Kameni river, and that diamonds were being dredged by suction from alluvial deposits in the bed of the stream. We had no information about the strength of the garrison, or about the area immediately surrounding the mine, but from the map the Kameni looked a major waterway.

Our own guys were riding in the two pinkies we'd flown out with us – long wheel-base Land Rovers, with windscreens folded down, all mirrors and lights hessianed-up, cam nets bunched and tied along the overhead roll-bars, and poles for the nets strapped along the sides. Everything had been stripped down in case we had to bomb-burst out of the vehicles. One pinkie had a .50 heavy machine gun mounted on the back, and one a Milan rocket-launcher post.

Our bulky kit was loaded into a seven-ton, four-wheel-drive Zyl lorry, sometimes driven by a local, sometimes by one of us. It was an ugly great lump of a truck, with a square-fronted radiator, a fore-mounted winch and an extra heavy angle-girder welded across the front, low down, to act as a bullbar. In spite of power steering, it was a brute to drive, but it was tough and reliable and had plenty of space. The cab was hot as hell, because it was all metal, with a turret opening in the roof on the passenger side. The back had steel sides about three feet high, and a canvas roof, rolled up on its frame to make a sun-shade. Most of Alpha Commando was travelling in similar vehicles, although they also had four Gaz jeeps of Russian origin.

One obvious problem was the inaccuracy of our maps. We already knew they were dodgy before we started south, but it wasn't until we started covering bigger distances that we realised just how much imagination they included. That first morning we wasted a couple of hours searching in vain for a dirt road clearly marked in yellow, heading south-east in the direction we wanted; either it had never existed, or it had been over-grown by bush, and we finished up making a three-hour detour along tracks to the west. That was the morning gone, and us scarcely any closer to our objective.

Another problem, we could see, was going to be water. We were carrying our own supplies in jerricans stowed under the false floors of the pinkies, along with our rations, and we had reserves in forty-five-gallon containers aboard the big truck. But the locals went through water like they were going to land up beside a nice big clean river every night, and I kept hearing their ruperts reading the riot act about it.

Even before the civil war the country south of us had been sparsely inhabited. According to Joss, only one village in fifty had a borehole. Now most of the villages had been burned down. Some of the few wells that existed had been deliberately wrecked, and others had been polluted with the dead bodies of animals or humans thrown down them, so that once again everybody depended on rivers or springs, and people thought nothing of walking three or four kilometres in each direction to fetch water every morning.

As we went further south, the air grew steadily hotter. With only short breaks we drove right through the first afternoon after Bakunda's departure, and on through the night. A couple of hours before dawn we came out on to a ridge commanding a big sweep of country, across which – according to our maps – ran a main road leading from the border in the direction of Gutu. So we stopped under a grove of sausage trees to get a good look at what lay ahead of us. Our vehicles deployed and cammed-up, with the heavy weapons sited in all-round defensive positions, and everybody got their heads down in turn.

When the light came up, we were disappointed to find that the ground in front consisted of a featureless sea of bush, dipping gently until it rose again to another low ridge in the distance. There were open patches of grassland between the trees and shrubs, but if the road was there, we couldn't see it and continuous observation revealed no movement of any kind. The only development before midday came at about 1130, when a column of smoke went up from beyond the far ridge, to our left.

'Bush fire?' I asked Joss, who was standing with me.

'I don't think so,' he answered. 'Smoke's too concentrated. A bush fire would be more spread out. Looks like somebody's burnt a village.'

It was Jason, the skinny tracker, who raised the alert. He was on stag in one of the forward OPs when he gave a sudden call.

I looked across, saw him pointing, and hurried over.

'What is it?'

'One man.'

'Where?

'Two tall trees, over there.'

'Got 'em.'

'To the right, open space.'

'Yes.'

'One minute, he come out.'

I glued my binoculars to the small, stony plain, not wanting to put Mabonzo down, but hardly believing that a single man could be moving on his own through that huge wilderness.

But hell, the tracker was right.

A tiny figure struggled into view, an African, bare-headed, in rags, limping heavily, leaning on a stick, dragging himself forward a step at a time, four or five hundred yards from us. He was heading vaguely north, on course to pass to our right.

'Hey, Whinge,' I called. 'Look at this.'

'The poor bugger's hurt,' said Whinger immediately. Then suddenly he shouted, 'No! For fuck's sake!'

One of the Kamangan sentries had brought his AK47 up into the aim.

'Don't shoot!' said Whinger fiercely. 'This guy may be some use to us. He's tabbed it from the direction of the enemy. Hey, Joss!'

The distant fugitive must have heard Whinger's first yell, because he'd stopped and looked around.

'Jesus!' I said. 'He's going to do a runner.'

'Like hell he is,' said Andy, who'd appeared beside me. 'He

couldn't run to save his life.'

'Let's get down to him, then,' I went. 'Andy and I'll go with Joss. The rest of you keep still and cover us.'

We watched for a couple of minutes to make sure the man was on his own. In the end, unable to identify where the sound had come from, he started lurching forward again, and Andy and I set off towards him, together with Joss and a man called Kaingo, who could speak several tribal languages besides his own. As we moved I kept a patch of thick bush between us and our target, so that he didn't see us, because I was afraid he might take fright and try to sheer off. The result was that when he finally came in view of us, he was only twenty metres off.

The sight of four armed guys in DPMs, two black, two white, gave him a horrible fright. He jumped backwards, tried to run, fell over, and then raised his hands in a pathetic gesture of surrender. By the time we got to him, he was on his knees, eyeballs rotating like crazy. We could see straight away that he was covered in cuts, with dust and dried blood crusting over them, and that he had metal shackles on his ankles. But it wasn't until Andy went round behind him and whistled in amazement that we realised how badly he'd been injured. His tattered blue shirt had been torn into vertical strips, and so had the skin on his back. From shoulder to arse he was ripped and scarified, with shreds of skin hanging off, as if he'd been dragged over a bed of nails. The backs of his legs were the same. The wounds were fresh, with some of the blood not yet congealed, and flies crawling all over.

'Tell him he's safe,' I said, and when Joss translated, the man's fear visibly declined.

'Water,' I told Andy. 'Give him a drink.'

Andy pulled a bottle out of his belt kit and handed it over.

Between gulps, the miserable creature choked out his story. His village had been destroyed by the rebels, he said.

'First they bombed,' Joss translated.

'With aircraft?'

'No aircraft. With guns. Shells. Some people were killed. Many ran away into the bush. Then the Afundis came and set fire to the huts. They raped the women – themselves first, then with knives in the belly. They cut the children into pieces.'

'Okay, okay. Where was it?'

The man turned and made a big gesture towards the south. 'Many days' walking' was the only way he could describe the location.

'How did he get here, then?'

He'd been captured and taken for slave labour, driven off in a truck to rebuild the road from Gutu to the border. Places where floods had washed it away in the rainy season. He'd escaped during the night when a gang of workmen was being transported to a new location further west. He'd managed to secrete a hacksaw blade, and had sawed through the chain of his shackles during the journey.

At first we got the impression he'd just jumped off the truck; then he explained that he'd wriggled down over the side, between the rim of the body and the canvas top, and clung there, not daring to drop because they were travelling so fast. A minute or two later they'd come to a place where thorn bushes had grown over, nearly closing the track, and suddenly he'd found himself being ripped to pieces, all along his back. When the vehicle slowed, he'd dropped off.

'Can you show us the road, then?' I asked gently.

The man pointed over the sea of bush ahead of us, and his answer came back via Joss, 'Half a day.'

'At his rate, half a day's only a couple of ks,' I went. 'Let's get down there and have a look.'

'Wait,' said Joss. 'He says he has something important to tell you.'

'Go on, then.'

'Tonight a convoy is coming back along this same road . . .' The refugee talked in slow, painful sentences, and Joss patiently relayed the details. 'From the border. It is bringing arms and ammunition for the garrison at Gutu.'

I felt a surge of excitement, but all I said was, 'How does he know?'

'He heard Afundi officers speaking.'

'Tonight – is he sure?'

The man nodded vigorously.

'How many vehicles?'

'He thinks three or four. One of them will be the truck he jumped off.'

'Right, then.' I glanced at Andy and saw he was thinking the same as me. 'Kaingo, get Mart to do what he can about his wounds. Andy and I are going down to recce that road.'

The reason we hadn't spotted the track was that it ran across our front in a long, shallow valley, out of our sight as we were advancing. But there it was, just as the man had described it: a narrow, sandy track, so little used that seedling trees and bushes had sprouted up all over it, and in many places vegetation had closed in from the sides, halving its width. This squared with descriptions we'd heard of how, before the civil war, Bakunda had deliberately let roads serving Gutu go to pot, in a clumsy attempt to increase the security of the mine, while he himself relied on aircraft to lift supplies in and diamonds out. But now, on this one, there were tyre tracks, and a litter of broken twigs that showed a vehicle had recently forced its way through.

One thought was uppermost in all our minds: ambush. Coming so soon after the exercise, this looked like a God-given opportunity to give the Kamangans live practice and prevent a load of weapons reaching the rebels. Joss was all for it. His eyes were gleaming as he said, 'Oh, wah! Let's just find a good site, and we'll get on with it.'

Our recce didn't take long. There were no footprints in the dust of the track, and we ourselves kept off it, moving parallel with its course until we came to a point where it swung left and right as it crossed a wide hollow, and then straightened as it disappeared over some higher ground beyond. Up there, thick bush was growing, but the depression was open – a great killing ground. For ten minutes we scanned with binoculars to make sure nobody else was on the move.

'Lovely thicket, just the ticket,' went Andy, imitating

Whinger, but letting himself down by giving both halves of the rhyme instead of one.

'Yeah,' I agreed. 'Let 'em come well down the slope into the open, and we've got 'em.'

In many ways the site was better than the one we'd chosen for the exercise, and Joss didn't need long to work out a plan. Positions for right and left cut-off groups suggested themselves immediately. For RPGs and heavy machine guns, the range was point-blank; if the enemy vehicles reached the bottom of the slope, none of them would escape. There was even a bit of a hill out to the left from which a rear cut-off group could put down fire across the track on top of the rise, to take out anyone who tried to run off along it, and also, in the opposite direction, cover our own backs.

With all the drills fresh in people's minds, everything seemed ridiculously simple. Nevertheless, we took all sensible precautions. Only once during our recce did we set foot on the road, and then we all crossed it together, brushing out our tracks behind us.

After scarcely an hour we were back at our bivouac site, and Joss again made careful models in the sand to brief his men. Then he took the commanders forward for their own recce, and Pavarotti helped them plan a cut-off barrier of claymores, with trip-wire triggers, in the bush on the south side of the track, to catch anybody who tried to break in that direction. We'd agreed that the SAS would take no direct part in the ambush itself, but that we'd be there close behind, in the background, to advise if anything went wrong.

Our best policy was obviously to leave our vehicles where they were, under guard, well out of the way, and move into position on foot. At 1630, after a meal, I gave everybody the same kind of bollocking as before, but tougher, telling them that this time the action was going to be for real, and they couldn't afford any NDs or general faffing about.

'The sky's clear,' I told them, looking up. 'That means it's going to be a fairly light night. The convoy will probably be driving without lights. If the wind gets up, we may not hear the engines until the last minute. So everybody needs to be on full alert. Your aim is very simple: destroy every enemy vehicle, and make sure no one gets out alive.'

With that, everybody tabbed forward, with three Kamangans humping the gun, spare barrel and tripod of their .50 machine gun, and two other guys carring spare ammunition.

Before the sun set at 1740 the whole party was in position. To keep things simple, I'd assigned the same back-ups as in the exercise: Pav behind the left cut-off, Andy behind the right, Genesis with the rear, Mart with myself and Whinger in the centre. We'd lent Joss one of our covert comms sets so that we could keep in touch with him, and we were close enough to talk to the rest of our lads, who stayed back with the vehicles, ready to move up as and when we called them.

Night fell as quickly as if a black curtain had been drawn down over earth and sky. Apart from the background chorus of crickets, not a sound disturbed the silence. I kept thinking about the big owl that had swooped over the village, expecting to hear that low *hoo-hoo* any minute – but if owls were flying, none called near us.

Whinger and I were lying at a comfortable angle – heads up, feet down – on a sandy bank that gave good protection from the front. If anyone started firing in our direction, we'd only have to lower our heads to be in dead ground. Also, we were far enough back from the Kamangan line to be able to talk in whispers without being heard. Not that we had much to say to each other at that point: we were both weary, and hoping the convoy would arrive early, rather than wait till four in the morning to put in an appearance.

Time dragged. To hurry it up I tried to imagine the map of Africa, fitting in all the countries like the pieces of a jigsaw. South Africa, at the bottom, was easy enough. Next up on the left came Namibia. I'd spent a week there once, and knew most of it was barren desert. Next up again was Angola, scene of one of the longest-lasting civil wars. Inland, beside Angola, was Botswana. I'd been there, too, and had spooky experiences in the Tsodilo Hills, where one of our guys had been killed falling off a mountain. I remembered how the RAF had flown a Hercules over the spot and how, when they tried to throw a wreath out the open back door, in tribute to the dead man, it had blown back into the aircraft three times, an uncanny fluke that left the crew twitching.

It was Andy, on our right, who heard the noise first.

'Green Two,' said his voice in my earpiece. 'Something moving ahead.'

'Vehicles?'

'Pass. Sounds more like people on foot, coming through the bush.'

'Has your squad heard it?'

'Sure.'

'Wait out, then.' I listened intently for a few moments. My watch was reading 2155. As I watched, a shooting star hurtled down the sky towards the south. Then I called, 'Green Three? Any noise in your sector?'

'Negative,' came Pav.

'You heard Andy?'

'Roger.'

'Green Four?'

'Definitely,' said Genesis. 'There's movement up ahead.'

'Green Five, you heard that?'

Joss took a moment to answer, maybe feeling for his pressel switch. Then he came up with: 'Roger. We're ready.'

'All stations, stand by.'

We listened, straining to catch the slightest sound. The air was completely still. The moon was well up, casting a black shadow behind every silver-grey bush and tree, pitting the land with inky patches. I held my breath and uttered a silent prayer that none of the Kamangans would open fire prematurely.

As I let my breath go, I felt wind on my right cheek, that sudden, curious night wind, starting again. Quickly a surge built up, gusting from the north, sighing through the scrub. But this little squall never reached the intensity of the one that had blown up during our exercise. In a couple of minutes it died away again, and silence returned, the huge, all-embracing silence of the African night.

Maybe, I told myself, it was only an eddy of air that the guys had heard. But soon, when nothing else happened, I got a different idea. I began to wonder if the breeze had betrayed our presence to rebel scouts, moving ahead of their convoy. Had they got our scent and quietly turned back? Surely none of the Kamangans could have been such an idiot as to light a cigarette? Most of them stank like polecats, and BO on its own might have been enough to raise the alarm.

'What d'you reckon it was?' I whispered.

'Animals, I expect,' Whinger murmured. 'Probably an antelope.'

He'd hardly spoken when, somewhere beyond the killing ground, a branch snapped. I knew instinctively that the crack was too loud to have been made by an impala or a puku. Antelopes are delicate animals that nibble at leaves and twigs; except when running for their lives, they do not break thick branches by treading on them.

'All stations,' I said again, 'stand by.'

I was expecting – hoping – to pick up the rattle of a truck travelling slowly, or the grind of engines turning steadily at low revs. The next sound we got was almost mechanical, but utterly different: a huge, raucous intake of air, like a giant snort.

'Firekin 'ell!' went Whinger out loud. 'Elephants!'

Before I could hit my pressel again, the night split apart in a blinding flash and the shock-wave of an explosion buffeted us in the face.

'Jesus!' I shouted. 'They're in the trip-wires!'

Boom! went another claymore. Violent screams burst out, as harsh and loud as if giants were tearing up sheets of corrugated iron. One, two, three, four – primeval cries of fear and alarm ripped out all over, building into a chorus of panic. Another booby trap exploded, setting fire to the bush in the background. All across our front the Kamangans opened up, pouring rounds into the killing area.

'*Stop!*' roared Pavarotti. 'Stop! Stop! Stop!'

His words were lost in the uproar. From being dead quiet, the night had turned crazy with noise. Like the elephants, the Kamangans had gone hyper. They were firing bursts of ten or twelve rounds, half of them high into the sky. The heavy hammer of the .50 was continuous. Two RPGs went scorching into the bush and exploded in brilliant flashes. A fourth claymore detonated, then a fifth.

Why the hell hadn't Joss switched on the ambush lights? Why hadn't he fired a flare? He had the shamoulis. I'd hardly had time to wonder what he was doing when I realised that hefty black shapes were hurtling towards us like tanks – not three or four, but dozens – crashing headlong through any scrub in their path as they charged across the killing ground.

One of them was coming straight for me and Whinger.

'Watch this fucker!' I yelled. But before we could move it veered to its left and swung off in a circle, like a truck with a punctured tyre. I knew it had taken rounds and was disabled. Another went down, head over heels, and rolled to a halt like a seven-ton truck with all four wheels seized. The rest of them kept coming.

At last a rocket soared up and a flare deployed, yet the sudden illumination only increased the chaos. Presented with a clear view of fifty charging elephants, the Kamangans leapt to their feet and ran in all directions, back, sideways, forwards, loosing off wildly. Human yells merged with the louder animal noises. The effect was to increase the general panic and accelerate the stampede. Huge creatures thundered forward, ears raised, trunks up, screaming all out in a rolling cloud of dust. My instinct was to get up and run, or join in the firing, but I knew that any movement would expose us to still greater risk of getting trampled or knocked over.

'Keep down!' I yelled.

Whinger and I clung to the earth, on the back of our little mound. I felt the ground tremble as the nearest elephant hurtled past, three or four yards to my left. With it came a hot, fierce, animal smell, like that of cows, but more intense. Spurts of warm liquid sprayed on to us. In a few seconds the whole herd was through our position and past us, crashing away into the distance along the line of the road.

When the firing died down, I found myself shaking from a massive charge of adrenalin, and my finger trembled as I hit the pressel of my radio.

'Come in, all stations.'

There was a pause before Pav answered, 'Green Three.'

'You okay?'

'Fine.'

'Okay. Green Four?'

'Roger,' went Genesis.

'Five?'

'No problem.' Joss's voice sounded high and strained.

'Get the fucking lights on,' I told him. 'Keep the shamoulis going. We need maximum illumination. Two, then. Come in, Green Two.'

I waited, tried again. No reply. Andy. It was possible his radio had gone down. It might have fallen out of its pouch if he'd had to move quickly. But deep down I knew at once something bad had happened.

I've seen the shit hit the fan often enough, but never as messily as that. Dead or dying elephants were scattered over the killing ground, some roaring and groaning as they struggled to get up. The Kamangans' discipline had gone like the night wind. Men had abandoned their positions and were running all over the place, putting bursts into the crippled beasts, already whacking into the dead bulls with machetes and commando knives as they started to cut out their tusks. It seemed highly unlikely that there could be an enemy force in the vicinity; if the convoy had been close, it would have turned tail by now. Just as well, because our party was wide open to attack.

'Fuck it!' I shouted to Whinger. 'It's not down to us to get these bastards back under control. I'm going to find Andy.'

Together we ran towards the spot where he'd taken station, behind the right cut-off group. 'Andy!' I yelled. 'Where are you?'

In the distance the claymore explosions had ignited several bush fires, but the crackling flames only made our immediate surroundings seem darker. The last shamouli had floated off to the west, so that its flare was filling every dip in the ground with black shadow, and we had to check each inky patch individually.

It was Whinger who found him. He gave a sudden yell of 'Here!' and stood still, with his torch-beam pointing straight downwards.

In a second I was beside him. Andy was lying on his back, head turned to the right, with his eyes shut and a trickle of blood oozing from his mouth. It was obvious what had happened, because his chest was almost two-dimensional, only two or three inches from top to bottom, crushed flat by a tremendous weight. An elephant must have knocked him down and put a foot right on him, or rolled over him. Kneeling beside the body, I ran my hands up its sides and touched the ends of snapped ribs jagging out under his smock. I saw his 203 lying in the dust a few feet away.

I felt choked. Andy, just married. My mind flew to the day of the wedding. All the blossom had been out in an orchard next to the churchyard. I looked down at his body and thought, 'Why in a godforsaken place like this?' I knew we'd had our differences, but he never deserved this. I thought of Penny, a bride of only two months. Now the Families' Officer would have to call on her. I remembered how they'd broken the terrible news about Kath's senseless death to me.

'Jesus!' I went. 'It's that fucking witch doctor. This is his number one, the first of ten.'

'Bollocks,' said Whinger. 'It was just bad luck. I bet the silveries have taken casualties as well.'

'The more, the better,' I said savagely. 'Stupid bastards. Why the hell can't they control themselves?'

'This wasn't their fault,' said Whinger, doggedly. 'It wasn't them who cracked it off. It was the claymores that panicked the elephants.'

I knew he was right, but that didn't make things any easier. I stood up, getting hold of myself, and used the radio to call our remaining guys together. I couldn't help feeling irritated when

Genesis started to recite a short benediction, commending Andy's soul to the Almighty, and I shouted at him to shut up.

'Where was God when the elephants charged?' I said bitterly. 'He wasn't fucking looking after Andy.'

Genesis opened his mouth to say something, but I poked him in the chest with my forefinger and snapped, 'Eh, just keep quiet.'

We unrolled our one para-silk stretcher and got the body into it, to carry it back to the holding area. By then darkness had settled back on the bush, except where the fires lit up patches in the distance and, closer, a couple of places where Kamangans were feverishly hacking at elephant corpses by torchlight.

'Joss!' I yelled. 'Where are you?'

'Here.' He answered from only a few feet away. He must have been coming in search of us.

I went, 'What a fuck-up!'

For the moment he didn't reply. I think he was choked as well. Then I was aware of him standing beside me, his black face invisible, only his DPMs showing faintly in the moonlight. He pointed at the shrouded body and asked, 'Who is this?'

'Andy.'

'Andy! Oh my goodness! I'm sorry. Was it an elephant?'

'Yep. What about you? Have you got casualties?'

'Two dead. Two broken legs, one broken arm, one flesh wound from a bullet.'

'What about casevac?'

'It will be difficult from here.'

'You've said it. Let's get back to the holding area and talk about it there.'

I should have bollocked him for letting his men run riot, but I let it go, because I'd seen enough of their behaviour to realise it was utterly unrealistic to expect the sort of discipline that prevails in British forces. Nor did I tell him to call off the guys who were carving up the elephants. I knew the whole Kamangan army was shit-poor, and hadn't been paid in months, so who was I to deny them the fat haul of dollars they might get from selling tusks?

*

At 2300 local time – 2100 in the UK – I called Hereford on the satcom phone to report our casualty.

'What d'you mean, it was an elephant?' said Pete Dickson, the Duty Officer, incredulously.

'We were on a night ex,' I white-lied. 'A herd of about fifty ellies wandered on to our position and stampeded. Came right through us. There wasn't time to move or do anything. Andy got knocked down and trampled.'

'Killed outright?'

'Instantaneously. When you see the body, you'll know. His chest is about two inches front to back.'

'Jesus!'

'Listen,' I went on. 'We need to get him out fast. He won't last a day in the kind of heat we're having.'

'You mean a charter aircraft?'

'Exactly. There's a firm called Kam-Ex, in Mulongwe. You can contact them through the embassy.'

'Are they going to be happy to fly into your area?'

I lied again. 'There shouldn't be any problem. We're still well north of rebel territory.'

'Okay. And is there a strip close by?'

'There will be. There's a straight bush road with a good level surface. It just needs a bit of scrub cleared, and we can do that at first light.'

I gave the coordinates, which I'd punched into my GPS as Waypoint Four.

'Right,' said Pete. 'We'll see what we can do. But we'll need a full report on the incident in due course.'

'Of course.'

'D'you want to speak to the CO in the morning?'

'Not unless he wants to speak to me.'

'Okay, then. Until tomorrow.'

Dawn saw us back on the bush road with a force of forty Kamangans. We'd chosen a stretch on which the scrub was light anyway, and now those razor-sharp machetes came into their own. In the cool of the morning the guys worked well – I had to hand it to them – and in little more than an hour we'd cleared a strip four hundred metres long, cutting back the shrubs on either side of the track to create an open corridor about twenty metres wide. Provided no strong cross-wind got up, a reasonable pilot ought to be able to land and take off without difficulty.

At that stage – 0630 – we had no confirmation that an aircraft was available, but I went ahead preparing the strip anyway. At 0945 I was relieved to get a satcom call from Hereford via the Defence Attaché at the embassy in Mulongwe, confirming that a Kam-Ex aircraft was on its way. Its estimated flight-time, the DA said, was one hour forty minutes, and he gave us a frequency on which we could establish comms with the pilot when he was approaching.

It seemed to me that Joss was observing our preparations with a slightly cynical air. He was sending his own dead and wounded back to the nearest military base by road, and obviously reckoned our reaction was over the top. At the same time, maybe he was ashamed of the way his guys had behaved, and so felt he wasn't in a position to start making criticisms. I didn't feel sorry for his casualties, even the two with broken legs. In fact, I hoped they'd have a rough ride home.

Our pilot came on the air when he was twenty minutes out. His name, he told us, was Steve, and by his accent he was an Aussie or a New Zealander. He was flying a Cessna 210, at 8,000 feet, and having no problems with his navigation as he came towards our location from the north-east.

'Hold that bearing,' I told him. 'We're ready for you. The strip we've cleared runs roughly east and west. Four hundred metres long. Level ground all the way. Wind at the minute is zero, but we'll light a fire at the north-eastern corner to see what the smoke does.'

'Roger,' he went. 'Sounds dinkum. Where's my passenger?'

'We'll have him by the fire. Suggest you come in from the west and taxi right along.'

'Fair enough. No rebel forces in the area, I suppose?'

'Not that we know of. We've had a patrol out one k to the south, and they're reporting the area clear.'

'Okay, then. I'll see you in a minute.'

The scrub we collected was so dry our marker fire went off like a torch, but the blaze produced practically no smoke, so we sent one of the Kamangans running to pull some branches off a leadwood tree which was growing a couple of hundred metres away. The dusty-looking leaves crackled fiercely and gave off dense black smoke; after a quick trial, we kept the rest ready until the plane arrived.

We heard it before we saw it. The sun was already high and brilliant, and we had to screw up our eyes against its light when we detected the far-off hum. Then we picked up a little dark dot which rapidly grew into a silver and blue aircraft, already descending.

'We have you visual,' I called. 'Come slightly right of your heading, and we'll be on your nose. You should see our smoke.'

'Okay,' he answered, 'but there are bush fires all over.' Then his voice sharpened as he said, 'Got it! Got the strip. Wait one while I take a look.'

Bringing the Cessna down low, he made a pass to the south, with the aircraft tilted over towards us as he scanned the makeshift runway. As he climbed again a covey of terrified guinea fowl exploded from the scrub beneath him, eight or ten heavy grey birds, scattering desperately.

The smoke from our fire was going up straight as a pillar.

'Looks okay,' he said.

I saw his undercarriage go down as he pulled round in a tight turn to line up for an easterly approach. Without further ado he came in low – so low that it looked as though his wheels were going to brush through the tops of bushes short of the strip. Then with twin puffs of dust he was down, bouncing a bit but well under control. He taxied steadily towards us, stopped about thirty metres off, closed down his engine, opened the door and jumped out – a stocky young fellow in bush shirt and shorts, with a shock of fair hair that flopped over his tanned forehead.

I went forward to shake hands, and said, 'Thanks for coming.'

'Don't mention it. Sorry you needed me.' He gestured at Andy's body, now zipped into a black bag. 'Trouble with elephants, I hear.'

'That's right.'

'Dangerous animals.'

'We thought there were none left. We heard they'd all been shot.'

'Don't you believe it. I flew over a big herd right back there.'

'Maybe that was the lot that ran into us. Well, where d'you want him?'

'On the floor. We've stripped out the seats.'

Four of us picked up the body, which had gone stiff as a board in the night, but now was floppy again, and hoisted it awkwardly through the passenger door.

'What are you going to do with him?' Genesis asked.

'The embassy's laid on an ambulance to take him straight to the city mortuary. They're arranging a flight back to the UK as soon as possible.'

That seemed as good as we could get. Steve said a quick goodbye and got back on board, but nobody else spoke. None of us had anything to say. We watched mutely as he started up, carried out his checks, turned, taxied and took off in the opposite direction, waggling his wings in farewell as he swung right-handed and climbed away to the north. I had a strong desire to jump into the co-pilot's seat and fly clean out of this mess, on the pretext that the body needed an escort. In reality I knew that such an action would never wash, and in any case, it wasn't in me to leave my own guys in the shit.

We'd sent nothing with Andy, because he had practically nothing to send – no money, credit card or wallet. The only personal items I kept were his watch – a good stainless-steel Rolex, which would certainly have been nicked in the mortuary – and a small folder of green canvas holding two photos of Penny, which I found in the breast pocket of his DPMs. Whatever happened, I'd make sure that those two items got back to the UK safely.

In a couple of minutes, the Cessna vanished into the sky, and our little group was left standing in silence under the hot morning sun. Just before we moved off I noticed that Genesis was fingering the crucifix which he wore on a fine chain round his neck, and that his lips were moving in prayer.

'Blessed are the dead which die in the Lord,' he was murmuring. 'Even so sayeth the spirit, for they rest from their labours.'

SIX

We started south again in a sober frame of mind. The fiasco of the ambush had been damaging on two counts: first, we'd taken casualties; second, far from achieving anything, we'd given our presence away. We had no means of telling where the arms convoy had been when things went noisy; but even if it was still too far out for the guys on it to hear the gunfire and explosions, they must have seen the concentration of bush fires raging up ahead of them, and they'd be bound to suspect that a military force was operating in the area. Nor did we know anything about their comms. Had they been in contact with the mine at Gutu and reported the disturbance? Even if they hadn't, the mere fact that the convoy had failed to come through must have told the garrison something was wrong. We needed to put space between ourselves and the ambush location.

In the morning we'd revisited the scene – and a horrible one it was. In the killing ground we found seven dead elephants: five mature animals and two babies, densely covered with flies, their stomachs blown out like grey barrage balloons. The one that sprayed blood over me had collapsed just past the spot where Whinger and I had been lying. Two more had been killed by the claymores: one had had the lower half of a hind leg blown off, and had dragged itself away for a couple of hundred yards before it bled to death. We found it lying in a gully in a pool of blood. The air was still too cool for the thermals to have got going, and most birds of prey weren't yet airborne, but something had already alerted two vultures, which were perched in a bare tree to the south, watching and waiting to begin a colossal feast.

The futility of the whole thing made me angry. I was feeling the loss of Andy, too, and although I said nothing more about the witch doctor, I felt certain that somehow the old bastard had put a spell on us.

'I can't figure out the rebels' strategy,' I said as I sat beside Whinger in the front of one of the pinkies. 'Bakunda reckoned they've got five hundred armed men, at most. With a force that size there's no way they could control an area as vast as this.'

'Not a chance,' Whinger agreed. 'All they can do is hold on to one or two key points. If they're getting diamonds from the mine, they can buy in weapons from other countries. Meanwhile, they terrorise the population by burning villages while they build up their strength. The arms convoy was supposed to be part of that build-up. Even if we only delayed it, we may have done ourselves a favour.'

'I wish to hell we'd hit it, though,' I said. 'It would have been nice to see a few tons of ammo go up in smoke.'

'By the way,' said Whinger, 'what did you make of Joss last night?'

'I don't know. Until then I'd thought the guy was all for us. But I suddenly got the feeling he doesn't like us that much.'

'Not a lot we can do about it.' Whinger beat a tattoo on the wheel with his fingers spread. 'And anyway, in about three weeks we can say goodbye to him.'

By noon that day we were well into rebel territory, and everyone was getting hyped up with the feeling that we were driving into danger. Our relatively carefree time of training, pure and simple, was over. From now on we might come under attack at any moment. Already we were exceeding our brief from Hereford, but I told myself that if anything did develop, we'd pull back and let the Kamangans handle it.

The overgrown track had swung more to the east than we wanted, but for the time being it still seemed our best option, and we followed it, moving cautiously in short bounds, conscious of the fact that somebody might be coming out to meet the missing convoy. One of our pinkies ranged ahead, with Pavarotti driving, Joss beside him, Phil on the .50 in the back, and two silveries sitting on the bonnet to watch the surface of the road for any sign of disturbance. It seemed unlikely the Afundis would have mined a track their own vehicles were using – but we weren't taking any chances.

The speed of our advance depended on the terrain. In places where the bush was thick, we moved slowly, but when vegetation was sparser and visibility better, we accelerated. The scout vehicle would press ahead until it came to a natural look-out point; there it would halt, and once Pav had satisfied himself the coast was clear, he'd call up the rest of the force by radio.

Stopping and starting, we progressed without incident until late in the afternoon. All the way Pav was following the single set of wheel marks left by the truck from which the wounded refugee had escaped. But then at about 1630, with the sun turning red as it sank towards the horizon behind us, he called a halt after only a short stretch on the move.

'Wait out,' he called. 'We've got more tracks here.' A couple of minutes later he came through with: 'We're on a Y junction. There's one road coming from the east, and another heading south. Quite heavily used. Fresh tracks. Several different vehicle types. Looks like the remains of a village in the distance as well.'

'Nothing on the map,' I told him.

'I know. But the place is real enough on the ground.'

'Okay,' I said. 'Stay where you are. We'll close on you.'

By the time we reached the burnt-out village, dusk was already falling. All that remained of the grass huts were black circles of ash, with an occasional stick of charred wood – the relics of home-made furniture – poking out of the pile in the centre. The one brick building, a single room, had evidently been a shop of sorts, for although its roof had gone, the remnants of two pathetic metal signs still hung over the open doorway: HOT CENTRE GROCERY and TWO BARS HEAVEN. There was no smoke rising, but when one of the Kamangans pushed a stick into a heap of ash, he found the middle of it still warm.

'We're pulling back out of here until we get a better look at the area,' I told Joss. 'The rebels can't have gone far.'

'Agreed.' He looked round and gave a shout of 'Mabonzo!', calling up the beanpole tracker.

'How long have the people been gone?'

Mabonzo examined various footprints and tyre marks, then held up his right hand, tilting his open palm alternately right and left. 'Maybe last night. Maybe this morning.'

'That settles it,' I said. 'That, and the evidence of traffic on the road. We'll take up a defensive postion on the rise back there, and move on in the morning.'

The night passed uneventfully. We heard hyenas, but no engines, and in the morning, as soon as the light was strong, we checked out the village more thoroughly.

'Look at this,' I said to Genesis, as we found the blackened skeletons of maize stores – little round enclosures with grass walls, built up on stilts to keep their contents safe from rats. The remains of charred cobs showed that the contents had been incinerated along with the structures. 'What sort of bastards deliberately burn people's food supplies? If they'd wanted the maize for themselves, they could have taken it. But why destroy it?'

'There's no accounting for human wickedness,' he said. 'Innate evil is the greatest problem in the world.'

I looked at him. His pale, freckled skin was glistening with sweat, and an angry-looking red lump had come up from a fresh bite on his throat beside his Adam's apple. From anyone else, remarks like that would have seemed platitudinous and balls-aching. But Gen radiated a kind of calm that usually had a soothing effect on everyone else. I never did understand how he reconciled his religious beliefs with his job, which was basically to be a killing machine, but somehow he managed it.

It was Genesis who made the worst discovery. In a hollow behind the remains of the village store he came on what looked like an innocent heap of brushwood, but, seeing that everything around it was black, and this pile of sticks was unburnt, he realised that something was odd and went over to it. The next thing I heard was the sound of him retching violently.

'Eh, Gen,' I called. 'What's up?'

I found him staring at a tangled pile of black bodies, half hidden beneath the wood. The flies were at them already, but they hadn't been dead much longer than the elephants. I felt my own gorge rising. The corpse nearest to us was that of a young woman, naked. Whatever else she'd been raped with first, she'd been terminally violated with a knife or a bayonet, and her whole torso was split open from crutch to breast-bone. The violence of the attack, which had carved her pelvis clean in half, was appalling. They hadn't spared the babies, either: several tiny, mangled corpses lay among the big ones.

I thought Genesis was going to start pulling bodies out, to see how many there were, so I said sharply, 'Don't touch them! There's nothing you can do for them now.'

'But we can't just leave them,' Gen began.

'We can, and we're going to. The only useful thing we can do is take the coordinates and hand them over to the UN when we get back. How many are there?'

'Looks like five or six women and three children – no, make it four.'

'Okay, then.' I scribbled the figures into my notebook, along with the GPS fix of the village. Was there any point in recording one small atrocity in the middle of a civil war? Not much, but you never know. Then I turned round and shouted, 'Joss! Look at this!'

I thought he was shaken when he saw the bodies, but he kept a hold on himself and just said, 'This is what they do, I'm afraid.'

'D'you want to bury them, or anything?'

He shook his head. 'We could spend the rest of the year burying bodies, and still there'd be thousands above ground.'

'Right, then,' I said. 'We're moving on.'

No doubt the village had had a name, but because the map was blank, we had only our GPS to give us our position. That put us almost due north of Gutu, which looked as though it was about fifty kilometres off. According to the map, a range of hills ran north-east to south-west across our front, with the river Kameni flowing parallel beyond them, and Gutu on its south bank – the far side from us.

'Ought to be able to see those hills from here,' said Mart.

'Yeah,' I agreed. 'We probably could if it weren't for all the fires. The air's full of smoke and dust.'

Abandoning the road, we motored slowly across country, this time with a Kamangan scout vehicle out ahead. The terrain was changing. We'd left the open mopane scrub behind us and were in tall grassland, with clumps of big trees dotted about. Not until midday did we start to see the hills; then gradually, through the haze that masked the horizon, we began to get glimpses of a high, dark-looking barrier which seemed to advance and recede as we moved towards it, depending on the clarity of the air. The closer we came, the rougher it looked, with a lot of grey rock showing among the scrub.

At 1230 Joss called a break. The vehicles pulled into the shade of trees for a quick brew, and it was because all the drivers had switched off that Chalky, who had the sharpest ears in our party, heard the noise of an engine.

'Aircraft!' he called.

I'd heard nothing, but I knew that years of firing weapons had left me slightly deaf. 'Sure it isn't a truck?'

He shook his head. 'Definitely an aircraft, and it's got problems. There – look!'

He shot out an arm, pointing to our left. In the distance a small white plane had appeared, flying very low on our side of the hills. My first thought, quite illogical, was that Steve, the Aussie pilot, had brought his Cessna back to pick up another body. Then I saw that this aircraft was larger, and twin-engined.

At once we knew it was in trouble. Its engines were running rough, spluttering and hiccuping, and it was losing height. As it came closer, we could see puffs of black smoke trailing behind it and hear its engines back-firing.

'That fucker's going in,' went Pavarotti.

'It's a Beechcraft,' said Danny, who had his binoculars on it. 'South African.' He read out the registration on the fuselage. 'G-SAF. The pilot's got his undercarriage down. He knows he's in the shit.'

For a minute the Beechcraft flew more or less level with the contours, but it was sinking gently as it passed across our front from left to right. Then the pilot turned away from us, towards the hills, as if trying to nurse his crippled machine back over the ridge.

'He'll never make it!' shouted Pav again. 'He's knackered.'

We stood in a line and watched, awaiting the inevitable. The end came quicker than I expected. With a final volley of back-firing the engines cut, and for a few hundred metres the plane glided on. Through my glasses I saw its starboard wing flick through the top of a tree. Debris flew – whether branches or parts of the wing, I couldn't tell. Then, in an instant, the aircraft vanished from view.

'It's down!' exclaimed Stringer.

'Wait for the bang,' said Whinger.

To our surprise, none came.

I'd seen aircraft go down in open country before – choppers, too – and every one had exploded. A pilot can get away with a belly-landing if he finishes up skimming a road or a level field, but in rough terrain like that, the plane had no chance. For several seconds we fully expected to see a cloud of smoke erupt, and hear the boom of a distant explosion. Yet neither materialised. Nothing further happened. The aircraft just disappeared silently into the hillside.

'Well damn!' said Pavarotti. 'Where in hell did it go?'

'Into a deep, dark hole,' I told him. 'Listen, I'm going up there to see if there are any survivors. I'll take Whinger and Phil. Pav, set up an LUP and get everybody under cover, okay?'

I took a bearing on the spot we'd last seen the plane, and we set off in one of the pinkies, weaving our way forward between trees and shrubs. But at the foot of the hills we found our way blocked by a series of rocky ledges; though each was only a few feet high, we kept being confronted by small vertical cliffs. There came a point at which we could drive no further, and for the last half a kilometre or so Whinger and I took to our feet, leaving Phil to guard the vehicle.

The chance that somebody might still be alive made us run, and by the time we reached the impact area we were sweating like pigs. Up there the terrain was still more broken. The shoulder, which looked smooth from a distance, turned out to be a series of shallow, scrub-covered, rocky ravines aligned up and down the slope. I stopped, panting, on a high point and took a back-bearing on to the grove of trees under which our force was parked. This showed we'd strayed a bit to the left of our line, so we struck out again right-handed.

The further we climbed into that harsh wilderness, the more certain I became that nobody could have survived the crash. The Beechcraft must have gone in with an annihilating impact. At last, as we came up on to yet another little ridge, we saw a single wheel sticking up above some rocks.

'Upside down,' Whinger gasped.

We scrambled on a few more yards. The aircraft was lying on its back in a grassy hollow dotted with bushes. Its dented nose was high in the air towards us. The outer end of the port wing had been torn off, the leading edges were full of dents, the glass of the landing lights smashed, both props crumpled. One wheel had disappeared, together with its mounting, and the tail fin was crushed down nearly to the level of the fuselage. Doors on both sides of the cabin were hanging open.

'Arse over tit,' I went. 'It must have hit these rocks we're standing on, and flipped. Yeah – look at this.'

Right under our feet were fresh, white scrape-marks. I glanced behind me and spotted the tree I'd seen the wing slice through: fresh white splinters jutted from the ends of smashed branches. The air around us was saturated with the high-octane smell of aviation gas.

'Watch yourself, Whinge,' I said. 'This fucker could go up any minute. Look at that – there's fuel dripping out of the wing tanks.'

The vapour seared our throats as we tried to recover our breath. Then Whinger said, 'If it hasn't gone already, it probably won't go now.'

'You'd better be right.'

Two more steps forward, and I could see a body lying face-down on the ground, then another, both well clear of the plane: two white men, both dressed much the same, in tan-coloured bush shirts and shorts, with knee-length stockings and desert boots. I ran to the first and started to roll him over. When I pulled at his shoulders, his torso turned, but his head didn't come with it, because it was only hanging on by a couple of strands of gristle.

'Nothing to be done for this bugger,' I said.

'Dead as a dodo,' Whinger agreed.

'We'll need to ID him,' I said. 'Grab his passport. There, in his shirt pocket. What about the other?'

The second casualty's crew-cut, mouse-coloured hair was a mass of blood; the top of his skull was pulp.

'Instantaneous,' went Whinger. 'Big impact. Flung on to a rock. I guess this guy was the pilot.' He pointed at the breast pocket, still full of ball-point pens. Then he added, 'South Africans. They must be.'

'Yeah.' I looked at the big, heavy whites, with legs like tree trunks. What else but Afrikaaners?

The smell of avgas was stronger than ever.

'Let's get out,' I said. 'Leave 'em.'

Just as I spoke, a noise came from the plane.

'Shit!' exclaimed Whinger. 'There's some other bastard in there.'

He started towards the fuselage.

'You're not going in there!' I snapped.

'I fucking am!'

A second later he was hauling himself up into the cabin through the open door.

'It's a woman!' he shouted. 'Hanging in the straps.'

'Alive or dead?'

'Alive.'

'Cut her down, then. But for Christ's sake, hurry.'

I heard him grunting with effort as he hauled himself upwards. On the ground, I watched fuel dripping from the port wing. The sun was beating down. If one piece of glass from a smashed light focused it, grass might start to smoulder, and in a flash the whole wreck would be alight. Whinger and the woman would be roasted. So would I, if I stayed where I was.

Every instinct told me to get back. I withdrew three or four paces, then heard Whinger cursing. I thought, I'll give him another ten seconds, then fuck off. But suddenly, he said, 'Coming down. Catch her.'

Legs clad in sand-coloured slacks appeared, dangling from the cabin. I ran in and grabbed them. A second later I had a woman's soft, inert body in my arms. I turned and stumbled away, half running, moving as fast as I could. I'd made about ten steps when *whumf!* a hot blast hit me from behind. I tottered forward another yard or two, then fell on to a patch of bare ground, coming down on top of the casualty.

I looked back. The aircraft was a ball of flame. Between it and me stood Whinger. He too was on fire, all down his right side. Suddenly he began to run, or tried to. He tripped over a rock, fell, struggled up, set off again, yelling and screaming. I'd seen this before and knew what to do. Guys on fire always run like lunatics, and you've got to stop them, cut off the air. Leaving the woman, I ran at him, dropped him with a rugby tackle and rolled on top of him, smothering the flames. Still he was yelling like a madman, fighting me, fighting the fire, fighting everything in creation. I held him tight, rolling over and over until the flickering flames were out.

Boom! Up went one of the tanks – thank God the one on the wing furthest from us. A fresh burst of fire seared up. Shooting out at ground level, it ignited the clothes of the man with the severed neck.

'Get up! Get up!' I shouted. 'Run!'

Holding on to each other, we staggered clear of the fireball. 'That way!' I pointed. 'Keep going.'

Whinger reeled away and collapsed on the deck. I darted back to the woman, lying stretched out on the ground. Even at that distance from the plane the heat was ferocious. Grabbing her by the hands I dragged her after me, face up, her backside bumping over the rough grass.

I found Whinger sitting on the ground, doubled up, holding his head in his hands, cursing all out. I left my burden and ran to him.

'How is it?'

At first he didn't make any sense. He was, like, 'Shit!' and 'Fucking hell!' But while he was sounding off I got a look at him and saw he had burns up his right forearm and the right side of his face. The hair on his arm had gone, and the skin looked red and raw. There were scorch-marks all down the right leg of his DPMs. In several places flames had burned through the material, and I could see blackened skin underneath.

As the shock wore off, he became more rational and started to laugh in reaction. 'Fuck me!' he went. 'That was a near one.'

Looking closely at him, I saw that his right eyelashes and eyebrow had been singed off. Blisters were already forming round his temple and on top of his head. I pulled a water-bottle out of my belt kit and poured the contents over him, in the hope that it would keep the swelling down.

'How's your vision?' I asked.

'Seems okay.'

'Close your left eye. Look at me. What am I doing?'

'Blinking,' said Whinger. 'You've lost most of your front hair as well.'

I reached up and felt short, frizzy ends.

'Shit!' I went. 'But at least your eyes are okay. I'm calling Mart up right away.'

It was Pavarotti who came on the radio. 'You lot all right?'

'More or less. See the fire?'

'We sure can. Any survivors?'

'One woman, unconscious. Listen. Whinger's got some bad burns, face, arm and leg. We need Mart up to where we've left our pinkie. Quick as he can. He'll be able to follow our wheel marks. Okay? We're on our way down. RV there soonest.'

For the first time I took a proper look at our survivor. She was dressed much the same as the men, in bush kit, but with a safari-style tunic and long trousers. As she lay on the ground, she stirred slightly but showed no other sign of coming round.

'She's taken a whack on the head.' Whinger pointed at a livid bruise on her right temple.

I knelt beside her, looking her up and down. With finger and thumb I opened her eyelids on the right side. Her eyeball showed no reaction. Cautiously, I moved her head, feeling with my fingers on the back of her neck. Had she taken a bang on the spinal cord as well? All I could think of was the little Kamangan boy who'd been hit on the head by the truck, and how he died in his mother's arms. Another head injury. Two more deaths. Two more *white* deaths. Jesus, I thought. This makes it three to the witch doctor. If this woman freaks out, it'll be four.

Whinger startled me by saying, 'What do we do, give her a bullet?'

'Hell, no!' I stared at him. 'We can't do that.'

'Why not? It might be best for her, as well as for us. She may die anyway.'

'She may. But also she may not. Until she snuffs it, she's coming with us.'

'Fancy her, do you?'

'Piss off, mate. She's better looking than you, anyway.'

Yet as I looked at her, I saw she wasn't that rough – jaw a bit heavy, perhaps, but a handsome, rather Teutonic face. Fine, straight fair hair cut short round the temples and left long on the back of her neck. She had elegant hands, too, no rings, fingernails short but in good nick. I guessed she was about thirty. I ran my hands over her arms and legs, checking for breaks, but couldn't detect any damage.

Behind us the aircraft was still burning. Cracking, clicking noises kept breaking out, but already the flames were dying down. The blaze had been so fierce that the skin on the fuselage and wings had melted or burned away, leaving the framework twisted, scorched and bare.

'That's the finish of any maps or documents they were carrying,' I said. 'Their kit's gone, too. Until our lady comes round, we won't know where they were from.'

'They probably put out a mayday call. Somebody may come looking.'

'I doubt it. Not out here. We're too far from anywhere.'

I saw Whinger starting to grimace again as the pain got to him, so I said, 'Come on, let's go.'

Grabbing a wrist and an ankle, I swung the woman on to my shoulder in a fireman's lift and started down the hill. With a last look back I noticed how the stony outcrops round the crash site had contained the fire and confined it to a small area. In that broken ground, with dark rocks everywhere, and the relics of bush fires scattered across the landscape, it would be difficult to detect the remains from the air. Only if a spotter plane or helicopter passed dead overhead would the crew have a hope of seeing it – a million-to-one chance in such a vast expanse.

Later that evening I passed Hereford such details as we'd been able to muster.

'The plane was a Beechcraft twin turbo-prop,' I told Pete Dickson over the satcom link. 'Registration G-SAF. That's all I know about it.'

'We'll check it out. What about the personnel?'

'We could only ID one of the guys. The other didn't have any documents on him.'

'Okay. So who's the one we have?'

'Surname, Pretorius. Christian names, Hermann Adolf. Born, Bloemfontein, 3 November 1954. Citizen of the Republic of South Africa.' The passport had been issued in Johannesburg.

When I'd given the date and number, Pete asked, 'And the woman?'

'Surname, Braun. Christian name, Ingeborg. Citizen of Namibia. Born Windhoek, 30 June 1969.'

'Is that all we know about her?'

'No, there was a business card in her passport. She's a rep for a firm called SWAG – South West African Game. Seems to be some kind of big-game management service. There's an address in Windhoek, too.'

'Okay, let's have it.'

I read it out, and said, 'Her clothes are a mixture of South African and German. The tunic's from David Lyndon Classics, the upmarket outfitter in Parktown, Joburg. Slacks from Powder Keg, in Melville. Her boots are Meindl – German.'

'Got that. What was the location of the crash?'

'Wait one.' I knew he'd want that, and to cover ourselves – to make it look as though we were less far south – I'd invented some coordinates that put the site about a hundred kilometres north of its real position. I persuaded myself it wouldn't make much difference: for the Beechcraft, it would have been only twenty minutes' flying time. But if the Kremlin realised how far we'd advanced already, they might start pissing about and ordering us back.

I gave the duff gen, and added, 'When we first saw the plane, it was coming from the east.'

'Okay. What state's the woman in?'

'Still unconscious, but stable. Mart reckons she'll make it.'

'Can't you find a hospital to put her into?'

'Hospital! You're fucking joking. There's no hospital within a million miles. There's no town, no road, no phone, no power, no water – nothing.'

'What are your plans for her, then?'

'Good question. We'll see what she says when she comes round. If we find out where she took off from, we may be able to call in another plane to exfil her.'

'How's Whinger?'

'Stable also. Mart's cleaned him up as best he can and given him pain-killers. It looks pretty bad, but it could have been worse.'

I was afraid Pete was going to ask why we didn't get the woman out by calling in the Kam-Ex Cessna that had lifted Andy's body. The answer was that I knew we were too far from Mulongwe, but I didn't want to admit it. Luckily he said nothing on those lines, and I ended the call by asking him to put over any information Hereford could dig out.

The plane crash and its aftermath had delayed us by several hours, and we didn't make it to the ridge of the hills by nightfall. Not knowing how the land lay on the other side, I didn't want to go over in the dark, so as dusk was falling our force deployed defensively in a level area just short of the crest.

Whinger was on his feet, but pretty miserable. After Mart had treated him he seemed in reasonable shape, but obviously he was getting a lot of pain, and there'd been an uncomfortable flare-up when Genesis had suggested going back up to bury the bodies and say a prayer.

'Fuck the bodies!' Whinger had shouted. 'I've just been fried, and if you come up with any more religious shit, I'm going to fucking drop you.'

The atmosphere was tense all round. I took Gen aside and said, 'Look, ease off the bible-bashing. You're starting to piss the guys off in a big way.'

'Sorry,' he went, innocently. 'I didn't realise I was annoying anyone.'

For the woman, we'd cleared space in the back of our mother wagon and put her in there in an American cot, in case we had to move out in a hurry. Mart had fixed her an IV drip, to keep up the level of her body fluids, and we arranged a rota of guys to monitor her, checking her eyes, making sure her pulse and breathing were okay. We all had the same instinct: to get her out, back to safety, as soon as possible, before her condition started to deteriorate. None of us wanted to be burdened with her. Whinger, who hated Germans on principle, nearly shat himself with rage when he realised that it was a Kraut he'd dragged from the wreckage.

'She's not a Kraut,' I told him. 'She's a Namibian.'

'Bollocks,' he went. 'All white Namibians are Krauts. How could she be anything else, with a name like that?'

He knew perfectly well that she was called Ingeborg – Inge for short, almost certainly – but because her surname was Braun, he started straight in, referring to her as Eva, like Hitler's girlfriend, Eva Braun.

'Firekin' roll on!' he cried, his temper not improved by the stinging of his burns. 'What do we want with *her*? She'll bring us nothing but bad luck. Better do what I suggested in the first place: put a bullet through her and leave her for the hyenas.'

'No way,' I told him. 'I want to have a little chat with her and find out what she was up to. I've been thinking about the scene of the crash. When we found the two guys lying dead, there wasn't a mark on their clothes. Those shirts and shorts were clean as clean. Whatever else that party was doing, it hadn't been on safari.'

SEVEN

We went over the hill at first light, and by 0700 we were established in an excellent OP, looking down through binoculars on the mine from a distance of seven or eight hundred metres. After so much dry, sandy terrain, our first sight of the river valley was quite something. Away to our left, upstream, the Kameni was wide and shining, flowing gently towards us between borders of brilliant green.

'Phragmites,' said Joss.

'What's that?'

'The reeds by the water. Spiky leaves. They can be ten feet tall.'

The surface of the river was dotted with what looked like dozens of little sandbanks, and it was only when some of them moved that we realised they were hippos, basking in shallow water. Beyond them, on the far shore, stood a small settlement: a square enclosure fenced with dried reeds, with the conical roofs of four grass huts showing above the walls.

A short way downstream, and close in under us, the land was higher. On our side, the base of the hills reached out to the river bank, and on the far bank rocky, scrub-covered outcrops rose from the water's edge, framing a shallow gorge, through which the stream tumbled in rapids. The mine was on the far bank at the bottom of that run, where the land levelled out again and the river reverted to a smooth flow. The sun, coming in low from our left, lit up ugly, corrugated-iron buildings clustered on flat ground above the water, with a long, covered gantry reaching out over the centre of the channel and down to river level. A rectangular central block with a pitched roof had been extended piecemeal by having sections of different shapes and sizes bolted on to it. The whole structure looked as though it had expanded bit by bit. Rising above it was a slender tower, square in section, topped by an open gallery under a flat roof. From the top of the roof rose a high, lattice-work radio mast.

Beyond that central assembly lay a compound surrounded by a security fence. Another large building, with two storeys of windows, stood apart, to the right as we looked – the accommodation, perhaps. There was also a dump of red forty-five-gallon fuel drums stacked inside a retaining wall built with concrete blocks. Further off, a low, white-washed bungalow range ran along inside the far perimeter.

Outside the fence a dirt airstrip stretched away into the bush downstream, to the south-east. The only road we could see left the compound in the opposite direction and followed the far bank of the river upstream before swinging off to the south. Transport didn't seem to the the outfit's strong suit: we could make out two old Gaz-type jeeps, a bulldozer and a couple of dump-trucks, and that was all. I guessed that because the place was so remote, most personnel and supplies came in by air.

The country beyond the compound was rockier than the terrain we'd come through: everywhere stony outcrops poked up out of the scrub and tall grass. There were also numerous black, burnt-out patches, and the vast, mottled plain faded off to a hazy horizon. The mine itself was particularly graceless: all vegetation had been scraped away to create a level, dusty, stony platform, without a single tree to soften its harsh outlines.

Looking down on the airstrip, I had a sudden idea.

'Eh,' I went. 'I don't suppose the Beechcraft came from here.'

'It was going in the opposite direction,' said Phil. 'When we first saw it, it was flying westwards, *towards* here.'

'True. In that case, was it *heading* for the mine?'

'Can't have been,' said Pav. 'I don't reckon the pilot knew this place existed. He was on the wrong side of the hills. If he *had* known about it, he'd have made straight for the strip when his engines started to fail.'

'True again. Bin that one, then. We'll have to wait on Inge to find out.'

Continuous noise rose from the plant. Even from a range of half a mile, the drumming of heavy machinery reached us loudly, augmented every now and then by violent outbursts of clattering, which sounded like rocks coming up the suction pipe from the river bed. I imagined a torrent of water, sand, rock and gravel pouring out on to a moving belt and being transferred automatically to a series of sieves or screens. From what I'd heard of the process, the whole lot got progressively washed and refined until diamonds were left glittering among the residue. From earlier briefings we knew that there was a secure area somewhere in the heart of the mine, where the diamonds were sorted and stored; now I made a mental note to take a supply of det cord and PE in my Bergen, in case we needed to blast our way in.

'Interesting,' I said, as we lay and watched. 'This whole flank's naturally protected by the river. No need for any defence on this side.'

'Yeah,' went Phil. 'But we can take some of the bastards out from this side.' He stuck an arm forward, and added, 'If we get guys on to that last little ridge down there below us, they can fire over the water and put rounds down anywhere in the compound, no bother. From that point the range can't be more than three hundred metres.'

'Sure,' I agreed. 'But the assault force is going to have to cross the river. How deep d'you think it is?'

'Up where the hippos are, not deep at all,' said Joss. 'You know they can't swim?' Seeing my look of surprise, he gave his high-pitched giggle. 'That's right – they just tip-toe along the bottom.'

'We could wade it, then,' I suggested.

'Never!' Joss was emphatic. 'Crocs. The water's full of them. When the sun gets higher, they'll come out on the sandbanks. You'll see.'

'Maybe we could drive them off with a few grenades.'

'Then you'd compromise us – tell everyone we're here to

join the party.'

'Show the crocs your arse, Pav,' went Phil. 'That'll put the frighteners on them.'

'*Zikomo*, mate.'

Joss was looking at Pav in consternation.

'He's got eyes tattoed on his backside,' I explained. 'One either cheek.'

'Oh, wah!' Joss grinned. Then his face turned serious, and he said, 'You know, my father was taken by a croc.'

'Never,' I went.

'He was.'

'How come?'

'He was a ranger in the park. Some old white settler guy used to hang about the river bank and go for a swim. One day he disappeared – all they found was his shoes. My father, he had to organise a hunt, and somehow he got snatched too. Eventually they shot the killer. It was a monster, twenty-two feet long. And when they cut it open, what d'you think they discovered in its stomach? Two hands, one white and one black.'

'Phworrh!' went Phil. 'How old were you then?'

'Five or six. If they hadn't got that croc, he might still be alive today. You know they can live to be a hundred? They go on growing all their lives.'

For a couple of minutes he went on chatting as he swept his glasses back and forth over the mine. He reckoned that after a croc hit you'd be be temporarily anaesthetised by shock; he didn't think you'd feel anything when the teeth crunched through your bones. I knew that was true of being hit by a high-velocity round, but a croc bite? I wasn't so sure.

'Leave the crossing for a moment,' I said. 'We'll get over somehow. What then?'

'Wait a minute.' Joss was eyeballing the straw hut settlement upstream. 'You know what that is? A pontoon station. You can see the boat in the water, down by the bank.'

'Oh aye,' I said. 'Great!' I could just make out a flat-bottomed wooden craft, like a wide punt.

'There must be a wire across the stream,' said Joss. 'Two men pull the boat across, back and forth, along the cable.'

'All right, then, we cross on the pontoon.'

'Got to get the fucker across to this side first,' said Phil.

'There'll be a rope that you can pull,' Joss told him. 'No problem.'

'We're across, then,' said Pav. 'Several trips, by the look of it. How many are you taking in the assault group, Joss?'

'Thirty? Could be more. Depends what we see in the next hour or two.'

'Sure,' I agreed. 'You'll need to get down there early – cross in time to attack at first light.'

'That's right!' Joss was becoming animated, talking fast and gesturing as he spoke. 'The assault group goes in left-handed, round the back of those mounds. See? We get them to within a hundred metres of the fence, in dead ground. Creep up to that ridge. We'll be slightly above the camp, looking down.'

'Good,' I went. 'Then what?'

'We wait there, in firing positions. The covering group stays this side, on that ridge you just pointed out below us.'

'What about the mortars?' I asked. 'They could stay right here, where we are, and crack things off with bombs into the main complex—'

'Hey!' Joss interrupted. 'We're not here to bomb anything. We don't want to destroy the plant. Don't want to damage it, even. We want to take it over in full working order. Same goes for any outside equipment. That bulldozer, for instance. That's going to be needed.'

'Okay, then,' said Pav evenly. 'Use the mortars as a distraction. If your guys start by putting bombs right over the top and landing them near the airstrip, the defenders may think you're coming in from that direction.'

'Yeah,' went Phil enthusiastically. 'They run out into the compound like headless fucking chickens, and the assault group drops them – *bom! bom! bom!* – just like that.'

'Just like that,' I said. 'That's the basis of it, anyway. Another thing you'd better put off-limits is the fuel dump, Joss. See it out the back there, that stack of drums with the wall round it?'

'Yeah, yeah. I've got it.'

'You don't want that going up in smoke. You'll need all the fuel you can muster to keep the mine going. Now, let's get down on this ridge beneath us and take a look from there.'

We spent the whole morning in that lower OP, getting baked and bitten, but also picking up an idea of the mine's routine. As we'd expected, the guard system was perfunctory. There were always two armed sentries on the main gate, but no patrol on the perimeter wire, and, except for the odd man walking around inside the compound, no other visible evidence of any military presence. The guys were wearing peaked DPM caps, so from a distance we couldn't see much of their faces. What we *could* tell, though, was that they were black as soot.

'So these are Afundis,' I said.

'That's right,' Joss confirmed. 'Our friends from the south.'

'They wouldn't show up much at night,' said Pav. 'That's for sure.'

'AK47s,' said Phil. 'They'll have gympis somewhere, as well.'

'Look at the tower,' I said. 'That open gallery, where the sandbags are. There's something nasty in there. Looks like a five-oh.'

'It is,' Phil confirmed. 'That'll need taking out right away.'

'Hear that, Joss?' I went. 'Put a good man on the RPG, and tell him to spray the tower.'

I began studying the fence with binoculars, looking for signs of an alarm system, but saw none.

'How many d'you suppose there are?' I asked.

'Guards?' said Joss. 'Can't tell. They'll be on a shift system, so half of them are probably asleep. Twenty altogether? And maybe the same number of workers.'

'What about *them*?' Phil asked. 'Are they Afundis as well?'

'Expect so. By now they'll have replaced any outsiders that used to work here.'

'They must have weapons as well – for an emergency.'

'Yeah,' said Joss scornfully. 'But we're going to hit them by surprise.'

'You reckon to drop any civilians as well?' I asked.

'Why not? They're only Afundis, and anyway, how do we tell which is which?'

I shot Phil a look, and said, 'Well, it's up to you.'

Joss didn't seem to hear that, or if he did, he paid no attention. All he said was, 'It's going to be easy!'

'Don't bank on it,' I told him. 'Lots of things can go wrong. But I tell you what. If you guys capture this place, you're going to have to strengthen the defences. Sooner or later, the Afundis are going to come looking to kick the crap out of *you*.'

'Sure, sure,' he went. 'First things first, though.'

'That blockhouse'll need sorting, too,' said Phil.

Beside the main gates a small building had been fitted into the perimeter fence, in the position the guardroom would occupy in a normal barracks. From far out it had looked like a tin shack, but from closer in we could see it was more solid, with an outer cladding of corrugated iron, inside which were walls of sandbags.

The big, free-standing building was obviously the cookhouse-cum-accommodation block. We deduced that from the way a trickle of blacks went in and out carrying their eating irons, mugs and so on. Because the far side of the main complex was out of our view, we couldn't tell exactly what everyone was doing, but Joss was obviously right: men were working shifts, for production to continue round the clock.

During the time we were watching, nobody left the compound on foot, heading for the pontoon. There seemed to be no reason for anyone to come in our direction – and that was good. The only event of the morning was the arrival of a four-truck convoy. When we saw a dust-cloud approaching from the south, my first thought was: shit – reinforcements.

'Watch this,' I went. 'Maybe they did hear the elephant rumpus. Joss, you may have to think again.'

But I was wrong. Two of the trucks drove to the cookhouse building and unloaded boxes which were obviously rations. The other two went to the fuel dump and deposited forty-five-gallon drums. The vehicles didn't stay long. The crews, two or three men from each, disappeared into the accommodation block, presumably for a meal, and within half an hour were on their way back.

'That's okay, then,' I said to Joss. 'Your plan holds. Your covering group deploys right here, where we are. They'll have one gympi and the five-oh with them. The mortars can fire from that hollow just behind us and put bombs down beyond the far wire. Keep off the airstrip, though. You're going to need that. The assault force will cross the river in the dark before dawn and deploy on those outcrops to our left. After the initial fire-fight, they'll go in from there to clear the buildings. Is that what you're thinking?'

'Fine, fine.' He nodded vigorously.

'When the shit hits the fan, your guys should be able to drop quite a few of the enemy straight away. But after the first couple of minutes the survivors will go to ground in one of the buildings, probably the main one. They'll barricade themselves in, for sure. Your lads are going to have to winkle them out.'

'RPG into the doors,' said Joss, laconically. 'Another couple of rockets into the tin walls. That'll get them jumping.'

'It might torch the place as well.'

Joss shrugged. 'If it does, it does. There's not much to burn inside – looks like it's all metal.' He turned to look at me, and said, 'By the way, I hope you fellows are going to join the party.'

'Well, we hope to. Phil and me are planning to come in behind assault force. We'll keep in touch and give you whatever back-up we can. Pavarotti will do the same up here with the cover group. The rest of us will remain on standby with the vehicles. How's that?'

'Fine, fine. No problem.'

'The most important thing is that nobody clocks on to the fact we're in the area. That means hard routine tonight: no fires or cooking. You need to get an OP on the ferry, too, Joss. We don't want any little bugger sneaking across in the night to raise the alarm.'

'We'll do that.'

'And you need to decide what to do if somebody comes this

way: grab him, knock him off, or what.'

Behind the OP in which we were lying, a gully ran back towards the hill, in dead ground from the mine; this made it easy for us to pull out and hand over to a relief observation team without any risk of being spotted. We were just about to go when Mart surfaced on the radio to say that Fräulein Inge was at last coming round.

'Great!' I said. 'Tell her I'll be with her shortly.'

'She's not that coherent yet,' he warned. 'Besides, she's talking German.'

'German!' snorted Phil. 'What did Whinger fucking tell you!'

'What's she saying?' I asked.

'Not too sure. We can't make much sense of it. She's hurt her ankle, though. She tried to stand up and went over on it. I see now it's pretty swollen. She must have sprained it in the crash.'

'Keep her comfortable. We'll be with you in twenty minutes.'

Walking back up the hill, Phil, Pav and I drew off to a distance on our own.

'Listen,' said Pav. 'That's not for real, is it? You going in with them?'

'Well . . .' I began.

'For fuck's sake!' he snorted. 'Let the silveries shoot hell out of each other. Leave them to it.'

'We don't want this first contact to go wrong,' I said. 'If we lose touch with Joss, he could blow it. Then we'd all be in the shit.'

'Give him a radio,' said Pav. 'Keep in touch that way. Don't get involved.'

'We're not planning on getting involved,' said Phil, stubbornly. 'That's the point. We're going to keep well back.'

'Bollocks,' went Pav. 'Once you get down on those mounds, you'll be in the thick of it.'

The argument continued till we were back in camp. Looking back, I realise it was Phil who was driving things. In spite of what he said, he was hell-bent on getting into a good fire-fight.

I should have put my foot down and vetoed the idea, but because I was tired I went along with his claim that our best chance of retaining control was to be on the ground with the assault force.

As we came in, Mart drew me aside until we were out of earshot of the trucks.

'She needs watching,' he said.

'What d'you mean?'

'I think she's bluffing. When she came round, the first thing she asked, was, "*Wo bin ich?*" Perfectly clear.'

'What did you tell her?'

'Nothing. I told her not to worry and that she was safe.'

'In English?'

'Of course. But after that, she went to gibberish.'

'She knows we're Brits, then. Maybe that's what turned her off. Make certain nobody says anything operational in her hearing. Nothing about where we are or what we're doing. Okay?'

'Sure.'

'How's her ankle?'

'Definitely sprained.'

'At least she can't do a runner, then.'

'Oh, no. The injury's genuine enough. She can only hobble. She must have caught it under the seats in the aircraft and wrenched it when the thing came down.'

'More important, how's old Whinge?'

'He's got a fever. That's only to be expected. I cleaned up his burns again as best I could, but there's always the risk a bit of shit has got in. I just hope the antibiotics'll keep him under control.'

I made a detour to see my old mate, but found that he'd dozed off on his cot, so I left him alone, lying on his back under a mozzie net with bandages all up his right leg and arm and a pad of gauze strapped over his right temple. Suddenly I realised that I'd never seen him out of action before, and the sight gave me a jolt. If the plane had blown up a few seconds earlier, I'd have lost him.

The woman was sitting propped up in the back of our seven-tonner, sipping at a mug of tea, with Genesis in attendance. Her eyes had a vacant look, and didn't seem to be focusing properly. I noticed her pupils were an odd colour, part grey, part yellow. The right eye was looking out level, the left one upwards. Now and then she muttered a word that sounded like German, but nothing I could understand, even though my own German's quite fluent.

'I'm Geordie,' I went. 'What's your name?'

No answer.

I tried it in German, but again got no reaction. Then, '*Wo kommen sie her?*'

Still nothing.

'*Das Flugzeug – wo kam es her?*'

Nothing. But hadn't there been a flicker in her eyes when I mentioned the aircraft? I glanced across at Genesis and got a faint nod, showing he'd seen it too.

'What about something to eat? *Essen?*'

Either she wasn't hungry, or she was playing dumb.

She – or somebody – had taken off her boots and socks. Her left ankle was swollen and black with bruises.

'How are *you* for food, Gen?'

'I've eaten, thanks.'

'Okay to stay with her a bit longer, then?'

'Fine.'

'I'll be back.'

As always, he was being saintly, and putting in more time with the patient than anyone else. But I didn't feel guilty as I went back to the others, who were sorting stores under a vehicle cam net. Maybe he was fancying the woman, too. Maybe he enjoyed being with her. As for me, I had a gut feeling that something about her didn't add up.

Pav and I sat under the net and ate some cold rations, discussing what to do about Whinger. Then Phil came over and started stirring up a debate about the woman.

'I mean, what are we going to *do* with her?' he demanded. 'We don't need this shit. If the rebels get hold of her, you know what they'll do to her. We can't have her round our fucking necks for the next two weeks.'

'Relax,' I told him. 'We'll shunt her somehow. And the first chance will probably be tomorrow.'

Our understanding was that when or if Alpha Commando recovered control of the mine, a transport plane or planes would come down from Mulongwe bringing engineers to take over the running of the plant, and troops to form a new garrison. Alpha would then be free to continue its marauding progress southwards.

'Don't worry,' I added. 'When that aircraft comes in from the capital, she's going to be the first passenger on the return flight.'

Phil said nothing, but shot me one of his looks. I could see he really didn't want the responsibility of looking after her, in case she came to a bad end. I knew his instincts tended to be pretty accurate, and when he said that this Krautish blonde was sure to foul up our plans, I didn't argue. I agreed with him that the sooner we got rid of her, the better.

A bigger worry, that afternoon, was Whinger. In spite of all the care Mart had taken cleaning his burns and covering them with Flammazine, an infection had set in up his arm, which was swollen and angry-looking, and his temperature climbed to 103. He didn't want any food, and it was an obvious effort for him to talk.

'Keep drinking, anyway,' I told him, 'and don't worry about the attack. It's going to be a cinch – and you're going out on the resupply tomorrow.'

As I came to the cookhouse area for supper, Mabonzo the beanpole tracker approached me shyly holding two little screws of paper in his right hand. We already knew he was the Kamangans' answer to Mart – an amateur quack who specialised in natural remedies – and now he was offering medicine for our patients.

'This one good for head,' he said, handing over the larger packet. 'Good for lady. And this one for fever.'

'Thanks.' I took them carefully and cupped them in my palm. 'I appreciate your help. How much do they need to take?'

'All.' He made a tipping-up gesture with his hand, showing the potions should be downed in one.

'Okay. We'll give them a go.'

Cautious investigation showed that each twist of coarse paper contained a small amount of powder. The dose for fever was white, the one for the head, grey. I thought of how the witch doctor's potion had blazed up that bilious green when I threw it on the fire.

'Bin them, for Christ's sake,' said Pavarotti, once we were out of Jason's hearing. 'You know what the head powder's made of?'

'What?'

'It's the bark of some tree, taken from down by the root, ground up and burnt together with dried dog-shit.'

'How d'you know?'

'Joss told me.'

'Delicious! Talk about kill or cure.'

'Give her some,' said Phil savagely. 'It might grow hair on her chest!'

'We'll see how she comes on,' I told him. 'I'll give Mart the stuff to keep for the time being, anyway.'

EIGHT

We were on the river bank at 0400, ninety minutes before first light. The stars were still bright in the sky, and the air was cool. Knowing how hot we were going to get, I'd stripped off my fleece jacket, but for the time being I was shuddering.

From the odd, quick remark that Phil let out on our way down the path, I could tell he was well hepped up. So was I. The argument about getting involved had lasted well into the night, but now it was too late. We'd taken the decision, and here we were, following the assault force down. Although I was apprehensive, I wasn't really scared. It wasn't as if Phil and I were going into battle; our role, I kept telling myself, was to stay at the back, out of trouble, and advise Joss if things started to go wrong. We'd done as Pav suggested, and lent him one of the covert radios. Keeping in touch should pose no problem.

The assault force of thirty-two men moved quietly through the dark, yet silence was hardly needed, because round that side of the hill we were well away from the mine, and in any case the hippos were putting on a staccato pre-dawn chorus. With their booming and barking they sounded like a flotilla of ships lost in fog. Without being able to see them, it was hard to tell what kept setting them off. One minute they were quiet, then suddenly they were honking all out.

Our first setback came at the water's edge. We found the end of the pontoon wire easily enough, but there was no rope to pull the boat across to our side. We knew the huts on the far bank were inhabited, because we'd seen cooking fires there the evening before. We couldn't shout for a lift, in case the guys over there raised the alarm. The only solution was for some of the Alpha guys to swim the river, take out the guards, and bring the ferry back across.

Joss had already selected three men for the task and dosed them with one of Jason's preparations that was supposed to ward off crocodiles. Rumour told us the stuff was made from snakes' bladders. At least it gave the guys full psychological protection. That was obvious as they stripped off and slipped into the water, armed only with their machetes, to carry out a silent attack. Far from showing any sign of nerves, they looked as though they were on a high and positively enjoying their role. At that point the river was about two hundred metres wide. Through binoculars I watched the three black shapes gradually diminish as they moved along the guide-wire into deeper water. After a couple of minutes only their heads and shoulders were showing.

From upstream the hippo chorus continued erratically. It was during one of the quiet periods that a croc put in its hit. I'd been more than half expecting it, but when it happened, the speed of the attack took my breath away. One second the surface of the river was smooth and calm; the next, a furrow was streaking diagonally across it from our left, heading downstream fast as a torpedo, with the water boiling at the point and a V-shaped wake spreading out behind. There was hardly a sound – just a splash, and one gasping groan that ended in a gurgle – but suddenly one of the men had gone, dragged bodily under water.

'Firekin 'ell!' went Phil, beneath his breath. 'I bet the other two aren't half shitting themselves.'

The Kamangan squaddies had no binoculars, so they could only guess what had happened, but they had a pretty good idea. Joss and a couple of his subordinate commanders knew full well that one of their guys had gone under, and they weren't going to put the wind up the rest. So nobody said anything. I found myself swallowing, from the thought of those jagged teeth slicing through human limbs. Would blood, spreading downstream, alert others and bring them speeding to the scene?

The two survivors forged on. By the time they were into the shadow of the far bank, even binoculars couldn't pick them out any more.

A tense wait followed. As if wanting moral support, Joss came up beside me.

'They must be ashore by now,' I muttered.

'Guess so. Let's get the boat over here!'

He sounded lit up by the prospect of action, as if he couldn't wait to reach the other side. I wasn't altogether happy: already I was thinking this could go wrong if he got too excited.

Between bursts of hippo talk, we listened intently. Nothing. Then Phil, who had a hand on the wire, said quietly, 'They're on their way back. I can feel the vibration.'

Through my glasses I saw the little ferry loom up square and black in mid-river. A couple of minutes later it came silently into the bank. Joss rapidly quizzed the pilots in Nyanja, then translated: 'They killed two guards with their knives.'

While the swimmers got back into their clothes, the first load went across. Until I saw the pontoon at close quarters, I hadn't realised how it was powered. Two crewmen sat on boards, one at the front, one at the back, each pulling on a single primitive wooden oar like a thick baseball bat, with a notch cut out near the end. The notch fitted over the wire hawser; when a rower exerted horizontal pressure, the oar locked on to the wire and pulled the craft forward.

The system was slow but effective, and soundless. With twelve men on board, the pontoon was almost awash, but I timed each crossing at only four minutes. The little craft was over and back inside nine minutes. Phil and I waited with Joss as the first two loads went across.

'Aren't hippos as dangerous as the crocs?' I whispered.

'On land, yes. If you get between them and the water, they charge. But I think they're used to the pontoon. It doesn't bother them.'

Back it came for the last time. We walked aboard and knelt down as two of the squaddies pulled us out into the stream. The current was running faster than it looked from the bank: I could feel it tugging us sideways against the guide-wire. On the far side we bumped gently against the bank and walked ashore.

'Okay,' I said quietly to Joss. 'On you go, and good luck.'

His teeth gleamed white in the darkness as he gave a quick grin, but I couldn't see the expression on his face.

His men set off silently in three sections, in line ahead. Phil and I waited till the last of them was moving, then tagged on behind. We followed the bank of the river, which swung out southwards round a headland before turning west again. At one point a loud bark burst out on our left, and a hippo, startled on its way back to the water, came blundering across our track. By sheer good luck there was nobody in its path.

After maybe five hundred metres we reached the outside of the bend and started to hear the mine's machinery running. Already the eastern sky was lightening behind us; in a few minutes the sun would rise, and when it did, it would shine low into the defenders' faces. Ahead, the small hills rose in knobbly, uneven hummocks – good cover. From low down they looked bigger than they had from above. Phil and I stopped and knelt down as the three sections deployed, fanning outwards. We could just make out the shadowy figures moving up into firing positions. Then Jason himself went on and disappeared. Looking up across the river to the dark bulk of the hill on our right, I imagined Pav and Stringer, on the OP with the machine-gun team. Their role was similar to ours: they were there to advise the Kamangans. The difference was, there was no way they could get involved in the battle, as the river was between them and the mine.

When my watch said 0515 I called Pav, and asked quietly, 'How's it going?'

'All good. We've got a great view. The compound's quiet – nobody in sight at the moment. There was a shift change while you were on the way down – guys back and forth between the accommodation and the main block – but now it's chilled out again. No movement on the perimeter.'

'Good,' I went. 'We're across the river. They guys are just getting into position.'

'Roger.'

'Stand by, then. As soon as Joss reckons the light's right, he'll give you the word.'

'Roger.'

The plan was to launch the attack in the grey twilight that preceded sunrise, when our own eyes would be accustomed to the gloom, and the defenders, stumbling outside, would be nearly blind for the first few seconds. It was up to Joss to judge the moment when it was light enough for our guys to see, but still dark enough to give us an advantage.

Once the Kamangans were settled, Phil and I crawled forwards and positioned ourselves hull-down behind a rock. We were less than ten metres behind the two-man RPG team, but lower than them, so that we'd be well protected from any incoming. Seeing how, in training, the guys had been inclined to fire their rockets high, I reckoned the RPG team might be the ones who'd need a bit of assistance.

Like the daylight, my adrenalin level came up by the minute. I glanced sideways at Phil and saw he was the same: face tense, eyes gleaming. 'Look out, you fuckers,' he was muttering. 'You've a nasty surprise coming.'

'One minute,' said Joss's voice in my earpiece. 'Covering force ready?'

'Roger,' went Pav.

'Stand by to open fire. Thirty seconds. Twenty. Ten . . .'

As he counted 'zero' we heard the distant *boomph* of the 81-mil mortars from high to our right. They were out of our sight, in dead ground, so we didn't see anything, but we heard the whistle as the first salvo of bombs arched high over the river. A few moments' silence, then bright flashes spurted from the ground way out in front of us. A volley of explosions split the dawn silence.

Joss had ordered his strike force not to open fire until they saw specific targets. But the tension got to them. The mortar detonations triggered their attack impulse, and before any human defenders appeared, they started putting rounds into the walls of the main complex. Maybe it made no difference. Within seconds of the first bombs landing figures emerged from buildings at the run. Three or four raced for the blockhouse at the entrance, coming towards us and crossing to our left. The rest headed away, deeper into the compound.

Presented with legitimate targets, the attackers opened up with short bursts and dropped one of the advancing defenders. But most of the firing was completely wild. Phil jabbed me on the arm and pointed to our right. One of the Alpha guys was standing upright behind a hillock, holding his rifle high above his head, trying to level it with both hands, and firing blindly over the mound without any clue as to where his rounds were going.

Bullets started snapping over our heads, uncomfortably close. From the loudness of the cracks and the heavy hammer in the distance, I realised they were coming from the .50.

'It's that fucker in the tower!' I shouted. I hit my pressel switch and snapped, 'Pav! Get some fire into the top of the tower. We're getting bloody murdered by the .50!'

The operator had pin-pointed our position. His first few bursts went high, but then, with a solid, heavy thump, a Kamangan twenty metres to my right took a bullet in the shoulder or chest. He'd been lying face down, but the impact lifted him bodily and flung him backwards down the slope. When he flopped to a halt against a rock, he didn't stir again.

On my left the RPG team were cowering behind a rock.

'Get up!' Phil roared at them. 'Get up and fucking *fire*!'

Gingerly, the Number One rose half into an upright position, took a perfunctory aim at the blockhouse and pulled his trigger. *Whoosh*! went the rocket, slightly to the left and miles above the target, so high that it flew free for the whole of its life until after four seconds and about nine hundred metres it self-destructed with a brilliant flash.

'Look at that!' I shouted. 'He might have been firing at a fucking aircraft!'

Flashes were spurting from the slits in the blockhouse. Now we were under fire from two directions. Our RPG guy was back on the deck. His Number Two was trying to stuff another rocket down the tube while retaining a horizontal position.

'Fire again!' I bellowed.

The second round went even higher than the first. I knew the team had only eight rockets between them. At this rate, they'd waste them all before they scored a hit. There was only one thing for it. All good resolutions left my head. There was no way I could keep back and watch such incompetence.

Phil was already putting in the odd short burst with his 203.

'Keep hammering the tower,' I shouted. 'I'm going on the RPG.'

At moments like that, instinct takes over. No matter how much Hereford had cautioned us about not getting involved, no matter how often we'd told each other we'd keep out of trouble, I was *not* going to lie there and wait to be turned into a rag doll by a round from the .50. The urgent necessity was to silence the big machine gun. Its operator probably couldn't see individuals, but he'd sussed out where we were accurately enough and was putting venomous short bursts into the rocks that stuck up round us. Splinters were flying in all directions, ricochets screaming away behind.

I wriggled back down the slope into dead ground, ran across, came up again behind the rocket team, held out a hand, and shouted, 'Eh, give it over!'

The guy with the launcher rolled his eyes, glanced at his mate, then, without speaking, handed the weapon across.

'Come on! Move!' I yelled, gesturing violently. 'For fuck's sake, get it loaded!'

With fumbling hands the Number Two got a rocket into the barrel. Swivelling to my right, I went up on one knee, settled the weapon on my shoulder, left hand awkwardly behind my right, and laid the cross hairs of the sight on the lower edge of the sandbagged machine-gun nest in the tower. The range was barely 150 metres – a cinch.

Whoosh! Away went the rocket. It hit the left-hand side of the structure and sent pieces of metal flying, but didn't explode. The contact could only have been a glancing blow. The explosion came a second or two later as the destabilised warhead plunged into the deck beyond the target.

'Reload!' I roared. 'Quick!'

This time the guy handled the rocket as if it was red hot,

loading in two or three seconds. I settled into the aim again, holding the upright wire of the reticle on the right-hand edge of the nest.

Impact! That second round went straight in with a brilliant flash. The explosion blew a cloud of shit into the air and enveloped the tower in smoke. As the cloud drifted clear, I saw the mast had been toppled and was hanging down like a minute-hand at five o'clock. The hammer of the .50 ceased. With luck, I'd done for the rebels' radio as well.

'Now the blockhouse!' I shouted.

This time I made no mistake. Again I held to the right, and the round went smack into the middle of the structure. Another big flash, another good explosion. The place burst into flames and began to belch smoke.

I handed the launcher back to its owner. 'Now one into the gate. The weapon's going left. Aim right of centre. This much.'

The range was shorter, so I demonstrated with my hands only a couple of feet apart. The Kamangan looked less terrified. He'd seen how effective his weapon could be. Maybe he was planning to take the credit for my hit on the tower. Whatever the reason, his next rocket blew hell out of the gate and left it a sagging wreck.

In the few minutes since things had gone noisy the light had grown stronger. Then, quite quickly, the whole scene turned pink. Screwing my head round, I saw that the sun was halfway over the horizon behind us – a huge, blood-red ball.

Abrupt volleys of small-arms fire made me look left. One poor hippo, taken unawares, had come lumbering back towards the river after its night's grazing. It didn't get far. Multiple hits brought it to a halt, then to its knees, and in the end it rolled sideways to the ground where it lay with its stumpy legs kicking feebly.

'What the hell are they doing?' I said to Phil.

'Maybe they're getting hungry.'

From the far end of the compound a column of black smoke was rising.

'Fucking roll on!' Phil shouted. 'Some stupid bastard's shot up the fuel store.'

Mortar bombs were still falling near the end of the airfield. Rounds continued to snap over our position, but now the fire was sporadic. What the hell was the Kamangan commander waiting for?

'Joss,' I called on the radio. 'Get 'em going!'

'Roger.'

He yelled out an order in Nyanja. His section commander passed it on. Leaving half a dozen guys to give covering fire, the rest jumped up and sprinted forward, blasting uselessly from the hip with their AK47s, wasting rounds by the hundred. One man went down before they reached the gate, but the rest piled through, fanned out, and dropped into firing positions inside the compound.

Phil and I stayed where we were, in relative safety. But suddenly I realised that accurate incoming fire was hitting the assault force from the left, from the direction of the accommodation block. One of the guys was slotted, then another. Somebody was shooting far too straight.

'Left! Left!' I yelled at the Kamangans still with us. 'Fire at the white block!' Rapidly, I scanned the windows, looking for snipers. Over the radio I called, 'Joss, you've got incoming from your left! Swing that way.'

He didn't answer immediately, so I went, 'Pav! We're getting enfiladed from our left. Incoming from the white block. Get the .50 on to it.'

'Roger,' he answered. 'Wait one.'

Seconds ticked past. Rounds were cracking in every direction. Then down came the heavy hammer of our own .50. Its big bullets swept back and forth along the front of the accommodation block, blowing plaster and cement out of its façade. In the middle of the turmoil our RPG let rip at one of the main doors of the equipment shed. The range was about thirty metres, and Number One must have learnt from his earlier cock-ups, because he blew the handle and locking mechanism clean out. With smoke and dust still swirling round the door, his mates rushed at it, ran it half open on its rail, and sprayed rounds inside.

Then suddenly Pav was on the air again. 'Listen,' he called. 'Watch yourselves. There's some guys out in the bush away to your left.'

'Outside the wire?'

'Well outside. They must have done a runner from the compound.'

'How many?'

'I've seen three. Could be more. They're in light-coloured DPMs.'

'Weapons?'

'Affirmative. Rifles or gympis.'

'Where are they?'

'There's a single bare tree with a big fork in the top.'

'Got it.'

'From here, they're on a ridge, two o'clock and fifty metres from the tree.'

'That puts them about four hundred metres from us.'

'Spot on.'

'Okay. We're going after them. Tell me if they move.'

'Roger.'

Phil needed no orders or encouragement. He'd heard the conversation and was on his way. Together we scuttled back off our hill, into hollows, and used dead ground to work our way fast round towards the south. We hustled along, twisting to keep in the hollows. Behind us, to our right, the battle was raging. Explosions that I reckoned were hand-grenades punctuated the small-arms fire. Then, as we came up to a ridge, I realised that some of the shots were going off from close in front of us.

'Bastards!' gasped Phil. 'Sniping from way out.'

'Get behind them,' I panted.

We dropped back and took another swing to our left. More single shots cracked out.

'There's the marker tree,' said Phil. 'Get up to that.'

Ten metres from the top of the bank, we dropped on to hands and knees. For the last little stretch we went into a leopard crawl until we could peep over the crest. Less than forty metres off three guys were down on their bellies in firing positions, weapons levelled, taking controlled shots at the compound. We were nearly abreast of them, slightly behind, so they were looking away from us, concentrating on their targets.

'Hey!' I whispered. 'Take the outer two. You the left, me the right. Count from five. Ready?'

'All set.'

I put my sight on the right-hand man's ribs, just behind his shoulderblade.

'Five, four, three, two, one.'

Crash! Our weapons went off simultaneously. Neither target moved, except to jerk and slump forward. Suddenly I realised there was something out of place about the man in the middle. He was white.

Before he could react I put another burst into the ground beside his head, and yelled, 'Throw your weapon away!'

For a few seconds he held on to it, glancing desperately to left and right. When he saw both his companions were dead, he pushed the rifle away to his right and left it lying on the ground at arm's length.

'Stay down!' I yelled. 'Get rid of your weapon! Right out in front of you! More! Hands on your head. Stay on your belly.'

The man did as ordered.

'Come on,' I told Phil. 'If he tries anything funny, slot him.'

We went forward with 203s levelled until I was a couple of paces from the broad back. Phil walked in front of him with his weapon pointed down at his head. I went and felt under him. My hand lit on a holster containing a pistol. I pulled it out – a Colt .45 with worn wooden grips. I pushed the weapon into my belt and told the guy to stand up.

He got up warily. He was older than I expected, in his forties, with a lined face and grey stubble on his chin.

'All right,' I went. 'Who the fuck are you, bonny lad? And what are you doing here?'

'No information.'

I gave him a kick in the groin, which made him stagger, then tried again. His answer was the same. The few words were enough to confirm he was South African – that edgy eccent.

'Listen,' I said. 'If you don't fucking talk to me, there are government forces down there, and *they'll* make you talk.'

A movement above us caught my eye. Another man had appeared on the skyline, a long way off. I saw him only for a second, but I realised from his build – his broad, stocky frame – that he couldn't be an African. Before I could react he'd ducked down and disappeared.

I hit my pressel, and called, 'Pav! We're by the tree. We've got one white guy, but there's somebody else moving above us. To you they'll be two o'clock from the tree.'

'Got 'em!' he cried. 'Two guys, three. Running like hell. Away from you.'

'Let 'em go,' I said. 'We'll bring this one down with us.'

We left the two bodies where they lay. The blacks had been firing AK47s, but the white guy had a good-looking sniper rifle with a vari-power telescopic sight. While he glowered at us in silence, I picked the weapon up and slung it over one shoulder.

Below us, the battle was fizzling out. The firing had become sporadic.

I wasn't going to waste time arguing.

'Get moving,' I told him. 'Back to the mine.'

With us two right behind him, I didn't think he'd try doing a runner – and if he had, we'd have dropped him without compunction. We steered him down the gullies by ordering 'Right' and 'Left' until we came up behind the covering force. Just as we reached them, Joss called them forward, and as they ran into the compound, we followed.

In spite of his orders not to cause unnecessary damage, the attackers had shot the place to pieces. The blockhouse was still smouldering, and a far bigger fire was blazing out of the fuel store: barrels of diesel had ignited and were sending a column of dense black smoke boiling high into the sky. The dredging machinery had ground to a halt. The doors of the main building, big enough to admit trucks, had been blown off their guide-rails and were hanging drunkenly. The corrugated-iron walls were riddled with bullet holes. No other prisoners had been taken. Bodies lay everywhere, most of them relatively intact, but several hacked into bloody lumps in an orgy of killing. Away to our left some of the Alpha guys were smashing their way into the single-storey block.

I grabbed the first two men we came to, and said, 'You two, guard this prisoner.'

They looked a bit shattered, so I added, 'Just stay here and keep him covered until I get Major Mvula.'

The air inside the main building was full of dust and smoke. Through it I made out inner walls – the secure area, a windowless box maybe fifteen feet high, with the conveyor belt from the dredger arm coming high over it and down through the ceiling. The place was full of men running around screaming and shouting.

'Joss!' I yelled. 'Where the fuck are you?'

Any answer he may have given was drowned out by a volley of shots, deafening inside the steel walls, as somebody emptied his magazine into the locks on one of the secure unit's doors, trying to blast his way in.

'*Joss!*' I roared. 'Get these guys under control. Get 'em out of here!'

It took him a few minutes to impose his authority, his men were on such a high. But in the end he managed it. Once all the shouting died down, it became possible to talk.

'Listen,' I told him as we stood in the main doorway. 'We've got one white prisoner outside. Take charge of him, and keep a good eye on him. We'll need to interrogate him to find out what the hell's been going on. And get some of your guys moving. We know three enemy at least made a breakout and got away to the south. There may have been more. The defenders may have broadcast an SOS before we took out the radio. A counter-attack may come in. Send out clearance patrols to check our immediate surroundings. Get people digging in on the perimeter. Leave the .50 section where it is, across the river, but bring the rest of your guys over soonest. You need an immediate resupply: ammunition and rockets.'

Joss nodded. But somehow he looked strange. His eyes were half closed, as if he'd just taken something or had a big drink. Suddenly I realised that in the heat of the moment I'd given him a stream of orders. Had I offended him?

'Look,' I said. 'I'm sorry. I didn't mean to tell you what to do. I was just saying what I thought ought to be done.'

'Fine, fine,' he said, but he sounded vague.

'Another thing. See that single tree on the rock up there? There's two bodies just this side of it. Let's get them brought in. First, though, I need some men in here with me and Phil, to help clear the secure area. Can you spare me five?'

I had a feeling I'd blown our relationship, and I wasn't sure whether he was going to detail anybody to help.

The next few minutes were tense. Inside, the dust was settling, but the heat was horrendous, like in an oven. I took off my Bergen and began sorting some det cord. The walls of the secure area looked pretty solid: there were concrete blocks on the outside, and I expected there'd be a lining of steel on the inside. The door was as solid as the wall, with a heavy-duty lock – a serious, precision-made combination job, with three dials. The bullets fired at it had bounced off, leaving practically no marks. Phil took one look at it, and said, 'We'll not pick that bugger.' So I made up a charge with a couple of ounces of PE, and I was taping it in position when five guys shambled in.

'Thank God,' I muttered to Phil. 'He's still on side.'

I turned to the Kamangans, and said, 'Okay, I'm going to blow the door. I expect some of the mine staff to be inside. Once the door's open, I want you to go in and round up anyone who's in there. All right? Take prisoners. No shooting unless you're fired at first. Understood?'

The senior man, a corporal, nodded.

'We're going to need these people to get the machinery going again,' I said. 'That's why it's important – no killing.'

With everyone round the corner out of the way, I cracked off the charge. Inside the tin walls, the noise and shock-wave were stupendous. The door swung ajar. Beyond it, black darkness. We needed torches. For a few seconds I stood with my back flattened against the outer wall, listening. Wild yells were still coming from the direction of the bungalow, but inside the building there was silence, except for the noise of water splashing. Then came a sudden rumble, a shuddering noise and a hum as, somewhere in the depths, a small engine started up. An emergency generator. Lights came on, dim and flickering.

Immediately inside the main door I could see a small, box-like cubicle partitioned off, with a window in the side – the place where workers were checked in and out. Peering cautiously in, I found the rest of the first room was empty – a kind of air-lock. I beckoned the others after me and slipped through the door.

Going into that enclosed space reminded me of a week I'd once spent on an aircraft carrier, when a simulated battle was being fought and the whole ship was sealed against nuclear, biological or chemical attack. Now I got the same feeling of instant claustrophobia, intensified by the fact that the air-conditioning system had gone down and the room was stiflingly hot.

With the five Kamangans lined up covering me, I tried the door in the far wall. Locked. But this was a flimsier affair altogether. Det cord round the lock and handle would sort it. Phil moved the Kamangans out of the way along one wall while I taped some cord into place.

I was on the point of cracking it off when suddenly I heard a movement on the far side. Somebody was fiddling a key into the lock. I whipped back against the wall, pulling my pistol out. The handle turned and the door opened slowly, inch by inch, as though the person pushing it was scared of what might lie beyond. There was a scuffling sound, as if several people were milling about. Then a hand appeared, and the sight of it amazed me, because its skin was white.

I stood transfixed as the owner emerged into view: an aged white ghost of a man, bent and shuffling, bald on top of the head, with a few wisps of long grey hair straggling down over his ears and white stubble bristling from his cheeks. He was wearing a filthy yellow T-shirt that hung loose over his bony shoulders, and even filthier grey trousers, with the remains of a pair of tennis shoes lashed round his bare feet. He looked as though he'd just risen from his grave, so deathly pale was his complexion.

When I made a sound, and he turned and saw me, he started, as if I'd stuck a knife in his ribs, and gave a croak of '*Mon dieu!*' For a second I wasn't sure what he'd said. I'd expected something in English, and didn't recognise the French. Before I could answer, he buckled at the knees, and the next thing I knew he was stretched out full-length, face down on the deck, still in the doorway.

'Pull him through!' I snapped at Phil. 'Get this door shut.'

In a flash I whipped out the key, closed the door and locked it from the outside. We dragged the old guy through the anteroom and sat him up against the wall in the main building, where the heat wasn't quite so devastating. He looked even closer to death, but when I poured the contents of a water-bottle over his head, he came round.

As his eyes opened, I said, 'Take it easy. You're all right.'

Phil handed him another bottle with the top open, and asked, 'Who are you?'

'Boisset,' he replied. After a long swallow, he added, 'François Boisset.'

'You're French?'

'*Belgique.*'

'Belgian! You speak English?'

'A little.'

'What are you doing here?'

'*Je suis l'ingénieur* . . . I am the engineer. I am in command of the *machin*, the machinery. You are who?'

'British,' I told him. 'We're helping the government forces.'

'*L'armée du gouvernement? Dieu merci!*'

Even in the dim light of the shed, the old man was having trouble with his eyes, screwing them half shut.

'You seem very weak,' I said. Maybe the blacks had been starving him. 'Are you hungry?'

'Hungry? No.' He sounded surprised. 'I am a prisoner. Since

more than a year I am a prisoner of these Afundis. In one whole year I have not seen daylight.'

In short sentences, often lapsing into French, he told his story. When the rebel forces took over the mine, they'd shot most of the staff. But they'd kept him and a few key workers to run the machinery. He himself had spent most of the time confined to a cell inside the secure area, only being brought out when something went wrong and his specialist knowledge was needed. Having no radio, he'd completely lost touch with the outside world.

'So who's inside the works now?' I asked.

'Seven men. Four workers, three Afundi guards.'

'Do they have weapons?'

'Two Afundis only.'

'Can you talk to them in their own language?'

'Of course. They sent me out to see what was happening.' A gleam came into his watery blue eyes as he added, 'So, for the first time, I have the key!'

I looked at Phil. 'Listen,' I said. 'Those guys have got to come out. I don't think the Afundis are going to have much chance once they get outside, but there's no way they're stopping in there.'

'*Salauds!*' exclaimed Boisset with surprising force. '*Je m'en merde.*'

At that moment, Joss appeared in the main doorway.

'Eh,' I called. 'Come here a minute.' Turning to Boisset, I said, 'This is the commander of the government force.'

Joss was pouring with sweat, but so spaced out that he didn't seem to register the fact that an extra European had appeared. 'Oh wah!' he went when I told him the score. 'Bring them out. We'll deal with them.'

'Okay,' I said to Boisset. 'Tell them to come out, and say they'll be all right.'

With a fine Gallic shrug, he said, '*Pourquoi pas?*'

The old fellow seemed suddenly rejuvenated. He heaved himself to his feet, lurched, steadied himself and turned back to the door.

'You send them out,' I told him. 'We'll wait here.'

In he went, calling out in Nyanja. Less than a minute later he was back at the head of a little procession. We hardly needed him to tell us which of the Africans were which. The first four looked downtrodden and apprehensive, and were wearing filthy T-shirts, shorts and flip-flops.

'The workers,' I said, and when he nodded, I motioned them to one side of the room. 'Stand over there.'

The last three were altogether different. Dressed in bush shirts and DPM bottoms, they had an arrogant look about them, and two carried AK47s. I'm afraid Boisset had told them that during the battle their own side had beaten off the attackers, and they thought they were walking out to a celebration. When they saw Phil and me standing there, they did a terrific double-take, but by then it was too late. In a flash our escort cut off their retreat, grabbed them, and wrenched their weapons off them. They also removed a large bunch of keys from the boss figure, and hustled all three out into the open.

Exactly what happened next, we never knew, but our ears told us enough. The three may have tried to do a runner. They may have just stood near the main doorway. All we heard was a burst of yelling, a volley of gunfire, very loud and close, and another roar of shouts and cheers.

Boisset looked at me and nodded, muttering, '*C'est fini.*' Then he turned to the mine workers and said something in Nyanja. For a moment they didn't believe him, and he had to repeat himself, using different words. Then the message got through, and suddenly all four were transformed from zombies into human beings, laughing and joking like they'd just got a year's extra pay.

'These men have not been outside, either,' Boisset told me. 'Not for more than a year.'

'You can go out in a minute,' I said, magnanimously. 'But you'd better wait till the excitement dies down. This wouldn't be a good moment. Now, how much damage has been done to the mine?'

'*Il me faut* . . . I must make checks. The main problem is loss of power. The generators have stopped.'

'That's because the fuel tanks have been ruptured.'

'*C'est ça?*'

'Yeah. The fuel depot's on fire.'

'No wonder we are *en panne*.'

At my request Boisset took the keys and led us on a quick tour of the mine. He showed us the machine room, where the conveyor belt came in from the river inside a big metal pipe and spewed its load onto a series of wire-mesh trays which normally had water washing through them. Huge fans suspended from the roof should have been keeping the air on the move, he explained, but with the loss of current they'd stopped, and the heat was formidable.

'Normally, the sieves are *agités*.' He held out a hand palm-down and moved it rapidly back and forth. 'The washed aggregate passes this way, into this next room.' He unlocked a door and let us through. 'Here, more washing, More shaking. *Enfin* . . .' He unlocked yet another door. With only the emergency lamps flickering, the light was very dim. 'Here, we are in the most secure area – and there are the diamonds.'

'Diamonds?' said Phil, scornfully. 'Where?'

'These.' Boisset reached down and scooped up a handful of what looked like gravel from the floor of a stainless-steel tank. '*Normalement* we have bright light.' He squinted up at the spotlamps close overhead. 'Specialist workers can see them easily. Look, this is one.'

Between finger and thumb he held up what looked like a crumb of broken glass, the size of a pea, which flashed brilliantly when he turned it.

'Yeah,' I went, suddenly remembering something I'd read. 'Guys with eyes like the shithouse rat stand here and pick them out.'

A faint smile lit up Boisset's face. '*C'est vrai*. But it is expert work.'

'Does this mine sometimes produce big stones?' I asked.

'*Mais oui!* We have had diamonds so large.' He held his thumb and forefinger at least an inch apart.

'Like an egg,' I said. 'One that size must be worth millions.'

'Of course. One stone like this would finance an entire civil war.'

Beyond that final sorting room lay a kind of laboratory, with raised benches on which the diamonds were sorted, and beyond that again a strongroom where they were stored. Apparently, an aircraft came in every week to lift out the loot.

'What sort of plane?'

'Myself, I have never seen it. But I am told it is of medium size. It always bring ten or twelve soldiers. A change for the garrison. Also it has a guard in case of attack.'

'And where does it go?'

'Sometimes to South Africa. Sometimes to Sentaba, the camp where General Muende has his headquarters.'

'General now, is he?'

'Leader of the Afundi rebels. Yes.'

'Has he ever been here?'

Boisset shook his head.

Without the primitive air-conditioning, the heat was becoming impossible.

'Let's get back into the open,' I suggested.

Boisset locked up behind us and led us back. As we passed the open sinks, I was sorely tempted to scoop up a handful of the diamond-laden gravel and stuff it into one of the pouches on my belt kit. Then I thought, set an example!, and carried on. Boisset diverted to show us the squalid little apartment in which he'd been held prisoner: two tiny, windowless rooms, with a cold tap and a hole in the floor for a bog. It seemed a miracle that he'd stayed sane.

'What did you eat all the time?' Phil asked.

'Filth. Whatever they brought me. My stomach has been very bad.'

Poor old bugger, I thought. On impulse, I asked, 'How old are you?', and I was shocked when he answered, 'Fifty-two.' From his appearance I'd have given him seventy at least.

'What about the keys?' I asked. 'You'd better hand them to Joss. Major Mvula, his name is. He needs to get a guard on the secure zone. There he is, coming now.

'Joss,' I went. 'Meet a great survivor.'

I explained who Boisset was, and what he'd done. Now Joss seemed in a raging hurry, far less friendly than usual. He greeted the Belgian in an off-hand way and made no enquiries about how he was feeling. Instead, he said, 'Water, man. What's the water situation?'

'We get it from the river,' Boisset answered. 'Naturally, it has to be filtered before use. The purification plant runs on electricity . . .'

Joss seemed to be only half listening. Without paying much attention to the answers, he fired off a whole lot of questions about how long it would take to get the mine up and running again. Then he ordered Boisset to draw up a list of any spare parts that would be needed. The old man listened meekly enough, then shuffled off.

'Listen,' I said to Joss as he moved away. 'That guy's had a hell of an ordeal. He needs looking after.'

Joss glared at me, and said, 'So does the mine.'

His attitude was starting to piss me off. But also I was worried. His emotional state seemed to be veering about. I had the feeling he might do something stupid at any minute. Hadn't we just helped him recapture the damned place? But it wasn't the moment to start anything, so I just asked, 'Okay. What's the drill, then?'

'We've been in touch with Mulongwe. The relief aircraft's coming down in the morning.'

'So when will you want to move on?'

'Maybe tomorrow evening.'

'That's fine.'

I walked out into the blazing sunshine. Then, on impulse I turned back into the building and sought out Boisset again. By then he was checking the big generators, which, as we thought, had shut down from fuel starvation.

'I'm sorry,' I began. 'That guy wasn't very polite.'

The Belgian gave a shrug, which said, 'That's Africans.'

'The thing is, what d'you want to do? I imagine you're

wanting out. If that's right, I'm sure we can get you back to Mulongwe on the relief plane.'

'*Mais non*!' came the answer, with some emphasis. 'I must stay to look after the mine. It is my child, almost.'

I was quite surprised. 'If that's what you want.'

'Certainly. If I can live once more in my bungalow over there.' He pointed in the direction of the single-storey accommodation. 'There is just one thing.'

'Go on.'

'Perhaps you can send a message to my nephew in Brussels. He is also Boisset, Alphonse, my brother's son. He is in the book. Alphonse Xavier. He does not know if I am alive or dead. Please tell him I am in one piece.'

'No problem. We'll get our headquarters to pass it on.'

'*Merci*.'

He had forgotten the telephone number, but wrote the address on a page of my notebook, and I left him pottering among his machinery. It crossed my mind that he must have some ulterior motive for wanting to stay on in such a hell-hole. Maybe, I thought, he's been burying the odd diamond over the years, and needs time to dig them out. Whatever it was, I hadn't got time to argue the point with him. If he wanted to stay, that was fine by me.

Outside again, I suddenly felt weak with hunger. I was astonished when I looked at my watch and found it was only 0730. The fire in the gatehouse had gone out, but the fuel depot was still burning well. Across in the bungalow some sort of party seemed to be in progress. There was a lot of wild shouting, laughter and singing. I thought of going across to check it out, but then I saw Banda, one of the black sergeants, heading out of the bungalow towards us.

Something bad seemed to have happened to him. He was moving unsteadily. I thought he'd been shot or had got into a fight, because there was fresh blood all over his face and down his shirt.

'Hey, Banda!' I went. 'What's the matter with you?'

'Join the party!' he shouted, giving a quarter-melon grin as he parroted Joss's war-cry. 'Big celebration! South African whisky very good!'

'What's all that blood? You been hit, or something?'

'White man's liver!' he cried. 'White man's liver very good!'

With that, he staggered past us and carried on.

'Jesus!' went Phil. 'He's pissed as arseholes. They must have found some hooch where the mercenaries were quartered.'

'Is that right about the liver?'

'You bet. That's what these guys do. Cut out their enemy's liver and eat it raw.'

'Fucking savages! D'you reckon they've topped the guy we brought in?'

'More than likely.'

'Let's leave them to it.'

Beside the wrecked gate a party of soldiers was filling sandbags and rebuilding the defences of the guard-post. At least some effort was being made. As we walked past, I called up Pavarotti.

'Pav,' I went. 'How're you doing?'

'Fine, thanks. All quiet up here.'

'Down here there's a fucking shambles. But it's Joss's show, so we're leaving him to it and coming back up.'

'Roger. There's one thing I'd better warn you about.'

'Oh yeah?'

'I just heard from Mart. The Kraut's come round. She's making perfect sense.'

'You're kidding.'

'Never. And you know what cured her? Mabonzo's medicine.'

NINE

We found Whinger stripped to his shreddies and bandages, stretched out on his American cot. Even from a distance I could see him shuddering with fever.

'How goes it?' I said.

'Average to fucking awful. Let's hear about the battle, though. Take my mind off this pain.'

'Basically it was all right,' I began.

'It sounded like Guy Fawkes night,' he croaked. 'Bloody brilliant!'

'Yeah. The silveries could have done worse.'

I filled him in on the various phases of the attack, then said, 'It's what happened afterwards that I don't like. The whole lot went bananas. Like after the stampede, only worse. They carved up one of the white mercenaries and ate him. Parts of him, anyway.'

'Who'd have thought it?' said Whinger, slowly. 'Mercenaries fighting for a shower like these rebels. Hardly worth their while.'

'I don't know,' I said. 'There's something bigger than we know going on here. Otherwise these guys wouldn't be involved.'

'They're after diamonds,' said Whinger. 'They're probably desperate for money. That's where you and me'll be in a couple of years' time – out on the wing for some fifth-rate black army.'

'Not if I can help it,' I told him. 'These bastards are that treacherous, once we get out of here, I'm keeping clear of Africa for a bit.'

'Me too,' went Phil.

'Another thing I can't understand is Joss,' I went on. 'He suddenly flipped. What bugged the bastard? Something happened to tip him over. Until then he'd been high as a fucking kite with excitement.'

Whinger gave a groan and a string of muttered imprecations as he shifted his position. Then he said, 'There's something strange about this woman as well.'

'Oh? What happened?'

'It was when the firing died down. I'd been trying to follow things from the noise. Then I must have dozed off, because when I woke up there she was, standing right beside me.'

'I hope you slid your good hand up her shorts.'

'Did I hell! I had the impression she'd been rummaging in my kit.'

'So what happened?'

'I asked what she thought she was doing. She said she was looking for something to drink. I told her to fuck off.'

'All good for international relations,' I told him. 'That's blown any chance of *you* getting your leg over. Not to worry. I'm off to sort her now.'

I found her sitting on an upturned wooden crate under a sausage tree; the cylindrical fruits were hanging down from the branches like vast green salamis. We knew from some we'd picked up that they weighed fifteen or twenty pounds, and it crossed my mind that if one dropped straight on to her head, it might solve a few problems.

We'd told her to stay on board the mother wagon, in case the rebels put in a counter-attack and we had to make a sudden move. But here she was, out in the open. Worse, there was no sign of the Kamangan who was supposed to be keeping an eye on her. She had her injured leg stuck out in front of her and her ankle resting on a rolled-up blanket. She was wearing an olive-green T-shirt and a pair of shreddies that one of the lads had given her. Little did she realise that she was dressed in a dead man's kit – the stuff was Andy's. If Whinger had put a hand up her shorts, it wouldn't have had far to go: the shreddies just about covered the ledge of her arse, and no more. Her face was pale under its tan. A rough crutch that someone had cut for her from the fork of a young tree was lying on the ground beside her.

'Look,' I began. 'You're not supposed to be away from the wagon. Didn't I tell you? We may have to get out quick. What happened to the guy we put here to mind you?'

'Oh,' she waved vaguely. 'He's over there, somewhere.'

I forced myself to chill out, and asked, 'How are you feeling?'

'I still have pain in the head. Quite bad.' She spoke with a strong German accent, and her voice had a harsh edge that grated on the ear.

'Did Mart give you aspirin or something?'

'I take the tablets, yes.'

'Good.' I couldn't help thinking of the ground-up dog-shit. 'Now, tell me about yourself.'

'What do you want to know?'

'How about a name, for a start.'

'Braun, Ingeborg.'

'And what do you do for a living?'

'Already I have this conversation, with your friend.'

'Tell me anyway.'

'Wildlife,' she said wearily, shifting her bad ankle. 'Animals are my business.'

'Safaris?'

'Not exactly. We give advice to game-parks, yes?'

'On what?'

'Numbers, culling. *Naturschütz* – conservation.'

'Who's "we"?'

'My company is SWAG.' She pronounced the letters *ess, vay, ah, gay*. 'That means South West Africa Game.'

'And where's it based?'

'Windhoek.'

Again, a very Germanic pronunciation: *Wint-herk*.

'We are affiliated with Conscor,' she added, as if that would make everything clear.

'Conscor?'

'The Conservation Corporation. They run the best game lodges: Makalali, Phindi, Londolozi.'

'So where were you going when the plane crashed?'

'Ach!' She drew the back of one hand across her forehead. 'So many questions!'

I waited, not wanting to give any leads.

Then she said, 'It is difficult to remember. When did we fall under?'

'Three days ago now.' I added a day deliberately.

'I am unconscious so long?'

I nodded.

'And my companions?'

'Killed in the crash, I'm afraid.'

'So. Their bodies?'

'We had to leave them. The area was very remote.'

Her pale blue eyes stared at me. I thought, she's trying to remember. Or maybe she's calculating, working things out. There was something about her that made the second alternative seem more likely.

'You have reported the accident?'

'Of course. We told Kamangan army headquarters in Mulongwe, and also our own people in the UK.'

'Kamanga!' Her whole body gave a twitch, as though she'd had an electric shock. 'I am in Kamanga?'

When I nodded, there was something peculiar about her reaction. For a second she looked almost elated, but then her face clouded. Later, I kept thinking back on that moment, and what it meant. But it was gone in an instant, and she exclaimed, '*Scheisse*! What happened to the plane? Normally it is reliable.'

'The trouble sounded like dirt in the fuel. The engines were misfiring.'

'And where did it happen?'

I shrugged. 'Hard to know. Our maps are so bad, they don't bear any relation to what's on the ground. All I can tell you is that the site is a day's driving north of here.'

'You cannot find it again?'

'Not a chance,' I said. 'Besides, there wouldn't be any point. The aircraft was a write-off. It caught fire when it went in.'

'My companions were burned?'

'No, they were thrown clear. They were killed by the impact.'

She stared at me, absorbing the information, then asked, 'You found their papers, their wallets?'

'Only one. A man called Pretorius.'

'So. And I?'

'You were caught in the straps, in the back seats. You owe your life to the fact the fire didn't start immediately. Fuel was leaking from the wing-tanks, but we just had time to get you out.'

'We?'

'Myself and Whinger. He was the one who found you. He got quite badly burnt by the fireball.'

'This man is who?'

'Whinger Watson.'

'Vincha? Is that an English name?'

'It's his nickname. His real name's Fred, but he's been Whinger ever since anyone can remember.'

'So.' Again she stared at me, and I thought, you devious bitch. Don't bother to tell me you had a conversation with him earlier today, will you? Don't own up to the fact that you were trying to search his kit.

'Our luggage?'

'Also burnt.'

'All? No bags thrown out?'

I shook my head. 'Nothing.' As an afterthought, I asked, 'Where were the cases?'

'Some inside, some in the nose compartment. The aircraft went arse over tit. The nose was crumpled first, then the whole thing burned.' I was thinking, I don't suppose she's going to thank us – and sure enough, she didn't.

'So where am I now?'

'Like I said, about a day's driving south, out in the bush. We brought you with us. It was the only thing to do.'

'And you are here, why?'

'We're training a unit of the Kamangan government forces.'

'These blex!' She spat the word out with a mixture of arrogance and scorn that was all too familiar: I'd heard any number of Southern African whites talk about natives with that tone.

'Some of them are all right,' I said defensively.

'Training for what? For the war, I suppose. My God, I would rather train dogs. At least they do not eat each other.'

'Well, it's our job.'

'All these shootings this morning, these explosions.'

'That was an exercise, a practice battle.'

'It is finished?'

'For the time being, yes.'

'Then you can take me back, perhaps.'

'Back? Where to?'

'To Gorongosa.'

'Where's that?'

'The Gorongosa national park. Where we came from. It is in Mozambique.'

'Mozambique! Jesus! You flew from there?'

'Quite sure.'

'But it's bloody miles away. The border's far enough. How far's Gorongosa inside Mozambique?'

'The park headquarters? Perhaps two hundred, three hundred kilometres.'

'How long did it take?'

She waved both hands in a gesture that said, 'How do *I* know?' Then, 'Maybe two hours, three hours.'

'What time did you take off?'

'In the morning . . . what time was the accident?'

'Lunchtime.'

'So, we take off at nine, nine-thirty, maybe. Not sure.'

'Heading for where?'

'Yes,' she said, as if still calculating. 'Now I remember. It was after breakfast. Nine exactly.'

'And where were you going?'

'*Endlich*, to Windhoek, but first to Gaborone, in Botswana. You have a map? I show you.'

'Okay. Just a minute.'

I walked back through the grove of trees and found Whinger

in precisely the same position, still shaking.

'Had her yet?' he asked casually.

'Twice,' I told him. 'Listen. She doesn't realise I talked to you before I saw her. She never mentioned coming over here. She's lying all the time. Where's our map of the area, the one without Gutu marked on it?'

'On the pinkie.' He pointed at a millboard slung round the windscreen pillar. 'Why?'

'I need to check her story. There's something about her that doesn't hang together. She says the plane came from Mozambique, and I don't reckon it can have. She's fucking curious about where we are, and I don't want her to know. I want her kept well in the dark about what we're doing.'

'What did she think all those bangs were, then?'

'I told her it was an exercise. Pass the word to anyone you see.'

'Roger.'

Back under the sausage tree, I asked, 'How long have you lived in Africa?'

'All my life. My grandfather came from Germany, 1946.'

Nazis, I thought immediately. Nazis on the run after the war.

'What did he do?'

'Skins. *Was heisst "Gerberei"?*'

'Tannery?'

'*Ja, ja.* He made animal skins. Zebra, cheetah, ostrich.'

I nodded. 'And what's Windhoek like now?'

'Quite small. There is the Kaiserstrasse, with hotels and shops. Otherwise, not much.'

'People speak German?'

'All. German and Afrikaans.'

'English?'

'*Wenig.*'

I opened the map and handed it to her, standing beside her to point things out.

'We're somewhere round here.' I indicated a large area.

First she spread the map over her knees, but then she held it out at arms' length, as far from her as she could reach.

'*Meine Brille*,' she said. 'My spectacles. To read, I need spectacles.' She reached to where the left front pocket of a safari shirt would have been.

'Short-sighted, are you?'

'Short, no. Long. I can read a newspaper one kilometre distance, but from close, no. You have such spectacles?'

I shook my head. 'None of our guys uses them.'

'And the blex?'

'Don't need 'em.'

She gave a snort of exasperation, and said, 'So where is the border of Mozambique?'

'Away over there.' I waved extravagantly to the right of the sheet. 'Well off the map. This is quite large scale.'

'And we cannot drive there?'

'Not a chance. We're too far from the border. And anyway, we haven't any permission to cross. The frontier guards would go bananas if us lot turned up.'

She glowered at me, as if her predicament was my fault. To lower the temperature, I asked, 'What were you doing in Gorongosa, anyway?'

'*Wildbemerkung*.'

'I'm sorry?'

'Game assessment. Many animals are killed in the civil war. We try to estimate how much game survives, for the possibility of hunting again.'

'But you say you don't run safaris?'

'No. We make totals – counts – from the air, to provide information.'

'And what did you see? Elephants?'

'Very few. Most have been shot. *Nashorn – total kaputt*.'

'*Nashorn?*'

'It is rhino. All gone. But impala okay, kudu okay, giraffe quite good. Zebra, *natürlich*. Warthog okay.'

'Well.' I folded the map. 'The only thing I suggest is that you go out on the plane tomorrow.'

'Plane? What is this?'

'A Kamangan military aircraft is coming down tomorrow on a resupply run. Maybe it could lift you out.'

'Where does it go?'

'To Mulongwe, or somewhere just outside.'

'Mulongwe! *Das ist ein Dreckhaufen*, a shit-heap. I don't go there.'

'You'd be better off there than here.'

'By no means. The Kamangans cancel all international flights because of the war. There is no way I can get out of Mulongwe. Probably they put me in gaol because I am Namibian. If I go to hospital for my leg, I catch Aids. Quite sure. Mulongwe – no.'

I was thinking, you'll go where you're fucking well told. In any case, how did she know what was going on in the Kamangan capital?

Luckily, someone forestalled further argument by shouting for me from our living area. I just said, 'Sorry, I'll see you in a minute,' and walked away.

I couldn't quite make out what it was that was making me feel so pissed off. The woman's arrogance didn't help, but if we were going to get rid of her within twenty-four hours, what did it matter? I also realised I was tired. We'd been up most of the night, and once the adrenalin of the assault had drained away, there was bound to be a sense of let-down. Yet none of this quite accounted for the black feeling that seemed to have settled on me.

I kept trying to analyse the reason. It wasn't the state of affairs at the mine; for the time being I didn't much care what was going on there. We'd helped Alpha Commando recapture it, and there our responsibility ended. It didn't take us to get the machinery going again or to keep an eye on the diamonds – that was down to the Kamangans. I wanted to help old Boisset, but if he preferred to stay put, that was up to him. We needed to get his message through, and maybe we could do that in the evening. The trouble was that for the moment our comms were down. You get these periods when satcom phones don't work, and there's nothing you can do but wait for the system to sort itself out.

Whinger was on my mind, as well. But suddenly I realised, or thought I realised, what the real trouble was. The day before, I'd taken my weekly anti-malaria tablet, Lariam. Back in Hereford the MO had issued each of us with two little foil packs of the big white bombers, one to be taken every week for eight weeks on end, without fail. Everyone said that Lariam was dodgy stuff, but that it was the only drug still proving effective in the part of Africa where we'd be working. The mozzies, apparently, had wised up to all the older drugs like Paludrine and Mepacrine. Several of the lads, particularly Chalky, had been quite nervous of the possible side-effects of Lariam, printed on the leaflet that came with each packet. They'd tried to take the piss out of the warnings, but they hadn't convinced themselves.

Now I remembered Pavarotti putting on a phoney doctor's voice as he read out, 'Most common unwanted effects: dizziness, vertigo, loss of balance, headache, sleep problems. Less common unwanted effects: psychiatric reactions which may be disabling and last for several weeks, unusual changes in mood or behaviour, feelings of worry or depression, persecution, crying, aggression—' At that point there'd been loud cries of 'For fuck's sake!', and he'd laid off. But I know that Andy, for one, had binned his tablets rather than swallow them, and I suspect a couple more of the guys had done the same, just as they'd rejected the anti-nerve gas stuff handed out before the Gulf War in 1991. I'd taken my Lariam regularly, and so far had had no problems.

But now I felt so peculiar that I began to wonder: was the stuff getting to me at last? If it was, there was nothing I could do about it, and maybe it was this thought that relaxed me. In any case, I drifted off to sleep.

I was woken by Phil shaking my shoulder.

'Rise and shine, mate,' he went.

I sat up, sweating all over. 'Christ! What's the time?'

'Midday.'

I'd been out for nearly three hours. I should have felt refreshed, but even when I'd scrubbed my face with a wet rag I still had the same thick sensation in my head, and Phil did nothing to clear it by starting in again about the woman.

'What's the matter?' I said as I sat there trying to get myself together. 'You had a run-in with her as well?'

'She fucking started it. She shouted at me as I was going past.'

'What did she want?'

'She's found out where we are, more or less.'

'How?'

'One of the silveries told her we were close to the river Kameni.'

'Fuck it!'

'Yeah, and now she's screaming about a place called Msisi.'

'Where's that?'

'Christ knows.' Phil scratched his head. 'She claims it's on the river. Therefore she reckons we can't be far from it. She says it's a hospital, run by Roman Catholic nuns.'

'A hospital? I thought such things didn't exist around here.'

'This is the only one, apparently. Part convent, part *Krankenhaus*.'

'So what?'

'She wants us to take her there,' said Phil. 'She reckons the nuns'll sort out her ankle.'

'I don't believe it. What does she think they've got? Fucking X-ray machines that work without electricity? Wait till they *hear* her. That'll finish her chances. What's wrong with Mulongwe, for Christ's sake?'

'Dunno,' said Phil. 'She just won't hear of it.'

'This place, Msisi. Is it on the map?'

'Not this one.' Phil picked up the bum map and scanned it. 'Not if it's on the river.'

'How does she know about this convent, anyway?'

'Her party was going to land there on their way across, just to make sure the nuns were okay.'

'In that case it must be to the west, somewhere downstream. Try the good map.'

While Phil dug it out, I was turning the idea over in my mind: a quick run down to Msisi would be one way to get Braun off our hands. If the nuns had an airstrip, they could get her flown out from there. Also, maybe they could give Whinger better treatment than we could. Certainly the environment of even a primitive hospital would be less dangerous to someone with major skin loss than the shitty conditions in which we were living. The nuns might have better drugs, too.

But then Phil came back, saying, 'Nothing. I've followed the river all the way down.'

'Is it supposed to be a village, or what?'

'No, just a group of buildings on some sort of bluff.'

'No wonder it isn't marked, then. Wait a minute, though. I tell you who'll know: the old Belgian. We'll go back down and ask him.'

'Fair enough.' Phil folded the map away. 'She's obsessed about the plane, too. Keeps asking questions.'

'Like?'

'It ken fly again, yes?' He imitated the German intonation perfectly. 'I told her, "Can it hell?"'

'She already knew it got burnt out. I told her that myself.'

'She can't seem to accept that. She was on about her passport and stuff. "Vot heff zey finded?" I told her you'd found bugger all. She started asking me about Whinger. Did he get into the plane? How did he get burnt? Then it was, "Ve can go back zere, yes?" "No way," I said. "We'd never find the spot."'

'It's as if she wanted to recover something,' I said.

'I suggested that. But she said no, she just wanted to see the place where her companions died.'

'Stick to that line, Phil. Tell her the place is impossible to find. And don't take it so hard. I know she's a pain in the arse, but think of it from her point of view. She's well in the shit, by any reckoning. Friends dead, plane *kaput*. Stuck in the middle of Africa. You can't blame her for panicking a bit.'

We were heading down to the river crossing again when a volley of shots rattled out from below.

Phil's eyes lit up. 'Maybe it's a counter-attack.'

'More like someone taking it out on the hippos,' said Pav.

He, Phil and I were on our way to check things at the mine.

Because we'd stood down the OP on the cliff, we had no eyes on the compound, and I wanted to know how Joss and his guys were getting on with the machinery. We also needed to quiz Boisset about the convent.

When we reached the bank, we were pulled up short. The pontoon was on the far side, and the Alpha guys who'd taken charge of it were lounging around, having a brew; but when we called to them to come across for us, they just gave us the fingers.

'Bastards!' I muttered. 'What are they playing at?' Then I yelled, full force, '*Get that boat over here, in double time!*'

At least that made one of them stand up. He started to yell back, and at first we couldn't understand him. Then we made out, 'Major Mvula say, no one across.'

'What the fuck's going on?' said Phil, angrily.

'Turds!' growled Pav. 'I'll wade it. I'll go over and fucking sort them out.'

'Nobody's wading,' I told him. 'You didn't see what happened this morning. The crocs are horrendous. Watch this, though. I'll soon put the frighteners on them.'

Moving slowly, I unslung my 203 and ostentatiously raised it to my shoulder.

'Come across now!' I bellowed. 'Or I shoot.'

The fellow who'd got up stood looking. The rest didn't bother to shift. I switched to automatic, aimed a yard to the right of the boat, and put two short bursts into the sandy bank, just at the waterline. The noise and the explosion of spray had the rest of them on their feet, sharpish. They considered doing a runner; we could tell that from the way they looked round behind themselves. But they saw that if they tried to get away, they'd be in our field of fire for at least fifty metres, and they weren't going to risk it. Seconds later two of them jumped into the ferry, settled at the little club-oars and began hauling themselves over.

'Listen, Geordie,' said Pav, urgently. 'I don't know what these cunts are up to, but there's something funny going on. Crossing could be bad news.'

'You mean, we could get stuck on the wrong side?'

'Exactly.'

'Fuck it,' I said. 'I'm not taking this kind of shite from Joss. We're going over.' Then, as the ferry was approaching, I added quietly, 'Don't take it out on these guys. It's not their fault. They're only doing what they've been told.'

The oarsmen looked scared to hell. Their eyes were rolling all round their heads, anywhere but at me. Plainly they were expecting me to top them at any minute for insubordination, and feed their bodies to the crocs.

'Take it easy,' I said quietly as we set off. 'Let's just cross.' I waited till we were halfway over before asking, 'When did Major Mvula give that order? What time?'

'Now.'

'Right now?'

'Half hour.'

'Okay.'

On the far side we set off for the hillocks which had been our firing position in the morning – that was the direct approach to the compound – and we headed for the back of the mounds exactly as we had before first light. Until our setback at the ferry, it hadn't occurred to me that we'd to have creep up on the mine like this for our second visit, but now I thought we'd take a shufti at what was going on before we walked right in.

Just as well. If we'd come into sight at that moment, things could have turned ugly.

'Fuck me!' exclaimed Pav under his breath. 'A kangaroo court.'

Out in the open compound, between the wrecked mesh gates and the main building, a huddle of twelve or so Kamangans were sitting on the ground in a horseshoe. Halfway round the ring, and just outside it, with his back to us, Joss was poised on a metal chair perched atop a packing case, as if on a throne. Opposite the ends of the horseshoe, like the pillar in the middle of a peepsight, a white prisoner was standing bound with rope to an upright wooden stake. Beside him stood another man wielding a heavy stick, and on the ground close by lay a body.

The prisoner was already far gone. His head was lolling

forward, chin on chest, and blood was dripping down his chest. As we eased into view Joss screamed some question at him, and when he didn't answer, the attendant belted him in the ear with his club, rocking his head violently sideways.

'Jesus!' breathed Phil. 'Isn't that the guy we brought in?'

'It is.' I took a deep breath. 'What do we do?'

My instinct was to take out the whole of the kangaroo court. With three 203s, we could have done it. Joss as well. But I knew we couldn't start topping the guys we were supposed to be working for.

'Rounds over their heads!' Phil urged. 'Cause a diversion.' Already he was pushing his rifle into position.

'No, no!' went Pav. 'For fuck's sake! They're so fired up, they'd go completely hyper if they thought we were shooting at them. There's three of us and about fifteen of them, plus more indoors. We'd get massacred.'

We'd arrived just in time for the final act of a violent drama. Joss screamed the same few words again and again in a high tenor voice, almost a falsetto. When the prisoner gave no answer, he stood up and appealed to the assembled court in a burst of impassioned ranting. Without understanding his exact words, we knew what he was asking: guilty or not guilty? In a single roar a dozen voices gave him the answer he was looking for. Instantly he raised his right hand in a kind of Nazi salute and shouted an order. Half his jurors came up on one knee and levelled their AK47s at the prisoner. Another yelp of command, and *cra-cra-crash*! A ragged volley riddled the victim, who jerked backward, then slumped into his ropes, with blood pouring from multiple wounds in the chest.

I shot a glance at Phil. His eyes were gleaming. '*Phworrh!*' he went. 'Didn't give the bugger much chance, did they? What the hell did he do?'

'He was enemy,' I said, 'fighting for the Afundis. And he was white. That's enough.'

We lay still as we watched the court break up and disperse. For the time being adrenalin had cleared my head. I felt apprehensive, but calm.

'Give 'em a minute or two to cool down,' I said. 'If they saw us right now, they might carry on firing.'

'Let's pull off,' Pav suggested.

'Not a chance,' I told him. 'We're going to sort the bastards out.'

We watched as somebody brought up one of the Gaz jeeps, cut down the body, slung it aboard and loaded up the one already on the ground. The vehicle drove off round the back of the big building, and Joss stalked away into it, throwing strange, dismissive gestures with his right hand. There seemed to be something peculiar about his gait. He was moving stiff-legged, as though on stilts. A couple of squaddies carried away the chair and box that had acted as the seat of judgement.

We gave it five minutes, sweating literally and metaphorically. The afternoon sun beat down on us, and we knew our position was dodgy to a degree. It looked as though Joss was high on something. Power? Drugs? The mercenaries' hooch? We could have withdrawn and returned later, but that would have entailed loss of face, because sooner or later he'd hear from the boatmen that we'd come across and had been hanging about, too scared to go on. There was only one thing to do: confront him.

We expected to be challenged at the gate, and we were. Two sentries put on a hostile front and barred our way, saying, 'No visitors to the mine.' But by then I was quite angry, and the message soon got through. One of them shouted across to the central building, and presently a man came out to wave us across.

'Chill out,' I told the others as we went forward. 'Play it cool.'

We found Joss sitting at a trestle table just inside the big doors, where he seemed to have set up a temporary office. He'd taken off his beret and laid it on one side of the table as he checked names on lists with a corporal standing at his elbow. He looked hot and harassed, and our arrival did nothing to improve his temper.

No cheerful 'Join the party!' this time. Instead, he demanded, 'What do you people want?'

'Courtesy call,' I said, easily. 'We came down to see if you needed any help.'

'If I want help, I'll tell you.'

'Okay, okay.' Inwardly, I was boiling. Who did this arsehole think he was? Who did he think had planned the attack on the mine in the first place and got his team through it with so few casualties? But all I said was, 'Sure, but I'd like a word with the old Belgian.'

'What about?'

'Private business.'

'There's no private business here.'

'All right, then. I want to ask him about the mission hospital at Msisi.'

'Msisi? Where's that?'

'That's what I want to find out. Somewhere down river. Whinger's burns need proper treatment.'

'Well, you can talk to the man in front of me.'

'Listen, Joss.' I kept my voice low, staring into his bloodshot eyes. 'Watch yourself. I don't know what's got into you, but there are one or two things you need to remember. The first is, your president's getting a full report on this campaign.'

He shot me a glance, but said nothing.

'We saw you execute those prisoners just now.'

He jerked in his seat, and said angrily, 'You had no business to be watching.'

'We didn't mean to. We stumbled on it. But those shootings might not be entirely to your credit.'

'The men had been stealing diamonds,' he said defensively. 'They were caught with their pockets full of them.'

I felt my scalp prickle, and I said a silent prayer of thanks that I'd fought off the temptation to load up myself.

'All right,' I said. 'The way you maintain discipline's your business. But I'm also reporting on your attitude in general.'

'You take it easy!' He pulled himself upright and swayed about, banging a fist down on the table. 'Don't try threatening me. You went into the strongroom. I'll have you searched as well.'

Still I kept my cool. 'Search away if you want,' I said evenly. 'But I can tell you, there's no point. I didn't nick anything, and even if I had, I wouldn't have it on me now. I'd have hidden it long ago.'

Joss slumped back into his seat. The man was obviously high on something, but the strange thing was I couldn't smell any alcohol.

I decided to up the voltage a bit, and demanded, 'Look. What the hell's the matter with you? Has one of our guys pissed you off or something? What's got into you? Calm down a bit.'

I saw his broad nostrils flaring with anger. 'You're telling a senior officer how to carry on!' he shouted. 'You've no business to give orders!'

From close beside me, on my right, Phil uttered a strangled curse. I sensed he was on the point of erupting. With his temper, he might thump the Kamangan commander any second.

I turned towards him, silently mouthed 'For fuck's sake!', and then said out loud, 'I'm not giving orders. I'm talking about common courtesy.'

'Courtesy!' yelled Joss, struggling to his feet again. 'The best courtesy you could show would be to get back to UK, pronto.'

Still I held my cool. 'If that's what you want, fine. We'll start tomorrow. But I don't think President Bakunda will be very chuffed if our assignment ends prematurely just because you can't keep your temper.'

The hands on the table top were clenching and unclenching. Beads of sweat were standing out all over the man's forehead. I stared at him, amazed that he could have changed so completely in such a short time.

He took a deep breath, sat down again, and asked, 'What is it you want?'

'Like I said, to speak to Boisset.'

'All right. We'll get him. But only in my presence. No private spying conversations.' Over his left shoulder he gave a rapid order in Nyanja, and the corporal departed for the inner machine sheds.

I almost added, 'I'll talk to him anywhere I bloody well like,' but I bit it back, and asked, 'While we're waiting, how many men did the rebels lose in the attack?'

'Twenty-seven,' came the prompt answer.

'All black?'

'Twenty-five black, two white.'

'Including the man shot just now?'

He nodded.

'No other prisoners?'

A shake of the head.

'What about the other whites?'

'They got away. But we found where they'd been living. Over there.' He gestured towards the bungalow.

'How many?'

'Seven or eight.'

'South Africans?'

He nodded.

Suddenly, going over details of the battle, he had become reasonable again. But when I asked, 'How many casualties on our side?' he took offence once more.

'What business is that of yours?'

'I need a figure for my report.'

'Damn your report! Anybody would think you were writing a history of Kamanga.' His tone was humourless, bitter. I said nothing, waiting for him to continue. He glared at me a couple of times, and eventually said, 'Four dead, and one flesh wound.'

'Pretty good,' I suggested. 'What have you done with the bodies?'

'Buried them.'

'Already?'

'You have to, in this heat.'

'With the bulldozer?'

He nodded.

On our way in I'd noticed that the bulldozer was in exactly the same position as when the assault started, but I said nothing. Instead I asked, 'When's the plane from Mulongwe due?'

'What's that got to do with you?'

'I wondered if we could put the South African woman on it, to go back? We need to get rid of her somehow.'

'Why can't she stay here with us? We can look after her.'

'She's wanting out, and her ankle needs treatment. The plane would be best.'

'It depends on the pilot. He may not want to take her.'

'Can't you order him to?'

'Hey, I said it already!' Suddenly he was screaming again. 'Stop telling me what to do!'

'I asked a question, that was all. What time's the plane?'

'Ten in the morning.'

'What aircraft?'

'C-130.'

I nodded. A big plane. An idea came to me. If Joss really wanted us out, our whole team could take passage and be back in Mulongwe by evening. If necessary we could bin our vehicles and go. Get Whinger to hospital that way. But I reckoned that such a suggestion might send the Kamangan ballistic, so instead I asked, 'Any clue about the involvement of the South Africans?'

'That fellow wouldn't talk. Only this.' He riffled through the pile of paper on his desk and slid one A4-size white sheet towards me. 'We found this in their kit.' The sheet was blank, except for a name and address printed discreetly in grey lettering across the bottom: INTERACTION, PO BOX 1189, JOHANNESBURG, S.A.

The name gave me a jolt. I knew the firm was one of the biggest private military contractors operating in Africa; it had contacts at the highest level in many countries, and in terms of international law it often sailed dangerously close to the wind. I remembered furious rows about its activities in Sierra Leone, Angola and other places. Was it being supported by the Foreign Office in Whitehall, or was it not? The issue had never been clear. Although nominally based in South Africa, Interaction was run from an office in London by a former army officer called Mackenzie. When one of the papers reported that he'd been a member of the Regiment, he never bothered to deny it, but in fact he'd no more been in the SAS than he'd visited the moon.

Glancing sideways, I saw Phil grappling with the same thought as me, that if Muende had hired guys from Interaction to bolster the rebels, it confirmed what I already suspected: there was something bigger going on than either Joss or President Bakunda realised. And if the firm was involved, we might find ourselves up against former American SEALs or even old and bold ex-SAS, because Interaction was exactly the sort of company guys of that calibre would work for after they'd left the forces.

What I *should* have said was that if Alpha Commando was about to run into opposition of this calibre, they were going to need us more than ever. But because the atmosphere had become so scary, I was thinking, well, if Joss wants to fight Interaction on his own, fucking good luck to him. I'd rather not get involved against people from our own background. All I said, casually, was, 'Oh yeah, I've heard of these people. They supply private armies – weapons and stuff.'

My train of thought was broken by the reappearance of Boisset, who came shuffling out from the back at quite a lively pace. In the few hours since I'd seen him his face seemed to have filled out and coloured up slightly. He looked less like a living skeleton, more likely to survive.

I tried to sound relaxed as I asked him, 'How's it going?'

'Not bad. We make some progress. One big emergency generator is running, at least.'

'Great! I wanted to ask something. Have you heard of a place called Msisi?'

'*Certainement.* It is a Catholic mission, run by the Poor Clares.'

'And where is it?'

'Down river, about sixty kilometres.'

'You've been there?'

'Once, yes.'

'What sort of a place?'

'Quite small. A few buildings above the river.'

'On a cliff?'

'*C'est ça.*'

I glanced at Joss to see how he was enjoying this private conversation. In the state he was, I thought he might take offence at the fact that I was ignoring him. Luckily, he seemed bored by my questions, and had started talking to his corporal again. Better still, when one of his junior officers appeared in the open doorway and called him, he got up and walked out.

I waited till he was clear, then asked, 'This mission, is it a hospital?'

'A small one, yes. It is funded by the Red Cross.'

'Which side of the river?'

'The north side. Opposite of here.'

'Is there any bridge, any means of crossing?'

Boisset shook his head. 'Not for many kilometres.'

'So how would we reach it from here?'

'First, you cross over here to the north bank, by the pontoon. Then there is a road . . . there *was* a road, a track. You have a map?'

'Here.' I pulled our good map out of the thigh pocket of my DPMs and spread it on Joss's table.

It took the Belgian a minute to find his bearings; then he pointed with a long, black fingernail, and said, 'We are here, above the big bend in the river. *Non*?'

'Looks like it.'

'Yes. Here is Gutu. And Msisi must be here.' Again he pointed to a spot on the river. 'You go along the north side of the river, past the so-called Zebra Pans. Yes, here.' He indicated two small oblongs coloured light green, in the middle of brown surroundings. 'Areas of flood in the rains, but dry now.'

'And the road?'

'Only a bush track. It leads round the south side of the pans, between them and the bank of the river. Perhaps it is grown over by now. But once you have found it, you need only follow it. In the end you will see a hill, with the mission on top. White buildings, with big mahogany trees growing round them.'

'Great,' I said. 'Thanks.'

'You go to Msisi now?'

'We may try tomorrow. One of our guys has got burnt and needs treatment.'

'Ah yes, the Poor Clares will treat him.'

Joss had reappeared in the doorway, still talking.

'François,' I said, in a low voice. 'What's the matter with him?'

Boisset gave another shrug. 'He is very angry.'

'You've said it. But why? Is he on drugs or something? He's behaving like a lunatic.'

'Maybe he does not like Gutu, the mine. He prefers to be somewhere else.'

Who wouldn't? I thought. I just had time to ask, 'The bulldozer. Is it working?'

Boisset shook his head. '*Mais non. Ça ne marche pas.* It will not go for many days. The fuel pipes are all shot through with bullets.'

'I thought so.'

Joss was back, swaying, no less aggressive. 'Finished your private conversation yet?'

'Sure.' I nodded. 'If there's nothing we can do here, we'll be getting back to camp.'

'Get back to camp. Stay in camp. I don't want to see you here any more.'

Did he mean today, or any day? I wasn't going to ask. I shot Boisset a glance and saw consternation on his face. He, too, was baffled by this head-on hostility.

'Come on,' I said to Phil, loud enough for everyone to hear. 'We'll have another chat in the morning, when the temperature's lower.' Turning to Boisset, I said, 'Thanks for your help. Be seeing you.'

With that I swung round and walked out. No thank you to Joss, no goodbye. If I'd had FUCK YOU written across my back in big white capitals, my message couldn't have been clearer. As we headed for the gate I tensed myself, half expecting somebody to open fire on us from behind. Going through the strongpoint I muttered to Phil, 'The bastards never buried anybody. They must have thrown the bodies in the river.'

Even when we were in dead ground behind the hummocks, I was uncomfortable. Only when the surly boatmen had landed us on the north bank of the river did I start to feel safe.

Reading my thoughts, Phil said, 'If we sank the pontoon or cut it loose, at least we'd confine the buggers to the far side.'

'Yeah,' I went. 'That might delay them, but it would really strop them up. I can imagine a couple of kamikaze swimmers braving the crocs to come over with special orders to take us out.'

We'd been expecting the resupply that evening; now it wasn't due until the morning. If a fresh infantry unit had come in, I'd have felt a lot safer: reinforcements might have calmed Joss down and made him feel more secure. As things stood, the situation looked so threatening that I changed our plans. It certainly wasn't safe to remain where we were: we might easily end up getting our throats cut by our nominal allies. So, instead of staying in camp with the Kamangans, we used the last hour of daylight to hive off our own vehicles and equipment and shift to a new site a kilometre away, higher up the hill. There we set up a defensive position and staked out the approaches with trip-wires.

Ever since our showdown with Joss, my mind had been on the witch doctor and his bones. The death of the South African mercenary brought the score of white casualties to four. I didn't bring the subject up with any of my mates, because I knew they'd think I was becoming obsessed. All the same, it wouldn't go away.

With Whinger out of action, we were down to eight fit men. By the time dark fell, I wasn't the only one feeling apprehensive. We'd put three guys out on stag, watching possible routes to our location, in touch by covert radio to give us early warning of anyone approaching. That left only five to hold a Chinese parliament on what we should do.

Once we'd got some food down our necks, we gathered round Whinger's cot so that he could join the discussion. With a big piece of gauze stuck over the right side of his face, and his arm and leg swathed in bandages, he showed up well in the dark. He was cursing steadily with the pain, but it chuffed everyone to have him with us.

Pavarotti, Chalky and Mart were on the first stag, so round the prostrate Whinger were Phil, Genesis, Stringer and Danny. The woman had eaten in the back of the seven-tonner, and I'd told her on no account to leave it. The arrangement suited all parties. Without quite putting it into words, she'd managed to give the impression that she didn't like being at close quarters with a group of dirty, sweaty soldiers. As for us, we were chuffed to have her out of earshot.

'All right,' I kicked off. 'How does anyone feel about binning the task and going home?'

'Won't the shit hit the fan if we do?' Stringer asked.

'Well, we're supposed to give Alpha Commando six weeks. We haven't completed three yet. But because Joss has gone bananas, there's a strong case for pulling out right away.'

'What's wrong with the guy?' asked Danny.

'You tell me. He's on something powerful, for sure.'

'He's gone round the fucking bend,' said Phil. 'You should have heard him yelling insults.'

'What did you do to annoy him?'

'Nothing. That was it.' Phil was full of indignation. 'We didn't give him the slightest hassle. It was as if the battle had got to him. The sight and scent of blood put him right over the edge.'

'You really think he might send guys to top us?' Danny sounded incredulous.

'I wouldn't put it past him,' I went. 'Like Phil says, he wasn't making sense. He was just mouthing off. But even if he was still on-side, I reckon we're too bloody close to the war zone to carry on as we have been. In fact, we're *in* the war zone. If we carry on any further, we won't be training the silveries any more, we'll be fighting their campaign for them.'

'You've got a point,' Stringer agreed. 'After today, training'll be too fucking dangerous. While our attention's tied up trying to get some discipline into these bastards, we could get attacked.'

'Yeah,' went Genesis. 'Caught with our pants down.'

'Christ!' exclaimed Phil. 'Just as we're getting to grips with these arseholes of rebels. Why don't we whack a few more of them?'

'Come on!' Gen needled him. 'You've had a good blast-off today. Won't that satisfy your blood lust for a bit?'

There was silence except for the crickets and the odd shot from the direction of the mine. Then Whinger croaked, 'It's unlike you, Geordie, wanting to chicken out.'

'You didn't hear Joss carrying on,' I told him. 'It was horrific. I'm not chicken. I'm just trying to be realistic.'

'All right,' he persisted. 'So what are we going to do? Tell the Kremlin we don't like it?'

'I'm not doing anything unless everyone agrees.' I looked round the darkened faces. 'Usual drill. We need a majority verdict. It's just our silvery friends are starting to behave like fucking apes. If you'd seen them shoot that guy . . .'

'Let's all of us go down in the morning and give Joss a right bollocking,' Phil suggested.

'That'd send him *totally* ballistic.'

'What if we do carry on?' Stringer asked. 'What's next on the agenda?'

'When the aircraft comes in with the relief garrison, Joss's guys are supposed to hand the mine over to them,' I said. 'Then, in theory, they'll be free to move on, and we're supposed to go with them.'

'To?'

'Good question. The next enemy base is reported to be at Kapani. That's a town about three days south of here. On another river. The objective is the bridge bringing the main road in from the south. If Alpha can capture that, or cut it, they'll have a stranglehold on the rebels' main supply route. I was planning to carry on with them at least as far as that.'

'Help them plan that attack, too,' went Phil.

'That's the obvious option.'

'And what if we quit?' Stringer persisted.

'We piss off back to Mulongwe under our own steam.'

'HMG wouldn't like that,' went Whinger. 'What if Muende gets the upper hand, takes over the uranium mines and starts shipping the stuff to Gadaffi? Then we'd look a *right* bunch of pricks.'

'Too bad,' I said. 'What does anyone think?'

Stringer began to say something, but before he got it out Genesis asked, 'What about the woman? She's hell-bent on getting to the convent at Msisi.'

'Don't I fucking know it,' I told him. 'But we can't head that way. If we're splitting with Alpha, we need to get our arses away to the north pronto.'

'Don't you think we ought to go and check things?' Gen persisted. 'I mean, if there's twelve holy sisters there, they could be in trouble.'

I looked at our walking bible and saw him staring into the darkness. Obviously he was fancying the chance of visiting a religious retreat and helping the nuns out. That'd give him a bigger kick than shagging them.

'What are Poor Clares, anyway?' I asked, playing for time.

'They're Franciscan nuns,' he replied, immediately. 'Named after St Clare of Assisi, who was a disciple of St Francis. They lead a life of prayer and spend most of their days in silence.'

Phil was fanning himself with one hand in sarcastic appreciation of such great knowledge. 'What the fuck do we do when we get there?' he demanded. 'Sing a few hymns, dig in, and spend the next six months defending the holy sisters, without talking to anybody?'

'They may be wanting out,' said Gen. 'We might need to organise an airlift.'

I turned to Danny, who was in charge of our transport, and said, 'By the way, make sure there's no keys left in dashboards tonight. I wouldn't put it past the Kraut to try doing a runner in one of the vehicles. Even if she can't walk, she could probably drive.'

'Sure, sure.' Danny looked faintly peeved at the suggestion that he couldn't be trusted to do his job. 'She'll not get far.'

'To hell with the convent,' Whinger announced. 'She's going

out on the fucking relief aircraft, even if you have to carry her aboard kicking and screaming.'

'At least Msisi exists,' I said. 'I asked the Belgian. Apparently he's been there, and it's only a couple of hours downstream from here.'

'Eh, Geordie,' went Whinger. 'You gone soft on the woman or something?'

'Piss off, mate,' I told him. 'I'm just considering options. What if the plane doesn't come tomorrow, for instance? What if it goes U/S? There's a very good chance of that. Then we'll be stuck with her.'

I paused, looking round the circle. Various ideas were chasing each other round my head.

'Try the satcom again,' I told Stringer. 'I wish to hell we could have a word with the Kremlin.'

Stringer stood up, went over to the pinkie with the comms equipment on board and began to fiddle with his aerials.

'Leave the woman out of this for the moment,' I said. 'She's only a side issue. We haven't answered the main question. What do we want to do? Go on or pull out? What's the crack on that? Whinger?'

'It depends on Joss,' he replied, his voice heavy and slow. 'He may have settled down by tomorrow. If he has, carry on. We've only lost one guy, and that was to an elephant. Pure bad luck. If we watch ourselves, there shouldn't be a problem.'

'But if he's still the same?'

'Then fuck off, fastest.'

'Okay. That's you. Danny?'

'I agree. If Joss pulls round, no reason not to carry on.' He shot me a look, and went on, 'I dunno about you, Geordie, but it strikes me there's something big going down here.'

'Like what?' I waited, knowing that Danny often had good ideas, but was slow to articulate them.

'The South African involvement. This company, Interaction. These guys wouldn't be pissing about with the rebels if it was just a question of diamonds. Southern Africa's full of diamonds.'

'So?'

'There must be some other agenda. Something that's really got them going.'

'Okay, I agree. But what are you saying? That we should stick with it, or what?'

'If Joss comes back on-side, yes, we should.'

'Right. Genesis?'

'I disagree. If we go any further south we could land ourselves in the shit. We might not be able to get back at all. And as we know, the chances of getting lifted out of the bush are zero. I'm for pulling off, first to the convent, then to Mulongwe. Bollocks to the uranium, and to the agreement.'

Next round the circle was Phil, and I knew before I asked him what his answer would be.

'Fuck Joss. Go for it! Get stuck in with Alpha and go for the bridge. Let's have another good shoot-out and hit the rebels where it hurts.'

Before I could say anything else, Mart's voice abruptly came up in my earpiece with 'Green One'.

'Green One, roger,' I answered.

'Got an intruder,' he said quietly.

I held up a hand to stop anyone talking, and asked, 'What is it?'

'Somebody coming up the track from below.'

'Sure it's not an animal?'

'Definitely human. I had him in the kite-sight.'

'Stand by. I'll be with you.'

Our meeting broke up as though a bomb had landed in the middle of the group. In seconds the guys vanished outwards into the darkness and took up prearranged positions – all except Gen, who grabbed Whinger's cot by the head-end and dragged it alongside one of the pinkies. I ran the few yards to the seven-tonner and hissed at Inge, 'Stay where you are. Don't move. We've got problems.'

Mart was about two hundred metres to the east. He'd stationed himself on a bank where the track came up over a steep little rise. He'd told us that from that vantage point he could see out over an expanse of open bush.

We hadn't expected any visitors, certainly no friendly ones. But the one thing we needed to avoid, above all, was any risk of a blue-on-blue – a clash between our own people.

My boots made no sound in the dust as I scurried forward. The moon was still low in the sky, but the starlight was strong, and I could see quite well. When I reckoned I was halfway to Mart's position I called him on the radio, and said, 'Closing on you from behind.'

'Roger,' he answered.

'Anyone in sight?'

'Negative.'

He must have been watching me through the kite-sight. Long before I could see him, he came on the air with, 'I have you visual. Keep walking.' A few seconds later I saw his head come up from behind a rock and I crouched beside him, looking out over the drop.

'Where was the guy?' I whispered.

'See the big tree?' He handed the sight over. 'Just to the left of it. The track's coming nearly straight towards us at that point.'

'What was he doing?'

'Walking slowly. Carefully.'

'Weapon?'

'Yep. At the ready. Looked like an AK47.'

'Where did he go?'

'Disappeared into that dead ground on our right.'

As he whispered, I was scanning with the sight, which gave out a faint, high hum. I searched the ground to our front, checking every shape, looking for a black figure moving across the fluorescent green background.

'Nothing,' I breathed. I switched the sight off. Its tiny scream died, and we crouched side by side without speaking, listening to the cicadas grinding away all round. The air was comfortably cool, but the mozzies were out and about. Every few seconds, one came whining past.

If any of the other guys got a contact nearer camp, we'd hear immediately over the radio, so I felt that our rear was covered. But who the hell was this, on the move out front? Because the area was devoid of civilians, it could only be someone from Alpha Commando. My stretched nerves told me it must be a scout, sent up to spy on us, or the lead man in an assassination squad.

Minutes passed. Nothing stirred in the dark landscape below us. Up above, the stars were bright as diamonds. Diamonds. The trouble they caused. I thought of the prisoner slumping under a hail of bullets at the kangaroo court. Seeing the guy killed like that had shaken me more than I liked to admit. It was one thing to be hit by rounds in the middle of a battle, another to be deliberately murdered in front of an audience.

Could Mart have made a mistake? I didn't think so – and I wasn't going to ask him again. He took the sight back and switched it on once more, waited for it to warm up, scanned, switched off. There was no point in calling the other guys to find out if they'd seen anything; they'd tell us soon enough if anything showed.

Suddenly, there was a noise behind us, a voice. Somebody had spoken, very close. We both leapt round, weapons levelled. A black human shadow was standing on the track about six feet away. My finger was on the trigger. I came within a split-second of firing, but in the last instant I realised that anybody planning aggression wouldn't have spoken in the first place – he'd have fired a round or come at me silently with a knife.

'Sir!' The voice was high, frightened, African. 'Sergeant Geordie.'

'Who are you?'

'I am Jason. Jason Phiri.'

'Mabonzo!'

'Yassir.'

'Jesus!' I let out my breath with relief and took a step forward. Even in the starlight, Jason's scarecrow frame was recognisable. At close quarters I could smell his body odour, acrid with fear. 'You nearly bought it then. What the hell are you doing here?'

'I come warn you.'

'What of?'

'Major Mvula, he has bad spirits.'

'I know.'

'They make him mad. He send men to kill you.'

'Kill *me*?'

'Cut throat. All British soldiers.'

'When?'

'Tonight. Twelve o'clock, a killing party will come.'

'Fucking hell!' I looked at Mart, then back at Jason, then at my watch, which was saying 2135. A shiver ran up my spine at the way the tracker had come round behind us and got in so close without our having the faintest inkling of his proximity. I supposed he must have heard the tiny whine of the kite-sight, and worked on that.

'Okay,' I said. 'Come back to camp. We need to talk.' Then I went on the radio with, 'Green One. We've found the intruder. He's friendly. We're bringing him back. All stations recover to base.'

In less than a minute we were back in our temporary camp, and in another couple we'd heard Jason's story. Joss had detailed an assassination squad, under Lieutenant Akuli, to come up and wipe out our entire contingent, and burn our bodies on a big fire.

'They coming with knives, guns,' the tracker added.

'Great!' I said.

'Fucking hell!' went Phil. 'Let's booby-trap them. Light a good fire to draw them in, and let 'em have it.'

'No thanks,' I told him. 'If we haven't got an international incident already, we'd definitely have one after that.' I looked round the anxious faces. 'Forget that. We're leaving now. I'm not messing with these turds any more. Pack up and get moving west. Where's the woman?'

'In the truck,' said Mart.

'Okay. She can stay there. Eh, Jason.'

'Yassir?'

'How did you know where we were?'

'I track you. Major Mvula send me tracking Brits.'

'Have you told him where we are?'

'Yassir.' He nodded.

'So you've been up and down, and up a second time?'

Again, he nodded.

'You must have shifted your arse. What are you going to do now?'

'Come with you, sir.'

I stared at him. His sharp cheekbones glinted faintly in the moonlight, but apart from them and his eyes, he was almost invisible.

'You're quitting? Changing sides?'

'Yassir. The major, he got real bad spirits.'

'What d'you mean?'

'Evil got into him. I come with you.'

Suddenly I felt choked. This guy had probably saved our lives, and was risking his on our behalf. I reached out and brought my hand down on his bony shoulder.

'Good on yer, Jason.' Then a thought occurred to me. 'What about your kit? Have you left it behind?'

'No sir. Backpack here.' He pointed into the bush behind him, then started rummaging in a trouser pocket. 'Old whitey, he say give this.'

'The Belgian?'

'Yassir.'

He pulled out a crumpled scrap of paper and handed it across. Opening it carefully, I turned the sheet to the fire. Obviously it was a message, but the handwriting was so small and scrawly that in the flickering firelight I couldn't read it.

'Torch, somebody,' I said.

Pav handed one over and I shone the beam on the paper. There were two short lines of irregular pencil scribble that seemed to be some sort of code.

Jvoltefaceparcequilcherchepierre
exceptgrandetrouveeilyaquelqjours

Jesus!' I went, 'What the hell is this?'

Stringer, peering over my shoulder, said, 'It's French, or a sort of French. He's run the words together to make sure the blacks can't understand it. Give it here. I'll sort it.'

I handed the note over with, 'Rather you than me.'

Apart from speaking some French, Stringer was a brilliant cryptographer, always working at his codes and doing crossword puzzles when he wasn't on the weights. If anyone could decipher the message, he would.

'Get everything squared away,' I said. 'We're rolling in five minutes.'

'Why we go now?' Inge's nagging voice grated out behind me at a moment when I least wanted to hear it. 'It is playing, yes?'

'Playing? You mean an exercise? Far from it. The blacks have turned nasty, and we've got to get out.'

TEN

We were away just after 2200, hoping we had nearly two hours' start, driving our two pinkies and the mother wagon we'd been using for our kit. This, of course, belonged to the Kamangans, but I told myself we'd hand it back to them at some later stage.

What would the Alpha guys do when they found our campsite deserted? Joss had overheard part of my conversation with the Belgian, so he knew we might have our sights on the convent and be heading that way. Almost certainly he'd order a squad to follow us up, and inevitably the tracks of our vehicles would show where we'd gone. But would the blacks have the guts to come after us in the dark? Would they wait around until daylight? Or would they let us go, pull back to the mine and sit there until the relief aircraft arrived?

'Hundred to one against them doing a follow-up at night,' I said to Pavarotti as we set out. 'All the same, we'll go off at a bit of a tangent. Head due west instead of south-west. As soon as it's light, we'll tack back down.'

The track we'd followed from the Kamangans' camp out to our temporary staging post was so overgrown that even in daylight it had been hard to pick out. Lack of use had allowed saplings and shrubs to spring up all over it, blending it back into the bush. Now in the dark it was untraceable - and in any case, it was no longer heading in the direction we wanted.

We piled up the fire, to make a good marker for the assassins, and slipped away into the night. Driving across country without lights was tricky until the moon climbed higher. Later its bright glare, coming at first from behind us, threw inky shadows across the ground ahead and made it difficult to spot holes. For the first hour the land kept falling away, and apart from a few short climbs out of gullies, we were mostly going downhill. Then the terrain flattened out, and I guessed we were back on a level with the river, which lay somewhere off to our left.

On difficult stretches, where we had to cross numerous small ravines, we had guys ranging ahead on foot, but whenever the going was better we kept the vehicles rolling at seven or eight kilometres an hour. It was a miracle that we had Jason with us: an extra driver, and the best spotter of obstacles anyone could hope for. All the same, with three men driving, three spotting and three tabbing ahead, we were stretched to the limit. Every hour we swapped around, but there was never a chance for anyone to get his head down properly.

One factor in our favour was the heavy dew, which had damped down the dust; without it, the trip would have been a nightmare for the guys at number two and three in the column. As it was, even for those in the rear, the night air felt cool and clean. The people I felt sorry for were the two invalids, who were being continually bounced around in the backs of the vehicles. Afterwards I suspected that the rough passage did a lot to accelerate Whinger's deterioration.

Our slow progress gave me all too much time to worry. Not only had our training task gone to ratshit, we were in deep trouble. With comms still down, we couldn't tell Hereford what had happened; there was no chance of the Kremlin getting a Herc on its way to exfil us. We weren't carrying enough diesel to drive all three vehicles back to our original start-point outside Mulongwe, and anyway, we'd now get a hostile reception wherever we pitched up inside Kamanga. If Joss's radio was working, and he'd already sent back messages heaping shit on us, it would be highly dangerous for us to approach any military camp or centre of population. We'd suddenly become pariahs, to be shot, or eaten, or at best locked up, by the first native force that could catch us. We badly needed to get a true version of events back to Hereford.

I knew several of the guys were wondering about Jason. Had he made up part or all of his story? We knew he had that habit of not coming out with important facts. Chalky, in particular, had been sceptical, and Danny also voiced his suspicions. I wasn't sure, but my instinct was to trust him. For the time being there was nothing for it but to put distance between ourselves and the assassination squad. At our first halt, soon after 2300, we switched off our engines and sat listening. After an hour of grinding movement, the silence was beautiful. Then, from somewhere not far ahead, came an extraordinary sound, a volley of harsh grunts, in and out, like somebody sawing wood.

'What's that, Jason?'

'*Kaingo*. Leopard. It is male, making territorial call.'

Moments later weird squeals and shrieks erupted out to our right.

'Hyenas,' said Jason. 'They dispute kill, maybe with lions.'

In the tension of getting away I'd forgotten that animals were going about their business all round us. The calls of the predators brought home to me even more clearly the fact that we, the foreign humans, were being hunted. Many times in my career I'd been on the run, and the sensation had never been a comfortable one. Now I got the feeling that takes over during escape and evasion exercises, when you have to keep going against the clock, driven by the knowledge that enemy forces are out looking for you, and that the consequences of getting caught will be extremely unpleasant. From being aggressive marauders, we'd abruptly turned into fugitives, committed to escape and evasion on a continental scale, with no safe house to aim for.

'Try the satcom again,' I told Stringer. 'I'd be a lot happier if the Kremlin knew what we're doing.'

'Come on, then,' he said. '*You* try. Check everything with me to make sure I'm not cocking up.'

We knelt on a patch of flat, sandy ground and set up the little dish aerial.

'What bearing do we need?' I asked.

'One sixty mills.'

'Okay. Elevation?'

'Forty-five degrees.'

I set the dish on those parameters, and went, 'Frequency?'

'Five point six eight nine.'

I punched in the figures, waited a few seconds, then squeezed the button on the hand-set, and said, 'Hullo, Zero. This is Sierra Five Four. Sierra Five Four.'

Holding my breath, I released the button. Nothing but a rush of static. I waited a minute, then tried again, with the same result.

'You little fucker,' said Stringer quietly, gazing at the brilliant stars as he addressed the satellite. 'You're up there somewhere. I can almost see you with the naked eye.' Then he turned to me, and said, 'With the sky this clear, you'd think we'd have continuous comms – nothing to block them.'

'I know. Maybe it's to do with the ionosphere.'

'Check all the connections, anyway.'

We did that next, undoing every one and tightening it again before we tried once more. I imagined the signallers sitting in the bomb-proof Comms Centre in the Kremlin, monitoring calls from all over the world. Why in hell weren't they responding to ours? There was no question of them having gone for a piss, or being asleep. The centre was run to the highest professional standards and continuously manned. The fault must lie in the atmospherics, or in our set.

'Try again in an hour,' I said, and on we went.

For the next stage it was my turn to drive the lead pinkie, and I needed all my concentration to avoid rocks, skirt depressions and weave between trees whenever the bush grew thicker. Towards the end I had a headache, and I felt so shattered I told Pav to keep talking to me so that I didn't fall asleep at the wheel.

Midnight brought a badly needed respite. We reckoned we'd put fifteen kilometres between us and our last camp site. Because there'd been no sign of any pursuit, it seemed safe to stop and get a brew on, so we lit up our solid fuel stoves and set about making hot drinks. The person who needed liquid most was Whinger. By then he'd more or less stopped talking; he'd only respond to a remark if really pressed, and we had to haul him into a sitting position to get some warm, sweet tea down his neck.

'Hang in there, mate,' I told him. 'We'll get you to the *Krankenhaus* first thing in the morning.' I made my voice sound cheerful, but it choked me to see my old mate sunk so low.

I'd just taken my first sip of cocoa when, very faintly, a dull splutter of small-arms fire popped off in the distance far behind us, then another. The sounds seemed to come from somewhere to the right of the line we'd been driving on.

'It is a battle? Yes?' Inge loomed out of the dark. She'd gone walkabout to have a pee, and I noticed she was moving more freely.

'I don't know,' I said, genially. 'It was a long way off, any road. I see your foot's on the mend.'

'It is stronger, yes. I think there is nothing broken. Only bruises.'

The distant noises spurred us on. Whether or not Jason's version of events had been correct, we knew now that some action was in progress behind us, so we reckoned we'd done the right thing, and I had no regrets as we motored on through the rest of the night, with the moon gradually moving across the sky until it was low over the horizon to our left front.

At the four o'clock halt Stringer came up to me, and said, 'Still no comms, but I think I've hacked Boisset's message.'

His normal handwriting was small and neat, but on the sheet of paper he handed me the letters were all over the place, thrown by the jolting of the vehicle. Even so, I had no trouble reading them by torchlight. What he'd done was to decipher the condensed French text by opening it out into separate words; then he'd added a translation.

J(OSS)'S VOLTE-FACE PARCE QU' IL CHERCHE (UNE) PIERRE EXCEPT(IONNELLEMENT) GRANDE TROUVÉE IL Y A QUEL(QUES) JOURS

JOSS'S ABOUT-TURN BECAUSE HE'S LOOKING FOR AN EXCEPTIONALLY LARGE STONE FOUND A FEW DAYS AGO

'Good on yer, Stringer,' I went. 'Hey, Phil, look at this.'

'What does he mean,' growled Phil, '"an exceptionally large stone"?'

'Don't you remember? The old Belgian told us that sometimes rocks the size of pigeons' eggs come up out of the river. I reckon they found one of those. If it doesn't have too many faults, it'll be worth a fucking fortune. This explains Joss's crazy behaviour. It's got to be this that flipped him.'

'No wonder the bastard wanted us out, then,' went Phil. 'He's after the stone himself.'

'That's right,' I said. 'He couldn't afford to have us know anything about it. That's why he had those two guys shot by the kangaroo court. Must be. He reckoned they'd got the big one, or knew something about it. You know how he kept shouting the same question at the second guy? I bet he was asking, "Where is it? Where is it?" He'll be doing his nut by now.'

'Fuck him,' said Phil, savagely. 'It's too much to hope that noise just then was him running into the rebels.'

'Not him,' I said. 'Not Joss. He'll be down there digging holes all over the compound, trying to find his magic rock.'

When we drove on again, I kept thinking about the diamond. If Boisset had been working in the heart of the mine, why hadn't he seen it when it came up out of the river? Maybe he'd been locked away in his cell at the time. And then, how had Joss found out about it? From one of the technicians we'd released, I supposed. They were the guys who would have seen it. And what had happened to them? If they'd refused to say where it had been hidden, they'd probably been fed to the crocs by now. The one fact of which I felt certain was that Joss himself wouldn't leave the mine until he'd found the big one.

Our plan was to keep moving until first light, and then take stock of our position. But things didn't quite work out that way. By 0430 we'd reached a dead flat area. The ground was smooth and level, and sandy to the touch, with patches of tall, dense grass scattered about. I realised we might be near the edge of what the map called the Zebra Pans, and that therefore the ground might be soft, so for a while we had a couple of guys walking ahead to test the going. Then, because it seemed firm enough, they climbed back aboard.

Trouble came without warning. Pavarotti, at the wheel of the lead pinkie, suddenly began cursing.

'Fucking hell!' he went. 'Puncture . . . no it isn't. We're going down!'

He slammed the gear lever down into second and gunned the engine, but the vehicle wallowed as if it was afloat and settled on to its belly. Pav revved some more, went into reverse, gunned again, and gave up with a yell of 'Shit!'

Twisting round, I saw the blunt bonnet of the mother wagon just behind us, also stationary. The roar of its engine instantly told me that it, too, was stuck.

'Switch off a minute,' I shouted. I jumped out, expecting my boots to sink in. To my surprise, the ground felt firm. But when I shone a torch at the pinkie's wheels, I immediately saw what had happened. We'd driven on to a crust of dried-out earth, and the weight of the vehicles had taken them through it. Round the tyres liquid mud was oozing up, glistening in the torch beam.

'Jesus!' I said. 'This is all we need.'

Genesis was still gunning the engine of the mother truck, which heaved and shuddered like a stranded elephant as all four wheels churned in the morass. Already our predicament was bad enough, and the mechanical scream made it intolerable. I waved my torch violently at him, shouting, 'Switch off, for fuck's sake!' Thank God, Stringer, driving the second pinkie, had been far enough behind to stop and back off before he too sank into the quagmire.

Behind us the sky was already starting to lighten. Looking all round, I couldn't make out a tree anywhere, only grass, grass, grass. Nothing to winch on to. Nothing to hide under. In every possible sense of the phrase, we'd landed in the shit. The only factor in our favour was that the ground round the vehicles was solid enough to bear human beings: we could walk about without our boots going through the crust. But the bedded vehicles were over their axles, down on their bellies.

'Pav,' I called. 'I vote we wait for daylight before we start any winching. What do you reckon?'

'Good decision,' he answered. 'Otherwise we could end up worse than we are.'

'Let's get some breakfast, then.'

Before I looked out some food, I went to check on Whinger. I found Mart with him in the back of the mother wagon, propping him half upright to make him drink some water. The right side of his head was still covered with gauze, but the other half of his face looked puffed-out and swollen. When I went, 'How're you doing, Whinge?' he didn't answer, and Mart had to fill in for him.

'He's going down,' he said. 'Unless we get him into a better environment, he's not going to last the day.'

For a few moments I couldn't speak. Then I took refuge in practicalities, and said loudly, 'We've got to get out of this mess, first. Then we'll see what we can do.'

I drew Pav aside, and said, 'I know we're wanting north. But I reckon the priority now is definitely to get old Whinge into dock.'

'Agreed.'

'Best if we can all go on to Msisi together then. But if we can't, it may come down to a couple of us taking the good pinkie and leaving the rest of you here. I don't like the idea of those turds following our trail and finding you stuck – but there it is.'

'No sweat,' said Pav. 'I don't think they'll come anyway. But somebody can nip back a couple of kilometress and mine the track. At least that'd give us early warning. Christ, look at that.'

Straight behind us, in precisely the direction from which we'd come, the rim of the sun was coming over the horizon, a blood-red crescent sitting on the rim of a black world. As we stared, it grew rapidly into a crimson hemisphere, then into a complete ball, and our surroundings took on a ruddy glow.

A GPS check gave coordinates that tallied closely with the location shown on our good map as the eastern end of the first Zebra Pan. We reckoned the river couldn't be more than a couple of kilometres due south, and the convent no more than fifteen downstream to the south-west.

With daylight strengthening, we recced outwards on foot and confirmed that we'd driven into the edge of the easternmost pan. The land round the stranded vehicles had obviously been flooded during the rains: although the surface was dry now, we could see it had been levelled and puddled by sheets of water. Genesis, returning from a quick sortie, reported that reeds eight or ten feet tall were growing in water a few hundred metres ahead. Behind us, in contrast, the terrain was quite different. Only fifty metres from the big wagon we found a definite demarcation line, where the bare mud ended and thick grass was established. Easy enough to see it now, but if we'd stopped half an hour earlier, and waited for dawn to break, we'd have been okay. As it was, exhaustion had blunted my judgement and let me blunder on.

All three vehicles were equipped with front-end winches. In theory the way to recover the stranded pair was to winch out the pinkie first, and then use both jeeps to pull the mother wagon out backwards. The trouble was, truck and jeep were one behind the other, in line ahead, both facing away from the pinkie on dry land. There was no way we could drive round in front, to give a pull from that direction, because the treacherous ground extended for hundreds of metres, becoming softer and softer as it approached the reeds. The only solution seemed to be to attach both pinkies' winch cables to each other and try, by pulling at an angle, to drag the bogged one round in its own length.

So began a dire struggle. While Pav went back along our tracks to cover our backsides, the rest of us dug, heaved and sweated until we were on our knees with filth and exhaustion. The mud beneath the crust was grey-brown and glutinous. The moment we began to dig, we were covered in it from top to toe, and as the temperature mounted, we got into a hell of a state, so plastered in slime that we looked like aboriginals going through some initiation ceremony.

Progress was alarmingly slow. Once the mud was disturbed,

it exercised terrific suction: when our boots went down into it, we had the devil's own job to pull them out, and the vehicles were held as if by glue. When we linked the two winch cables together with shackles and pulled in opposite directions, trying to heave the front of the stranded pinkie round, all that happened was that the free vehicle got dragged bodily forward, with the clutches of both winches squealing and overheating. Next we tried digging so that we could get our perforated steel strips of sand-track under the wheels, but as soon as we opened a trench, water seeped into it and dissolved the mud into thick soup, leaving the tyres nothing to grip on, with the belly of the vehicle held as fast as ever.

As the sun rose, tsetse flies swarmed out of the grass and increased our desperation. Their easiest target was Whinger, who was too comatose to notice when they landed on him, so we carried his cot out of the back of the stranded pinkie and set it in the shadow of a clump of grass, with mozzie nets rigged up over him. He never made a sound while we were moving him, but every now and then, as we worked, he'd start shouting gibberish.

The nightmare would have been bad enough without the German woman, but she nearly sent us ballistic, hopping about, making idiotic remarks, apparently panicking about the time, as if she was going to miss a plane.

'I think we are late,' she kept saying. 'We should go now. Push harder, please.'

'Late for what?' I replied, only just managing to keep expletives out of it. 'And can't you see we're doing our best?'

At around 0830 Pavarotti reappeared, chuffed to bollocks at having laid what he called 'a couple of nice ones'. He'd buried the mines at places where we'd driven through dry river beds, and he'd raked out the sand above them so that our wheel-tracks appeared to run straight through the hollows. When he saw the state we were in, he was amazed. 'Christ!' he exclaimed. 'You lot remind me of that cabaret we went to in Berlin: hermaphrodites wrestling in mud.'

'You come and try it, mate,' Chalky snapped. 'You won't

think it so fucking funny.'

Pav got stuck in. By 0900, after repeatedly digging away the mud beside the wheels, rather than in front of them, and then winching, we'd dragged the stranded pinkie about halfway round. But the guys looked totally knackered, covered in mud and sweat and visibly drooping, so I called a break and lay down flat on my back, looking up at the sky. High above us two large birds of prey were effortlessly circling, gliding round and round in huge sweeps with no perceptible movement of their wings. There was something faintly ridiculous about their shape: their tails were so short that it looked as though they were flying backwards.

'What are those, Jason?'

'Bateleur eagles,' he answered. 'Snake eaters.'

'Some flyers. If we could fly like that, we'd be at Msisi in a couple of minutes.'

When I closed my eyes, I got a sudden, clear vision of the convent hospital. I saw a compound shaded by trees, an airy ward open to the breeze, nuns in white habits ministering to the sick, a sister in an office working the radio. I knew it was wishful thinking, but the pictures were startlingly real, and as I lay there some sort of compulsion took hold of me. We couldn't wait any longer. We had to get Whinger to this place. We had to get the woman out, for her own safety. We had to send a radio message to the outside world.

I opened my eyes. The eagles were still circling, as if keeping an eye on our puny struggles, or maybe hoping we would flush out some prey.

'Pav,' I croaked.

'Hullo.'

I turned my head and realised he was lying on the ground a few feet away.

'We can't fuck about any more. We've got to get Whinger into dock. As soon as we get the pinkie out, I'm going to drive on with him and Genesis, and leave you to carry on extracting the mother wagon. D'you have any problem with that?'

'Fine by me,' he went, 'but take the woman with you too,

eh? She's driving the guys round the bend, and if the Alpha guys follow up, the last thing we need in the middle of a fire-fight is a hysterical Kraut.'

'Will do, mate.'

'How long will you be?'

'Can't say. We've got to find the place first. But I'll be surprised if it's much more than an hour ahead of us. Maybe three hours for the round trip.' I looked at my watch. 'If we leave at midday, we should be back by 1600 at the latest. Well before dark, anyway.'

'Okay.' Pav sat up and slapped at a tsetse fly that had landed on his shin. 'Supposing we get out, what d'you want us to do?'

'Stick around,' I said. 'If there's anything wrong with the hospital's radio – if we can't get Whinger casevacked, for any reason – we can't just leave him there. We'll get what drugs we can for him, but we may have to bring him back for the time being.'

'We'd better RV on higher ground,' said Pav. 'Up there, for instance.' He pointed to the north, where a tree-covered ridge formed the skyline. 'See that single tree standing out on the little shelf? If we get clear, we'll make for that and get cammed up in the best location near it.'

'Fine,' I agreed. 'Provided we get back in daylight, no problem.'

Pav asked, 'What's your route going to be?'

'Good question.'

I dug out our reliable map. Its scale was too small for it to be much use, but it gave the general lie of the land.

'All we can do is head straight south, for the river, which I reckon should be just out of our sight.' I indicated the spot where I thought we were. 'Then we turn right and follow the north bank, as closely as we can.'

Looking back on that terrible day, I realise how vague and speculative our plans were. We didn't have any precise idea of where we were; we didn't know where the convent was; we weren't confident that the mother wagon could be rescued; and we knew that a strong Alpha force might well come on the scene. Our little party was in an extremely dangerous situation. Yet necessity drove us on. Necessity and exhaustion: we were all too worn out to see the risks or take rational decisions.

At last we managed to turn the bogged pinkie round. Once we'd got it lined up in the right direction, we started to make slow progress by digging in front of its wheels, slipping sand-tracks under the tyres at a slight upward angle, and winching the vehicle forward two or three feet at a time. The process was desperately laborious, but it worked. Gradually, as we drew near the edge of the pan, the mud became shallower and the rate of advance speeded up. At last Phil gunned the pinkie the final few yards under its own power, and a cheer went up, half ironic, half relieved, as it went up on to dry land under its own power. The time was 1145. Every part of the undercarriage was packed with mud – axles, steering arms, track rods, hubs, brake-tubes – but nothing seemed to be damaged, and as we had no spare water, any attempt to wash parts clean was out of the question.

It took Genesis and me only a few minutes to get organised. Because we wanted to travel light, we left most of our kit behind, taking only our weapons, ammunition, basic rations and a jerrican of water. Rather than take off the Milan post, we left it in place, even though the chances of our firing it seemed negligible.

Gen had already recced a route to the river bank, and away we went, with him in the back to keep an eye on Whinger, and Inge sitting up front beside me. Tired though I was, I sensed she was in a peculiar mood, almost on a high, twisting around on her arse and making bright remarks. I put it down to the fact that she thought she was about to get away from us.

Anyone who'd seen us would have thought us quite crazy. I was still caked in dried grey mud from head to foot (my plan was to have a quick plunge in the river, provide we could find a croc-free pool). Gen was also caked. Whinger was fairly clean, but wearing nothing except a pair of shorts. We were carrying more clothes for him, and sweaters for ourselves, in case it got cold at sun-down.

Our first sight of the river sent Genesis into ecstasies. 'Look at it!' he cried. 'It could be the Garden of Eden.'

Impala grazed on the far bank. Troops of baboons were scattered along the shore, with babies sitting on their mothers' backs or hanging round their necks. Crowned cranes paced the sand, and a flight of duck went away low upstream.

'Okay,' I agreed. 'But where's the serpent?'

'He's about,' Gen admitted. 'And so are the crocs.'

Every sandbar was carrying what looked like a dead log, which sprang to life and slithered into the water at speed the moment we came into view. I wondered about the bodies thrown in upstream the day before. Had they already been eaten? Or would they have passed this point and gone on downstream by now?

Crocs or no crocs, I had to agree with Gen: the scene was idyllic. At the point where we hit the river the stream was sweeping in wide coils between banks about ten feet high, and the ground on top was almost bare of vegetation. Turning right, I drove for a few hundred metres downstream, sending the baboons racing for cover. The current looked quite fast, especially in shallow stretches, and the water was opaque with grey silt. Gen stood up in the back, spotting for a good place to fill the jerricans, and presently he said, 'There, that'll do.'

We pulled up above a little bay, where the stream had carved a sweep out of the bank. The pool was manifestly too small and shallow to harbour a croc, and it was cut off from the main river by a sandbar.

'My life's in your hands, Gen,' I said as I slithered down the bank.

'Fear not,' he replied. 'If it moves, I shoot.'

With him poised above me, 203 at the ready, I walked through the pool, just to make sure it was uninhabited, then lay down full length and scrubbed myself furiously. Never mind that the water was full of decomposing bodies, crocodile shit, bilharzia and other delicacies, its coolness was sheer delight. When the relatively stagnant pool turned the colour of milky coffee, I rolled sideways into the faster-flowing shallow race and let the current sweep away all the grit, dirt and sweat. With all the grunge went a lot of my anxiety and exhaustion, and I came up feeling renewed.

Genesis followed me in, fully dressed, and washed his clothes on him, knowing they'd dry in minutes under the burning sun, while I stood over him with a weapon loaded and cocked. The German watched all this with a condescending air, as if we were lunatics; we ignored her and climbed back into our seats, dripping but refreshed. Whinger hadn't stirred. His eyes were open, and he turned his head slightly when I told him we were moving on, but otherwise he was frighteningly inert.

The drive took far longer than we'd anticipated. We were never lost, as we always had the river to follow, but it swung back and forth in huge loops, and we were constantly forced away from the bank by tributaries coming down to it from the north. Most of them were dry – just beds of sand - but many were deep, with vertical sides, and some still had water in them, so we had to search for places where we could cross. Each time, before we committed ourselves, we took it in turns to walk ahead and check the ground, because we couldn't afford to get bogged again. As the flies were still a pain, I put some clothes back on, and by then Gen had fully dried out.

At last, about 1630, with the sun going down straight ahead of us, we hit on our first trace of civilisation: a dirt road running along the bank. By the look of the dust, no vehicle had been up it for months, but at least it was a man-made track. Gratefully we rolled on to it and increased our speed. Then, in the hazy distance ahead, we made out higher ground above the river, a little plateau, with tall trees growing on it, silhouetted black against the sun.

'The bluff!' we both said simultaneously.

'This is Msisi?' went Inge.

'Looks like it.'

'*Wunderbar!*'

'We'd better get some covering over Whinger,' I said, pulling up. 'Don't want to give the nuns a fright.'

He gave a couple of delirious curses as we pulled a blanket

over him. His body was hot to the touch, his breathing short and laboured. When I accidentally brushed my hand against his burnt arm, he gave a groan of pain.

The closer we came, the higher the plateau seemed to loom over the river. Probably the cliff was only a hundred feet tall, but in that flat environment it looked enormous. Perhaps that's why they put the hospital up there, I thought: healthier, away from swamps and mozzies, catching the breeze. I felt adrenalin driving off some of my exhaustion; the sheer relief of having found the place was exciting.

As we approached, the dying sun was straight in our faces, so that we couldn't make out details. But we caught a glimpse of white walls, and a flag flying from a pole among the trees. Also, joy of joys, we spotted a latticed radio mast. Then we were in under the shadow of the cliff, and following the track up a natural ledge which rose across it, until at the top we came out on the level.

Looking back, it's easy to see what we should have done. We should have stopped well short of the bluff and concealed the vehicle under a tree. While one of us stayed to guard Whinger and the woman, the other should have recced forward and taken a good look at the convent. The fact was, we were in desperate straits, and too far gone to carry out SOPs. We'd set our hearts on reaching what we thought was a haven, and now we'd found it, relief swept caution away.

Low, whitewashed buildings with corrugated-iron roofs were ranged round a compound. The place looked fairly run-down, with big blotches of mould on the walls and fallen branches lying about. We seemed to have arrived at the back door. Between two of the buildings, set at right angles to each other on a corner of the compound, was a gate of rusty wire mesh.

'Can't see any lock,' I said. 'We might as well drive through. Try undoing that loop of wire.'

Genesis jumped out, wrestled with the primitive fastening, eventually got it free, and pushed the gate open. I drove forward a few yards and stopped, waiting for him. By evil chance Whinger chose that very moment to surface and say something.

I couldn't make sense of it, but the sound of his voice made me turn to look at him, and when I faced forward again, I got a dreadful shock.

Black soldiers were running at us from both sides. With a glance to my right I took in a line of military vehicles parked down the inner side of the compound.

'Gen!' I yelled. 'Get back in! We're compromised!'

I slammed into reverse and let out the clutch with a bang. But Gen had just got the gate secured, and it caught the pinkie like a fishing net.

Seconds later the blacks were all over us like baboons, yelling, screaming, brandishing pistols and machetes. I tried to drive forward, but three or four sets of hands seized me by my shirt and dragged me out sideways. As my foot came off the clutch, the vehicle gave a bound and the engine stalled. Everything happened so fast that I didn't even have time to grab my 203 from its place down beside my right hip. Gen never made it back to the vehicle; other guys were dragging Whinger out of the back.

For a few seconds I was convinced we were going to get lynched. Then the strangest thing happened. Inge pulled herself to her feet, holding the top of the windscreen, and began bellowing in some African language. Quickly the hubbub died down. Into the moment's silence she shouted something else. The next I knew, we were all face-down in the dust and getting our wrists and arms bound behind our backs. I felt hands going all over me, nicking my watch, pistol, knife, GPS set. Afterwards, I couldn't think why we hadn't offered more resistance, but the truth was we were numbed by the suddenness of the attack, too shocked and tired to react quickly.

Once our captors had got us trussed, they heaved us back to our feet. At least, they tried to. Whinger, wearing only his shreddies, just fell down again. Once more the German woman called out some order. I was amazed and horrified to see a couple of the Africans salaaming at her, as if she were some sort of goddess or white witch.

My mind reeled. What the fuck was going on? These soldiers

must be rebels. They *were* rebels: on the epaulettes of their DPMs they were wearing green-and-white stars – Muende's emblem. And yet they seemed to know her. From the way they were greeting her, it was almost as if they'd been expecting her. How in hell did *she* know *them*? How had she got such a hold over them?

I shot a glance at Genesis and saw him looking equally bewildered. Then anger surged up inside me. Somehow the woman had betrayed us. I couldn't see how she'd done it, but by God, she had. It was she who'd brought up the idea of Msisi in the first place, she who'd gone on about the place being a hospital, she who'd urged us to come here. Dimly I realised she must have known all along the place had been captured by the rebels. She'd shopped us, delivered us into the hands of the enemy.

'*You fucking bitch!*' I roared.

She was still standing in the front of the pinkie, high above everyone else, with a gloating smirk on her face.

'English soldiers,' she said, in a mocking voice. 'You should be pleased. You will now have the privilege of meeting the leader of the Afundi rebels, General Gus Muende.'

With that she turned and gave another order. Our escorts frog-marched us forward, past our abandoned vehicle, into the compound itself. Too late I saw that the flag, which to us had been just a black rag against the sunset, bore the same green-and-white design. Too late I saw that the whitewashed walls were pock-marked with bullet holes, and that the sign proclaiming MSISI HOSPITAL – CONVENT OF POOR CLARES had been riddled with small-arms fire. A couple of soldiers began dragging Whinger like a sack of coal, but when Inge spoke sharply to them, they picked him up and carried him. That puzzled me, as well. Why should she care what happened to Whinger?

The sun was setting, and the light was already dim, but not so dim that I couldn't see, lying along one wall, a line of bodies. Somebody had thrown a sheet over them, but it didn't cover the legs, and the legs were those of elderly white women. White under-garments had been ripped off and thrown aside. The nuns. I felt sick. The nuns, butchered. No doubt they'd been raped as well, probably with bayonets. What the hell were these people going to do to us?

There was a brief delay as we were herded into a small room close to the main gate, Whinger on the deck, Gen and myself hemmed into a corner by a crowd of stinking soldiers, all jabbering with excitement. From the notices pinned on a wall-board, still listing patients and treatments, I saw the room must have been the hospital office. Where had the patients gone, for God's sake? Probably they'd been murdered, too.

Next door somebody was trying to get a voice transmission through on the radio, yelling the same message over and over again. Then I heard Inge take over, talking in a native language, until suddenly she said in English, 'Yes, they are coming now . . . No, but we make them talk.'

I was thinking furiously, how wrong can you be? Somehow it had never occurred to us that the convent could be in enemy hands. We'd believed all along that the rebel forces were away to the south, that the mine at Gutu was the most northerly point they'd reached. In our eyes, the fact that the convent was on the north bank of the river had given it extra security. In any case, we'd assumed that a religious hospital wouldn't come under attack. All of us had been totally blind.

Minutes later, all three of us were face-down on the steel floor of an open-backed truck, Whinger in the middle, and we were driven out of the compound with four or five armed soldiers ranged along the seats on either side, stamping their boots on us whenever they felt a need to relieve their feelings.

ELEVEN

Think positive. That's what I've always been taught. When you're in trouble, think as hard as you can about possible options. For one thing, the process takes your mind off present hardships, and for another, it may produce a good idea. The trouble is, when you're face-down on the steel floor of a truck being driven at lunatic speed along African bush roads in the dark, it isn't easy to think of anything except immediate survival.

The first few minutes of that marathon journey were relatively gentle. The truck ran downhill for a minute or two and then on to a pontoon. We never saw the ferry, but we could tell from the movement we were afloat. The driver switched off his engine, and after a quiet five-minute crossing we thudded ashore against the far bank. That's one thing the Boisset slipped up on, I thought: he'd said there was no means of crossing the river at Msisi. That was one of the factors that had encouraged us to believe it was a safe place to visit.

On the far side, all three of us were soon getting severe stick from the bumps in the road: we were repeatedly thrown in the air and smashed down on the deck, without having our hands free to steady ourselves or lessen the impacts. If I lifted my head, or tried to turn on one side, or spoke, I got a boot between the shoulderblades or on the backs of my knees. Oddly enough, as I realised after a while, Whinger was probably suffering the least of the three. He was so far gone with his fever, and so full of pain-killers, that he didn't seem to care much what anyone did to him.

As we were getting thrown into the truck, I'd hissed at

Genesis, 'Estimate the time.' I got a clout in the ear with a rifle butt for my pains, but he registered my message: that to find out where we were being taken, we needed to guess the time the journey took. Gauging our speed was difficult: from the violence of the ride, it felt like seventy or eighty kilometres an hour, but I reckoned that because of the roughness of the road, we weren't doing more than forty, if that, and would probably average twenty-five. At one point we went up a long hill, or over a range; the driver kept changing down, grinding upwards in low gear, and negotiating sharp bends. Then came a protracted descent, with the brakes squealing as we approached corners. From the way we were continually enveloped in a dust-cloud, I assumed another vehicle was travelling ahead of us as escort or leader.

After one almighty bump, which threw all our guards into the air, as well as us, I managed to get my head up far enough to catch a glimpse of the stars. There, ahead of us and slightly to the right, was the Southern Cross. As I expected, we were heading south-south-east.

Obviously we were in for a bad time, and I tried to prepare for it mentally. It would have helped to talk to Gen, but that was out of the question, as any attempt at communication put our escort into a frenzy of stamping.

Everything seemed desperately uncertain. Did the rebels know who we were? Did they know what we'd been doing? Did they know that we'd set up the attack on the mine? I suspected the woman was telling someone all about us. Ever since she'd come on the scene our own guys had been very guarded with her, but I was pretty sure some of Joss's men had blabbed. Even they hadn't known, or shouldn't have known, that we were SAS. Our cover story was that we belonged to an infantry training school based at Hythe in Kent, and we'd stick to that as long as we could.

Not that details of regiments would make much difference if Inge had found out about our involvement at Gutu. If she had, we'd be accused of butchering the defenders. Altogether, I didn't give much for our chances of survival. It wasn't as if we knew any vital secrets the rebels would want to pry out of us, and we'd seen what a low value Kamangans put on human life, so to knock off a trio of Brits would be just a nice little evening's entertainment for them. People with a greater sense of responsibility might have been inhibited by fear of the international repercussions that such murders might create, but not the Afundis.

Another big worry was the fate of the rest of our team. Virtually my last words to Pavarotti had been an agreement to RV with him on the high ground above the northern end of the Zebra Pans, whether or not they'd managed to free the mother wagon. The worst-case scenario was that they'd be unable to shift it, in which case they'd un-ship as many of the stores as they could carry, move them to the RV site, and booby-trap the truck. If the satcom came alive and they got through to Hereford, they'd ask the Kremlin to get a Herc moving in our direction and try to arrange for it to stage through some friendly capital like Harare. Then, when they found any flat area that would do as a makeshift strip, they could call it in to exfiltrate them.

Them. I was thinking 'them'. I should have been thinking 'us'. I had agreed with Pav that if Genesis and I hadn't returned to the area of the pan by first light, he would follow up our tracks and come looking for us. Now that looked a seriously bad option, but there was nothing we could do to cancel it.

Our transport eventually pulled up after a journey which I estimated at nearly two hours. Gen guessed it was only ninety minutes. Splitting the difference, I reckoned we'd travelled fifty-something kilometres. With a squeal of brakes our driver came to a halt. There was a brief exchange of shouts, and a gate or gates scraped open. Then we went forward again into some sort of a compound. By then we'd already taken a fair hammering and were half-choked with dust. When our guards dragged Whinger out, I saw he'd got a bloody nose – no doubt from being too comatose to prevent having it banged on the steel deck.

I only got a brief glimpse of our surroundings, but they

looked like a barracks. We'd debussed just inside the gates, which were made of weldmesh, with barbed wire on angle-irons at the top. The perimeter fence was the same. Inside, five or six identical single-storey buildings were ranged parallel to each other, about fifty metres apart, but it looked as though they were disused, because the windows were all dark; beyond them there was a big open space that could have been a parade ground, and higher buildings in the distance, up a slight incline. The whole place was poorly lit, with the occasional dim electric bulb slung from drooping wires. The lights kept flickering, as if the generator powering them was on the point of going down.

More shouting broke out among our guards, obviously an argument about where we were to be taken. In the middle of it I saw Inge limping off into the distance. As her fair head passed under one of the lights, I realised she must have been riding in the wagon that led our convoy. Again I wondered what the hell she was doing, mixed up with the rebel forces. Clearly she was in cahoots with them – but how, and why?

We found out soon enough. After a wait of maybe half an hour, during which we were held in a bare room that stank of piss, we were taken out again and hustled up the compound. Gen and I were frog-marched by guys holding either arm, with more in front and behind, all carrying AK47s, but Whinger was carried on a stretcher. I had a wild hope that he was shamming, and would suddenly leap to his feet, scattering our escort, but that was just a dream.

On the higher level we came to an area where the buildings were closer together and some of the windows were lit. Then, as we passed another building, a door opened, and out came a white man. Just for a second I saw him clearly – and he saw us. In fact he must have seen us better than I saw him, because to me he was little more than an outline, with the light coming from behind him and falling in our direction. Our escorts moved sharply up beside us, trying to block his view, but there was no doubt that he'd got eyes on us. He was only ten or twelve metres off, and he half raised his right hand, as if in surprise or greeting. I got the impression of a big, middle-aged guy in a short-sleeved shirt, and opened my mouth to shout something, but before I could utter a syllable I was knocked sideways by a stunning blow on the jaw. I almost went down, and by the time I was in control again, the guy had vanished.

Seconds later, we were in a ramshackle lecture room, with a low stage and metal chairs set out in rows facing it. A few tattered charts and diagrams hung on the dirty white walls, but I was too confused and preoccupied to take in what they were about. On the stage, already seated beside a plain trestle table, was the German. Behind the table a second chair, a more elaborate one, with arms, stood waiting, as if for the judge who would take charge of the proceedings.

The moment we appeared Inge began cracking out orders in some native language, and her guys jumped to it, scraping the other chairs away across the bare concrete floor until three were left lined up in the middle of the room. Gen and I were pushed down onto two of them, with our bound arms and hands forced behind their backs. Whinger was dumped on the middle chair and similarly trussed, rolling to right and left. With his head lolling on his chest, he was snorting through his bloody nose. The gauze had long since come off his face, and he looked a right mess, the skin hanging in filthy bulges. I could hardly bear to look at him. But suddenly, to my amazement, he came round, straightened up, and said loudly, 'Where the fuck are we?'

I just had time to say, 'In the shit,' before the woman barked, 'No talking! Only answers!'

I had to fight down an impulse to jump up and rip out her throat. But I stopped myself doing anything at all, because I knew if I moved or spoke out of turn I'd only get another clout over the ear. Always be subservient during interrogation – that's what I'd been taught. Never get the questioners' backs up unnecessarily.

For a few moments there was silence. The atmosphere was like in a classroom when kids are waiting for the teacher to arrive – everyone teed up with expectancy, laced with a dose of fear. After a bit, people began to talk in quick whispers. Then a door at the back of the stage opened, and everyone abruptly went quiet again.

In strode a tall, heavily built man, bare-headed, dressed in plain, oatmeal-coloured uniform. The people were obviously in awe of him, and his sheer size gave him a commanding presence, but there was something about him that didn't add up. Although his features were definitely negroid, his skin was no darker than milky coffee, and his short, crinkly hair was a peculiar dark yellow.

At his entry the guards alongside us came more or less to attention and stood rigidly upright. Inge hauled herself to her feet and gave a peculiar bob forward, half bow, half curtsey. Jesus, I thought, she's doing him obeisance – and I knew he must be the infamous General Muende. He was the right age, early thirties, and his half-Scottish background would account for his strange colour. His movements were peculiar, too: he rolled, rather than walked, as though he had problems with his balance. In his right hand he was carrying a dark-green, army-type water-bottle, which he put down clumsily on the table, and when he sat in the chair he hit it heavily, then slumped forward on his elbows. Jesus, I thought, the guy's pissed out of his mind.

Behind him came two big, square-arsed lads wearing DPM fatigues and slung about with weapons, who stood to one side, slightly behind him, followed by a single white. Was this the guy who'd raised a hand as we'd gone past? No, that fellow had had what I'd call a normal figure. This one was squat and broad, and had a bullet head with it. Was he one of the three who'd escaped from the mine? Possibly. Whoever he was, all he did was lurk in the background, glaring at us.

My mind was spinning. The German was in league with this drunken, half-caste creature of a general. What did we know about him? What else had Bakunda told us, besides his age and his part-Scottish descent? More came back to me from our evening of rum-drinking round the fire: Gus Muende had been to West Point, in the States; he was the arsehole of the Afundi tribe; he was a friend of Gadaffi.; he'd been fêted as a star guest in Libya. He was *dressed* like Gadaffi, anyway, in a tunic with a turned-up collar and general's insignia on the epaulettes, and he carried a pistol in a holster on his belt.

'Soldiers of Her Majesty,' said the arsehole. 'What are you doing in Free Kamanga?'

His voice was hoarse, and too high for his size, his accent definitely American. He sounded excited, or angry, or both.

'We're a training team, sir,' I said.

'A training team? Is that right?' He turned to the woman, who spoke briefly in dialect. Then he went, 'Uh huh,' and faced us again. He seemed to be having difficulty summoning words and collecting himself to speak. 'Mercenaries, I suppose.'

'No, sir. We're here on an official tour, invited by the Government of Kamanga.'

'The Government of Kamanga!' Muende shouted. 'I might have known. That neo-colonialist bum Bakunda has been licking the ass of the British Government again.' He reached for his bottle, unscrewed the cap and held the neck to his mouth. Whatever it was he drank, it made him gasp and blink. Then he said, very loud, 'What's the goddamn difference, anyway? You're being paid to kill people, just like if you were mercenaries.'

'No, sir. We're not being paid to kill anyone. We're serving members of the British army,' I said, evenly. 'We were sent here by the British Government.'

'I don't care who in hell you are!' Muende was getting more worked up by the minute, shouting louder and louder. 'You ought to be shot. You've been killing our people. Killing an Afundi is a capital offence.'

I was going to deny that we'd killed anybody, but I held off, because I didn't want to provoke him. What we needed to do was soothe him down, flatter his ego. Subservience, I told myself again.

Suddenly, his manner changed. His tone became friendly, conversational. 'But look,' he said. 'I don't want to shoot you. Tell me what you think of Kamanga.'

I was taken aback. What was he trying to do now? Make some friendly overture? I had to think fast. Better not tell him it's the arsehole of Africa. 'You have tremendous potential, sir,' I said.

'That's right. We got the resources. We just need to develop them. What we don't need is these sonofabitches in the north messing us up.'

'I'm not up in Kamangan politics.' I tried to sound naïve. 'I don't know what the war's about. What's wrong with the north?'

'What's wrong with it?' His voice rose again. 'What's *right* with it? That crazy bum Bakunda, hiring people like you to fight for him.'

'We're training,' I repeated. 'Not fighting.' I should have left it at that, but I made a bad mistake by adding, 'And anyway, you hire whites to fight for you.'

'I do not. That's an insult.'

'Listen,' I went, growing reckless. 'We've seen them. And who's that guy behind you?'

Muende glanced round at the heavy in the background, glared at me, and ostentatiously drew his pistol. I thought he was going to shoot all three of us there and then, but he laid the weapon on the table in front of him.

Then, with a kind of snarl, he said, 'You're lucky.'

'How's that?'

'We need to do a deal.'

'Sorry, I'm not with you.'

'Your lives in exchange for the stone.'

'What stone?'

'What stone?' He echoed my words with a tenor shout and crashed his fist on the table. 'See here, Englishman! I'm not taking any shit from you!'

Still I was determined not to provoke the bastard, so I said nothing. When he glowered at me, I lowered my eyes submissively. The bare bulbs hanging from the roof flickered down very faint, then came back bright again. Then, into the silence, Whinger mumbled, all too audibly, 'Tell him he's a cunt, from me.'

I saw Muende's bloodshot eyeballs bulge. With shaking hands

he unscrewed the stopper of his water-bottle again and raised it to his mouth. Genesis, obviously feeling the tension needed to be lowered, said mildly, 'General, if you tell us what you're on about, we may be able to help.'

'You better,' he said. 'Have you got families?'

'Families?' I was taken aback. 'No. None of us.' In a kind of lightning flash I saw Tim's face looking back at me from the door of the departure lounge at Birmingham airport, the last time I sent him back to Belfast. But I thought it better to pretend we were all single.

'Just as well,' said Muende, with heavy menace. 'But look, all you need do, to get out of here alive, is say what you did with it.'

I felt panic threatening. The guy was making no sense, and I reckoned his patience would soon run out. I should have gone on being obsequious, but instead I said sharply, 'Come on! This is ridiculous. Stop pissing about and tell us what you want.'

Muende gave an upward flick with his right hand. A second later a crashing blow caught me on the left cheekbone and sent me lurching against Whinger. For a few seconds the light bulbs spun and swam.

'You went to the airplane!' Muende shouted. 'Do you deny that?'

'What airplane?'

'The Beechcraft. When it crashed.'

'Of course. Yes. I mean, no.'

'Yes or no? Were you there or not?'

'Of course I was there.'

'Why deny it, then?'

'That's what I meant. I don't deny it. My colleague was with me. Both of us were there together. That's where he got burned. He nearly killed himself rescuing this bloody woman.'

That brought a signal from her, and another clout. I felt a trickle of blood run down my temple.

Muende shouted, 'Where is it, then?'

'What?'

'The diamond!'

At that moment the lights went out. Instantly there was a stir all round us. Guards moved in and gripped us by arms and shoulders, as if we might try to do a runner in the darkness. Outside the hut distant shouting started up. Inside, the woman barked out an order. I heard one man detach himself from our group, hurry to the door, feel for the handle and let himself out. Under cover of the commotion, I whispered to Gen, 'The guy's pissed, and getting worse.'

'Don't wind him up any more,' he answered. 'He's right on the edge. Highly dangerous.'

Once again, Whinger muttered, 'Tell him he's a cunt.'

Luckily his words were muffled by the general hubbub, but out of the darkness, the woman shouted, 'No speech without questions!'

So, Muende as well as Joss now – both having a seizure because neither knew the whereabouts of the diamond the old Belgian had told us about in his coded note. It had obviously been somewhere on the crashed plane, otherwise why was the general – and Ingeborg Braun, for that matter – so manically concerned about it?

For the moment I kept quiet, thinking furiously. Then the outer door opened again, and a man came in carrying an oil lamp, which he stood on the corner of the table. Knock it off, I thought. Set the place on fire. Make them all scatter. I measured the distance. The lamp was about eight feet from me. Tethered as I was, I'd never make it. But at least, with the generator down, they couldn't start giving us electric shocks.

In the faint lamplight beads of sweat were shining as they trickled down Muende's plump jowls.

'General,' I said. 'Now I know what you're talking about. The big diamond found in the mine at Gutu.'

'So!' Inge gave a yell of triumph. 'I told you! This man knows. He is all the time lying. He knows absolutely.'

'Where is it?' Muende repeated.

'I haven't a clue. I've never seen it.'

'You took it from the plane.'

'I never got near the plane. The bloody thing was on fire.'

'*Nein*!' shouted Inge. 'It was this one, the middle one! The sick one!' In her excitement she broke into German. '*Er war in dem Flugzeug*!' Seeing Muende hadn't understood her, she translated, 'He was inside of the plane.'

'Search my kit,' said Whinger, thickly. 'That's what you were doing in the camp, anyway. Search it again. Search the vehicles. You'll find fuck all, because it isn't there.'

'No, of course!' she cried. 'You have hidden it in the bush. Tell me where! Tell!'

She shouted an order at the guards. Two of them started to beat Whinger about the head with rifle butts, one from either side, with sickening thuds. He made no sound as his head was hit to and fro like a football.

'Stop!' I roared. 'You fucking bitch! Tell them to leave him alone!'

I'd have done better to keep quiet. A second later, Inge was on her feet, limping down off the stage, coming at Whinger, jabbing at his face with her nails.

'See!' she screeched. 'He is burned! Because he was inside! He knows the diamond, where it is. He has hidden it in a special place.'

The next thing I knew, she'd started pulling patches of dead or dying skin away from Whinger's cheek. 'Tell!' she shouted. 'Tell!'

Doped though he was, Whinger gave a roar and rocked away from her, knocking Genesis over sideways.

'This is the one who knows!' she cried, turning back to Muende. 'Quite sure! He tells us! I make him tell us!' With her long nails she peeled off another flap of skin and threw it towards the side of the hut. Again Whinger bellowed like a wounded bull.

That was too much. With all my strength I lunged forward and sideways. The chair I was tied to brought me down almost in my own length, but I had enough forward impetus to head-butt the woman in the flank and put her flat on the deck. Immediately a rush of guards swarmed over me, kicking and stamping at my head and body. By the time they hauled me upright again I was bleeding freely from nose and scalp. One trickle ran down the middle of my forehead into both eyes, blurring my vision.

I could see enough to know that Muende was on his feet, drinking again. He held the bottle high for several seconds, gulping. Then he smacked it down on the table and lurched towards us. Inge was also on her feet, bent and gasping, holding her ribs, white in the face. I reckoned she was coming for me, but she was confused, and thought it was Whinger who'd attacked her. She screamed at him from close-up, but this time in Afundi, or whatever African language she was using. Then she turned and screamed at Muende.

The noise and the drink seemed to get to him, and he too suddenly began yelling orders. The whole room erupted into movement, a nightmare scrummage. Two or three men cut Whinger free from his chair, picked him up bodily and carried him to the stage, where they laid him flat on his back on the table and held him down. The poor bugger made no effort to resist: he hardly knew what was happening. Muende lurched round the far side of the table, bent over the prostrate figure until his face was nearly touching Whinger's chest, and flung his arms out, sweeping them round and back as if swimming breaststroke. Three times he did it, giving loud grunts: '*Uh! Uh! Uh!*' Then he stepped back and his place was taken by another man brandishing a machete. Its curved blade gleamed in the lamplight as he raised it aloft. I thought he was going to whack Whinger's head off with one downward sweep, so I gave an almighty roar and tried to surge upright again. My reward was a stunning blow on the back of the neck, a rabbit punch delivered with the butt of a rifle, which put me down and out for several seconds.

Perhaps it was a mercy in disguise. When I came round on the deck, the whole room was buzzing with noise. Our guards were chattering with excitement. Through a forest of legs I could see half the platform and part of the table. Inge was standing over it with her mouth gaping in a wolf-like grin of triumph, holding out a hand. A black hand passed her a long, thin strip of what looked like dark meat, shiny and dripping. She took it between finger and thumb and handed it to Muende, who raised it high over his head and lowered it into his mouth.

I couldn't believe what I was seeing. My eyes were still cloudy with blood. I blinked again and again, trying to clear them. The result was that I made out a tangle of grey, slippery intestines sliding down over the side of the table, reaching to the floor. The coils were moving, twitching. My gorge rose and my stomach heaved up into my mouth, but there was nothing to come up except bile. I lay gasping for breath. God almighty. What I'd seen was Whinger's guts. They'd disembowelled him. Did they think he'd swallowed the diamond and was hiding it in his gut? No. Jesus Christ! They were eating his liver. Was he still alive? I hadn't heard him yell out. Had they cut his throat? Or coshed him?

It's a terrible thing to pray that your oldest, closest mate is dead. But I did then. I wished him dead with all my might so that he wouldn't suffer any more. I told myself that he was going to die anyway, from his burns. I closed my eyes and felt sweat break out all over my upper body. Then I started to shudder uncontrollably. One of the blacks gave me a couple of kicks, but I couldn't stop shaking.

It was anger that came to my rescue, sheer rage at what these people had done. As the shudders subsided I seemed to go cold with fury and the desire for revenge. At the first opportunity I got, I was going to kill this man. The woman, too. The woman first. In a flash my hatred of her had become all-consuming. Whether I shot her full of holes or blew her into vapour, I'd make fucking certain she never saw Windhoek again.

My head, neck and jaw were aching, but my mind had cleared. From what Muende had said, the big diamond must have been on board the Beechcraft. How in hell had it got there? The answer came in a flash: the woman and her South African escorts had picked it up from the mine. That's what they'd been doing. That's where they'd just come from when we first saw them. That would account for the course the aircraft had been on. They'd just cleared the ridge, coming away from the river, and were heading west. Her spiel about flying from Mozambique had been a load of bollocks. She was Muende's courier. On his behalf, with his instructions, she'd been trying to smuggle the stone out of Kamanga, away to Namibia or South Africa.

Would it have survived the crash? Yes. Diamond is one of the hardest stones on earth, well able to withstand fire. In any case, the fiercest blaze had been in the wings, around the fuel tanks, and if the stone had been stowed in the cabin, or the luggage compartment in the nose-cone, it would have escaped the hottest flames.

Lying on the floor, I shut my eyes, and tried to shut my ears to the repulsive gurgling, slurping noises coming from the stage. So much for an education at West Point. Whatever it had taught Muende, it hadn't stopped him being a cannibal.

I needed a plan. The start of it was simple enough. Without my help, he and his sidekick might search for weeks before they found the wreck. Only I could locate it quickly. If I offered to lead them to the site, they'd have to accept – and somehow, on the way, I'd call in the rest of the lads to knock them off.

I was racking my brain to think how we could make contact when a sudden recollection drove into my plan like a dagger: my GPS. The thieving soldier bastards at the convent had nicked it. And in it, marked as Waypoint Seven, was the precise location of the crash. Anyone who realised that Waypoint Seven was the vital spot, and understood how the device worked, could make his way directly to the place. The GPS would give him bearing and distance to target – a dead giveaway.

They had Whinger's GPS as well. Or did they? No – we'd left it behind with the rest of his kit in the mother wagon. And anyway, I was pretty certain he'd never punched in a waypoint for the plane; he'd been too busy trying to come to terms with his burns. The only other GPS with the coordinates in it was Mart's. Who'd got mine by now? With any luck, some dickhead of a black squaddie, who would run the batteries down by trying to figure out how it worked, and have no means of recharging them.

For a few moments, chasing possibilities in my mind, I'd managed to attain a state of more or less suspended animation. I was brought back to reality by scraping, bumping noises. By squinting sideways I could see that men were dragging Whinger's body out through the door. Instinct screamed at me to go after it, take possession of it, to hold it, keep it. Reason told me none of that was possible. Reason said the only way Geordie and Genesis could get out of this alive would be to appear to cooperate.

Gen! Where the hell was he? From my position on the floor, I couldn't see him. He'd done nothing to provoke Muende, but I hadn't heard a sound from him, and I was afraid they'd knackered him as well. At last I was dragged upright and dumped back on a chair, arms down over the back once again. There was Gen, right beside me, where he'd always been. He'd had a good beating, too. Except where it was blooded, his face was sheet-white and had a stricken look, as if it had been frozen by cold. But his lips were moving. Was he muttering out of sheer terror, or was he saying a silent prayer?

Muende was back in his chair, wiping his chin with a handkerchief. There was blood down the front of his swish tunic, but he looked more in control than before, as if the act of eating had left him calmer. Inge, the bitch, was also back in her seat. The sight of her sent a new current of anger racing through me, but I steeled myself to remain cool, to negotiate rather than argue, to ignore the filthy deed they'd just done.

Muende cleared his throat loudly, and said, 'Now, the diamond was in the plane.'

'Please,' I begged. 'You have to believe me. We never saw it.'

I was talking with a lisp, due to the fact that my lower lip was swollen and split on the left side.

'You must explain,' I went on, obsequiously. 'We don't know what happened. Did your friend here collect the diamond from the mine at Gutu to take it out of the country?'

The woman started as if she'd been stung in the arse by a scorpion, and said, 'Who has told you that?'

'Nobody. I put two and two together.' When she didn't answer, I went on: 'If you'd told us to start with, it would have saved all this.'

'Then the diamond is where?'

'I don't know. I told you, we never saw it.'

'But you went to the aircraft.'

'Yes. But I never got into it. The only one who did was Whinger. And now you've killed him, he can't tell you anything.' I nodded in the direction his body had disappeared. 'We didn't have time to search the plane. It was far too dangerous. Fuel was leaking everywhere. We knew there was going to be an explosion any second. It was touch and go. Getting you out was the bravest thing I've ever seen anyone do.'

She took that with a stony face. She didn't know whether or not to believe me. I could have been lying to cover myself. On the other hand, she'd seen for herself that Whinger had suffered horrific burns. To put the ball in her court, I asked, 'Where *was* the diamond?'

'In the front. A special compartment.'

'The nose-cone?'

'Yes.'

'Well, I can tell you this much. After the crash that part of the aircraft was crumpled but intact. I expect it's still inside. How big was it?'

She glanced at Muende before answering. 'Like this. Like a ball for golf.' She held her finger and thumb more than an inch apart.

'In a special container?'

'Yes. A box of steel.'

Muende had been listening intently. Now he asked her something in dialect, and she translated, 'You can find the aircraft again?'

'I think so.' I didn't want to sound too confident. 'It should be possible, provided we can get into the right area, north of the river.'

'You can drive to it with the car?'

'No.' I shook my head. 'The ground's too rough. The site's

on the side of a mountain, all rocks and small cliffs. We'll have to walk the last few kilometres.'

Again she conferred with Muende.

To make the journey sound more difficult, I said, 'It would be best if we could go back to Gutu and retrace our route from there.'

'That is not possible. Government forces have captured the mine.'

Acting dumb, I shrugged my shoulders, and said, 'In that case, I don't know.'

Didn't the bitch realise where she'd been, after all? Or was she playing some deep game?

'Well,' I went. 'If you can get me back into the area, I'll do my best to find it.' Apparently as an afterthought, I added, 'Of course, if the general has a helicopter, that would make it easier.'

'He has one, but it is broken. Now, show us.'

She spoke to one of the bodyguards, who stepped forward and unfolded a map, laying it out on the table. Two guards hoisted me up, chair and all, and carried me forward.

In the dim lamplight the map was hard to read, and with my hands tied behind me I couldn't indicate, so I had to operate by remote control. When Inge put the tip of a pencil on Gutu, all I could say was, 'Up. Up. Now, left. More. Up again.' Soon she was pointing to an area well north of where the Beechcraft had gone in, on the wrong range of hills.

'Now you must be getting close,' I told her. 'All right, on that slope there. I should say that's about it.'

'So,' she went, 'we work out a route.'

'Keep the party small,' I warned her. 'We'll be in enemy territory and we don't want to attract attention.'

'Of course,' she agreed.

Muende, who seemed to have relapsed into a stupor, roused himself, and said, 'How do we know you're telling the truth?'

'You don't,' I said. 'But you will when we get to the plane. The diamond must still be there.'

'Your friend.' Muende jerked a hand towards Genesis. 'Why doesn't he talk?'

'He wasn't at the plane. He never saw it on the deck, because he didn't get anywhere near it. You can keep him out of this.'

I looked at Gen and saw he was about to say something, but I cut him off by grunting, 'Cool it.' If he started telling the general he'd sinned in the eyes of God and man, he could easily crack off another bout of thuggery.

Once again, Inge spoke to Muende in dialect. Then she faced us, and said, 'So, at first lighting tomorrow, we go. All together to find the diamond.'

'Suits me,' I went. 'And if we find it? What then?'

'You will be free. But tonight you will remain prisoner.'

'We need some water,' I told her. 'Both of us.'

'That can be arranged.'

With that, we were cut away from our chairs and dragged off, leaving the boss figure slumped at his table. The electricity system was still down, and only a few fires and lamps flickered round the compound in the warm darkness. By then I realised I'd pissed myself during the beating: my left trouser leg and sock were soaked.

The next we knew, we were in a proper lock-up. One guy stood with the barrel of a rifle in the small of my back while two others cut away the ropes round my arms and replaced them with metal handcuffs, which bit into my wrists. Then, with my arms still behind me, they made the cuffs fast with a short length of chain to a shackle mounted in the wall. Somebody else fixed Gen up the same, to the next shackle, a couple of metres away.

Our gaolers went out, but they didn't lock the door, and I felt sure they'd be back in a moment. Sure enough, in came the guy who'd escorted me, carrying a mug or cup.

'You want drink?' he said, and shoved the mug hard into my face, so that the metal rim grated across my front teeth. Being thirsty as hell, I took a sip. It was fresh piss, with a hot, acid stink. I went *phworrrh!* and spat out the little I'd taken in.

'Don't touch it, Gen,' I went.

The guy didn't even offer the mug again. He didn't speak any more. He just threw the contents into my face, went out, and rattled some locks into place behind him.

Gen gave him a minute to get clear, then said quietly, 'How are you doing, Geordie?'

'Fucking awful,' I answered. 'How about you?'

'Not great. My ribs are in a mess. I've shat myself, too. Are you hurt much?'

'I'm hurt, but I think it's only bruises. Fucking stiff neck, too.'

'Can you sit on the floor?'

'Not a chance,' I told him. 'Can't reach.'

'Me neither. Kneel?'

'Just.'

'Ditto. We're in for a long night.'

We'd hardly got a glimpse of our surroundings, and now we were in almost total darkness. The only glimmer of light came in through a ventilation space left between the top of the walls and the roof, high above our heads. The opening was a perfect entrance and exit for mozzies, which were soon whining in to attack us. I could feel that the wall was made of bare concrete blocks, and by scraping with my boot I could tell that the floor was earth, but that was all we knew.

Soon I realised we weren't alone. Rustling noises started up on the other side of the room, and at first I thought they were being made by another prisoner, maybe as his last gasp from thirst and hunger. Then I heard some squeaks as well, and I said, 'Fucking rats!'

'Yeah,' Gen went. 'I just had one run over my foot.'

By their noise, the rodents were everywhere – not only at floor level, but around the roof as well. For some time we were both silent, busy with our own thoughts. Try as I might to banish the image, my mind kept returning to the horrific sight of Whinger's innards sliding down in coils over the side of the table. After a bit, I said, 'Gen, did you see how they killed him?'

'The guy with the machete slit his belly open and carved out the liver. That was what killed him. Loss of blood.'

'Thank God I was on the deck when that was happening. I never saw it. I never heard him shout, either.'

'I don't think he made a sound. He must have been unconscious already. They'd given him some battering. I don't reckon he felt a thing.'

'Gen, these people are fucking animals.'

'No, Geordie. They're lower than animals. Animals don't behave like that.'

'Fair enough,' I agreed. 'But if I get the slightest chance, am I going to level the score!'

'"Life for life,"' Genesis intoned in his singsong Welsh, '"eye for eye, tooth for tooth, hand for hand, foot for foot, burning for burning, wound for wound, stripe for stripe."'

'Who said that?'

'It was God, giving the law to Moses in the Book of Exodus.'

'That's what it's going to be for me.'

'But that was the Old Testament, Geordie. Jesus said the opposite. He said, "Turn the other cheek."'

'That can't apply to someone who did what this guy did.'

'Geordie, that man's mad. He was also pissed out of his mind.'

'I know. But he's got a brain. He's been expensively educated. That makes him all the more dangerous. Gen, it's going to be him or us.'

'He said if they find the diamond, we'll be free to go.'

'Bollocks. Muende knows we saw him kill Whinger. If we take him to the plane and he gets his diamond, the first thing he'll do is top us, to make sure we don't talk.'

'What's your plan, then?'

'We'll have to go with them. Make as if we're playing along. Get them relaxed. Maybe we'll become confused, won't be able to find the site. We'll play for time by taking them to the wrong area. The longer the trek, the twitchier they'll get. They won't tab far, either of them. The bitch is lame, and he's fat as a pig.' I stopped, then added, 'Of course, everything will be different if they get their hands on my GPS. If they did that, and got the thing to work, they might put two and two together and dispense with our services altogether.'

'What if we do take them to the plane?'

'I don't know. Maybe we bounce one of the guards, grab a weapon, drop them. It depends what route they take. We might even meet the rest of our own guys, coming the other way.'

Gen didn't answer immediately. But presently, he said, 'I wonder how they're doing.'

'So do I. My gut feeling is they've got the wagon free. I just hope to hell they don't go looking for us around the convent in the morning.' Again there was a silence. Then Gen asked, 'What's the relationship between the two?'

'Muende and the German? God knows. They can't be shagging. Or can they?'

'Anything goes,' said Gen. 'You never know. Maybe she's after the diamond for herself. Maybe, if she'd managed to get it out of the country, she'd have just pissed off over the horizon.'

What with thirst, headache, exhaustion, aching arms and wrists, mozzies and rats, it was hard to follow any train of thought for long. But my mind kept going back to Whinger. I couldn't stop thinking of how the machete must have sliced through his stomach muscles. Again and again I saw those intestines, still alive, slipping down over the side of the table and landing in coils on the floor.

Another worry began to needle me. 'Gen,' I said. 'Was it my fault that he got killed?'

'What d'you mean?'

'If I hadn't butted the woman . . . if I hadn't created that disturbance.'

'No, no, Geordie. Forget that. It was going to happen sooner or later. The woman was gunning for Whinger all along.'

'You're right there. And now I've thought of something else.'

'What's that?'

'Yesterday, in camp, she went trying to search Whinger's kit while he was asleep. He woke up to find her standing over him. She must have convinced herself he had the bloody diamond all along.'

In the next silence I heard a faint scurrying noise as a rat moved across the floor towards me. I raised my right foot into the air, standing on one leg, in the hope that I could crack down on the animal if it came right close. A moment later I felt it touch the toe of my left boot. I stamped, but only half connected; the target gave a squeal and scuttled away.

'What was that?

'Fucking rat.'

'They're everywhere.'

Again we endured a few minutes' silence.

'Gen?'

'Hello.'

'I'm thinking about the delay when we arrived here.'

'What about it?'

'The woman must have been briefing Mr Arsehole on who we were and what we'd been doing. Obviously she'd been in cahoots with him before. But it was only when she got to the convent that she could make contact with him. That was her first chance since the crash.'

'Sounds about right. What's her role, though? What's their relationship?'

'You tell me. I reckon she's been acting as a courier, taking diamonds out. Maybe she's a dealer. When she came for the big stone, the guys in the plane were just pilot and escort. The stuff about big-game surveys was a load of crap. Ditto the story about coming from Mozambique. I reckon they nipped in from Namibia early that morning and were on their way back out.'

Genesis gave a muffled curse as he shifted position, trying to ease his arms. 'A stone that size has got to be worth millions.'

'Hundreds of millions. That's what Boisset said – one of those would finance a whole war.'

We both went quiet again for a while. My ribs were aching all down my left side. I'd got quite a few kicks there when I was on the deck. The cuts on my head had stopped bleeding, but my left eye was puffed and swollen, my mouth the same. The back of my neck felt rigid, swollen from the blow that had knocked me down.

After a while, I said, 'What have they done with his body?'

'They won't waste energy burying him. That's for sure.' For once Genesis allowed a cynical edge to sharpen his voice. 'If this place is on a river, they'll have thrown him in by now.'

'It'll be the same for us if they top us in the open. The crocs or the hyenas.'

Another silence. I didn't want to ask Gen what he thought the time was. The answer might be too depressing. We probably hadn't been in the nick for more than an hour; we must have about seven or eight hours to endure till first light.

Soon my mind was going down another alley. 'I'm thinking about the old magician, Gen.'

'The witch doctor?'

'Right. We've had another white death. Whinger makes the score five. If us two go, it'll be seven. Not far to ten.'

'Ah, bollocks!' said Gen, with sudden emphasis. 'That was a load of shite, Geordie. I keep telling you. Pay no attention. I mean, what's a white death and what isn't? There must be hundreds of white mercenaries fighting for the blacks all over the continent: South Africans, Germans, Russians, Czechs, Americans, Brits – everything. There's whites here in Kamanga, we know that. They're in every country. I bet you more than ten have gone down already, since we arrived in Africa.'

'Maybe. But the witch doctor meant in our lot.'

'Okay. So we've lost two – Andy and Whinger.'

Gen's down-to-earth good sense was a comfort, as always. But I sensed that, for once, his faith in the supremacy of good had taken a bad knock. He might talk about God working in mysterious ways, and battling against the power of Satan, but he'd become confused by the apparent influence of the witch doctor. Where did the *sin'ganga* stand in the scale of good and evil? In our predicament, the devil definitely seemed to have the upper hand. As for me, lacking all religious conviction, once I'd started to believe that events were being governed or directed by some sinister paranormal influence, it was impossible to put the idea from my mind – especially when our very survival was threatened by a crazy dictator and his slapper of a hand-maiden.

TWELVE

I didn't realise I'd been asleep, but I must have drifted off, because I came to with a jolt, in pain all over. Something had woken me. Rats? No. They were still on the move, back and forth across the floor, but I was used to them already. I listened. A faint thud came from outside the door. Then a chain or padlock rattled briefly. I assumed Muende had got his hands on my GPS, worked out that Waypoint Seven was what he needed, and decided he could bin us without further ado. Now he'd sent someone to take us out and shoot us. I started shuddering, partly from nerves, partly from cold.

'Gen?' I whispered. The first try brought no response. At the second he gave a grunt. 'Something's happening outside,' I croaked. 'I hope to fuck they're not coming to beat us again.'

There was practically nothing we could do to prepare ourselves for an assault. But at least we were awake. If someone had come to top us, he'd get a good kick in the crotch first.

The next sounds from the door were the scratch of a key turning in a lock and another faint clink of chains. I was still bracing myself for a confrontation when I realised that the noises were furtive; not the confident clang of a gaoler going into his charges, but the careful tinkering of somebody who had no business to be there.

A moment later, the door opened inch by inch, and a voice said in American-accented English, 'You guys there?'

I tried to speak, but couldn't. My mouth was so dry that no sound came out. I swallowed a few times, and at last managed to croak, 'Who's that?'

'Friend,' came the answer. 'Hold quiet. I'm coming right over.'

There was a scraping sound as he dragged something into the cell, and a scurry of rats departing. Then I felt, rather than saw, a man approaching along the wall. A hand settled on my left arm and ran gently down to my wrist.

'Cuffs,' whispered the voice. 'Okay. I have some keys.'

I smelt the fresh, minty tang of chewing gum. Hope surged up inside me as I heard and felt unseen fingers trying different keys. At last one turned in a lock, and my wrists came free. With incredible relief I brought my arms slowly round in front of me and flexed them.

'Wait there while I see to your buddy.'

Starlight was flooding through the open door. In it lay the bundle our rescuer had dragged in: the body of the guard. Moving stiffly, I went across and ran my hands over it, searching for weapons. No luck there. The man was wearing a holster, but it was empty.

From across the cell came the scrape of a key and whispered curses. I stepped back from the dead gaoler and tripped over something else. Crouching down, I reached out a hand and felt a boot, a bare leg. Another corpse, but this one was cold. Whinger! Instinctively I whipped my hand away, fearful that my fingers might come up against his congealing intestines. Then another horrible thought hit me. That was where the rats had been heading all night; it was Whinger they'd been eating.

I knew where his legs were. I ought to be able to find his head, without running my hands up his body. Aiming off about four feet, I reached down again. My right hand landed on the side of his face. I felt the puckered, slimy skin. I ran my fingers down his neck and got them under the paracord that held his ID discs. I was so absorbed in my task that I hardly noticed the movements behind me. Then came a touch on my shoulder, and a soft voice said, 'Okay. We gotta go.'

With my left hand I lifted Whinger's head, and with the other slipped the loop of cord free.

'Leave him!' said the voice. 'Move!'

The head fell back on to the earth floor with a thud. I stood up, and the voice whispered, 'Follow me. Keep right on my ass.'

Outside, the cool air made me feel less sick, and the starlight seemed bright as day. We waited a moment while the American reset the outer padlock; then, pocketing the keys, he led us silently along the side of the building and across an open space towards some big sheds in the distance. Behind us only a couple of fires were glowing, and the camp was almost entirely dark.

Walking was an effort. In order to keep going, I began to count the steps, and reached two hundred before we came to the sheds. In deep shadow behind them, out of line-of-sight from the rest of the barrack blocks, our escort stopped and turned to us, letting out a big breath of relief. 'Okay,' he announced, quietly. 'We made it so far.'

'What about the guard?' I went.

'He got a broken neck.'

'Yeah, but won't someone find his body?'

'Not for a while. He's locked in there for the duration, and I have the keys. How're you doing?' He shone a torch briefly on my face, and exclaimed, 'Boy, you got a beating!' He gave Gen a quick scan as well, saw he was much the same, and asked, 'Well, what do you need?'

'Water.'

'Okay. Something to eat?'

'Maybe, but water first. Any liquid.'

'Sure. Stay here. If the alarm goes up, head thataway.' He pointed to the south. 'There's a group of trees right out there. If you have to, hide in them, and I'll come get you. Otherwise, stick around here. I'll be back.'

He slipped away round the corner of the shed.

I felt breathless, barely able to believe we were out. 'Gen,' I whispered, 'somebody answered your prayers.'

'I know. Geordie, how are you feeling?'

'Stiff as hell, specially my neck. Bruises all over. You all right?'

'I wouldn't say that. But I don't think anything's broken.'

Gingerly, I touched my lip, which seemed less swollen than it felt from inside. Next I swung my arms round vertically, slowly at first, then faster, to loosen cramped muscles and get circulation going.

In less than ten minutes our saviour was back. 'Nothing much,' he said, 'but it's liquid, anyway.'

He held out his hand, and I took what I could feel was a water-bottle.

'Are we okay here?' I asked.

'Long enough to take a drink.'

'Go on.' I passed the bottle to Gen. 'You first.'

He unscrewed the top, took a swallow, and said, 'Champagne!'

In fact it was sweet lemonade, better than anything in the world. I took two long swallows, then handed the bottle over again.

'I got some food as well,' said the American. 'Only MREs, but there you go.'

I took two squashy foil packets and slipped them into the thigh pocket of my DPMs. Genesis pouched a couple as well.

'Thanks,' I said. 'What time is it?'

'Ten of three. You guys gotta get out of here. They're planning to kill you once you've done whatever it is they want. Which way d'you want to head?'

'North, I suppose. Back towards the place we left the rest of our team. Where are we?'

'This goddamn dump's called Chimbwi. It's a decommissioned bauxite mine. The rebel army's taken it over as a forward base.'

'How far are we from Msisi?'

'Never heard of that. What is it?'

'A convent. It *was* one, at least. Not a nun left now. That's where we ran into trouble. We didn't know the rebels had captured the place.' I took another drink and asked, 'Who are you?'

'Sam Kershon, former SEAL.'

'A SEAL!' I peered at him, trying to see his features in the starlight. All I could make out was a neat crew-cut head and powerful-looking shoulders. 'My God,' I said, 'what the hell are you doing here?'

'I'm with an outfit called Interaction.'

'Interaction! We know it. Based in London.'

'Yep. London and Joburg. This guy Muende hired us to smarten up his rabble.'

'Some job.'

'You said it. Are you guys British special forces?'

'Correct. Part of a training team.'

'For the government forces?'

'Exactly.'

'That means we're on opposite sides. But when I saw you being brought into camp, I thought you looked like Brits. I said to myself, shit, this is too much. Say, what are your names?'

'I'm Geordie. This is Genesis.'

'Genesis! Good one! First book of the Bible.'

'Spot on!' Gen agreed. Then he asked, 'How did *you* get here?'

'Trucked up from Sentaba, the Afundi headquarters. That's a hundred miles or so. Eight-hour ride. What about you guys?'

'We came the opposite way, from the north.'

Talking in fast whispers, I filled Sam in with an account of the crash, the attack on the mine, Joss's volte-face, the discovery of the big diamond, and his plan to cut our throats in the middle of the night.

'Nice way to treat your guests and allies,' Sam said. 'Sounds like there ain't much to choose between the two sides.'

'No,' I went. 'But this damned diamond is twisting everything. Until that came into the reckoning, Joss was okay – wasn't he, Gen?'

'Better than okay,' Gen replied. 'He was good.'

'Well,' said Sam. 'Big money always talks loudest.'

A single shout came from the camp behind us. We listened for a few seconds, but the disturbance died down.

'Look,' I said. 'We've got to get the fuck out of here.'

Then Sam sprang a surprise. 'All right if I come with you?'

'Why, are you wanting out?'

'Too right I am. I'm through with this lot.'
'Well, it's up to you. It's going to be some hike.'
'How far's this Msisi?'
'It's got to be about fifty ks from here. The Zebra Pans about the same.'
'Sixty ks!' The American gave a low whistle. 'That's over thirty miles. You have any equipment – compass, GPS?'
'Nothing. The bastards who captured us nicked everything.'
'Well, I've got a compass. Know what heading we want?'
'Not exactly. Where's Gutu in relation to Chimbwi?
'Gee, let's see. I'd say about forty ks north-east of here.'
'Then I reckon we need to head north until we hit the river, then turn downstream. Can you get us out of camp?'
'Oh, sure. That one's easy. There's plenty holes in the fence. But we've only got three hours of darkness. There's no way we can make it back to the rest of your guys before first light.'
As the elation of getting free wore off, exhaustion was clamping down on me, and I sat on the ground to think.
'Any chance of nicking a vehicle?'
'Tough. The transport's kept in a compound of its own and guarded pretty good. You'd stir up a hornets' nest if you tried to get in there. Tell you what, though. Can you fly a plane?'
'Depends what it is.'
'A light aircraft,' said Sam. 'Very basic.'
'Christ, that could be okay. Don't tell me there's one here.'
'Sure is. They had it for prospecting.'
'Is it operational?'
'Absolutely. Somebody took it up a couple days back.'
'Jesus!' I felt my adrenalin stirring. 'Where is it?'
'Right over there.' He pointed. 'In an open shed.'
'Any security on it?'
'Nothing. There's only one guy knows how to fly it, and he's an officer, so they trust him.'
'What about a strip?'
'Right in front of it.'
'Fuel?'
'Should be plenty.'

'Can we go and look at it?'

'Sure. Come on.'

He led us to the end of the shed, took a cautious scan round the corner, and set out across the open ground beyond. The moon was already well across the sky. As I looked up at the stars, it seemed incredible that only twenty-four hours earlier our whole team had been driving though the dark. It felt like a month ago.

In three or four minutes we came to a perimeter fence, weldmesh on steel posts. As Sam had said, it was full of holes, and we found one easily enough. Behind us the camp lay silent, but out in the bush hyenas were howling. Walking was hard work for me; I was bruised all over, and my legs hurt when I moved them.

Soon, another large shed showed up ahead of us, black against the sky.

'This is the hangar,' Sam whispered. 'Wait here while I check it out.'

Gen and I knelt down. Being so used to carrying weapons, I felt defenceless and vulnerable, lacking even a knife. Without thinking, I raised my left wrist to look at my watch, remembering too late that it had gone. I glanced behind us, trying to estimate how far we'd come from the main part of the camp. Half a mile, anyway.

Presently, Sam loomed up out of the dark, and announced, 'All clear.'

The shed was open-fronted. Just inside it, with its perspex bubble of a canopy glinting in the moonlight, stood a very basic-looking aircraft.

'Jesus!' I went. 'This is all right. You have a torch?'

'Sure.' He handed one over.

'I'm going to have a quick look over it. Keep an eye out while I switch the torch on.'

'Keep it short, then. Just point it away from the camp.'

I ran the beam quickly over the little plane. It wasn't any make I recognised, but it looked much the same as other small aircraft I'd flown.

'Only two seats,' said Gen.

'Don't worry. Sam can sit on your lap. We'll squeeze him in somehow.'

'Will it take off with that weight?'

'Should do.'

A quick inspection showed the plane had a nose-wheel and two main wheels, an ignition switch but no electric start – just a hand-pull on the side of the engine – and a squeeze-ball pump for priming the carburettors.

'Think you can hack it?' Genesis asked.

'Try it, anyway.'

I doused the torch, eased myself into the left-hand seat and felt the controls: accelerator arm, joystick, pedals, handbrake. Everything moved freely. I shone the torch on the transparent tube that served as a fuel gauge. The level was fairly low; it looked as though there were only twenty or twenty-five litres in the tank.

'We could do with more gas,' I said. 'Is there any around?'

'In the back.' Sam pointed into the depths of the shed. But there, for the first time, he was wrong. The day before, he said, two forty-five-gallon drums had been standing in the corner. Now they'd gone.

'Too bad,' I said. 'We'll have to make do with what we've got.' I looked back towards the camp, calculating our chances. 'It's too dark to take off at the moment. If anything went wrong with the engine, we'd kill ourselves trying to land. Our only chance is to wait until dawn's about to break.'

'If we wait till it starts getting light, chances are someone will spot us,' said Sam.

'I know. But it's a risk we've got to take.'

Because I was the only one of us who could fly, I was taking charge of the situation. But I didn't want to put the American down, so I added, 'If it's light, and something does happen once we're in the air, at least we'll have a chance of getting down again. Okay, Sam?'

'I'm in your hands, skipper.'

'That's the plan, then. What we can do meanwhile is push the thing further away from the camp, give ourselves that much more of a start, and keep the noise at a distance. How long's the strip?'

'Maybe five hundred yards.'

'Better check it out. We'll need to take off westwards. I don't fancy flying back over the camp. Step it out to the far end, Gen.'

'Fine. What do you need for take-off?'

'Two fifty yards. Two hundred at a pinch. As there's no wind, and we'll have a heavy load, two fifty would be better.'

As Genesis set out, taking long strides, I let off the hand brake, and the two of us rolled the little aircraft forward. It trundled easily, making hardly a sound. I reckoned we'd pushed it nearly two hundred metres when we made out a dark figure coming back towards us.

'Three hundred paces more beyond here,' Gen said quietly.

'This'll do, then. What is there at the far end?'

'Nothing. The ground just gets rough.'

More than anything else, I wanted to see if the engine would start. But I knew that the moment it fired, we'd probably be compromised: the noise would be almost bound to give us away. So all I could do was show Sam the hand-pull on the side of the engine.

'It's just like a lawn-mower,' I told him. 'All you need do is pull when I say, and keep pulling until she fires.'

'We need a contingency plan,' Gen said. 'Supposing we can't start it? What do we do then?'

'Head north from here on foot, and keep going,' Sam replied, pointing. 'Right out there. There's nothing to stop us. We're already through the wire.'

'You got a GPS?'

'Sure.' He patted his chest pocket.

'Okay,' I said. 'Good. How's the time?'

He glanced at his watch, and replied, 'Twenty after four.'

'What time's first light?'

'First light around here is twenty after five. Sunrise a quarter of six.'

'An hour to go, then. What about the guard on the cell? Won't someone miss him?'

'His relief won't come on till six o'clock. Then he'll find his mate's disappeared, along with the keys. Probably he'll think he's gone to sleep someplace. By then we'll be up and gone.'

'Touch wood.'

The tension was electric, but somehow we had to pass the time. We sat on the ground under the wing of the aircraft and chatted in quick, nervous whispers.

'The guy they killed,' Sam said. 'Good buddy of yours, was he?'

'More than that. We'd served together for fifteen years – Russia, Ulster, Colombia, everywhere.'

I began thinking about Whinger's family. His mother was dead, but his father was still alive. If I got back, it would be down to me to go and tell him what had happened. I might never reveal *exactly* what they'd done to him; it would be bad enough without going into details. That unpleasant task was in the future, though. Our first priority was to get ourselves out. Had the lads got the satcom up and running? Was a Herc on its way to lift us out?

My mind kept returning to our flight. The last time I'd flown was eighteen months ago, when we'd done some pilot training with the Army Air Corps. Luckily for me, the Regiment had had a ridiculous idea that they wanted to train guys to fly, but nothing came of it, because at the end of the course one of the lads wrecked an aircraft. Now in my mind I ran through some standard drills.

'Sam,' I said, 'those hills to the north. D'you know how high they are?'

'The Makonde Hills? In the day you can see 'em in the distance. How high? Nothing great. Six, seven hundred feet. Why?'

'I was thinking. We're going to burn a load of fuel clearing them. It's a question of how much we have left after that.'

I borrowed his torch again for another check of the fuel gauge. It had no calibration, just the curved, transparent pipe, so judging the supply was a matter of guesswork. By wishful thinking, I confirmed my original estimate of between twenty and twenty-five litres. Five gallons to lift us to freedom.

At about 0440 I suddenly felt ravenous and cracked into one of the ready-to-eat meals. My lip hurt as I took each mouthful, but never had cold, congealed corned-beef hash tasted so good. Genesis wasn't so lucky: his foil pack contained spaghetti bolognese, which he said tasted like wallpaper glue, but he got it down his neck all the same.

Feeling revived, I asked, 'Sam, were you in the Gulf?'

'Sure,' he replied. 'SEAL Team Six, in the Western Desert.'

'Never!' I exclaimed. 'That was our location, too. Deployed from Al Jouf? Amazing! What were you on?'

'Air-sea rescue. Picking up downed aircrew.'

'Some hairy trips, I bet.'

'You said it. Had one near-miss from a SAM. Twice we nearly didn't make it out.'

'Ninety-one,' I said, trying to remember a name. 'Did you ever meet a guy called Tony Lopez?'

'Sure did! Hell of a guy, Tony. I spent some time with him in Panama. He a pal of yours?'

'Absolutely. He gave us a big hand in Colombia. Then he came over to the UK on attachment, and stopped a bullet at Chequers, of all places.'

'Chequers?'

'The Prime Minister's country home.'

'No kidding?'

'Right there, in the park.'

'What in hell were you doing?'

'Tangling with the IRA.'

'Oh, *those* choirboys.'

After a short silence, Genesis asked, 'How many of you guys are there here?'

'Mercs? Twelve. Only one American, though. Me! The rest are hairy-assed South Africans. Supposed to be some Russians coming in, too.'

'So what's your brief?'

'Good question. They hired us to help fight the war against the north, but in the past couple of days that campaign's pretty much taken a back seat. There's a new agenda now.'

'Which is?'

'The thing's going nuclear.'

'What d'you mean?'

'Somebody's stumbled on a cache of warheads near a place called Ichembo, out west. I don't know who found them, or how, because the site's outside the war zone.'

'Warheads?' I asked

'Nuclear heads for tactical weapons. Muende's desperate to get his hands on them. He's pissed off with the slow progress of his campaign. But now he reckons with medium-range nuclear capability he could knock out the north in a couple of weeks. A few missiles into Mulongwe, and all will be dandy. The north will be on its knees.'

'Jesus!' I went. 'I bet they're shitting bricks up there, then.'

'They don't even know about the stuff, yet. Nobody knows about it except us - that is, Muende's force.'

'How many heads are there?'

'Supposed to be about fifty.'

'What size?'

'I dunno – like so, maybe.' Sam held his hands about four feet apart to indicate their length. 'I guess they're like hundred-millimetre shells.'

'Has Muende got the means to deliver them?'

'Oh, sure. He has plenty Russian rockets. That's how the warheads got here. Left behind by the Russians when they pulled out in a hurry. Then forgotten. Or, put it another way, deliberately not remembered. Apparently they're in an underground silo, but they're deteriorating – going unstable.'

'If that arsehole Muende does get his hands on them,' I began. 'When he's been drinking, he's not rational any more. He might turn round and start on South Africa.'

'That's right. And the South Africans on the team know that. From what I've heard, they're cooking up some plan of their own. Muende thinks they're going to help him recover the warheads. They are, but once they've got them, they're planning to hijack them for their own purposes.'

‘What do *they* want them for?’

‘You tell me. Maybe they’re working covertly for their government. Maybe they’ve got some private agenda. But this whole thing’s getting to be too big a fuckin’ mess. That’s why I’m wanting out. Ordinary fighting’s one thing. Nuclear is something else.’

‘Don’t blame you,’ I said. ‘What’s the timing of the operation?’

‘Immediate. The Afundis are going for the warheads tomorrow. Correction, today. They’re gonna start right out this morning. The great commander’s going to direct the operation in person. It’ll be some circus, I tell you.’

‘Where is this place?’ I asked.

‘Ichembo? Not that far west of here. North-west, I should say. Maybe a hundred miles. But the main force has got to come up from the south, and then they’ve got to cross the river.’

‘So when do they reckon to get there?’

‘Evening, I guess. Why, you gonna join the party?’

‘Some chance!’

‘Sam,’ said Genesis. ‘How did you get involved with this shower, anyway?’

‘Answered one of Interaction’s ads. Simple as that. Came out of the military and found civilian life a bit tedious. I guess I was looking for some excitement. But I tell you something: if I’d known what a shithole Kamanga was, I’d never have gotten involved.’

‘The same goes for us,’ I said. ‘Except that we didn’t have the choice, we just got sent.’

The conversation drifted on. I was in a peculiar state. Lying flat on my back, looking up at the stars, I felt exhaustion pressing in on me like a heavy atmosphere from outside. I had that thick, cloudy feeling in my head that I’d been blaming on the Lariam. But at the same time apprehension was needling me internally and keeping me awake. I had to discipline myself not to go on asking Sam the time; after two enquiries, it was still only just after 0500, and there was at least half an hour to kill. My biggest worry was the rest of our guys were about to fall into the same trap as we had. Unless we got back to stop them, they'd set off in search of us soon after first light, and drive head-first into the shit at the convent.

In spite of everything, I must have dozed off. Suddenly, Gen was shaking my shoulder and saying, 'Watch yourself, Geordie. Something's starting up.'

He and Sam were already on their feet, looking back at the camp, where torches were flashing and people were running about.

'Sounds like they've broken in to the cell and found the body,' said Sam. 'We better get set.'

Above the camp, in the east, the sky had started to lighten, but the moon had set, and around us the land still looked black as coal.

'Can't we get off right away?' Gen asked.

'Not yet,' I said, looking at the sky. 'Have to hang on for a bit.'

'We've got a few minutes,' said Sam, calmly. 'They'll run around the huts like blue-assed flies, looking for you. There's nothing to draw anybody in this direction. When they find you're missing, most likely they'll head for the transportation section. They'll think you're trying to steal a vehicle.'

'You'd better be right.'

The longer we held on, the more I managed to convince myself that the aircraft's engine wasn't going to start. Given the Kamangans' abysmal standards of maintenance, the chances of it firing up and running properly seemed infinitesimally small.

Now, more than ever, precise timing was going to be critical. If we took off prematurely, in the dark, we could be committing suicide. If we let the light get too strong, and then couldn't start the engine, we'd almost certainly be spotted and picked off by trigger-happy guards.

Dawn seemed desperately retarded. Daylight strengthened with impossible slowness, the greyness hardly able to infiltrate the black. The sky was clear – not a cloud anywhere – so I knew the apparent slow-down was psychological, but that did nothing to speed things up or ease my nerves.

Back in the camp, the commotion kept increasing. Vehicles had started to scud about. Horns were blowing, torches and headlights flashing, orders being shouted, doors slammed.

'Let's flit,' said Sam. 'Let's do it.'

Looking at him, I could just make out his features for the first time: dark hair, thick eyebrows, broad, humorous face.

'Okay,' I agreed. 'This is good enough.'

I'd hardly spoken when a pair of headlights swung out of the camp and came straight for us. They were five or six hundred metres off, but moving fast. Clearly, their objective was the hangar.

'That's it!' I shouted. 'Get in, Gen. Sam, on the starter!'

I jumped into the left-hand seat, squeezed the ball to pump fuel through the carbs, and called, 'Pull!'

Sam pulled. Nothing. Again. Still nothing. At the third attempt the engine fired, backfired and cut. I stole a glance over my shoulder. The headlights were bouncing around, speeding towards us. I pumped again, and shouted, 'Keep pulling!' Once more the engine fired up and cut. In the silence I heard two sharp cracks snap out behind me. Screwing my head round, I saw the headlights boring in on us.

'Pull, Sam!' I bellowed. 'For fuck's sake, pull!' My adrenalin was well up. My hands were shaking on the controls. As the engine fired again I whipped up the accelerator arm and sent the revs sky-high. 'Okay! I yelled through the sudden scream. 'Get in!'

More rounds were cracking past us. Sam, in front of me on the left, let go of the handle and ran round the front of the aircraft to jump in on top of Genesis. But as he came level with the open doorway, he gave a sudden yell, slumped forward and went down. From the way he buckled, backwards then forwards, I knew he'd got a round through the chest.

Gen made a move to get out and grab him.

'Stay put! I yelled. 'Leave him! He's fucked.'

I ran up the revs, released the handbrake and got the little aircraft rolling. The acceleration felt sluggish, and the track was rough, but at least we were moving. I glanced over my shoulder once more and saw the pursuing headlights veer wildly from side to side. Then the beams whipped straight up into the sky, like searchlights, before they wheeled over and were snuffed out. The vehicle had hit a rock or gone into a hole.

By then the sky was fairly bright. What light we had was coming from behind us, so forward visibility was adequate and I could see my instruments. I fixed my eyes on the airspeed indicator and watched the needle pick up: fifteen knots, twenty, twenty-five. In a few moments the ASI was reading thirty-five. Mentally, I urged it upwards. Only five more needed for lift-off. Suddenly, on my left, a stream of glowing green spots zipped past from behind and went looping away into the distance.

'Tracer!' I yelled. 'The bastards are firing at us.'

I ducked instinctively as sharp fragments rained down on my head. At the same instant I felt the nose lifting. Tracer on the right now. Suddenly, the perspex bubble in front of us starred: a round had come right through the cabin from behind. Forty knots. I eased back on the stick, and we were airborne.

I planned to stay as low as possible until we were out of small-arms' range, in the hope that we'd be less visible and offer a more difficult target, so I levelled off at about a hundred feet and kept going due west. For the first few seconds there was open bush beneath us, then a higher, more solid wall of vegetation loomed ahead.

The engine noise was deafening, so I shouted, 'Forest! Can't stay so low. Got to climb.'

I pulled back the stick, lifting the nose. Dark tree canopy flashed beneath us. The ASI was showing fifty-five knots. We'd been flying for nearly a minute. We were easily one kilometre clear of the strip. A few more tracer rounds came floating past, but they were hopelessly wide of the mark. Every second we went further west was a waste of fuel. Surely it was safe to swing round on to the heading we wanted?

Gently I banked to the right, holding the turn until the compass needle settled on zero. As we came round, I could see the dawn breaking, away to our right: the rim of the sun was showing crimson on the horizon. Ahead lay the range of hills we had to cross. They rose in front of us, grey and crumpled, raked by long black shadows. I glanced across at Genesis, but his head was turned away as he too looked at the dawn, and I couldn't see his face.

I started a gentle climb, easing the aircraft upwards in an attempt to conserve fuel by ascending as slowly as possible. Every few seconds I glanced at the cylinder-head temperature gauge. The needle for No. 1 had always been slightly higher than the one for No. 2. Now it began to climb, slowly but ominously. Up and up it went, to the edge of the red danger area. If the engine blew, that was us finished; I'd have no option but to glide down and land on the first level stretch we could find.

'Starting to overheat!' I shouted. 'Nothing we can do.'

At that moment I saw two huge birds coming in at us from the left front, big black silhouettes, almost on collision course. At the last moment they peeled off and fell away, to the left and below. From their long necks and trailing legs I reckoned they were storks, probably weighing twenty or thirty pounds. One of them into the canopy would have made a fine mess of us.

I straightened up and got back on course, so intent on watching the gauges, the ASI, the compass and the sky ahead for more birds that I ceased to think about the light. All the while the sky had been growing brighter, but then, because we were climbing, came a sudden, dramatic change. One moment we were still in the shadow of the earth, the next, the sun was over the horizon, and its radiance exploded all round us. In an instant it had flooded the whole of Africa with light.

'Hey!' I shouted in a moment of exultation. 'How about that!'

Genesis turned half towards me, and said, very loud, '"To give light to them that sit in darkness, and in the shadow of death."'

A moment later I felt him shudder violently. My right shoulder was pressed against his left, so the tremor was transmitted straight to me. I turned to look at him again. His head had dropped forward and was rolling back and forth across his chest.

'Gen!' I shouted.

I reached for his left hand with my right, lifted it, shook it. When I let go, it flopped off his knee and hung down, lifeless. I shouted his name again and twisted round to look at him. The only way I could get a proper view was by releasing my harness and coming half out of my seat, still holding the throttle and the stick. By doing that I got a sight of his chest, and saw blood seeping out down the front of his DPMs from a point just below the heart. I knew in an instant he was dead. The bullet that shattered the windshield had gone right through his torso from back to front.

I felt shaken to bits. I couldn't believe it. Why hadn't he said something when he was hit? Why hadn't he yelled? Even if he had, I couldn't have done anything to save him. But at least I'd have known the score. How typical of him not to complain. He must have known he was mortally wounded. Typical Gen to conceal his own trouble so that he didn't disturb my concentration. Typical above all, in his last moments of consciousness, to come out with that quote from the Bible.

I felt choked, exhausted physically and emotionally, pissed off to the final degree with Africa and all these feuding savages. For a few seconds I thought, there's one easy way to end this: climb to a thousand feet, point the nose down and open the throttle. That would be the finish of your worries, Geordie Sharp. Then, instead of self-pity, I felt shame, and said to myself, what about your mates, Geordie? They're in the shit, nearly as deep as you, and they need your presence fast. Concentrate. Get back to them. Retrench. That was easier said than done. I'd begun to shake so violently that I could hardly hold the stick still. The cause wasn't the cold – already the sun was hot on my right cheek and arm – it was more to do with shock and reaction.

Almost without noticing it, I cleared the highest point of the ridge, which was covered in grey rock and nearly bare of trees. Until then I'd hardly bothered with the altimeter. While waiting for take-off, I hadn't been able to see enough to wind it back to zero, and I knew any reading it showed would be only approximate. Now it was giving me 1,200 feet, which was obviously my height above sea level, rather than above the ground.

As I eased off the power, the temperature gauge began to sink back from its danger level, but the fuel in the transparent gauge was looking perilously low. I'd been planning to descend, following the lie of the land as it fell away towards the river valley, but I changed my mind and held the same altitude, with the idea that I'd get a better view of the ground ahead and see the river earlier.

Down the far side of the hills the bush thickened again, and the terrain reminded me of the area in which the Beechcraft had crashed. All the better: there must be thousands of scrub-covered ridges just like this one, scattered all over central southern Africa, and Muende's chances of finding the wreck without my help were practically zero.

Thinking about the diamond, I realised I didn't want the damned thing for myself. It had landed us in enough trouble already. No matter what it might be worth, I had a feeling it would always bring bad luck to anyone who owned it. What I *did* want, though, was to get my hands on Muende and the woman. If it was the last thing I did, I'd exterminate the pair of them.

My mind was becoming confused. I was too tired to think things through. Off to my right I spotted a dirt road twisting about like a grey ribbon, but running roughly north and south. Was that the track we'd been bounced along the night before? Must be. I checked the compass needle for the umpteenth time and made a small deviation to the left, aiming a few more degrees west of north. However small the risk – and by my calculations it was pretty much non-existent – I couldn't afford to hit the river at the mine, or anywhere near it. If Joss's guys saw a light aircraft approaching from the south, sure as hell they'd open up on it, thinking it was part of an Afundi attack.

Thank God, the air was completely smooth, the visibility perfect. At one point, to my right, I saw three startled giraffes set off at that curious, floating canter that makes them look as if they're swimming. I could even make out the puffs of dust knocked up by their pounding hooves.

Then, at last, across my front, I saw the river. Or rather, instead of muddy water lined by trees, I saw a long, white, winding streak of what looked like cotton wool. Fog! Above the stream vapour had condensed in the cool night air, and the valley was filled by a blanket of mist.

'Shit! Shit! Shit!' I shouted. This was the one, knackering circumstance I hadn't foreseen. For the hundredth time I glanced at the fuel gauge. It was showing all but empty. I'd only got a few minutes' flying time left.

Desperately I searched for a landmark that would tell me where I was before descending. The layer of mist looked shallow, but if I went down into it, I'd be blind. Any attempt to land in it could prove fatal. Beyond the fog rose a low mountain barrier. That was the western edge of the range of hills we'd come over before we attacked the mine. But where in hell was the spur on which we'd established our OP – that prominent feature from which Pavarotti had directed the mortar fire? Where was the track down which we'd approached the pontoon? Well away to my right, I hoped.

I estimated that, by air, the mine and the convent were no more than fifty kilometres apart. Now, unless my navigation was all to blazes, I was heading for a point roughly halfway between them. The eastern end of the Zebra Pans was about thirty-five ks downstream of the mine and fifteen kilometres short of the convent. If, as I hoped, I reached the river about thirty kilometres west of the mine, all I'd have to do would be to turn left and fly downstream until the pans appeared ahead.

Every few seconds I reviewed my options. What if the engine cuts *now*? Swing left, head out over the mist to the far edge, and look for a landing place on the other side of it, beyond the river. Then continue downstream on foot. What about Gen's body? Deal with that when the time comes. What if the engine dies *now*? The same.

The river was less than a kilometre ahead. Not a landmark in sight. The decision could wait no longer. I turned left and flew parallel with the edge of the white blanket, two or three hundred metres out. Now the low sun was blazing from straight behind me. Without thinking I'd come down to a couple of hundred feet. Buffalo below – a big, slate-grey herd churned up the dust as my approach set them running, and a cloud of ox-peckers wheeled after them.

Gen's torso was lolling to the left in its straps, leaning against my right arm. I shoved it away. The engine spluttered. Fuel gauge on zero. Must be a reserve. Then a gleam of hope: through the fog I saw grey-green water. The mist was thinning and breaking. In a few minutes the sun would burn it off. More glimpses of the river, which was swinging in wide loops, not running fast and straight as it did near the mine. That looked good, more like the flat terrain around the pans. I positioned the aircraft over the centre line of the coils and flew on downstream.

I'd quit looking at the fuel gauge. There was nothing more it could tell me. The temperature gauges were steady, so I could concentrate on looking ahead. Then, in the distance I saw that the fog blanket spread out to cover an area far wider than the river. The pans! That broad stretch of mist must be hanging above the water, the shallow lake, where Gen had found the reeds growing. Feverishly I scanned the high ground to the north, searching for the little shelf that Pav and I had designated as our RV. From this height it would look different, and I tried to allow for that.

Here, too, the mist was breaking. I was fast approaching the eastern end of the pans, the point where the vehicles had got bogged. My spirits leapt. Through a gap I saw the very spot where they'd gone in: a patch of ground freshly churned up, with semi-liquid mud showing dark in the middle of the lighter crust, like chocolate in the middle of coffee, and vehicle tracks all round. From above it looked as though elephants had got bedded and flailed their way out. The main thing was that the mother wagon had got out and had gone.

Now that I had my bearings, I knew where to look for the RV point. I banked hard right and headed for the hill. Sure enough, there was the shelf, with a rock face rising behind it.

Even if the lads had the vehicles well cammed-up, there was a chance I'd see them – I was that low and close. But no, the location was empty. Either they'd never been on the spur, or they'd been there and gone.

Morale sank. They *must* have been on it. I knew Pav would not have moved from that location until first light, as we'd agreed. That meant they must be on their way to the convent.

I banked hard left, coming back towards the river. There was only one route they could have taken: the one that Gen and I had used the evening before. I assumed they'd picked up our vehicle tracks; they must be following them along the bank. At all costs I had to stop them.

The engine faltered and cut, then picked up again. I was on the way down. I had just enough power to reach the river and turn right above the near bank. All I could do now was line up above the track and keep going until I finally ran out of fuel, then glide in and land. In that crisis, my mind became clear as glass. I wasn't worried about finding a place to put down; there were patches of open, level ground between the scrub, easily big enough for my purposes. All that mattered was that I should overtake the lads before they blundered into hostile forces at the convent and got captured, just as we had.

It was only in my final seconds under power that I saw them: two vehicles, one large, one small, crawling right-handed away from the river. Obviously they were looking for a route across one of the tributaries. As I turned towards them, the engine cut and died. In sudden silence, broken only by wind whistling past, I put the plane into a glide.

Now the sun was hot on my right cheek, the mist rapidly clearing. The vehicles were heading away from me, but I knew they'd turn at any moment, as soon as they found a crossing point, and come back towards me. I aimed for flat-looking ground on the left of a dry sand river, where I could intercept them. Without power, I was committed. I had only one chance. I picked my spot: a patch of bare earth at least a hundred metres long, with a thicket of thorn bushes at the far end which would act as a safety net if need be. I pushed the stick forward and dropped the nose, getting the attitude of the aircraft settled and aiming to maintain a forty-five-knot rate of descent. In the final instants of the approach I thought, Christ, I hope the lads can get to me quickly if this aircraft goes up. But at least it's got no fuel to start a blaze.

It was too late to worry. I tried not to look down over the nose, as I knew that would produce the illusion known as ground rush – of the earth tearing past too fast for the eyes to focus on anything properly. Instead I concentrated on my peripheral vision, looking outwards and ahead, with the result that the ground seemed to be coming up round my ears, but at a speed that I could manage.

With a few feet to go I eased the stick back, flared the aircraft and held it there, letting it sink. As the wheels hit and bounced, I was aware of our pinkie coming past in the opposite direction, scarcely twenty metres to my right, as though on the other lane of a motorway, with Jason the tracker in the driving seat and an expression of utter astonishment on his face. Then he was gone and I was down. The aircraft bounced twice before it slewed sideways and slid right-handed, coming to a halt, still on its wheels, just short of the thorns.

Within seconds, the guys were all round me. Phil, Mart, Danny and Chalky on my left, Pav and Stringer beside Genesis. They were covered in dry grey mud from head to foot. There was also a fearsome noise; everyone seemed to be shouting at once.

'Christ almighty!' went Phil. 'What the fuck's happened to you?' At the same time Pav was yelling, 'Gen! Gen! Wake up! You've made it!' and pulling at his arm.

'He'll not wake up,' I said dully. 'He's dead.'

'Dead?' roared Pav, incredulously. 'Never! Come on, boyo!'

But when he undid the harness and tugged, Gen's body crumpled toward him and tumbled to the ground. The next thing I knew, I too was on the deck. I had no recollection of unbuckling my straps or of getting out of the seat. I seemed to have passed out, and came round flat on my back, with faces staring down at me. I felt annihilated, as if I'd had a total anaesthetic.

'Where's Whinger?' Pav was asking.

'Dead.'

'For fuck's sake! How? Where?'

'I'll tell you. Any chance of some water?'

'Yeah, yeah.' Danny sprang to it and started rooting about in the pinkie.

'Get a guy on stag towards the convent,' I croaked. 'The bastards are in there. They may come out looking for us.'

'Who?'

'The rebels. The place is in rebel hands.'

The faces above me started to revolve. I'm sure Mart thought I was about to die on him, because he grabbed my wrist and held it, feeling the pulse, and opened up one of my eyelids with finger and thumb.

'Geordie,' he went. 'Your face is a mess. You look like the phantom of the fucking opera.'

'That's how I feel.'

'Stay there while I get something to clean up the cuts.'

I heard him get up and move away. For the time being nobody else spoke. I think they were in shock, nearly as badly as I was. Then Mart was back. He sponged the dried blood and dirt off my face with water, and when he dabbed antiseptic solution on to my cuts, the sting tweaked me sharply back to life.

'The one on your temple's not much,' he said. 'More of a bruise. The one on your cheekbone's deeper. Ought to be stitched, really.'

'Fuck that,' I said. 'Cover it over.'

He put on gauze pads and taped them in place. A couple of minutes later I was sat propped against the front wheel of the mother wagon, in the shade, gulping down water by the pint. Somebody had pulled Gen alongside the rear wheel and zipped him into a black nylon body-bag.

Except for Chalky White, who'd gone on ahead to act as an early warning, the rest of the lads crowded round to hear what had happened

'It's all down to that German woman,' I began. 'When I catch up with her, her feet won't fucking touch. That I guarantee.'

I looked round the haggard, unshaven faces, trying to collect my thoughts.

'We drove right into it,' I went on. 'Came up to the back of the convent, and suddenly these blacks were swarming all round us. It happened so fast we never even got to our weapons. They had us on the deck, cuffed us, nicked everything – watches, GPSs, knives, the lot. They'd already massacred the nuns. There were bodies lying around everywhere. Old, white bodies. They didn't touch *her*, though. She swaggered about giving orders like she was a fucking general in their army.'

'She's not a general,' said Stringer. 'She's a crook, pure and simple.'

'Eh? Did that come from the Kremlin?'

'Yeah. In the end the South African police turned up trumps. That guy in the plane whose ID we got – Pretorius – he was wanted by Interpol for embezzlement, international currency rackets and so on. The woman the same. She's got a record as long as her legs.'

'That makes sense,' I said. 'Anyway, at the convent she was frightening the shit out of these blacks, bollocking them in their own lingo. Next thing, all three of us were dumped in the back of a truck and driven to some clapped-out bauxite mine.'

'Was Whinger with it?' Mart wanted to know.

'Not really. He was coming and going. Mostly going – lucky for him.' I paused, thinking back. 'The thing was, the woman must have known where she was, all along. During the time she was with us, I mean. She was never as confused as she pretended. All that crap about needing glasses to read. It was shite. She knew bloody well we'd attacked the mine, and that the rebels had captured the convent. She was just waiting to get back there, to join up with them again.'

I held out the mug in a silent request for more water. 'Anyway, from the convent, she went ahead in another vehicle. She was at the next place when we arrived. There was a delay – twenty minutes or half an hour. Then we were taken into a hut like a classroom, and in comes Mr Big himself.'

'Muende?' said Danny.

'Him.'

'What does he look like?'

'A right half-caste. Pale skin, hair like tow. Yellow. Colour's wrong, but otherwise he's pretty much Afro-looking. Like the rest of these fuckers, only fatter. Quite sleek. Well oiled in every sense.'

In other circumstances, the lads might have laughed, but none of them even smiled. They knew something horrible was coming. Hardened though they were, the story of Whinger's end left them looking shattered. As for me, I could hardly tell it. I kept feeling I had to make excuses for not having prevented the disaster.

'The trouble was, the slag really had it in for him,' I said. 'She hated his guts. It didn't seem to occur to her that killing him was the worst thing she could do. Because he'd got burnt dragging her out of the wreck, she was convinced he'd found the fucking diamond. She was out to get him somehow.

'Gen and I were knackered, the pair of us. As I said, we were tied to the chairs. There was nothing we could do. Whenever we tried to help, we got hammered with rifle butts, or kicked. The way she handed Muende strips of liver – it was the filthiest thing I'll ever see.'

Pav, who'd been fond of Whinger, suddenly turned and walked away into the distance. I think he cracked up for a moment – I couldn't see. When he came back, he was together again, and muttering, 'Fucking arseholes!' over and over.

'What time did you get out of the mud?' I asked.

'Midnight,' Stringer said.

'Hell of a struggle.'

'You can say that again. Everyone's creased. Who's this bloke who got *you* out, then?'

'The Yank? Sam something. Former SEAL. That poor bastard's gone as well. They dropped him just as we were lining up for take-off.'

Phil handed me more water. 'So the villains are going for the diamond.'

'No. I mean, I don't know. I'm sure they will, in time. But without a chopper it'll take them days to find the wrecked plane. Even if they get hold of my GPS, they may not make anything of the waypoints. In the meantime, there's a new deal.'

I told them about the cache of nuclear warheads. Then I amazed them, and myself, by saying, 'I reckon we'd better go for that and clean it up before Muende does.'

Where the idea came from, I'll never know. It just jumped into my mind, fully formed.

'*What?*' Pav was astounded. 'Have you gone fucking mad? I thought we were on our way out of here.'

'We were,' I agreed. 'But now the goalposts have moved. We need to pull our fingers out and get after those missiles.'

As I said that, I felt myself changing. It was as though I'd been supercharged with rage at Whinger's death. In the past I'd never been really vindictive, but now I felt mean as sin: I'd dedicate myself to rubbing out the German woman and Muende, along with all his plans, if it was the last thing I did.

'He's not fucking getting away with it,' I announced to the company in general. 'There's no way he's going to get these weapons. You'll see.'

Pav shot me a peculiar look, as though he thought I'd gone round the twist. By then rehydration had got my brain going again, and I felt well in control of the situation.

I reckoned I'd better give the lads a minute to adjust their ideas, so I said, 'The first thing is to clear out of here. If the people at the convent have had a message about our escape, they could be out like a swarm of bees at any moment. Before we commit ourselves anywhere else, I need to talk to the Kremlin. Where's the best place for a temporary LUP? Pav? Phil?'

'Back up on that ledge at the RV point. Apart from anything else, it's a great OP, with a view down over the pans and the river. If anyone's coming, we'll see them.'

'That's it, then. Let's go.'

'What about this?' Mart pointed at the aircraft.

The thing was knackered. Without fuel, it had no future. We couldn't hide it, and even if we tried to burn it, the tell-tale skeleton would remain.

'Leave it,' I said. 'It's done its job.'

Half an hour later we were up on the ledge, with the vehicles cammed up between two thorn bushes. As Phil had said, the outlook was brilliant: through binoculars we could see baboons feeding on the river bank, hippos feuding in the water, crocs crawling out onto sandbanks to bask in the sun. If any vehicle had moved, we'd have spotted it at once.

When I first looked into a mirror, I got a shock: my left eye was nearly closed, my mouth stuck out in a pout, and much of the rest of my face was covered by Mart's dressings. My ribs were bruised black and blue all down my left side, but a check showed none was broken.

I made a quick inventory of the weapons and equipment we'd lost: one pinkie and all its gear, including the Milan post and half a dozen missiles; two 203s, two pistols and six badly needed jerricans of fuel. Needing to re-equip myself, I dug out Andy's watch, which I'd stowed in the mother wagon for safe-keeping, and took over Whinger's 203, commando knife and GPS. I still had the Colt .45 which I'd taken off the white mercenary.

'Eh, Stringer,' I went. 'Any joy with the satcom?'

'Yeah, it's fine. Didn't you hear? The Kremlin told us about Pretorius and so on?'

'Oh yeah. What was wrong with it?'

'I took the handset apart and found a wire had broken inside.'

'No wonder the bastard wouldn't work. So you've been through to Hereford?'

'Sure.'

'What's the buzz?'

'We asked for an exfil. There's a Herc on its way down. It's going to stage through Harare and wait for us to call it in.'

'What's its ETA?'

'Dunno yet. We need to get confirmation.'

I thought for a moment, then called, 'Phil, where's the good map?'

'It was in your pinkie.'

'Ah, shit. What about the other?'

'Here.' He brought it over. 'What are you looking for?'

'Place called Ichembo. Somewhere to the west. Christ, there it is. I found it straight away. That must be a sign.'

'A sign of what?'

'That we're supposed to go there.'

Phil shot me a hard look as he asked, 'What is it?'

'The dump where these nuclear warheads are lying.'

By the time I'd got sorted, Andy's watch was reading 0745.

'What time will it be in Hereford?' I asked Stringer.

'Minus two – 0545.'

'Let's go through to them.'

'What, now?'

'Yeah. I need to catch up on things.'

This time the satcom worked perfectly, and in a few seconds I was talking to a signaller in the Comcen at Stirling Lines.

'Who's the Orderly Officer?' I asked.

'Max Davidson.'

'Oh, right.' I'd met the man – a tall, sandy-haired rupert who'd recently joined from the Parachute Regiment – but I hardly knew him. 'Put him on, then.'

'There's been a runner sent to get him. He was talking to the DA in some dump called Mulongwe.'

'Christ, that's us. I mean, it's to do with us. I'll hold.'

From where I stood waiting, I could see the body-bag in the back of the truck. I was thinking, we can't take Gen with us in this heat. We're going to have to bury him, and then, if we can, come back for him later.

'Orderly Officer speaking,' said a Scots voice in my ear.

'Hello. Geordie Sharp here.'

'I've just been talking about you.'

'What was the buzz?'

'You're blacked,' said Davidson, jokily.

'Great! What have we done?'

'You attacked the Kamangan government forces without provocation and ran away. Now you're deliberately fomenting civil war.'

'Like fuck we are. Listen, you've not swallowed any of that shit, I hope?'

'Of course not.'

'I'm glad to hear it. Reality's different. The Alpha commander suddenly turned round and told us to bugger off. We heard he was sending an assassination squad after us in the middle of the night, so we did a flit.'

'Quite right,' went Davidson. 'Where are you now?'

I gave him our coordinates, and filled in more background. Then he said, 'We've got problems at this end as well. Kamanga's broken off diplomatic relations with the UK.'

'Charming,' I said.

'Yeah. They're refusing landing rights to British aircraft. The FCO are trying to negotiate. But if push comes to shove, the Herc can nip in across the Namibian border, permission or not. How are things with you?'

'Bloody awful. We've lost two more.'

'Oh, God! Since midnight?'

'One before, one after.'

'Who? Tell me.'

As quickly as I could, I brought him up to speed. I didn't tell him about the diamond, and I didn't say exactly what had happened to Whinger. I couldn't. I just said he'd been murdered at the instigation of the German, that Gen and I had escaped in the light aircraft, but that Gen had collected a bullet.

'But listen,' I ended up. 'The thing now's this dump of nuclear missile heads. We've got to go for it.'

'Say that again.'

'We've got to grab the stuff before this nutter Muende gets his hands on it. We're well placed. The location's only about three hours west of where we are now. We can beat the opposition to it.'

'Wait one. I think you need to talk to the Ops Officer and the

CO before you go ahead on that.'

'If we're going, we can't piss about. It's now or never.'

'What are you proposing?'

'To lift the stuff out before anyone else gets there. What we need to do is find an LZ near the site and guide the Herc in.'

'Geordie,' went Davidson, as if he was speaking to a kid. 'Take it easy. Your ideas are running away with you. All *we're* looking to do is pull the remains of the team out before anyone else goes down.'

'Where's the Herc, then?'

'Right now' – he paused, as if looking at some schedule – 'it's en route to Harare. ETA there zero five hundred Zulu.'

'That's all right then. It can easily make it here by midday. But we're going to need NBC suits for all crew members, and our own guys.'

'Geordie, I say again: you need clearance on this one.'

'Clearance!' I shouted. 'For Christ's sake, we need help, not clearance. We're trying to avert a fucking nuclear catastrophe.'

As I broke off the call, I again saw Pav looking at me in a strange way, but he didn't make any comment, and I said, 'Before we do anything else, we'd better get Gen underground.'

Nobody argued about that; we'd all seen what the heat and flies did to a body. Flies would be into the nose, eyes and mouth and lay eggs in a matter of hours. In a day or so the eggs would hatch into maggots, the maggots would start eating away, and the belly would explode with gas. Our immediate future was so uncertain that burial was essential. The only question was, where to excavate the grave. We could see that digging would be easiest down in the sand and mud around the pans, but for one thing we didn't want to go down there, close to the river, and for another we reckoned there would be less risk of animals digging the body up again if we put it in the rocky ground high up. I kept remembering how the warthog had erupted from a hole at the site of the training ambush, and how Joss had told us that aardvarks make enormous excavations every night.

After a search, Phil found a site which he reckoned would do – a level patch, with a little grass growing out of sand – but Jason immediately told him there was rock close beneath the surface.

'How far down is it?' Phil asked.

'Like this.' The tracker held his hands about a foot apart.

'How do you know?'

'I feel.'

Phil glared at him, not liking to be contradicted, and started to dig anyway, with one of the short-handled, pointed shovels that we carried on the pinkies. Sure enough, just over a foot down he hit solid rock and had to admit defeat.

His second choice of site met with Jason's approval, and there, taking turns, sweating like slaves, we got down nearly four feet before we again hit living rock, while those not digging assembled enough flat pieces of stone to cover the body.

'That'll do him,' said Pav. 'Nothing can come at him from underneath. If we put these lumps on top, he'll be fine.'

Sorting through Genesis's kit, we found his precious bible in the mother wagon. Our first idea was to bury it with him. Then I thought, no, there's a good chance we'll come back for him, so we'll keep it with us and return it to his family.

I don't think any of us had actually buried a mate before. Going to a funeral is one thing, doing the work another – and anyway, the body is usually inside a coffin. For Genesis we had no such luxury: he had to go under as he was, and there was no rush to take hold of him. In the end it was Pav and myself who picked up the body-bag and lowered it into the rough-cut hole. We'd dug it only just wide enough for his shoulders; his body had already gone stiff, and we had to wriggle it about to make it go down to the bottom. Once he was settled I leant over and pulled the toggle of the zip down far enough for us to see his face. His eyes were closed, and apart from some dried blood on his forehead, he looked peaceful enough

All eight of us – me, Pav, Danny, Chalky, Mart, Stringer, Phil and Jason – were shoulder to shoulder in a tight semi-circle, looking down. Nobody wanted to be the first to shovel earth in, to put him out of sight.

'Give him our thoughts for a minute,' I said gruffly. 'Say goodbye.'

Seconds ticked past. I was conscious of the sun growing hotter on the back of my neck, of bird calls and insect noises. I was grateful to Pav when he broke the silence.

'If it'd been one of us, he'd be praying,' he said. 'Let's pray for him now.'

'Yes,' I went. 'And save a thought for Whinger.' Then I added, 'The last thing Gen said, after he was hit, was, "To give light to them that sit in darkness, and in the shadow of death."'

'He would,' said Pav. 'And that's where he is now: in the shadow of death. RIP.'

That cracked Stringer up. I saw tears come into his eyes. I bent down, gave the pallid, freckled cheek a pat, and ran the zip of the black bag shut. Then I started lowering flat rocks into place above the body and shovelling like there was no tomorrow.

THIRTEEN

In retrospect, I can see we were crazy to carry on. We were all so shattered by exhaustion that our judgement was seriously flawed. We still had the .50 machine gun and nearly a thousand rounds of ammunition, as well as one RPG and a couple of dozen grenades, besides our personal weapons, but with our team down to seven men – eight including Jason – and only two vehicles, we were hardly an effective fighting unit, and certainly not strong enough to take on a major Kamangan force. We should have sat tight in our elevated LUP, waited until the incoming Herc was poised for a short last leg, and then gone out to find an LZ to mark with smoke grenades to guide the pilot in.

We did none of those things. Instead, we held an impromptu Chinese parliament in the shade of a leadwood tree and by a unanimous vote decided to head for Ichembo.

For me, the decision was easy. By then I was being driven by personal hatred of Muende and the German woman. I was rational enough to recognise this compulsion and see its dangers, but reason wasn't strong enough to prevent me trying to gain revenge for Whinger's death by topping both of them. After what they'd done, I'd have walked the length of the continent to get level with them, but after listening to Sam, I'd got it firmly in my head that the rebel leader would be leading the raid on the nuclear cache in person. Furthermore, having seen how he and Inge worked together, I felt certain she'd be coming with him. Therefore, if we reached Ichembo first, we'd have a good chance of ambushing the pair of them.

I was also needled by a dislike of failure. With our training task in ruins, and three of our lads dead, we'd got nothing to show for our month in Africa. It went against the grain to head for home with three lives lost and bugger all achieved. If, on the other hand, we managed to avert a nuclear showdown among such volatile states, we'd have a big plus to our credit. If we secured the weapons and topped Muende at the same time, all my goals would be achieved at once.

I was perfectly open with the rest of the guys. I told them exactly what I was thinking. Like me, they felt frustrated at the way the original task had collapsed under them, through no fault of their own; to have quit at that stage would have left a bad taste in their mouths. They also saw that immediate action was needed to secure the nuclear arsenal, and that to let it fall into Muende's hands would be criminally irresponsible.

Yet beyond these practical considerations there lay a different pressure. I didn't realise it at the time, but Pav told me later that from the moment I tumbled out of that little aircraft and collapsed on the deck, the rest of the team thought I'd changed. They felt I was somehow different: more ruthless than usual, almost fanatical. There were moments when they feared I'd lost the plot completely. They put it down to the experience I'd been through during the night, and luckily they were sympathetic. If they hadn't been basically on-side, they might have mutinied. I know, now, that at one stage, when my behaviour became too outrageous, they did discuss ganging up on me and putting me under open arrest, but because they felt nearly as bad about Whinger and Genesis as I did, team loyalty held everyone together.

When I say 'everyone', that included our new recruit, Jason. He was as loyal as anybody, but again, his reasons were different. Having thrown in his lot with us, he seemed determined to come with us wherever we went, to stick with us to the bitter end, whatever that might be, and then come back to the UK. 'I come work for you in England' became his constant refrain. He had no conception of the difficulties involved: immigration laws, work permits, the northern climate – all way beyond his ken. But none of that fazed him in the least, and as for us, because he'd saved all our lives, we felt bound to do our best for him, and we kidded him along with jokey enquiries as to how he'd deal with his family if he did leave Africa.

'How many wives have you got, Jason?' Danny asked once.

'Two, sir.'

'What about children?'

'No children.'

'What, none at all?'

'No sir.'

'How's that, then?'

'Woman's no good!' He flipped up a skeletal hand, as though throwing one of the useless creatures over his shoulder, and everybody laughed. The fact that he had no young family to support made the idea of him emigrating seem less far-fetched, but still none of us took it seriously.

Yet he was the one who finally tipped us over in the direction of carrying on. We'd held the usual discussion of pros and cons, reviewing our options, and when I went to sum up, I expected opinions to be evenly divided.

'So,' I began, 'we're okay for ammunition and food. Water – have to be careful, but we can manage. Fuel's the diciest. We've got enough to reach the area of the cache, but not much more. What we need is to hijack another vehicle without blowing it up, and nick its supply. We haven't the fuel to return to Mulongwe, and in any case, my guess is we'd be thoroughly bloody unwelcome there. The main problem is to find the nuclear site. I vote we carry on to Ichembo and grab somebody with local knowledge who can give us directions. What does everyone think?'

Phil, as always, was for pressing ahead. So were Pavarotti and, to a lesser extent, Stringer. Chalky, Danny and Mart were more cautious. But, as I say, it was Jason who swung the vote when he said quietly, 'I know Ichembo.'

'You know it!' went Pavarotti. 'How?'

'One brother-law, he come from that place. I visit his family there.'

'What is it?' I asked. 'A village?'

'No village – *boma.* Small town.'

'Can you find the way there?'

Jason nodded.

For a moment I felt seriously pissed off with him for not having divulged such vital information sooner. Again, it was out of habit of holding things back, but I didn't bollock him on it because I knew it was his nature to be self-effacing, and also because he was shy about his limited English, and didn't like speaking it more than he could help.

'Wait a minute,' I said. 'I've just thought of something. The Yank, Sam, said the place was outside the war zone. If we beat Muende to it, maybe we can just cruise in and get some legit fuel from a garage.'

Again, Jason nodded, and said, 'I think so.'

'That's it, then. Let's go.'

'What about the Kremlin?' Stringer asked. 'Shall we tell them what we're doing?'

'Not yet,' I told him. 'We'll find out the score first and tell them after.'

'Another suggestion,' said Chalky. 'Why not call your friend Back-hander and chat him up? If you went through to the embassy on the satcom, they might pull him across to talk to you. You could tell him Joss has flipped, and we're in the shit. He might believe it, coming from you. It might stop him swallowing whatever crap Joss has sent back through his own headquarters. He might even send his chopper to lift us out. After all, you and he were great buddies when he came to the ambush.'

'Yeah, well,' I went. 'It's an idea.' I remembered how we'd laughed when Bakunda had said, 'Some of these fellows are not long down from the trees.' Now I thought, too fucking right.

'*Good* idea, Chalky,' I said. 'Let's try it.'

When we punched in the number for the DA in Mulongwe, the call went through like clockwork. But the response was not what we'd hoped for: instead of a live human, we got a female voice on a tape honking, 'The British Embassy in Mulongwe is temporarily closed. Urgent calls should be redirected to the

British Embassy in Harare.' There followed a string of numbers, but I switched off in the middle of them.

'Cancel that one,' I told the lads. 'Like the Ops Officer said, they've broken off diplomatic relations. We're on our own in glorious Kamanga. We'd better shift our arses, because if what Sam said was right, we're in a race.'

Any race is easier to manage if you know what competition you're up against. If you can see the other runners, and watch how they're performing, you can at least pace yourself. But on that blazing hot morning we had only a hazy idea of what the enemy were up to. We believed that Muende was heading up with some sort of a force from the camp where I'd been held prisoner. Whether his South African mercenaries were still with him, or whether they'd formed a splinter group, we couldn't tell. What we knew for sure was that Joss and his Alpha Commando were somewhere behind us, to the east, probably following our tracks. Had *they* got wind of the weapons cache, and of Muende's new agenda? Again, we had no means of knowing. In the circumstances, all we could do was crack on as fast as possible.

Thanks to Jason, our move westwards went perfectly. How he navigated, I never quite made out. Riding in the front of the pinkie, with Pav driving, he never looked at the map, still less at a compass. His eyes were constantly sweeping the horizon, and every now and then he would glance up at the sun, as if to check his bearings. For the first hour he directed us through the bush, not on any road, but twisting and turning along one game trail after another. Then we came on to a sandy, overgrown track and followed that to the north at a good speed until we came to a T junction and joined an earth road leading east and west.

Half an hour westwards along that, and at last we saw signs of normal African life. After days without setting eyes on a civilian, it gave everyone a lift to find patches of cultivation and meet men and women walking along the road with bundles on their heads. When we stopped beside a little group and Jason made enquiries, the news was electrifying: the next village ahead possessed a borehole, and had plenty of fresh water. I was frantic to press ahead, but, whatever happened, we needed water, so I called a quick halt. The community was tiny – only twenty or thirty grass huts – but somehow it had been awarded a development grant, and there in the centre stood the borehole: a hand pump with a chute that ran water off into a galvanised metal tank, all under a conical grass roof set up high on wooden posts.

The moment we pulled up beside it, dusty, barefoot children began to assemble, struck speechless by the sight of these peculiar grey men caked in mud. Danny grabbed the pump handle and began to rock it back and forth. Up came a gush of water, cool and crystal-clear. Mart and Pavarotti started filling jerricans, but after days of mud, sand, grit and sweat, the sight of the clean water was too much for Phil, who ripped off his shirt and poured bowlfuls over his head. Stringer and Chalky followed his example. The spectacle of them furiously scrubbing away, and quickly turning white, sent the kids into paroxysms of delight.

Adults appeared from nowhere. One of them – elderly, tall and dignified - introduced himself as the head man of the village. Clearly he fancied a good exchange of news and a lengthy chat.

'Explain we're in a hurry,' I told Jason. 'And ask if he's heard anything about the war.'

As the two were talking I dug out a handful of boiled sweets and distributed them to the junior fans. The first little boy made to put the gift straight into his mouth, paper and all, and I had to show him how to unwrap it first.

'First time the poor little bugger's ever seen a thing like that,' I said to Phil. 'Eh, work the pump while I stick my head under the spout.'

By the time I'd given my head and neck a scrub, and sponged cautiously at the least sore parts of my face, Jason had established that the head man knew nothing about any fighting. He'd heard there was trouble away in the east, but that was all. The rumours hadn't been bad enough to make his people desert their homes.

We tried to get him to pin-point the position of his village, but the map meant nothing to him, and all he could confirm was that Ichembo was straight on in the direction we were pointing.

'Let's pay for the water,' said Pav, as we were about to roll.

The suggestion irritated me. 'Don't be ridiculous,' I told him. 'They're not expecting anything.'

'No, but Christ, look how poor they are.'

'Well . . .' I saw the sense of what he was saying, and felt ashamed of my own grudging attitude. From the general float, kept in the mother wagon, I dug out a ten-dollar bill and presented it to the head man, who held it up in front of his chest in both hands, beaming as if he'd got hold of a million dollars, and bowing his head repeatedly in thanks.

'He says he buy football for the boys,' Jason translated.

'Good, and thanks!' I smiled, shook the scrawny old hand, climbed back aboard, and off we went. We'd lost ten minutes, but gained a big lift in spirits and a supply of the best water we'd seen in Africa.

Until then, members of the party not driving or navigating had tried to get their heads down and catch up on lost sleep, but after the halt the tension was too great for anyone to relax. Not knowing what lay ahead, we were going to have to rely entirely on the speed and intelligence of our reactions: stealth, speed and surprise would have to be our weapons. There was no disguising that we were some form of army unit. Two military vehicles moving in convoy, the jeep with a .50 machine gun mounted on the back – what else could we be?

Another anxiety lay heavily on me. The rebel column advancing on course to meet us was one thing, but what was going on at Gutu? Had a relief force arrived and taken over the mine? If it had, what were Joss and his crew up to? Was Alpha Commando again moving southwards, according to their original plan? Or was the assassination squad still on our tail? Or had the South African mercenaries also found out about the nuclear stockpile, and diverted Joss's hunt towards Ichembo? We'd seen Joss having one of them shot, but had the three we chased off into the hills rejoined his force? Because we had no means of answering such questions, they were preying on my mind.

'This cache, or silo, or whatever,' I said to Pav as I drove the pinkie. The surface was fairly good, and we were doing thirty, so I had to pitch my voice loud. 'It can't be in the town, or anywhere near it. Not even the Russians would have been such cunts as to locate a nuclear dump in an inhabited area. There's the health hazard, for one thing. And then, quite separate, there's the question of security: people would have been walking into it all the time. No, it's got to be tucked away in some remote area that the locals don't have any reason to visit. Eh, Jason!'

The tracker leaned forward from his place in the back, and I explained my concept to him in short, shouted takes.

'As soon as we get to the edge of this town . . . we need to grab some guy . . . someone who looks sensible . . . find out if such an area exists.'

Jason's answer was 'Yassir.' He said that to almost all enquiries. But I was sure he'd got the point.

Ever since we'd come on to the east-west road the terrain had remained flat: kilometre after kilometre of featureless, fairly open bush, with dry, sandy ground showing between the vegetation. But then, through the haze far out to our right front, I began to make out higher ground – some kind of a plateau.

'Jason,' I called. 'Is Ichembo down on the flat, or up there in the hills?'

'Flat, flat,' he said emphatically, moving his open hand from side to side.

'So what's all that high ground?'

'Is called Meranga Plain.' Again he indicated level ground, but held his hand higher.

'Do people live up there?'

'No people. Ground bad for crop. Too much rock. No water.'

'So it's empty.'

'Yassir. Only army training.'

'A training area?'

'One time. Now left.'

'And is there a barracks in town?'

'One time,' Jason repeated. 'Many Russian soldiers here. Training army.'

'You mean the camp's closed now?'

'Yassir.'

Again I felt pissed off with our faithful tracker. Why the hell hadn't he said the magic words 'Russian' and 'training area' before? All the same, I felt the adrenalin rising.

'Hear that, Pav?' I went. 'That's where our stuff will be.'

'Yeah, yeah.' Pav's instincts had responded the same as mine. He was sitting up high and eyeballing the country all round for a possible landing strip.

'Listen,' I said. 'I just had an idea.'

'Like what?'

'About how news of this cache suddenly came to light. If the warheads have been lying around for a dozen years, the locals must have forgotten all about them. But someone else remembered. I bet I know who it is – some bloody Russian who's recently joined Muende's private army.'

'One of the mercenaries?'

'Exactly. Sam said something about there being Russkies in the mercenary team. It's a hundred to one there's a guy who served out here in the Soviet army, finished his tour in the forces and signed up with Interaction, just like the South Africans, the Yanks and all the others. And now they've sent him to Kamanga because he knows the place. '

'Possible.'

'More than that: it's bloody probable. And, of course, the trouble is, that guy will remember exactly where the stuff's stored.'

Pav continued eyeballing for a bit, then asked, 'You got a plan, Geordie?'

'We need to ID the site first. Then it'll depend on the strength of the opposition. If we find it, we'll defend it until we can call in the Herc and an NBC crew.'

'If, if, if,' went Pav.

'I know.'

In the last few minutes we'd started to meet pedestrians again, which made us think the town couldn't be far ahead. Then came a hoot from Chalky, driving the mother wagon behind us. Stringer, standing up through the turret of the cab, was pointing energetically to our right front. From his high position he'd seen something we couldn't. I slowed to a halt in a cloud of dust; no need to pull off the road, because we hadn't seen another vehicle all morning.

'What is it?'

'On top of that bank. There's a long open area that looks good for an LZ.'

'Not another flood pan?'

'Well, it could be one. But it's worth a shufti.'

Stringer was right. Parallel with the road was a strip of ground at least two hundred metres wide which ran on for several kilometres. It appeared to have been levelled by a flood at some stage. Only a few isolated tussocks of grass grew out of the sand, and the surface turned out to be extremely hard. After our experience at the Zebra Pans we were dead cautious about driving on to it, but the seven-ton mother wagon rolled smoothly along for half a kilometre, leaving scarcely a mark.

'This'll do,' I agreed. 'Get the coordinates, Mart. And Stringer, now we've stopped anyway, get through to the Kremlin. First, though, let's get under those trees, just in case Muende has got his precious chopper airborne and does a fly-past.'

The time was 1125 local – 0925 in Hereford. Because we'd been stirring the shit internationally, I guessed the bigwigs would already be at their desks. As Stringer set up the satcom dish, and I took another look at our one surviving map, Jason came across from the roadside, where he'd quizzed a passer-by, to announce, 'Ichembo, one hour.'

'One hour walking?'

'Yassir.'

'Five or six ks, then.'

I was right about the Kremlin. Everyone there was buzzing and bobbing like the shithouse fly. But the good news was they'd got their fingers out, and a Herc with crew equipped to handle NBC material was already on the ground at a military airfield just inside the border of Namibia.

'Brilliant!' I told Dave Alton, the Ops Officer. 'We're a bit north of that, but it can't be more than two hundred ks – less than an hour's flying time.' I gave him the coordinates of the LZ, and a brief description of the area. 'We're calling the feature the Mall,' I said. 'It's that flat and straight.'

'What about hazards?' he asked. 'Hills? Power-lines?'

'Nothing. No hill more than a couple of hundred feet within miles, and as for electricity, there ain't none in this part of Africa. Listen, you don't have any info on the cache site?'

'Nothing's come up yet. We're still trying, but we doubt there's any record.'

'Roger. We think we've got the area pin-pointed, and we're about to start a CTR.'

'Good work. What have you done with Genesis?'

'Buried him. I hope it's only for the time being. We're planning to go back for him if we get a chance.'

'Roger.'

We agreed to open up the satcom link for five minutes every hour, on the hour. Then we shut down.

'Why not call the Herc in now and fuck off out of it while we've got the chance?' Danny suggested.

'*You* can, if you like,' I told him. 'Personally, I'm staying to sort that bastard Muende.' I didn't mean to sound anti-Danny, but that was how the remark came out, and I saw him looking a bit pained. 'Nothing personal, mate,' I added. 'But you weren't there when he had Whinger butchered. You didn't see what a barbarous fucking ape he is.'

By 1150 we were on the move again, with the pinkie leading, and soon the outskirts of Ichembo came into view – the usual string of shacks made from corrugated iron, cardboard, packing cases, pallets and so on. Also in view, and clearer now, was the low escarpment to our right, where the land ran up to the plateau Jason had described.

'Eh!' exclaimed Pavarotti suddenly. 'Look at this: the bloody barracks.'

On our right ran the remains of a two-metre chain-link fence. Stretches of wire had been taken down and carried off, and holes cut in the parts that remained. Inside the perimeter lay the wreck of a barracks, long, low huts with doors and windows ripped out, roofs collapsing. Around them was a flat, weedy wilderness of former drill squares and vehicle parks. Under the glare of the sun everything looked baked and dusty and dead.

With minimal warning to Chalky, who was driving behind, Pav swung the pinkie right-handed through one of the gaps in the fence and headed straight across an old parade ground.

'Stands to reason!' he shouted. 'There must be access from this place, straight out on to the training area at the back.'

In less than two minutes his hunch proved correct. The rear fence had scarcely been vandalised, and a pair of exit gates was still closed by a rusty padlock and chain. Rather than alert the neighbourhood with an explosion, we chopped through the chain with bolt shears and hauled the gates open, squealing on their hinges. Beyond them a dirt road went up through a cutting, between walls of grey-brown sandy rock. From the weeds that had sprung up on the track, we could see it hadn't been used in years.

'Jesus!' I shouted to Pav. 'This is it! We've hacked it!'

The little canyon was no more than a hundred metres long, and towards the top our expectations rose even higher when we found the road blocked by a sagging wooden pole, painted pale blue and bound with barbed wire. A metal notice which had once hung on it had fallen off and lay face-down in the dust. I jumped out, picked it up and turned it over. Half the writing had gone, but the red letters that remained were in Cyrillic script.

'Stringer!' I yelled, holding the sign up. 'What does this say?'

'No entry,' he translated. 'Danger. Keep out.'

'Shit hot!' went Pav. 'We're closing in.'

Again there was no need for a demolition charge. The posts supporting the barrier were made of wood, which had been eaten away to a skeleton by termites. One push from the front of the pinkie and both snapped off in puffs of dust. We crunched over the remains of the barrier and motored to the top of the bank. A wilderness of withered shrubs and knee-high dead grass stretched off into the distance. The plateau had a blasted, lifeless, desolate look.

By then everyone was well hyped-up, but Pav was cool enough to look behind us and see that, from this higher ground, there was a long view out over the town. Even better, through the heat haze, we could see a road coming up from the south to join the one we'd just left. The junction was seven or eight hundred metres from where we were standing.

'Let's split in two,' Pav suggested, pointing at the southern road. 'If Muende comes, that'll be his route. We can OP it from here and keep the rest of you informed while you recce ahead.'

'Right,' I agreed. 'Better cam up, just in case.'

Pav backed the mother wagon between two tall patches of shrubs, aligning it so that the crew could watch both our own track and the southern approach road from the cab. Stringer, Danny and I left them slinging cam nets from the bushes, and drove on into the wilderness.

For the first few minutes I remained on a high. The place obviously had been used as a training area. Rusting sheets of metal riddled with bullet holes lay around. Roofless concrete-block buildings, without doors or windows, had been assaulted time and again. A pistol range had been excavated from a high sandbank. All this was encouraging, and I felt we were hot on the scent.

Then I began to realise how large the area was. The further we went, the more uneven the terrain became. Low hills restricted our view. We seemed to be driving along the main drag, but branch roads ran off to left and right, disappearing into the wastes of rock and dead grass. Black-and-white painted wooden signpost arms had once pointed to various outlying destinations, but now they had either fallen down or lost their lettering, and they gave no indication of where all the side tracks led.

After five minutes, and about five kilometress, I went on the radio to Pav, and said, 'This place is fucking enormous.'

'Yeah, well,' he went. 'It's not surprising. One thing the bastards aren't short of is space.'

'I reckon it runs out into the desert and goes halfway to bloody Namibia. There's tracks leading off in every direction. Wait one, what's this?'

Stringer was pointing to our left. Below us in the distance, carved out of the face of a low hill, was a semi-circle of what looked like bunkers: pairs of corrugated iron doors, about fifty metres apart, faced on to a wide-open flat area the size of a football field.

'This looks better,' I told Pav. 'Something like an ammunition storage area. This could be it. Stand by while we recce it.'

'Roger.'

With my pulse speeding up I drove down the access track and on across the open ground to the right-hand pair of doors. Each of them was about ten feet square, an entrance high enough and wide enough for large trucks to drive in. Most of the pale-green paint had peeled off the metal, and patches of rust were eating away at it.

As soon as we drew up alongside, my excitement started to wane. The doors were mounted on rollers and held together by nothing more formidable than one big hasp. There was a ring which would have taken a heavy padlock, but no lock in place. It took a big heave from Danny and me, pulling in unison, to shift one of the doors along its track. Metal rollers squeaked and groaned as we forced it open half a metre. Inside, the heat was phenomenal.

'Torch,' I called to Stringer, and he flipped me one from the vehicle.

The beam reached out into a cavernous interior, with a curved roof of concrete sections which came down almost to ground level on either side. The shelter certainly looked as though it had been used to store ammunition, but now it contained not a thing.

'Drawn blank at the first one,' I reported to Pav.

'What was there in it?'

'Two thirds of three fifths of fuck all.'

'Try the others, then. How many are there?'

'Six. Will do. Nothing moving on the road?'

'Negative.'

We kept trying, with equal lack of success. Stringer drove the pinkie slowly forward across the front of the complex as we forced open one set of doors after another. We'd just reached the fifth when Pav suddenly came on the air with, 'Stand by. There's a heli approaching.'

'A heli! Jesus, where is it?'

'Coming up from the south, along the line of the road. It's going to miss us, but I'd say it's heading your way.'

'Roger. How far out is it?'

'Three ks max. You've got about a minute.'

'Roger.' I looked quickly round. There were no big trees to provide us with cover.

'Inside!' said Stringer.

Without another word all three of us put our shoulders to the door and forced it open wider. The rollers ground and groaned, but the gap was just big enough. Danny leapt back into the driving seat, reversed, lined up the pinkie and crawled it in. But could we close the door again? We pulled like lunatics, but the rollers, jammed with rust and sand and sundry shit, wouldn't move.

We stood in the doorway, gasping from the effort. It was too late to do a runner. We were trapped. We could already hear the distant scream of a turbine. By the sound, the chopper was very low. We held our breath as the noise swelled to a roar and the thudding beat of a rotor buffeted the air. If the aircraft passed in front of the store sheds, the crew was bound to see the pinkie; if it passed behind the hill into which the bunkers were dug, they'd probably miss us. For a few seconds we waited breathlessly, weapons at the ready. Then, suddenly, the storm of noise was diminishing, and I knew we were safe for the time being.

I ran out into the sunlight and just got a glimpse of the

aircraft, big and heavy and painted dun grey, as it disappeared over the horizon. A moment later it reappeared in the distance, turning right-handed. Instinctively I ducked, but then I realised that, with the heli banked towards us, the crew couldn't see in my direction. As I straightened up, it went in to land, somewhere beyond the skyline, and the scream died away as the pilot cut his engines.

'It's landed,' I told Pav. 'Did you get a proper look at it?'

'It's a Hind. There was a guy sat in the open door with a gympi, but that was all I could make out.'

'It's got to be a recce,' I said. 'I bet Muende's on board. He's come to check out the site. I'm bloody sure of it. I'm going after him.'

'Eh, Geordie!' said Pav, sharply. 'Chill out!'

'What d'you mean?'

'You sound as if you've gone all hyper. Take it easy. Don't tangle with that machine-gunner, or we'll not see you again.'

I didn't reply to that, but I demanded of Stringer, 'What's he on about?'

'He's right,' said Stringer, coolly. 'You're letting it get to you.'

All at once I was angry: angry with Pav, angry with Stringer – who was a dozen years younger than me, for Christ's sake – angry with the whole situation. I had a sharp ache in the back of my head. I glared at my companions, trying to fight down feelings of rage and frustration.

'All right,' I said savagely. 'What do we do, then? Just let them fuck off with their loot?'

'No,' went Stringer. 'I've had an idea.' He pointed back along the semi-circle of doors, and said, 'Look at those.' He was indicating the pinkie's tracks, which showed up like a dog's bollocks, freshly printed in the dust and sand. 'If the heli takes off in the same direction it landed, and swings back low towards its original course, there's a bloody good chance the crew will see our wheel-marks. If they do, they'll wonder who the hell's got in here. There's no way they can leave without investigating.'

'So we'd better shift our arses out of it?'

'Yes, but bait the trap. Leave the pinkie inside, so there's only one set of wheel-marks. None leading away. That'll screw them. Deploy with our weapons into the scrub opposite. Then, if the heli lands out there in the open, we can whack the crew from behind when they get out to see what's happening.'

'Stringer,' I went. 'Your name should be Einstein. Fucking brilliant!'

My anger evaporated as we shifted the pinkie to one side of the shed, away from the line of the open door, grabbed our weapons and belt-kits, and put through another call to Pav, explaining our plan.

'We'll be off the air while we're away from the vehicle,' I told him. 'Call you as soon as we're back. Wait out.'

We scuttled out across the open area and took up firing positions on the edge of the dunes, well concealed under swathes of long grass, seventy metres from the door, only thirty or forty from where the chopper was likely to land.

We didn't have long to wait. I'd just looked at my watch and seen that it was after midday. We should be calling Hereford. Then we heard the heli's engines start up. The roar deepened as the aircraft took off, and we could tell by the change in the note that it had turned in our direction. We'd loaded grenades into our 203s, but I'd told the others not to smack the chopper unless it looked like getting away from us. My aim was to make sure of Muende, if he was on board, and, if he wasn't, to grab the crew and find out what the plot was.

By the noise, the heli pilot was aiming to pass behind us, very low. Twisting my stiff neck to the right, I peered through the grass and saw the aircraft skimming the dunes. Shit, I thought. He's too low to see the wheel-marks. He's going to miss them.' For a few bad seconds, I thought he had. Then the engine scream changed note and stopped moving. The thudding beat of the rotor increased. The pilot was hovering. The crew must have seen the fresh tracks in the dirt on the road.

Now they were coming back. I had a momentary panic that they'd fly right over our heads, and the downdraught from the rotor would expose us by blowing away our grass camouflage. With my left hand I gathered a bunch of long, dry stems and pulled them down over my back, holding them in place. In fact, the pilot was following the trail we'd laid. He flew back above the road, turned over the side-track, heading for the first of the bunkers, then swung towards us along the front of the complex and went into a hover directly between us and the open door. Never had I had a more tempting target in my sights: one grenade into the flight-deck – curtains.

Sand and dust boiled up in dense clouds as the Hind settled in to land. It was all that airborne shit that gave us our chance. If the ground had been clean, I'm sure the pilot would have kept his engines turning and burning for a rapid take-off. As it was, he obviously didn't want all that rubbish sucked into his intakes, and he shut down.

'Danny,' I said.

'Aye.'

'Stringer and me will deal with anyone who gets out. The pilot's your business. I don't want him dead or hurt. Just under control. Okay?'

'Fine. I'll sort him.'

The rotor blades drooped as they swung slower and slower, gradually winding down. The dust cloud began to disperse. Through it we saw movement, figures emerging from the belly of the aircraft. Moments later four of them were walking towards the open door. I was amazed that they didn't make any attempt at a tactical approach. I expected two or three to go down and cover the others as they went for the door, but no. They were so far from any battle zone they just weren't expecting trouble. Maybe they thought some crazy farmer had been using the bunker to store maize. Whatever main weapons they had, they'd left them in the chopper, and were armed only with holstered pistols. In any case, they moved as a loose bunch, two blacks and two whites, all bare-headed, all in DPMs bar the taller white who was wearing a light-blue overall. I didn't need binos to tell me that neither of the blacks was Muende. Both were youngish guys with short black hair, walking springily, far darker and slimmer than the rotund rebel leader.

Everything had happened so fast that I'd made no plan for dealing with this party. But by then my blood was up. Four was too many for us. We needed to thin them out. I guessed that the whites were mercenaries, the guys with expert knowledge, the blacks just guides or liaison officers. Whoever they were, we couldn't afford to have any of them reach the open shed and see the pinkie.

'Drop the silveries,' I whispered to Stringer. 'You take the right. I'll take the left. Ready? Now!'

Our two short bursts were intermingled. The blacks were cut down like blades of grass, flat on their faces, and hardly moved. The whites leapt in the air as if they'd been electrified and came down facing different ways. But they were temporarily bemused. Echoes or ricochets made them think the shots had come from the bunker, ahead of them. Instead of pressing on towards it, they turned and ran for the helicopter, straight towards us.

I aimed into the ground between them and put another burst just ahead. The rounds ripped up puffs of sand and dust. At the same moment, I roared, '*Stop! On the deck!*'

I don't know whether they went down voluntarily, or tripped. Either way, both dropped, and before they could collect their wits Stringer and I were on top of them.

'Hands behind your back!' I yelled. 'Nobody move!'

I stood over them with my 203 and fired another burst into the ground less than a metre from their heads. Dust erupted and hung in the air. I kept the weapon levelled while Stringer bound their wrists with para cord. A glance at the helicopter reassured me that Danny had the measure of the pilot. Then we relieved the two of their pistols and got them on their feet.

I recognised one immediately: it was the fat, fair-haired South African who'd stood in the background while Inge had ripped the skin off Whinger's face. When he saw me, he must have nearly shat himself. His mouth fell open and he gave a kind of croak. I could see him trying to work out how in hell I'd got to this place ahead of him. I blasted him with a look and concentrated on the other. In a flash I realised this guy must be Russian: a tall man, dark-haired, with a prominent forehead, hollow cheeks and sunken, pale blue eyes that made me think of the mad monk Rasputin, minus the beard. My adrenalin was already well up, but it ran even faster when I realised what the tall man was wearing: some form of NBC suit. No wonder sweat was running down his lean face and neck.

I went closer to him, and said, 'Russki?'

He looked amazed, as well as shit-scared, but he nodded.

'Great!' I went. 'You speak English?'

'A little.'

'Right. Where's General Muende?'

The guy looked blank.

'The rebel leader. Commander of the Afundis.'

The black eyes moved slightly. He'd understood the question, but he wasn't planning to answer.

'How about you, shitface?' I went up close to the South African and jabbed his bulging gut with the muzzle of my 203. 'Feel like answering a few questions?'

'*Vokken soutie.*' As he spat the words out, giving me a blast of dead-man's breath, his yellow eyes flickered back and forth.

'Listen,' I told him. 'I haven't got time to trade insults with a pig. We're going back on board your chopper. Your pilot will then fly us back to the stockpile of warheads. Understood?'

Again the guy didn't answer, but again I saw that flicker of comprehension.

'Get moving.' I jerked the muzzle of my rifle in the direction of the heli.

The South African shot his mate a look. I could see he was calculating his chances if he lunged at me with a head butt.

'Don't try anything,' I warned him. Suddenly, I put a three-round burst past him within inches of his right cheek. The noise and blast made him flinch, but he stood his ground: a hard case. 'Any trouble,' I told him, 'I'll make the sun shine through you. Now go!'

He turned and began to walk to the chopper. The Russian fell in behind him. As we came round the starboard side of the body,

I saw a 7.62 gympi mounted on an extended arm. Danny was standing behind the pilot, another white, on the flight-deck.

'Okay, Danny?' I called.

'No problem, except that this guy doesn't speak any known language.'

'Of course he does. To be a pilot, he must do. Another bloody Russian, for sure.'

I helped Stringer tether our prisoners to safety rings in the heli, well apart from each other, then told him, 'Keep an eye on them while I stir up Biggles.'

I nipped up the two steps to the flight-deck and sat in the co-pilot's seat. I could see at once the pilot was another Russian. He reminded me of Sasha, the great guy who'd got us out of trouble when the Kremlin mission went to ratshit. He had brown hair and a flat, wide face. He even had a couple of grey metal false teeth, one up, one down, in much the same places.

'I got this off him,' said Danny, handing me another pistol.

'Thanks.'

I slipped it into the thigh pocket of my DPMs, where it made a heavy bulge along with the others. Then I waded into the pilot.

'Don't fuck about,' I told him. 'Just start up and take off.'

With the barrel of Danny's 203 below his ear, he was already looking like a beaten spaniel. Now he spread his hands, and said miserably, 'No fuel.'

'Of course you've got fuel. You were airborne just now, no problem then.'

He shrugged, leant forward and flicked a couple of switches, lighting up the instrument panel. He jabbed a finger at the dials. The lettering was Cyrillic, but after our Russian task I could read basic words. The fuel gauges were showing about a third – plenty for a short trip.

'Your fuel state's fine,' I shouted. 'Get going!'

He stared at me as if I was mad – and probably, at that moment, I was a bit mad. I think stress and anger had sent me temporarily off the rails. The pilot seemed to sense it; he appeared to realise that no good would come of trying to resist me. He shrugged, and said, 'Maybe we crash.'

'Maybe we do,' I told him. 'I couldn't give a monkey's.'

'Where to?'

'Back to where you've just been.'

Again he made a hopeless gesture. 'Today we are in many places.'

'The weapons store.'

This time he tapped his head. I glanced back into the body of the chopper.

Stringer was crouched beside the open door, covering the two others.

'Listen,' I said, as menacingly as I could. 'If you want to stay alive, get moving. And don't try to pull any phoney malfunctions shit on me.'

'Okay'. He shrugged again, and went into his start-up routine.

'Danny,' I went. 'Stringer and me can handle this. Hop out. Get on the inter-vehicle radio. Call up Pav. Tell him we're hijacking the heli to find the cache. Ask him to bring the mother wagon forward and RV with you here.'

'Roger. What'll you do?'

'Depends on what we find.'

FOURTEEN

The heli's turbines fired. The pilot let the engines warm up for half a minute, then engaged the rotor, increased revs, put on pitch and lifted away. Below us, dust boiled out to fill the football field.

Back in the cabin, I buckled myself into a safety harness on a long tether. Next, ostentatiously, I threw all three pistols out through the open door, one by one. Looking quickly round, I saw two sub-machine guns in clips on the bulkhead, and hurled them out as well. Then I went close up in front of the fat Afrikaaner, and shouted, 'Tell him to go back to the cache!'

My only answer was a bear-like glare. A glance through the door told me we were heading out over the line of bunkers. The pilot was deliberately going the wrong way. I waited a minute, letting the aircraft gain height. Then, without another word, I jumped across the cabin, whipped out my knife, cut the South African free from the shackle and propelled him physically towards the open door.

As soon as he saw what I was planning, he began to struggle and bellow obscenities, half in English, half in Afrikaans. '*Jou moer!*' he shouted. 'You shit!' And then, '*Vokken soutpiel!*' He was a big guy, and heavy with it, but I was so fired up that I held him like a child, standing behind him in the middle of the gap, with his bristly, bull neck in front of my face.

'I'll count three!' I yelled. 'If you don't give the pilot an order, you go out. One!'

He tried to zap me again, this time whipping his shaven head backwards in the hope of catching me in the face, but I'd anticipated the move and leant away to my right, out of his range.

'Talk, cunt!' I yelled, punching him in the back of his meaty ribs. 'It's your last chance. Two!'

I left a gap of two or three seconds, then shouted, 'Three!'

At the same instant I gave his shoulders a violent shove and kneed him in the small of the back. His hands were still well tied behind him, but somehow he managed to grab hold of my DPMs around my right knee. By then his weight was carrying him out and down, already he was falling, but his grip was so desperate that he dragged me out with him. The next I knew, I was dangling face-down in mid-air on the end of the tether, with the South African below me, also face-down, clinging like a lead weight to my right knee, and the slipstream tearing past.

The guy was screaming like a lunatic. So was I, because I felt like I was being torn in half, with the tether heaving at its anchor-point high on the back of my waist, and a two-hundred-pound burden dragging at my leg. I had a moment of panic that the combined weight was going to snap the nylon strop or drag it from its moorings.

There was no way I could reach down with my hands to unlock those desperate fingers. With a terrific effort I brought up my free left foot, and stamped at the guy's shoulder. He must have been strong as a gorilla. I caught him a savage kick, but still he hung on. *Stamp!* I went. *Stamp! Stamp!* At last, by luck, my heel caught him on the base of the neck: his grip dissolved and he dropped away towards the ground. With his hands still tied behind him, he immediately went unstable. His screams faded as he tumbled head over heels, hurtling downwards.

I'd hardly had time to feel scared. All the same, it was a fantastic relief to be rid of the weight. I felt jerks coming down the tether. The slipstream was so ferocious that my eyes were streaming. Twisting round, I had a blurred vision of Stringer crouched at the side of the open door, hauling me up, a foot at a time. We seemed to be travelling at a phenomenal speed. The air pressure was horrendous, and I was swinging around like a leaf in the wind.

'Tell the pilot to slow down!' I roared.

Stringer cupped a hand to his ear, showing he couldn't hear.

I bellowed the same thing again. That time he nodded his head.

At last I came within reach of the doorway, grabbed the sill, dragged myself back on to the metal floor and lay there like a stranded fish.

'Why's he going so fucking fast?' I gasped.

'I told him to hover, but he did the opposite.'

'Lucky we need the bastard to fly this thing. Otherwise he'd be next.'

By then we were at least five hundred feet up. Unless by a miracle the South African had landed in a springy tree – and there wasn't a tree in sight – he stood no chance. I had a vision of his gut bursting like a ripe melon as he hit the deck, and derived a moment's satisfaction from it. Whinger, I thought, I've got our own back on one of them.

'Your turn next!' I yelled at the Rasputin character. 'Fucking *talk*!'

I cut him free and started wrestling him towards the doorway. He seemed to be paralysed by terror and didn't resist at all.

Then I happened to glance at Stringer. The look on his face was so awful – horror mixed with disbelief – that it stopped me half-way across the cabin. It came home to me that I'd just committed a cold-blooded murder. I hesitated for a couple of seconds, then decided I couldn't give a damn. The man I'd pushed out had stood by and seen Whinger killed, and was as guilty as anyone else.

I pulled Rasputin back into the centre of the cabin and tied him to a shackle again. He began screaming hysterically in Russian. In spite of the racket, the pilot heard him and put the heli into a hard turn to starboard. I had the impression we'd already flown halfway to Namibia, but in fact we were only a few kilometres off course, and in a minute or two we were back over the main drag of the training area. Another minute brought us over a major junction, with six earth roads radiating off it to all points of the compass.

Rasputin was shouting something at me.

'Say again.'

'Number twenty-one. You need road number twenty-one.'

'Okay. Is this it?'

He nodded. The pilot had gone down low and was flying up a narrow valley, almost a ravine, with big grey boulders sticking out of the dead grass on either side. After two more minutes he turned his head and shouted something over his shoulder.

'Here the site,' Rasputin translated.

'Tell him to land.'

We made one left-handed circuit, which gave us a good view of the valley-end through the open door: a natural cul-de-sac with walls maybe a hundred feet high enclosing a large, circular area of level ground. From the air it was obvious that the site had been shaped artificially: the ground had been bulldozed flat, and the bank at the northern end of the ravine had been cut or blasted off to form a vertical wall, in the middle of which was a big doorway.

We touched down gently in the inevitable cloud of dust. I motioned to the pilot to switch off. He made his gesture of futility, meaning he didn't have enough fuel for repeated start-ups. What he was thinking, I could see, was that if I got out to check things on the ground, he'd do a quick take-off.

'*Off!*' I bellowed, reinforcing the command with a thrust of my 203 towards the back of his neck. Reluctantly, he obeyed. As the noise died away, I said to Rasputin, 'All right. What have we got here?'

This time there was no pissing about. 'Medium-range warheads,' he replied. 'For small rocket.'

'What state are they in?'

'Bad. Already dangerous. You should wear clothes.' He pushed up his right shoulder, as if offering to take off his protective suit and hand it over. I waved the offer off. No way was I going to untie him.

'I'll just take a look,' I said. 'You have keys?'

This time he stuck out his right hip, and I found two keys on a ring in his overall pocket.

'I'll do a quick recce,' I told Stringer.

'For Christ's sake be careful.'

'Don't worry. And if the pilot goes to start up without me, whack him.'

The padlock on the door was new and shiny. I guessed Rasputin had brought it with him and put it in place as he was leaving. Yes, there on the ground was an old one, forced open somehow.

This installation was far more solid than the one we'd looked at before, but, bar the new lock, everything was in a state of advanced decay: the heavy metal frame of the doorway was rusted, the concrete-block wall surrounding it cracked and pitted. The outer cladding of the double-skinned, corrugated-iron doors had rusted right through in places.

All that remained of a warning notice-board was the ghost of a skull and crossbones on a sheet of tin which had fallen to the ground.

The doors were too heavy to slide. They swung outwards from the centre, each on a broad metal wheel which ran along a curved rail. Somebody, presumably Rasputin, had already scraped most of the accumulated sand out of the first couple of metres of the track; I cleared the rest with the toe of my boot, and then with a big heave got the right-hand door open enough to slip through the gap.

Inside, I immediately became aware of a sharp, acidic smell. At first I could see nothing. Then, at the furthest reach of the torch beam, something light-coloured showed up. A few steps forward, and I made out pointed white nose-cones facing towards me.

A shiver went down my back. Shells about six inches in diameter had been stored on heavy-duty wooden shelves, a honeycomb with partitions like a giant wine rack. The top shelf was half empty and carried only five, but the other four shelves were full: forty-five missiles in all. At the right-hand end of the stack some of the lower woodwork had collapsed, so that all the rows were tilted, on a slope, and the missiles in the bottom corner had been forced down into a tight-packed heap. Even from a distance I could see that liquid of some kind had seeped out of one or more of them and had crystallised on the casings.

I stood and stared at them, holding my breath, hoping that would protect me from the worst of the radiation. The points of the warheads were within fifteen feet of me.

I backed out, hauled the door shut behind me and turned the key in the lock. My mind was moving at speed. I assumed Rasputin, or the South African, had radioed news of the cache back to base the moment they'd checked it, and that Muende's snatch party was already well on its way. Back in the chopper, I greeted Stringer with a non-committal 'okay' and said to Rasputin, as a matter of fact, 'Muende's force is coming to pick these things up.'

He nodded.

'When?'

'They are coming now.'

'What time will they arrive?'

'One hour, two hour.' He pointed at his wrist, with circling movements of his forefinger.

'Is Muende with them?'

Rasputin shook his head.

'What's he doing, then?'

'He goes to other place.'

'What about the white woman?'

'She goes with him.'

'So neither of them's in the convoy?'

'*Nyet.*'

I took a deep breath. They must have gone looking for the diamond. I felt a stab of disappointment. I'd really been hoping to clobber the pair of them. Too bad. Sod the diamond. That was only a personal vendetta. We were on to something bigger now. We'd committed ourselves to the nuclear snatch and had to go through with it.

'Start up,' I told the pilot.

The guy seemed to have run out of arguments; this time he went through his checks without protest, and only when he had the engines running did he ask where he was to go.

'Back to the place you found us.'

The flight lasted no more than two or three minutes. Throughout the short transit Stringer stared at me as though I was lit up by radioactivity. All I could manage in return was a sickly grin. Was I feeling ill already, or was it my imagination? I had a headache, for sure, but I'd had that ever since I could remember. Also, I had that leaden feeling brought on by prolonged loss of sleep. But was this lethargy something worse than mere exhaustion? Don't be stupid, I kept telling myself. Even if you are contaminated, you wouldn't be feeling the effects yet.

Morale lifted when I saw our two vehicles side by side on what we'd called the football field. Pav had done his stuff and brought the mother wagon forward, and Danny had driven the pinkie out beside it. Someone had dragged the two black bodies out of sight.

'Over there!' I shouted to the pilot, pointing at the far end of the open space. He put down in the usual cloud of dust.

As the rotor slowed, I told Stringer to stay put, jumped out and ran across to the mother wagon. There, perched on the passenger's side of the bench seat, was Jason. In the general panic I'd forgotten all about him.

'Mabonzo!' I went. 'What the hell are you doing there?'

'I come with you, sir. I help.'

'Don't be ridiculous. Get out! It's far too fucking dangerous. You'd risk getting contaminated.'

'I have medicine.' He gave a slow smile and patted the breast pocket of his DPMs. 'Medicine make me safe.'

'No!' I told him. 'You don't understand. Radiation can kill you. You can't see it, but still it can kill you.'

'I know,' he said calmly. 'We have lecture on atomicals. Sir take medicine.'

He was holding something out in his long, thin fingers. Abruptly I felt on the verge of tears, choked by this man's loyalty, his determination to stick with me. Jesus, I thought, never mind the warheads, it's me who's going unstable. I took the offering – a small, grey, rough-cut block the size of one square of chocolate. What if it's hyena shit? I thought. But I put it in my mouth and took a gulp of water to wash it down. For a second I had a sharp, bitter taste, and then it was gone.

'Thanks,' I said. 'You'd better come as co-driver and security, on the basis you don't go into the silo, and don't try to touch the warheads. All right?'

Jason nodded, again giving that secret smile. There was something about his unshakeable confidence that bolstered my morale. Even if his imperturbability was based on ignorance, it was still reassuring. I felt that, whatever happened, he would never panic.

I noticed a few odd looks as I joined the rest of the team. There was evidently something about my appearance that spooked them. But I ignored it, and said, 'Right. We're going for the weapons.'

'Who's going?' Pav demanded.

'Me and Jason. We've captured two Russians. We'll take them with us and make them do the loading. I'll keep one tied up while the other works.'

'*What?*' Pav spoke for all the lads when he yelled. 'You're fucking mad!'

'Don't touch that stuff!' said Phil. 'Geordie, you'll kill yourself. No kidding. Blow the dump up. Booby-trap the doors. Let the villains blow it up. Anything but go back in there.'

'What?' I said. 'And let loose a bloody great cloud of nuclear fall-out over half of southern Africa? Forget it, lads. Anyway, I'm not going to touch it. Rasputin's going to handle the warheads. Him and his pilot.'

There must have been something about my manner that cut argument short. Normally, if one of us had made a proposition as outrageous as that, the rest would have ganged up on him and suppressed the idea. For a brief moment I thought Pav was going to come at me physically, but I think he saw that if he did, I'd put him on the deck, and he checked himself.

Everybody was staring at me. I glared back at them.

'The plan is this,' I said. 'The Herc's due overhead the Mall at 1430 our time. We drive the mother wagon from here to the dump now, load it as fast as possible, bring it out and head for the Mall. The rest of you go back on the pinkie. Get on the OP and position the vehicle so you can cover the road junction with the .50. Get the best protection you can. If Muende's convoy appears, you've got to hold it up at least until the Herc's on the deck and loading. Then break, belt for the Mall, jettison the vehicle and get aboard the aircraft. Any questions?'

'Comms,' said Chalky.

'We'll keep the vehicle link open. You'll have the satcom. You'll need to keep Hereford briefed on progress. Get a frequency for the Herc and talk to the pilot.'

I looked round, and asked, 'Anything else?', but everybody seemed to have been struck dumb. 'Okay, then,' I said. 'Let's raise the Kremlin on the satcom.'

The call went through without a hitch.

'We found the stuff,' I told the Ops Officer. 'Forty-five warheads.'

'Christ! How big?'

'Six-inch diameter. Six feet long.'

'Weight?'

'About seventy-five pounds, something like that.'

There was a short pause. Evidently he was doing calculations. 'Under two tons in all, then,' he went. 'Okay. The Herc's standing by.'

'Does it have permission to land?'

'Negative. It's coming anyway.'

'What's its estimated flying time?'

'One hour twenty to an LZ overhead at Ichembo.'

'In that case, it wants to take off soonest.'

'Where's your present location?'

'Just north of the town. But listen. The cache is in an old training area. There's nowhere to land round here. The terrain's very uneven, all low hills and re-entrants. We're going to bus the stuff out to the LZ we gave you. The Mall. Okay?'

'Yeah, yeah. I have that.' He read off the coordinates we'd passed him. 'But wait a minute. You can't handle stuff like that without protective clothing.'

'It's okay,' I lied. 'We've nicked some gear off the Russian mercenaries who came out on a recce.'

'You sure? Can't you wait till the Herc comes in? They've got spare suits for all you guys on board.'

'Not a chance. There's a rebel column on its way up from the south to grab the warheads. If we hang around here, the odds are we'll get into a big fire-fight. It's touch and go whether we can swag the stuff away quick enough as it is. We haven't the fire-power to hold anyone off for long.'

'Well, it's your decision. What are your timings?'

'Half an hour to load. Half an hour to drive back to the Mall. One hour from now, we'll be on the LZ.'

'Roger. I'll pass that to the captain of the aircraft. Have you marked the strip?'

'Not yet. We'll need to get some smoke going. The strip runs east and west, and we'll have smoke going at both ends. Wind state zero. Ground temperature around thirty-six. Wait one.' I did another calculation in my head, and added, 'Better allow another twenty minutes. Make it ninety minutes from now to the LZ overhead.'

'Roger. I confirm ninety minutes. And take it easy.'

Dave Alton was a sound enough guy, but the poor bugger could have no idea of the true situation. I expect he had visions of our lads lining up on the edge of the runway, all nice and clean, like a rugby team before kick-off, to receive their poncy new NBC suits from the head loadie before they tackled the cache all together and drove in convoy to the Mall.

I switched off the set and looked round the anxious faces. 'That's it, then,' I said.

'What about the chopper?' Phil asked.

'Torch it.'

'What, now?'

'Why not? White phos into the cockpit.'

Phil wasn't the man to miss an opportunity like that. He dived into the back of the mother wagon, came out with a white phosphorus grenade, ran the fifty metres to the Hind and tossed his little bomb through the pilot's open door. Moments later there was a hefty *crump!* Dense white smoke erupted from doors and windows, followed by brilliant sparklets of flame shooting out in all directions. In another couple of seconds the front half of the aircraft was in flames.

'Okay guys, let's do it. And good luck.'

FIFTEEN

We tied the two Russians together with their hands behind them, hoisted them on to the front seat and jammed them in between myself and Jason. Then I started up and rolled the heavy truck forward. Black smoke from the burning Hind was billowing over the track, and I crawled through it in second gear until we reached the main drag. There I turned left, accelerating out through the wilderness.

'Number twenty-one,' I told Jason. 'Keep your eyes skinned for a sign. That's the branch we need.'

'Yassir,' he went, and I knew that if anybody could find the way, he would.

Soon, however, I began to be alarmed by the distance we were travelling. In the chopper, the journey had felt like nothing; in the lumbering seven-ton truck, the pitted dirt road seemed to stretch for ever.

Minutes flicked away. Five had gone before we reached the first junction. There, four minor tracks converged on the main route, but only one signpost was still standing: it pointed vaguely to the left and said '12'. Ours, I knew, would be to the right.

'Is there a sign?' I shouted above the noise of the engine. 'Number twenty-one?'

'*Nyet,*' went Rasputin, but he nodded to the right.

Three more minutes brought us to the next junction. This time the markers were intact: Routes 16 and 18 went off to the left, 17 and 19 to the right.

'Next crossroads,' I told Jason. 'It should have six side tracks.'

It was already 1342 when we reached the key junction:

twelve minutes gone. I retained a mental picture of the intersection from flying over it, and I recognised it the moment I saw it from the ground. But where the hell were the sign posts? Not one survived.

On our right we had three possibilities. Without hesitation, Jason pointed to the first track, and said, 'This one.'

'Okay?' I asked.

Rasputin nodded. I changed down into second, hauled the wheel over and accelerated up the overgrown dirt road.

Sweat was pouring down my face and torso. The cab of the truck was an oven on wheels, and the four of us were crammed tight together. Luckily I'd had the foresight to load up two full water-bottles. I got Jason to unscrew the cap of one and hand it to me. After I'd drunk, I unhooked the mike of the inter-vehicle radio from the dash, and called, 'Green One. How're you doing?'

'Green Two.' It was Stringer's voice. 'We're in the OP with a good view of the road junction. Well cammed up.'

'Roger. Nothing showing yet?'

'Negative.'

'What's the range to the junction?'

'About seven fifty.'

'Brilliant.'

'Where are you?' he asked.

'Approaching the cache. Wait out.'

I probably sounded quite cool, but in fact I was shitting bricks that we were on the wrong road and were going to have to turn back, wasting more time. The terrain looked too flat. Then at last we reached the beginning of a deep gully, and I recognised the ravine with big, smooth boulders along its flanks. At the point where the sides closed in, we came to a wooden pole-barrier carrying one of the blue-and-white danger signs. I didn't even slow down to look at it, but drove straight through. Under the impact of our bullbar the flimsy pole exploded. Pieces flew into the air and landed among the rocks.

The time was 1347.

'Nearly there,' I said, half to myself, half to Jason. 'But Jesus!

It's going to take twenty minutes just to get back as far as the OP.'

My stomach contracted as the battered grey doors of the cache came into sight. I pulled up opposite them, switched off, and said, 'Okay, Jason. We'll both get out. You cover these two while I separate them.'

I opened the driver's door and slid to the ground.

'Out!' I told the two Russians.

They both began shifting and wriggling along the seat towards me. It had been awkward enough getting them in. I'd foreseen that getting them out was going to be worse, and I was expecting them both to tumble on to the deck before they got themselves sorted.

Far from it. Suddenly Rasputin was on the ground, free, and running. Somehow, during all the bumping of the journey, he'd worked himself loose. Before I could react he was well away down the approach road. The pilot was still on the seat. I gave a yell, dragged him forward out of the way and snatched my 203 from its clips. By then, Rasputin was fifty metres off.

'*Stop!*' I yelled.

But I knew he wasn't going to. I was too hot, too worked up, too mad to piss about any longer. Instinctively I opened fire. The first short burst missed. The second knocked him down, head over heels, and he lay kicking violently in the road.

By then the pilot was also on the move, running as best he could with hands still tied behind his back, not making much progress. Dimly I realised that if I went after him I could catch him easily enough. But I wasn't in the mood for running anywhere.

'*Stop!*' I yelled again.

He kept going a few more unsteady paces. I brought the rifle up and put the sight on the centre of his back. Suddenly he pulled up and started turning towards me, but it was too late. At that very instant I squeezed the trigger, and the burst caught him full in the chest. He crumpled to his knees, went down into the dust and lay there hardly moving.

I was trembling violently – hands, arms, knees. I glanced to my left and realised Jason was standing close to me. He didn't speak, but his eyes said it loud and clear: I should never have mown down that defenceless man, at the very moment when he was surrendering.

'Jason,' I went. 'I know. I know. But I'm out of my fucking mind with fright.'

All he said was 'Yassir,' but from the way he nodded, and from the expression on his face, I knew he wasn't blaming me. He understood.

I realised I was hyperventilating, and made a deliberate effort to steady myself down. I was horrified by what I'd done, though more for practical reasons than for moral ones. Feelings of guilt came later. The immediate problem was that I'd killed both the men I was going to use as human shields. In committing a double murder, I'd reduced our options to two: either we had to cut and run for it – and allow a stockpile of nuclear warheads to drop straight into the lap of a mad silvery – or I had to load the weapons myself.

I took the decision in seconds, without conscious effort. No way was I going to quit now. I didn't feel martyred or heroic or any shit like that; it was just the way things had turned out, this was something I had to do, no matter what the consequences might be.

'I'll handle the weapons,' I told Jason. 'But first I need that overall.' I pointed at Rasputin's body and set off towards it, expecting to find the torso perforated by bullet holes. In fact my rounds had gone high, and only one had hit him, in the back of the neck, so the suit was intact except for a single puncture in the collar.

I rolled the dead man on to his back. His black eyes were wide open, and I had to avoid their stare. There was one long zip down the front of the suit, and others up the inside of the legs, from ankle to knee. Limb by floppy limb, I worked the body out of it. Underneath, Rasputin had been wearing a green linen shirt and thin DPM trousers. All his garments were sodden with sweat. So was the lining of the protective suit, and its collar was sticky with warm blood.

The garment was made of cotton, with a rubberised finish on the outside. It looked far too flimsy to be capable of blocking radiation – and maybe, I thought, the manky thing was radioactive already, from when Rasputin inspected the weapons earlier. Did I really need to wear this filthy thing? I hesitated, then pulled it on. In a pouch on the front I found a pair of gloves and a floppy helmet made of the same material, which zipped on to the collar.

Back at the wagon, I said to Jason, 'Whatever happens, you are *not* to enter the silo, you understand?'

'Yassir.'

'Equally, you're not to help me load, or get into the back of the truck. Okay?'

He nodded.

'Get back up in the cab. Monitor the radio. If any message comes, relay it to me. Watch out for anyone approaching the site. If you see anybody, drop him.'

Again Jason nodded.

My first task was to open the heavy doors. I knew it couldn't be done by hand, so I started up, swung the wagon round and backed up right close. As I made to get out, Jason also started shifting his arse.

'No!' I said sharply. 'I told you, stay put!'

My hands were shaking again as I brought out Rasputin's key and fumbled it into the new padlock. With that open, I attached a tow-rope to the big hasps on the right-hand door, jumped back into the cab and drove forward in bottom gear, dragging the inner end of the heavy door round its track. Then I had to repeat the process: back up, unhook rope, re-hook it to second door, climb into cab, crawl forward again. All that took up what seemed desperate amounts of time.

At last, the entrance was clear. Cautiously, I backed in until the tail of the wagon was under the roof, within three metres of the racks. It was a relief – not much, but something – to find that the cab was still just outside the doorway. One last time I ordered Jason to keep still. Then I brought out the helmet and pulled it on over my head, zipping the bottom rim to the collar of the suit. Instantly, I was hit by a sense of claustrophobia. The thick plastic of the visor was so scratched and hazy that I could hardly see through it, and the primitive filter mask made every breath a labour. My instinct was to rip the damned thing off, but I told myself I had to try it. With my watch buried beneath the tight cuff of the protective suit, I couldn't read the time, and I had to keep asking Jason what it was. As I pulled on the gauntlets, I held up my left wrist for another check.

'Thirteen fifty-nine,' Jason called.

Taking a deep breath, I slid to the ground and walked into the silo. The truck took up so much of the open doorway that little light could filter in round it. After the blazing sun outside, the interior of the cache seemed dim as night.

It must have been temporary madness that drove me on. On the road I'd been wondering how I could force Rasputin to close in on the weapons without getting too close to them myself. Now I seemed to have got a terrific psychological boost from Jason's dose. For the time being, I felt impervious to harm.

I advanced on the rack of warheads and checked the number. As I thought, there were five in the top layer and ten in each of the four lower layers: forty-five all told. I grabbed the nose cone of the one on the left in the uppermost row. The white enamelled surface was so slippery that I couldn't get a firm enough grip to pull the whole shell forward. Looking closer, leaning right over the stack, I realised that the thing was being held in place by a set of four stubby fins which sprouted from the fuselage a third of the way down. When I lifted the nose vertically, the fins came clear of the timber cradle in which they'd been laid. Chocks of wood, curved to match the diameter of the barrel, fell away, and the warhead was free.

At its rear end was another set of fins, long and slender, and round the centre Cyrillic letters were stencilled in black. I didn't waste time trying to read the message. Drawing the missile forward, I held it in my arms, balanced across my chest, and moved crabwise to the tailboard of the truck. The weight was about what I'd estimated, and manageable: maybe seventy-five pounds. The length of the carry was only three metres, but Jesus Christ! The mental pressure of having that amount of warhead right up against my body!

The lads' last action, before the parties split, had been to clear the rearmost seven or eight feet of cargo space in the back of the wagon. Non-urgent kit had been binned, and the rest piled up further forward. All I had to do, then, was slide the warhead in along the floor, tail first. The fins scraped over the bare steel, and I thought, shit: by the time we've driven them to the Mall, these things are going to end up bent and deformed. Then immediately I realised that if we got the weapons out of the country, nobody would want to use them anyway; they'd be scrapped in some safe location, so that minor damage was of no significance.

I got the first six warheads loaded without too much difficulty. But all the time my body temperature was rising; inside that damned suit I was being boiled alive. I could hardly breathe, and there came a point when the volume of sweat on the inside of the visor made it impossible to see what I was doing. There was no way I could continue with the helmet on, so I ripped it off and threw it to one side. My hair was plastered to my head, and rivulets were coursing down my neck and back, but the return of fresh air revived me, and I carried on.

The ninth warhead completed the first layer across the floor of the wagon. They didn't fit together neatly, like pencils, but were held apart by their fins. At this rate, I could see, there were going to be five layers, the top one at the height of my head.

'Time, Jason?' I shouted.

'Fourteen eleven.'

Christ! I ran back to the stack, snatched the warhead next in line, cradled it, scuttled across, decanted it, ran back. Some of the casings felt rough and puckered; brown spots showed where rust had pitted the surface. Three more like that, and I was panting desperately. The chemical smell in the air seemed to be accumulating in my mouth, producing an acid taste and making my throat sore.

With the score at fifteen, there came a sudden shout from the cab.

'What is it?'

'Radio, sah. They seen the convoy.'

I ran out into the open, stood on the step below the open driver's door and reached up for the mike.

'Green One, say again.'

'Green Two.' Now it was Pav on the other end. 'The fuckers are in sight.'

'How many?'

'Two Gaz jeeps at the front. Then three big wagons – four- or five-tonners. Another jeep at the back.'

'What are you planning?'

'We're going to let them come nearly to the junction, then hit the lead vehicle.'

'Roger. Who's on the five-oh?'

'Phil.'

'Great.'

'How are things your end?'

'Tough. But we're winning. Loaded a third already. Done in twenty minutes.'

'Roger. Wait out.'

I wasn't going to tell him about the Russians' death. That could wait.

Jason pulled the mike back up on its springy, coiled lead.

'Water!' I croaked. 'Throw me a bottle.'

He lobbed one out. I filled my mouth, swilled the water round and spat it out, then drained the rest at a single swallow. The liquid revived me and I tore back to work, pulling, lifting, carrying, loading, shoving.

I'd just shifted the twenty-fifth warhead, clearing the third row down, when Jason shouted again. This time, when I emerged, he yelled just one word: 'Shooting!'

I stood by the cab door and listened. Even without a commentary I could tell what was happening from the noise exploding over the open radio link. The .50 was firing in short bursts, four or five rounds at a time, its heavy hammer roaring out of our loudspeaker. In my mind I could see the green tracer, every fifth round, looping away into the distance, to curl in and smack the target.

My first call went unanswered, but at the second Stringer came on the air.

'What's on?' I demanded.

'Phil's taken out the first jeep. It's on fire in the middle of the road. There are guys deploying into the bush.'

'Any incoming?'

'Not yet.'

'Keep at it.' I ran back to work and pitched into the fourth layer. The heat was threatening to finish me. I was sweating as I'd never sweated in my life.

With nearly the whole of that layer on board, and only twelve warheads to go, I heard another yell from Jason. The cry caught me in mid-carry. I didn't dare drop my burden on the ground, and I took several seconds to slide it into place before I could hustle outside. Seconds before I hit the open air, there came a burst of fire – not over the radio, but live, from close at hand.

'What the hell's that?'

I rushed into the open and called again. Jason didn't answer. The blaze of sun made me screw up my eyes. When I opened them again, the first thing I saw was a third body lying in the open some fifty yards off, a black body, clad in DPMs, dead or dying, but still twitching, with a weapon on the deck beside it. The guy's legs were moving as he tried to run. For a horrible moment I thought it was Jason. Just as I realised the DPMs were the wrong colour, lighter than his, another burst clattered out from above my head.

My 203 was in the cab of the vehicle. With rounds going down, I wasn't going to expose myself by climbing up to get it. Instead, I dropped flat on the ground, wriggled inside one of the wagon's big wheels and lay still in a pool of sweat, eyeballing the approach to the site. How in hell had somebody managed to bypass the pinkie and penetrate this far into the training area?

At the other end of the radio link the battle was still raging. At our end the body in my view stopped moving. Then, from somewhere high above me, came Jason's voice: 'Geordie, sah!'

'Here!' I called. 'Under the wagon. Where are you?'

'I come down.'

I waited a few moments, then heard scuffling noises as he slithered off the rocks above the doorway.

'Who was it?' I asked from my prone position.

'Two men. Coming for truck. I kill both.'

'Brilliant. Where's number two?'

'Up top.' He pointed.

'Are you sure that was all?'

'Don't know, sah. I saw two. Nobody more.'

'I bet they came in the chopper on its first run,' I said. 'Probably left to guard the site. Let's hope no more of the bastards are lurking about.'

I eased myself out from under the truck and took a quick look round. I wasn't going to waste time checking the bodies.

'Go back up where you were,' I said. 'You'll be safer hidden in the rocks than sitting in the cab. There's only a dozen warheads to go. Ten minutes, and we'll be on our way.'

I never got through that last dozen. I shifted another five, gasping with the effort, but the task took me to the point of collapse. My stack in the back of the wagon had risen to head height, and I only just managed to lift the fifth missile on to the top. The strain left me totally drained, hardly able to walk.

Mental pressure was increased by the sounds of battle pouring from the radio loudspeaker. Even from inside the cavern I could hear heavy firing and the occasional loud explosion. The racket made me desperate to get moving. Further pressure derived from the fact that the last shell I had loaded was slippery with the clear liquid I'd noticed when I first saw the cache. The remaining seven were coated in transparent crystals. It looked as though the casings had cracked when the wooden shelves crumbled, and some of the contents had leaked. No way was I going to touch those faulty specimens. I told myself that they couldn't be serviceable, so it wouldn't matter if Muende did get his hands on them. He'd never be able to use them.

I slammed up the tail-board, and tried to shout, 'Jason!' All that came out was a squeak. I cleared my throat, and called again. 'That's it! Let's go!'

I didn't bother closing the door of the silo. Instead, I threw the padlock away into thick bush, scrambled up into the driving seat and started the engine. The moment Jason slipped into the other seat, I let out the clutch and set off.

'Okay, sah?' He shot me an apprehensive look.

'Yeah, yeah,' I lied. 'No problem.'

Big black flies had already swarmed on to the bodies lying in the open; a cloud of them burst off Rasputin's as I drove past. With every movement of the wagon, every bump or hole in the track, our cargo clanked horrendously. I was gripped by fear that more casings would split, even that one of the warheads would be detonated by concussion. Was that possible? I just didn't know, and cursed the fact that our training in nuclear matters had been so perfunctory.

By then, I was in a horrible state, soaked to the skin inside the suit, dehydrated, shaking with exhaustion and reaction. I longed to rip the clammy overall off and throw it away, but fear of the possible consequences stopped me. The trouble was, I was so damned ignorant. Would the suit give me adequate protection? Or was wearing it even more dangerous than removing it, now that the front and arms were smeared with leaked chemicals? Would the suit itself contaminate Jason, sitting beside me? And would the steel of the cab protect him from the deadly load a few feet behind him?

'Time?' I demanded.

'Fourteen thirty-six.'

Jesus! We had less than half an hour to reach the LZ. We'd never make it in time. With my right hand I grabbed the mike, pressed the switch and called, 'Green One.'

There was quite a pause before Pav answered, 'Green Two.'

'We're rolling,' I told him. 'But we're going to be late. Any news of the Herc?'

'Affirmative. Stringer just spoke to the pilot. He's ahead of schedule.'

'Warn him we may be late to the LZ.'

'Roger. Shift your arse, though.'

'I'm doing that. How are things your end?'

'Plenty of incoming, but it's all over the place. Some RPGs as well, but they're falling short.'

'Has the convoy moved?'

'Negative. One of the big wagons is on fire as well. The only snag is, the Gaz that was at the back has detached itself from the rest of the column and headed off across country. For the moment it's disappeared into dead ground. It could be trying a flanker, to cut off our retreat.'

'Which way?'

'Going to our left.'

'Shit,' I went. 'That's towards our exit road.'

'Exactly.'

'How's your ammo?'

'The five-oh's getting low.'

'For fuck's sake keep some to give us covering fire when we get out on that road.'

'Roger. Wait one. Stringer's got something.' There was a pause, then, 'He says the Herc's already approaching the LZ. He's come in low-level, two fifty feet, to keep below any radars on the border. He's going to pop up to a thousand feet to get a look at the terrain.'

'Tell him I'm on my way.'

I was driving as fast as I dared, inhibited by the rough surface and by the rattling and clanking from our load. I kept glancing over my shoulder through the rear window of the cab, as though I could settle the warheads by glowering at them. I winced at every lurch and nursed the big wagon along, swerving continuously to avoid rocks and potholes.

Pav came back on. 'The pilot's seen the LZ. He reckons he can hack it. He could do with some smoke before he lands, though. How soon can you make it?'

'Ten minutes.'

Another pause as my message was relayed.

'Roger. He's willing to lose ten minutes in a circuit. Get your foot down.'

'It's down. I'm closing on you.'

'Roger. We'll give you max covering fire when you hit the road.'

On that rough track, at the speed we were doing, the mother wagon took some holding. The jolting was diabolical, and my arms ached from wrestling with the wheel. We passed the OP without seeing the pinkie or any of our lads - they were all up on a ledge above us – and dived down the channel that cut through the escarpment, then diagonally through the derelict camp and out on to the road.

The battle had cleared the highway of pedestrians; there wasn't a man, woman or child in sight. I held my foot on the deck until the engine was screaming in third, then crashed into top and forced the speed up to ninety kilometres an hour. The first half-minute was the danger time. We were broadside on to the enemy, but every second we managed to survive increased the range, and after about thirty seconds we'd be out of reach.

'Keep down!' I shouted at Jason. 'Keep below the window!'

He was on the right, our vulnerable side. He doubled himself down so that he was half lying across the bench seat, with the top of his head near my hip and his bony arse to the door. On the driver's side I had no option but to stay upright. I pressed myself as far back into the squab as I could go, trying to keep the door pillar and the rest of the cab between me and the enemy.

With a quick glance to my right, I took in the stranded convoy, no more than three hundred metres away. Columns of black smoke were rising from the wagons set on fire, but flashes of gunfire were spurting from improvised positions round the others. Until we appeared on the road, the enemy had been firing in the direction of the pinkie, up on the ledge. Now they had a beautiful new target, lumbering across their front in easy range.

Within seconds I saw something that looked like a big black dot whip across in front of us, right to left. It went so fast that for an instant I couldn't identify it properly. I just had time to shout, 'Eh! Look at that!' when an explosion cracked off a couple of hundred metres to our left.

'Rocket!' I yelled.

One of them into our cargo, and we'd be well stitched. I grabbed the radio mike, and shouted, 'Incoming RPGs! Keep their heads down!'

My right boot was flat on the steel floor. The speedometer needle was hovering on the hundred mark. The truck bucked and bounced like a speedboat in rough water, jumping bodily from one side of the track to the other. Less than thirty metres ahead dust-puffs erupted in a line across the road as a burst of small-arms fire raked the surface. Instinctively I hit the brakes. There was somebody out there who could shoot. Like a shotgunner swinging ahead of a distant pheasant, he was giving us a long lead, and nearly getting it right.

I was fighting the wheel too hard to count seconds, but I knew near enough when thirty had gone. I eased the speed down to eighty. We were already at extreme range, and in as much danger of crashing as of getting hit.

'Coming clear,' I reported.

'Roger,' answered Pav, coolly. Then suddenly, in a sharper voice, he said, 'Stand by. The Herc pilot's seen something he doesn't like.'

What the hell was this? All I could do was keep going. Thirty seconds more, and we were out of range.

'You're okay,' I told Jason.

He came up off the floor with a big grin.

Then Pav reported: 'He's seen military vehicles approaching from the east. At least a dozen.'

'Joss!' I shouted. 'It's Joss, and Alpha. How far out are they?'

'He estimates fifteen ks. He's turned away to the north to come back round and land.'

Fifteen kilometres. The enemy must have seen the plane, but for the moment there was nothing they could do to harm it. If the convoy was managing forty, that gave us twenty minutes to reach the Mall, guide the plane in, load the weapons and get airborne.

'Hear that, Jason?' I yelled. 'It's your old friends, following up our tracks, on collision course.'

'Yassir.'

Pav was on the air again. 'Closing down the show here!' he shouted. 'As soon as everyone's on board, we're coming after you.'

'Roger,' I went. 'Estimating one k to the start of the Mall.'

I became aware of a disturbance beside me. I glanced across and saw Jason twisting round to pull down his 203 from the clips behind his head.

'Eh!' I went. 'What's the matter?'

'Car coming, sah!'

He nodded forward. A single vehicle was streaking through the bush, coming in at an angle from our right front, aiming to intercept us. A plume of dust trailed behind it.

'Contact!' I shouted to Pav. 'That fucking breakaway Gaz, it's trying to head us and block the road.'

'Your pigeon,' Pav answered. 'We're rolling.'

Somehow Jason had got his head and shoulders out of the window and twisted them forward with his weapon levelled. It was an amazing gymnastic feat. Only someone as thin as he was could have managed it. I saw that his right-side ribs must be getting hammered on the door frame, but he seemed impervious to the pain.

'Wait!' I roared. 'Too far!'

The jeep was being thrown about by the rough terrain, jumping and twisting. As we converged I could see it had no canopy, but there were two men standing in the back, clinging to the tubular framework.

My right foot was flat down. We were doing ninety again – a crazy speed on that surface. It wasn't safe to take my eyes off the road for more than a second at a time. In spite of our pace, the jeep was going to reach the road first, before we passed the point where its line intersected ours, unless the driver suddenly stopped so that his crew could open up on us broadside as we went past. In the final seconds of convergence I realised he wasn't going to. He'd committed himself to blocking our path. Along that stretch the road was built up on a low causeway, maybe a couple of feet high, with sandy banks sloping down into the scrub on either side. We were less than a hundred metres from convergence when the jeep reached the right-hand bank, bounced up it and slithered to a halt at an angle across the carriageway. The driver must have thought the block would make me slow down. Some chance.

Beside me, Jason hammered off three short bursts from his 203. Dust spurted on our side of the jeep.

'Get in!' I roared. 'Get back in!'

He saw that impact was imminent, and wriggled back inside the cab. Just in time he dropped the weapon and braced himself, hands and feet. I did the same, gripping the wheel with all my strength and forcing myself against the backrest.

We went in at the jeep with terrifying velocity. I felt I was looking through a zoom lens, so fast did the target grow. Thank God for our bullbar, I thought. I just had time to see the guys in the back of the Gaz struggling to sort themselves and bring their weapons to bear on us when, *WHAM!*, we hit them broadside with shattering force. The impact lifted the jeep clean off its wheels and flung it away to our left like a toy. I caught a glimpse of the standing guys being jack-knifed over the bars they'd been holding on to. Their vehicle was whipped sideways with such colossal energy that the bars drove into their chests and stomachs, doubling them forward. As for us, we took a terrific jolt, but the mother wagon's weight and impetus were such that it hardly slowed. We came out of the crash still doing seventy. In the mirror I saw flames and smoke rising from the wreck.

'Fucking take that!' I yelled in triumph. Then I shot a glance at Jason and saw blood running down his cheek. 'Hey!' I went. 'You okay?'

'Sure, sah!' He was grinning and patting his left temple, showing where he'd nicked it against the roof of the cab.

I snatched the radio mike, and called, 'Green One. We've disabled that rogue jeep you saw go cross-country. It's on fire. But watch yourselves when you pass it. There could be survivors.'

'Roger,' went Pav. 'We can see the smoke ahead of us.'

For nearly half a minute after the smash I thought we'd got

clean away with it, that our truck was intact. The engine hadn't faltered, and the steering felt fine. Then I noticed the temperature gauge creeping up.

'Shit!' I yelled. 'We've holed the radiator!'

At that moment, Pav came on with, 'The Herc's nearly round its circuit. Looking to land in figures two minutes.'

'Roger,' I went. 'Which way's he coming in?'

'West to east, from behind you.'

'Roger. I'm almost at the end of the Mall. Tell the pilot I'll try to give him smoke at both ends of a good strip. Got a problem, though. Truck's overheating. Stand by.'

Eyeballing frantically to my left, I recognised the start of the Mall and swung left-handed off the road towards the flat ground. On the temperature gauge the needle was up into the red. Before we reached the level area we had to cross an old river bed. Over the bumps I changed down into second. Steam began pouring from under the bonnet. Fifty yards short of the flat, the needle went off the dial. I sensed that if I gunned the engine for another few seconds, it would seize. Somehow I'd got to get the truck on to the flat ground so that the Herc could pull up beside it. No way would the incoming crew be able to carry every missile a hundred metres or more.

I switched off, and said to Jason, 'Got to get some water into it. Here, take these.' I pulled out two smoke grenades which I'd had stowed in my Bergen, down beside my feet. 'The plane's coming in this way.' I made a sweeping movement, indicating an approach from behind us and to the left. 'Run! Crack one off over there, on the flat. Then run again. Minimum five hundred metres straight along. Six hundred if you can make it before you see the Herc coming. Okay?'

'Yassir!' Jason's face was all lit up. He slipped the grenades into his pouches, jumped down, and ran like a grey spider, stumbling over the tussocks.

'Green One,' I went on the radio. 'Tell the Herc he'll have one lot of smoke anyway, maybe two. If it's only one, that's his touch-down point; if it's two, they'll mark both ends of the strip. Stand by.'

I leapt to the ground. Steam was still pouring from the bonnet. With the catch released, the damage was obvious: some sharp edge driven into the front of the radiator. The whole engine was dangerously hot. I was still wearing Rasputin's protective gloves, but first I smothered the radiator cap with a piece of sacking as well, then turned it. Jets of steam spurted sideways. I ran round to the back of the wagon, unhooked the cage that held the jerricans under the false floor, dragged a can out and lugged it to the front. The first few pints of water exploded in steam, but the rest took the temperature down and the system began to fill.

As I stood there holding the heavy can level, I heard the engines of the Herc. I glanced behind me towards the beginning of the Mall. Green smoke was billowing, going almost straight up, and in the distance Jason was running.

Fresh water started to dribble from the hole in the honeycomb of metal on the radiator front. I stopped pouring, flung the can away, stuffed sacking into the puncture, replaced the cap, slammed the bonnet down and hauled myself into the driving seat. The engine fired. I went into first, crawled forward, and changed into second.

With my own engine running, I could no longer hear the plane. How far out was it? Jason had cracked off the first grenade well out on the flat ground. Fifty yards short of it, I stopped at right angles to the line of approach and craned forward in the cab, peering to my left. Nothing in sight.

A thought struck me. If I could get the wagon to the far end of our makeshift runway, the Herc could load up from it there, without having to taxi back the length of the strip. Because there was zero wind, the pilot could take off again in the opposite direction, and not overfly the convoy approaching from the east.

I revved up, rolled forward and turned right along the designated runway. Up ahead Jason had vanished into the heat haze. Too late, I glanced down at the temperature gauge. Once more the needle was high in the red. A second later I was getting steam again – a big cloud of it this time, spurting up in front.

No chance of stopping now. I had to keep going. I was maybe halfway along the strip when I heard what I'd been dreading: a horrendous, grinding scream from the engine, followed by a noise like chains being pulled fast through iron railings, then a single, devastating crack.

The wagon hiccuped to a halt. I grabbed the radio. 'Green One,' I shouted. 'I'm fucked! Where are you?'

'Right behind you,' came the answer. 'We have you visual. What's your problem?'

'Engine's seized. Can't move.'

'Stand by. We'll get a towline on you.'

Within seconds, the pinkie came up with a rush on my right and scorched to a halt a few metres ahead. Dust swirled up round it. Pav was driving, with Stringer beside him. The rest of the guys – I noted with relief that we'd suffered no casualties in the shoot-out – jumped off the open back and ran out a rope. Above the noise of the jeep's engine idling I could hear Stringer shouting over the satcom. I caught a glimpse of Danny with blood on his face. Holding the rope in place, he waved the jeep forward. Pav twisted round in his seat, then turned back and eased his vehicle forward to take up the strain. In the distance ahead a second column of green smoke was rising.

I already had my gear shift in neutral, and to minimise resistance I held the clutch pedal down on the floor. Still spouting steam, the mother wagon rolled forward, slow as a crippled elephant. Suddenly, from behind, from right above our heads, came an almighty roar and a blast of hot air as the Herc thundered over, not fifty feet up. Its undercarriage was down, but even as it cleared us I saw the flaps come up and heard the pilot increase power as he lifted away.

'What's he doing?' I shouted.

'Jesus Christ!' Pav shouted back. 'How can he land with you in the middle of the fucking runway?'

I felt faint, as though I was going to pass out. My left leg was shaking violently with the effort of holding the clutch pedal down. I let the pressure off, and we continued to roll. Without any power the steering had gone heavy as lead. We were doing only eight or nine kilometres an hour. At that speed I had time to reach out for a water-bottle and get the contents down my neck. Far out in front, the Herc was lifting away in a hard turn to the left, with black exhaust trails streaming behind its engines.

The liquid gave me new heart.

'Tell him we'll be ready for him next time round,' I said to Pav. 'And tell him the black guy on the runway's one of ours.'

'Roger,' Pav answered. 'We're in the shit already. The plane's just taken fire from the enemy column. The pilot reckons they're within three ks of the strip.'

I measured the distance from us to Jason's second smoke grenade. Two hundred metres. For another few seconds I held on. 'Keep going,' I called. 'Keep going . . . This'll do. Pull off! Pull away to the right.'

Pav turned. He had the sense to keep going until he'd towed the mother wagon well off the strip, at right angles to it, tail-on. The moment he stopped, Danny leapt off and slashed through the rope with a knife. Then Pav drove off twenty or thirty metres.

I jumped to the ground, ran to the back of the wagon and unhooked the fastenings of the tail-board. At a glance I could tell that several of the warhead casings had cracked during our violent transit. The whole load seemed to be coated in transparent slime.

The roar of aircraft engines made me look behind. There was the Herc, coming round in a hard turn, almost at zero feet, banked like a huge, heavy fighter, with the tip of its port wing flicking over the bush.

'Shit hot!' I shouted. 'That's some flying!' But when I moved towards the pinkie and the other guys, to get the crack, they edged rapidly away, staring at me as if I were a lunatic.

'What's the matter?' I called.

'Keep your fucking distance, Geordie!' Mart shouted. 'There's NBC suits for us all on board the Herc. Until we've got them on, just stay clear of us and the wagon.'

The Herc was already coming in. Having made the tightest possible circuit, the pilot straightened up and banged his big aircraft down just past the first smoke grenade. Smoke and dust exploded as the tyres bit. So hard was the first impact that the plane bounced and flew another fifty metres before it smacked down again. There was a terrific roar as the pilot reversed the thrust of the props, and the aircraft disappeared in a whirling cloud of dust, sand and debris.

By the time it trundled level with us it had slowed to a walking pace, and it swung hard round, right-handed, turning back to face the way it had come, before rolling to a halt no more than thirty metres from the mother wagon. Already the tail ramp was on its way down. From the side door burst a team of men in sand-coloured NBC suits, complete with helmets, masks and respirators. The two guys in the lead carried armfuls of spare suits. Ignoring me, they ran for the pinkie and threw the garments at the rest of the lads, who immediately started struggling into them.

The remainder of the NBC team came in my direction. The leader shouted something in my face, but the combination of his mask and the scream of the Herc's engines deadened his voice, and I didn't get what he said.

Instead of replying, I pointed at the back of the mother wagon. The guy ran towards it, stopped a couple of metres short, took one look at the load and made a colossal 'no way' gesture with his gloved hands, flinging his arms out wide to either side, on a level with his shoulders, like a member of a ground crew telling a pilot to shut down his engines. Then he turned and did the same towards the flight-deck of the aircraft.

He must have given a radio order to his mates. Three men ran forward with a hold-all and began rigging explosive charges on the noses of the weapons in the top layer. As they worked, the leader made violent gestures towards our team, pumping his right hand up and down and pointing at the plane. 'Get in!' his signals were saying. 'Move! On the double! All aboard!'

The lads stumbled towards the pinkie, half in and half out of their sandy suits, to grab their weapons. Pav must have realised that he wasn't going to need any protection after all, because he ripped his kit off and threw it on the ground with an angry gesture before he seized the .50 from its mount, then snatched his own 203 and ran for the plane, clutching both weapons. Stringer was already fully dressed, but Danny and Chalky moved awkwardly, with their legs encased, holding the upper halves of the suits around their waists. The Herc sat there, big and heavy, with all four props spinning.

As for me, I felt zombiefied. I couldn't move. I stood and watched the demolition guys taping their det cord into position and setting a timer. Stringer was right: we should have blown the missiles in the cache, without ever bothering to move them.

One of the demo team gave me five fingers: five minutes to get clear. Still I was rooted to the spot. I watched him, and all the NBC team, sprint for the tailgate of the Herc and up the ramp. I seemed to be caught in a dream. Everyone else could move, but I was frozen. Through the swirling dust I saw Pav and Chalky come out on to the ramp and make frantic gestures, ordering me, begging me, willing me, to go aboard. Their mouths were wide open, yelling. Another guy, unrecognisable in his NBC kit, was giving a similar performance from the side door. But something made it impossible for me to do what they wanted.

At last I came to life. I grabbed my 203 from the front of the doomed mother wagon and ran – not for the Herc, but for the pinkie. I slotted my weapon into the clips above the dash and jumped into the driving seat. The ignition key was in place. I switched on, started up and scorched off towards the far smoke pillar. As I accelerated away, the note of the Herc's engines rose and it started to move in the opposite direction. The side door had been closed; the tail ramp was going up.

I found Jason flat on his face, in a firing position, with his 203 levelled towards the east. Great guy – he was preparing to take on the Alpha column single-handed. I pulled up beside him with a yell of 'All aboard!', and hardly gave him time to scramble into the passenger seat before I shot forward again, hell bent on getting out of sight before the rebel convoy came into view. Instinct sent me due north, into a patch of dense bush, where thickets of thorn grew two or three times the height of the vehicle.

As soon as we were out of sight of the road, I stopped and switched off.

'If they've seen us, we're fucked,' I said. 'But I think we're okay.'

We grabbed our 203s, jumped out and scuttled to the edge of the thicket, at a point where a gap in the bushes gave a view of the open ground.

The roar of the Herc's engines under full power rumbled back at us. The aircraft was taxiing straight away into the far distance, trailing dust. Then it lifted off, leaving all the debris behind it. Seconds later a brilliant flash spurted from the mother wagon, and the *BOOM!* of a big explosion buffeted past us. Pieces of metal erupted into the air, falling back over a wide area. A grey, mushroom-shaped cloud soared upwards, and beneath it the wreck of the truck was enveloped by flames.

'The buggers won't fancy that,' I said, half to myself, half to Jason. 'Now they see the aircraft's away, and there's nothing left for grabs on the strip, they'll keep going, to check the cache. They've nothing else to go for.'

My hunch was immediately put to the test. Within a minute the first vehicle appeared, a Gaz jeep, proceeding quite fast along the road, with two guys standing in the open back. Obviously a scout – it was well ahead of the rest. Before it came level with the burning remains of the wagon, it stopped.

'They're radioing back,' I said. 'Reporting the situation, asking for orders.'

After a pause, the jeep went forward again. When I saw it wasn't deviating from the road, but heading on for the town, I breathed deep with relief. A minute behind it, the rest of the convoy lumbered into view: two more jeeps, four heavy trucks with their open backs full of troops, four closed lorries, a tanker and two more jeeps bringing up the rear – quite a force. Which vehicle was Joss in, I wondered? I dearly wanted to launch a 203 grenade and take the bastard out.

All Jason and I had to do was keep still until they'd disappeared, then slip away to the east. I felt momentary exultation at the thought that this lot of pricks was about to run head-on into the survivors of Muende's convoy, but then, with the abrupt release of tension, exhaustion hit me. Lying flat out, with my face on the backs of my hands, I closed my eyes and let out a deep sigh.

'Okay, sah?'

I opened my eyes, to see Jason staring at me with a worried expression.

'Yeah, yeah,' I went. 'A bit tired, that's all. And Mabonzo, you know what we're going to do now, don't you?'

'Yassir. Go get the diamond.'

SIXTEEN

Our basic need was to head north-north-east across country. I didn't want to use the road, for fear that Joss might have a back-up convoy coming along behind him. Alpha Commando certainly possessed more vehicles than we'd seen. At the same time, I did want to put distance between ourselves and the burnt-out truck, to get clear of any radioactivity released by the explosion. I knew I must already be contaminated to some extent, but I saw no point in taking unnecessary risks. So I pulled off Rasputin's sodden suit, buried it as best I could, and for an hour drove carefully through the bush, parallel with the road but out of sight of it, following a gully which twisted and turned more or less in the right direction.

With the immediate threat gone, reaction set in. I realised I was physically exhausted, and knew I had probably exposed myself to a fatal dose of radiation. What I didn't appreciate was that my mind and motives were totally confused.

To start with I felt angry with myself for screwing everything up. It was my fault entirely that I was stranded in the middle of a hostile country, my fault we'd gone after the arms cache in the first place, my fault I hadn't boarded the Herc when I had every opportunity, and the rest were desperately urging me to shift my arse and join them. Self-pity soon gave way to guilt. Thinking back, I knew full well that I'd been secretly planning this breakaway ever since Sam sprang Genesis and me from the cell. It was in the light aircraft, just after Genesis died, that I'd conceived the idea of peeling off from the rest of the team to go in search of the diamond. I'd kept the scheme hidden in my mind all through our approach to the weapons cache. The worst thing was that I'd deliberately deceived my mates. Never before, during sixteen years in the Regiment, had I done anything like that. I'd had disagreements and rows, of course, but they'd always been in the open. I'd always remained a good member or leader of the team; never had I double-crossed the rest of the lads about my intentions.

Now I told myself that if Whinger had been alive, I wouldn't have done it. I'd have confided fully in him, and almost certainly he would have talked me out of such a wild idea. But Whinger had gone, that was the whole point. It was his death that had thrown me off balance. If only we hadn't rescued the German woman. If only Whinger hadn't got burnt. If only we'd never gone to the convent. If, if, if . . . As Pavarotti was fond of saying, if my Auntie Nel had had two balls, she would have been my Uncle Arthur.

Now, of course, I had the satcom. I could always call the Kremlin. But what good would that do? Some rupert would only start in, bollocking me. Whatever else I needed at that moment, I didn't need advice or orders from Hereford.

Contradictory thoughts whirled round and round my head until, giving in to exhaustion, I came to a temporary halt under a grove of trees bearing dark-green leaves.

'Got to take a break,' I told Jason. 'We'll stay here till dark. We'll be safer moving at night, in any case.'

He nodded. Except for a small cut beside his left eyebrow, his long, thin face looked no different from normal; but in the past forty-eight hours he'd had as little sleep as I had, and I knew he must be worn out.

'Get your head down too,' I told him.

'Yassir.'

I should have asked him to do an hour's stag, while I had a kip. But by then I was so far gone that I'd developed a fatalistic attitude. It was a million to one against anyone finding us, I thought, and even if they did, I didn't care. I dug out a mozzie net, rigged it over my head and chest, stretched out on the bare earth, and within seconds was dead to the world.

*

When I came round, I couldn't think where I was. Then I looked out through the canopy of the sheltering trees, saw the sun was setting, and remembered.

Jason was sitting against a tree-trunk, knees drawn up, with his 203 on the ground beside him.

'Been asleep?' I asked.

'Yassir.'

I didn't believe him, especially as he said 'Big shooting!' and pointed into the distance towards Ichembo, indicating that some major contact had taken place while I was out cold. The noise had been too faint to rouse me. I reckoned the faithful bugger had sat there guarding me all the time. But I wasn't going to argue. I felt one hell of a lot better. The fog of exhaustion had cleared from my head, and, except for a patch between my shoulderblades, on which I'd been lying, the sweat had dried out of my clothes.

I was hungry for food and keen to get moving, so I dug out a couple of boil-in-the-bag rations, lobbed one to Jason and got the other down my neck. Seldom had cold Irish stew tasted better, and I chased it with pears in syrup.

With the meal came new energy. My first task was to make a mental inventory of what the pinkie contained, before darkness fell. The results were encouraging. We had half a tank of fuel and three full jerricans – enough for at least 200 kilometres. We had rations for several days, plenty of fresh water, cam nets, and several of the lads' spare sweaters. There was more 203 ammunition than two of us were likely to fire, two boxes of grenades and sixteen eight-ounce sticks of plastic explosive, together with det cord and timers. We had the satcom, and, best of all, Andy's GPS, into which I'd punched the waypoints recorded by Stringer in his own set.

Our last map had gone up in flames with the mother wagon, but because of the GPS its disappearance hardly mattered. I plugged the leads into sockets on the dash, so that I didn't drain the set's batteries, and once I'd got fixes on three satellites and established our new location, I was amazed to find how close to Waypoint Seven we were. Through all the violent swings of the past few days – our advance to the mine at Gutu, our flight from Gutu to the Zebra Pans and the convent, my capture and journey to Chimbwi, then from there to Ichembo – I'd had the impression that we were moving more or less in a circle. Now it turned out I was right. The GPS revealed that we'd ended up only seventy-eight kilometres from the site of the downed Beechcraft, and needed to advance on a bearing of forty-seven degrees to reach it. We were on the wrong side of the hills, it was true, but so close we could almost walk there in a night.

Also, I had Jason. I'd already seen that he possessed outstanding skills as a tracker, but now I began to realise that he also had an uncanny sense of place and direction. When I asked him, 'Do you remember where the Beechcraft is?' he replied, in a matter-of-fact voice, 'Yassir.' And when I said, 'Which way is it?' he instantly stuck out an arm, with fingers outstretched. When I stood behind him with a compass, I found he was pointing within one degree of the course the GPS had given me.

'Jason,' I went. 'Have you been here before?'

'One time Ichembo.'

'But not *here*, where we are now?'

'No sah.'

'Then how the hell can you be so sure about your directions?'

'Sun,' he said, pointing up at the sky. 'Moon, stars – and head.'

'Any obstacles on our route?'

'One river.'

'Jesus! Not that big one?'

He shook his head. 'Small one.'

'Can the pinkie drive across it?'

'I think so.'

I didn't let on that the GPS agreed precisely with his analysis of our position. I just pretended to go along with his estimate of the course we should take.

We needed to wait a few more minutes, until the moon was high enough to give good light, and as we sat in the dark, we chatted in a desultory way. I already knew about Jason's wives, but something made me ask about his family.

'What about your father?' I went. 'Is he still alive?'

'No sah. I show you.' He began scrabbling in the breast pocket of his DPMs and brought out a small, flat box, which he opened with a pop. I shone my torch on it, and saw it was made of aluminium, battered and dented. From it he took a piece of paper, which he unfolded delicately, with great care, before handing it across.

Like the tin, the paper had seen much service. It was a sheet torn from a ruled school exercise book, frayed at the edges and covered with smudgy finger prints. But the message, written in capital letters, was still perfectly legible:

HORNED MADAM
MAY IT PLEASE YOU TO KNOW YOUR
HUSBAND SHOOTED BY STUDENT AUGUSTUS
MUENDE IN FIGHT ON ACADEMICAL RANGES.
THIS IS TRUTH. YOUR FATEFUL FREIND
FELLOW STUDENT A.N.OTHER
ANNO DOMINI JANUARY 1985

Puzzled, I skimmed through it twice, then asked, 'Who was this addressed to?'

'My mother.'

'Jesus! So Muende killed your father? Is that what you're saying?'

'Yassir.'

'But how?'

'He was weapons instructor at college. Muende was student.'

'The military academy in Mulongwe?'

Jason nodded.

'What happened?'

He spread his hands, meaning he'd never known. 'I was only boy then. Nine years.'

'And now you're out to get Muende?'

'Yassir.'

'So all that stuff about wanting to come to England was a load of crap? You just wanted to join our team.'

I said it in a jokey way, but he lowered his head rather than answer.

'Don't worry,' I added. 'I'm glad you did. But how the hell did you know what we were going to do? At that stage we weren't after Muende at all.'

'You say you make personal attack.'

'Did I? Oh yes, that was *way* back, when we did the training ambush. But then it was only a joke.' I folded the paper carefully, and handed it back. 'Let's go,' I said. 'Let's get after him.'

For a couple on honeymoon, it would have been a perfect night. The air was pleasantly cool, the stars brilliant. The complete absence of human habitation would have given lovers the feeling they were the only people in the whole of Africa.

On me, though, all that was wasted. As Jason drove the first stint, weaving steadily through the bush, one anxiety after another crowded into my mind. Foremost was the possibility that Muende might beat us to the crashed plane. He might already have reached it, found the diamond and gone. Again, it was IF, IF, IF: IF the man who nicked my GPS had been discovered with it, or had handed it in; if Muende or Inge had had the sense to recognise the significance of Waypoint Seven; if they'd managed to cross the river, avoid the government forces, and find the site.

That was one of the needles that stopped me admiring the velvety night. The other was the witch doctor. The past twenty-four hours had been so frantic that he and his prophecy had gone largely out of my mind. But now, perhaps because we were heading back in his direction, they loomed up large again. I kept thinking about the abrupt, inexplicable blast of cold wind that had blown across the backs of our necks at the moment that kid expired.

In my head I went through the list of white deaths associated with our presence in Kamanga. Andy's was the first. The South Africans in the Beechcraft made the score two and three. The guy Joss's kangaroo court had shot was the fourth, Whinger the fifth, Sam the sixth, Genesis the seventh. The guy I'd pushed out of the chopper made the total eight, and the two Russians I'd topped made it ten. Or did it? It depended on whether you counted the pair in the Beechcraft. Their deaths had nothing to do with us; they happened before we arrived on the scene. But even if I left them out of the calculation, at eight we were getting perilously close to the predicted score – and now, with the rest of the lads gone, there were only two whites left in the action: the German woman and myself. Were both of us destined to go down?

It would have helped to share my anxieties with my companion, but I knew that if I started on about witchcraft, Jason would only give his secret smile and offer me dog-shit medicine to ward off spells. Instead, I tried to take my mind off the question by guessing where Pav and co. had got to. By now they must be in Namibia, at least, or on their way north towards home. They must think I'd lost the plot entirely. God alone knew what they'd tell the Kremlin about me. I couldn't give a flying monkey's, because it seemed unlikely I'd ever see them or Hereford again. For the time being my whole world was bounded by the need to reach the Beechcraft first.

Jason drove brilliantly, stopping to investigate every time we saw a black shadow that might conceal a deep hole, but keeping up a good pace overall. His navigation was amazing. The GPS, slotted into its cradle on the dash and framed by a shroud round its little screen, didn't seem to interest him. As far as I could tell, he never looked at its wavering green arrow, which constantly gave us our heading; rather, he kept glancing up at the sky. However it worked, his system enabled him to hold a course with incredible accuracy; when we stopped to change over just after 2100, the magic box showed that we'd covered twenty-eight kilometres, and that Waypoint Seven was only fifty ahead.

The night air was completely still, and in the silence of our break we heard hyenas howling away to the north. Then I took over and drove up into an area with more trees, until we hit on an overgrown dirt road running nearly north and south. Its pale line showed clearly in the moonlight, and Jason indicated that I should follow it, even though its direction was far from ideal. I couldn't make out whether he'd known about the track beforehand, or whether our finding it was a fluke, but I turned on to it, and for a while enjoyed the relief of being on a relatively smooth surface.

The further we drove to the north, the more sharply the arrow on the GPS swung to our right, until it was pointing at right angles to our line of advance. In twenty minutes the distance to target remained exactly the same, and I was on the point of remonstrating when Jason stood up, holding on to the grips on the dash, and told me to go slow. For a few seconds I crawled on in second, then he pointed sharply to the right, and said, 'Road to river.'

We were at a T junction – although without Jason, I'd never have known it. Even when he told me to turn, I could scarcely make out any opening between walls of bush, but when I pushed the nose of the pinkie into a gap, the vegetation parted, and a moment later we were rolling along a smooth pathway, with the vehicle's belly-plate scratching over grass and scrub.

The river took me by surprise. No dramatic valley opened out ahead; we just kept going on the level until suddenly we were on the bank, with fast-moving water glittering in the moonlight ahead of us as it flowed from left to right. The sight sent a spurt of adrenalin round my system as I tried to estimate the width of the stream. Eighty metres? A hundred?

'Jesus!' I went. 'Where's the pontoon, Jason?'

'No pontoon, sah. Now dry season, water very shallow.'

'*How* shallow?'

'So much.' He held his hands a foot apart. 'It is sand river,' he added, as if that would reassure me. 'Sand on bottom.'

'Crocs?'

'No crocs, sah.'

'Hippos?'

'Hippos gone to big river for dry season.'

'You'd better be right.'

'I walk first.'

Already he had taken off his boots. Leaving them on the seat, he got out and strode down the bank ahead of me, into the stream. At once the water was up to his knees, deeper than he'd indicated. I waited till he was four or five metres out before rolling the pinkie forward in first and easing it into the river.

The stream was surprisingly fast. Even though the tyres were on the bottom, I could feel the current lifting and tugging at the vehicle, pushing it bodily to the right. Moonlight flashed and glanced and glinted off the eddying surface, with disorientating effect. My surroundings were suddenly so mobile that I found it impossible to judge speed or distance.

Jason moved steadily ahead, sometimes ankle-deep, sometimes in as far as mid-thigh. Water invaded the floor of the pinkie, but I knew the air intake was level with the top of the engine, and I wasn't worried. Twice Jason stopped when he came to deeper holes. Each time he moved crabwise upstream to go round them, and I followed him, three or four metres behind.

Everything went fine until we were within twenty metres of the far bank. Then I felt the wheels starting to judder. Without any guidance from me the pinkie slewed round until it was facing straight upstream, and came to a halt with water surging past either front mudguard. I gunned the engine furiously: no result. The same in reverse. Even with the current helping, the vehicle wouldn't move backwards. We'd run into a patch of softer sand and bellied.

'Shit!' I went. 'Shit! Shit!'

At my shouts, Jason turned and waded back alongside.

'Have to winch it,' I said. 'I need to keep the engine running fast, to stop water coming up the exhaust. D'you know how to release the cable?'

'Yasir,' he went.

Round the front of the vehicle he plunged his arms into the water, feeling for the catch. I felt a prick, sitting there in the dry as he waded off with the shackle in his hands. Luckily, there were trees growing on the far bank, and when Jason went ashore he disappeared among them, swallowed by the moon shadows. I waited till a call came over the water, then engaged the winch, hauled the steering wheel over to the right, in the direction of the bank, and gunned the engine. The cable juddered and jumped on the drum as tension came on it. Inch by inch the vehicle rotated. Then the tyres again got a grip and hauled it forward. In a couple of minutes I reached the bank.

Beyond the river the track continued eastwards for a couple of kilometres, then turned away to the north. By then the GPS was giving a course to target of ninety-eight degrees, south of east, and a distance to target of twenty-three kilometres.

'We can't afford to head any further north,' I said. 'We've got to go straight for it.'

Jason said nothing, but threw out an arm, again on precisely the right heading.

On we went, following the green arrow, climbing gently now. We were back in mopane scrub. Hundreds of slender saplings bristled up all round us, black in the moonlight, but they were growing well apart, and it was easy to weave between them. I remembered Joss telling me that areas like this had been destroyed by elephants when the population was excessive. Over-browsing had killed off huge tracts of forest. But that was before the civil war. Now that most of the elephants had been shot out, the trees were re-establishing themselves.

The ground was hard and bare and scattered with loose stones. Several times a pebble was squeezed out from under one of the tyres and flew into a larger piece of rock with a sharp crack. Again and again a smell of soot told us that we were crossing areas where fires had swept through the scrub, and at one point, as we cleared a low ridge, we saw flames on the skyline far off to our left. After that the terrain kept rising.

'Eh, Jason,' I went. 'Are we on the back of the Totani Hills already?'

'Yassir. These the hills. Broken aircraft other side.'

I felt a surge of excitement. We were closing in on the target. I was pretty certain we'd have to complete the last few kilometres of the trip on foot; remembering how steep the ground was on the north side of the range – all those rocky ledges – I reckoned it would be impossible to drive over the ridge. In any case, it would be safer to leave the pinkie on the south face of the ridge and tab over. That way, we could creep down on the site from above in a silent approach.

By 0230 the GPS was giving us a distance to target of only seventeen kilometres. With three hours to go before first light, we had time in hand. All the same, we didn't hang about. Having changed places, we carried straight on, with Jason driving.

Fifteen minutes later, he gave a sudden exclamation. The pinkie was veering off to the right, downhill, and when he heaved on the steering wheel, trying to straighten up, it kept going.

'Puncture?' I went.

'Yassir.'

'Stop, then.'

I jumped out. Sure enough, the tyre was flat and the wheel-rim had buried itself in gravel.

'Grab the jack,' I told him. 'On the bulkhead between front and back seats. The brace is there too, in the clips. I'll get the spare.'

The spare wheel was held in place by a jumbo-sized wing-nut. I'd just started to turn it when I put a hand on the tyre itself and with a jolt realised that it, too, was flat. Obviously the lads had had a puncture earlier, and had had no chance to repair it.

'Jason!' I called. 'Stop. Bin that. This one's down as well. We're fucked. It's feet or nothing now.'

All at once, from being ahead of the clock, we were under pressure. I was determined to be on target at first light. Fifteen kilometres to go, and less than three hours in which to cover them. Before we started, I had to get the coordinates of our position, so that we'd be able to find the vehicle again. The wait for satellites was agonising, but in fact three came up pretty fast, and I pushed the button to save the figures as Waypoint Eleven.

Then, rapidly, we stowed essentials into belt-kits and Bergens: GPS and spare batteries, satcom, ammunition, explosive, det cord, food, water bottles, mozzie nets, torches. My final act was to pull out the ignition key and hide it under a flat stone a few metres away .

'See that?' I said. 'If either of us ever comes back here, that's where it will be.'

With that we set off uphill, walking hard across the contours as the lie of the land became steadily steeper. Thin as he was, Jason moved easily under his loaded pack. He was as wiry and tough as anyone I'd ever seen.

Somehow, the problem of getting out of there, of returning to civilisation, didn't worry me. I was so hell-bent on nailing Muende and Inge that nothing else seemed to matter. At the back of my mind was the fact that I had the satcom, and could always call for help if I had to; but the urgency of the task in hand stopped me pursuing the idea of exfiltration very far.

We were coming off the ridge when first light began to break in the sky ahead of us. At ground level the dark was still too intense for any landmark to be visible, but as soon as we started down over that series of ledges, the terrain felt familiar, even though we were approaching the site from the opposite direction. When the GPS began giving us four hundred metres to target, I put it away so that I could concentrate on eyeballing the slope ahead.

I knew the remains of the Beechcraft were lying in one of the hollows beneath us. The more I'd thought things over during the night, the more I'd convinced myself that we were going to find Muende and the woman bashaed up on the site. I just felt sure they'd reached the place as dark was falling, and made a camp beside the wreck. The danger was that we'd come on them suddenly, with our heads showing over the skyline, so we moved down inches at a time. As I'd expected, Jason was excellent at stalking: his feet made no sound, and his eyes never stopped ranging about.

In the end, it was the smell that told us we'd reached journey's end. Jason, a step ahead of me, turned his head, pointedly holding his nose between thumb and forefinger. Then I got it: a stench of rotting meat foul enough to make my gorge rise. When he held out a hand, indicating to our right, I just made out the hunched form of a hyena skulking away up the hill.

The light was still grey and thick when I eased my head round a rock and peeped over into the hollow, fifty metres below. There was the wreck, just as I remembered it. I was seeing it from above rather than below, but everything corresponded to the images in my mind: the broken fuselage, upside-down, with its nose high off the ground, the crumpled tail fin, the skeletal, blackened wings with the left tip ripped away, the scorched grass. The sight brought back a searing memory of Whinger on fire. I fought it down and continued to search.

The only pieces missing from the picture were the bodies of the South Africans. They'd been moved. No – they'd been torn apart. In the growing light I made out a scatter of bones and, further off, a heap of what had been sand-coloured clothes. That was the source of the stench. The bundle contained the last small remnant of a body, no doubt now heaving with maggots.

For five minutes I stood still, watching for any movement in the hollow or on the hillside below. The eastern horizon was flaring crimson. Then, I whispered, 'Stay here and cover me while I take a closer look.' Jason nodded, and settled his 203 over a rock.

I was just starting to move when a noise brought me to a halt. It was very faint – a soft, distant pop – but definitely not natural.

'That sounded like a shot,' I said. 'A long way off, but a shot all the same.'

Jason didn't answer. After another wait, I set off. Carefully picking my way down, I came out into the hollow – and part of my fantasy died. Nobody could have bashaed up there: the smell of death was suffocating. Trying to ignore it, I moved towards the front of the plane.

I stopped short. Under the nose cone was a pile of rocks. With horrible certainty I knew they hadn't been there before; somebody had collected them and piled them to a height of half a metre to make a platform, so that he or she could reach up to the front of the fuselage. I looked up. Sure enough, the small door in the side of the nose, giving access to the luggage compartment, was slightly open. I slipped off my Bergen, stood on the rock pile, reached up, pulled myself up on my hands and looked in. The small, white-walled compartment was empty.

Bastards! They'd beaten us to it. Disappointment and anger crashed down on me like a ton of lead. All the fantastic effort we'd made, only to reach the site too late.

I looked up towards Jason and waved at him to come down. In a few seconds, he was beside me.

'They've been already,' I said, quietly. 'That pile of stones wasn't there before. They built it so they could reach up high enough.'

Jason said nothing, but dropped into a squat and studied the ground intently, first round the stones, then in a wider circle. I moved off and got behind a rock that commanded the immediate area. As I leant on it, feeling knackered, the sun burst over the horizon with its usual flamboyance and flooded the hillside with light. My mind flew to Genesis and his final utterance.

Presently, Jason moved up to me, and said, 'Three persons come.'

'*Three?*'

'Yassir. Two mens, one woman. Woman with bad foot.'

I felt the hair on my neck bristling. The woman with the bad foot was Inge, presumably with Muende. But who was the second man?

'How can you tell?' I asked.

Leading me, he pointed at a faint mark in a patch of dust. 'This woman foot. Left side, turning in.' With his hand he demonstrated a twisted ankle. Then he moved on and showed me two other marks, one in some grass, one among pebbles, both almost invisible. 'One man here, one here.'

'When were they here? Yesterday?'

'No sah. In the night-time.'

'Just now?'

'Yassir.'

'Jesus! Let's get after them. They must have gone down. And listen, Jason.'

'Yassir?'

'If we catch up with them, we're going to drop all three. Okay?'

'Sure, sure!'

That was the most enthusiastic remark I'd ever heard him make.

SEVENTEEN

We went forward to the next little ridge, scanning down. By then the sun was fully up, shining right in our faces, making it difficult to see.

'That's where the rest of you waited while we came to investigate the crash,' I said, indicating the stand of trees under which Alpha had parked.

Jason nodded, but he seemed disinclined to head that way. I stood still, on the lookout, while he made a few casts downhill. He came back frowning and moved off in the opposite direction, going left-handed along the contour. Almost at once he looked back with a grin and beckoned me forward.

Once again, I could scarcely make out the evidence he'd spotted, but he was confident. 'All come this way.' He pointed ahead decisively. He was speaking in a very low voice, as if he thought our quarry was close in front.

Soon I realised how phenomenally sharp his eyes must be. He would point to a single stalk of grass bent over, the faintest impression in dry gravel, and read a whole story from it. His method was basically the same as mine, but his perception was on a different level. It was as if he could see everything through a magnifying glass – and, of course, he'd been practising every day of his life.

Now, with the early sun on our backs, the ground ahead was brilliantly illuminated. My instinct was to hustle on and overtake the party ahead of us. The trouble was, our forward visibility was limited by the curve of the hill bending away from us, and by the constant rock ledges, dropping down; if we hurried, we might lose the trail or, worse, come on the others unexpectedly. Our paramount need was to move so stealthily that we took them by surprise. If we managed that, we'd catch them with the diamond on them, whereas if they got any warning, they might have time to drop it, throw it into the bush or conceal it under a rock.

Jason was advancing in small spurts: he'd gaze at the ground, go forward a few metres, pause and gaze again. Then he stopped altogether. His body stiffened. Looking ahead intently, he unshipped his 203 and brought it to bear. I followed his gaze and caught a flicker of movement beside a shrub, fifty metres ahead. It hadn't been grass waving – there wasn't a breath of wind.

We stood still, watching. Another movement, uphill to the left. Something came up above a smooth rock. Pointed ears, then a whole head, looking back at us. Another hyena, or the same one circled back. It watched us for a few moments, then ducked and disappeared.

Jason lowered his weapon, but still he did not move. Clearly he was puzzled by the scavenger's behaviour. When nothing else stirred, he at last went forward again. Fifty metres on, part of the mystery was explained. In a depression among the rocks lay a body: a black soldier, face down, wearing DPMs, with an AK47 on the ground beside him.

For fully a minute Jason kept still. From my position beside him I could see his eyes flickering back and forth as he studied our immediate surroundings, searching, calculating possibilities. Only when he felt secure did he go down to the casualty.

One glance was enough to tell us what had happened. The man had been shot between the shoulderblades, point-blank. The muzzle of the weapon that killed him had been pressed right against his back: around the bullet hole in his tunic scorch marks radiated. At our approach flies rose in a cloud from the wound, but the body was still warm. When we turned it over, we saw the blood from the exit wound had hardly started to congeal.

'How long?' I asked.

'One hour,' went Jason. 'Maybe less.'

'That was the shot I heard.'

He nodded. The man looked young – barely twenty – and fit, with a lean face and just the shadow of a moustache. Obviously a squaddie. But why had he been murdered out here?

My imagination, working overtime, rapidly constructed a scenario. Muende had brought this guy along as a bodyguard, maybe because he understood how to use a GPS. Perhaps this was the very guy who'd nicked my GPS off me at the convent, and he'd been forced into the expedition as a penance. Anyway, once they'd got the diamond, Muende decided to dispense with him, to stop him talking. Or maybe he became scared that his bodyguard might turn on him and the woman and murder both of them, to get the big rock for himself. Whatever the precise motivation, the fact that the others had left the AK47 lying by the body showed they themselves were well armed, and needed no more weapons.

All this I communicated to Jason in short takes. Several times he nodded agreement. As I talked, a peculiar look came into his eyes as his normal calm gaze turned into a glare of hatred or anger.

We left the body and rifle where they were and moved on. After four or five steps Jason bent down and retrieved something from the grass – an empty 9mm cartridge case ejected from a pistol or a sub-machine gun. Even I could tell that the smell of cordite coming out of it was absolutely fresh.

The line Jason was following began to take us down across the slope and towards the trees. Now we could look out from the side of the hill over the flatter terrain below, but the scattered forest covered quite a large proportion of the ground and provided any number of hiding places.

We moved on yet again. Then the changing perspective abruptly revealed something shiny, something man-made, showing through a gap in the canopy of a sausage tree. I touched Jason's shoulder and pointed. At once he sank down on his haunches.

'Car,' he said, quietly.

The shiny object was the windscreen of a vehicle. The leaves on the tree were so still that we had to keep going forward, a few metres at a time, before we lined up on an opening that allowed us to see more of it. The fifth or sixth short advance revealed the outlines of a Gaz jeep.

'That's them,' I whispered.

Looking back below us, I saw that if we withdrew out of sight and dropped down, we'd be able to close in on the vehicle unseen from behind a gravelly mound that lay below us. I started to whisper my plan to Jason, but I'd hardly started when he nodded vigorously, and I knew he'd had the same idea.

Ten minutes later we crept up the back of the mound, raised our heads with infinite caution, and peered round the loose stones on the top. The jeep was rear end-on to us. It had a canvas top, but the back was rolled up so that we could see straight through it, over the front seats and out through the windscreen. There was no human in it or near it.

For five minutes we lay and watched. As the seconds ticked by, I became possessed by the feeling that somebody was watching us from the clumps of trees and bush round about. I convinced myself the jeep had been left there as a decoy or booby-trap, that if we approached it the enemy would open fire on us from somewhere close, or it would blow up.

'D'you think there's anyone around?' I whispered.

Jason shook his head. 'People gone, sah.'

Maybe my own feeling was sheer imagination. By then I'd learned to respect Jason's intuition. I knew he could notice things and pick up vibes that passed me by. So I didn't ask, 'How d'you know?' Instead, I said quietly, 'Okay, then. Cover me while I go forward.'

There was no point in moving slowly now. I hustled into the open quite fast, 203 at the ready, ran to the vehicle, dropped down beside it. Lying there, I could see under its belly. As I looked out through the opening framed by the front wheels, I realised something was out of place: a slender rod, coming down to the ground at an angle. The track-rod was broken. The jeep's steering was knackered. It had been abandoned.

I jumped up. Sure enough, the key was in the dash. I beckoned Jason forward and showed him what I'd found. We opened the bonnet and laid hands on the engine. Its temperature was hardly higher than that of the air.

'This happened on their way in,' I said. 'In the early hours of the morning. They walked from here, and now they're walking out.'

We made a quick check of the vehicle, but there was nothing in it to give a clue as to the nature of its crew. The occupants had taken whatever kit they had with them.

'Where can they be heading?' I asked.

Jason spread his hands.

'No town anywhere near? No villages?'

He shook his head. 'Next place is Narombo – small town.'

'How far's that?'

'Four day good walker. Sick woman six, seven day.'

'They'll never make that. Muende can't walk that far. He's fat as butter.'

For the first time in days Jason gave a little laugh. I grinned back, and pulled a water-bottle out of my belt-kit. We were going to have to watch it with our water; expecting a short, sharp contact, I hadn't brought very much.

'They won't walk all day,' I said. 'They'll stop soon and sit out the midday heat. We'll catch up with them then.'

The diversion caused by the vehicle cost us dearly. By the time we'd climbed back up the hill, the trail had gone cool, almost cold. Bent stalks of grass had straightened, and the dew had long since burnt off. Even Jason had a job to detect traces, and he made frequent moves that turned out to be false: he'd go ahead on a speculative quest while I stood still to mark the end of the sure route, then come back and cast about again.

I kept thinking, Muende must have been desperate, to come out here with a lone woman, one jeep and no back-up, and then to shoot his only able-bodied accomplice. Once again I saw what damage colossal wealth, or even the promise of it, does to you. It stops you trusting anybody else, so that you immediately become isolated and get forced into crazy actions.

By 1100 the heat was ferocious. The sun was beating straight down on us, and tsetse flies were bombing out of every bush we passed. Lines of sweat were running down Jason's scrawny neck from behind his ears, and he was stinking like cat's piss. High above us enormous birds had begun to ride the thermals, swinging in wide, wide circles. When I pointed up at them and suggested, 'Eagles?', Jason said, 'Vultures. White-headed vultures.' Any minute now, I thought, they'll be plummeting on to the fresh corpse behind us.

I happened to have looked at Andy's watch a moment earlier, so I know it was 1124 when, in the middle of quite a fast advance, my tracker stopped short and raised his right hand with index finger extended to our right front.

'Go-away bird,' he said, softly.

I had to listen for several seconds before I heard it. Then I picked up the raucous *go-wee, go-wee* of a grey lourie scolding some interloper who had trespassed into its territory.

'Has it seen us?' I whispered.

Jason shook his head. 'Too far. Other persons.'

That bird was a star. For the next half hour, as we worked our way steadily forward, it kept calling. Every now and then it moved to a different tree, but it hung around the same area, persistently giving out its mocking cry. We saw it once – a flash of pale grey, with a spiky tuft on the back of its head, as it looped from one perch to another – and at the end we knew there was a chance it had started to mob us as well. But by then it had done a brilliant job, leading us to a particular spot and putting us on maximum alert.

It was Jason who saw the pair first. They were sitting on the ground in an ebony grove, their backs against a big tree, looking utterly knackered. Inge had her head thrown back, resting against the trunk; Muende's was hanging down, chin on chest, as if he were asleep. His peculiar, yellowish hair was unmistakable. Beside each of them was an open haversack.

The sight sent a huge surge of adrenalin round my system, part excitement, part hatred of the pair who had murdered Whinger. We could easily have dropped both of them from where we stood, behind some bushes sixty metres off. They had no clue that anyone was near them, and there was no way we could have missed. A couple of bursts from the 203s, and that would have been that. But it would also have been too easy. Before I killed them, I wanted to look in their faces and let them see me. I wanted to tell them what I thought of them. I wanted them to know that retribution had caught up with them and run them down. So I breathed 'This way' to Jason, and we moved silently round to our left until we were behind them, hidden by the trunk of their own tree. Then we walked straight in. Whatever else happened, I was going to make them shit themselves with fright.

Twenty metres short of the tree, I motioned Jason to stay put and cover me. I eased myself out of the straps of my Bergen and lowered it gently to the ground. Then I crept forward alone with my 203 at the ready. The lourie was still calling away to our right front. Apart from that there was no sound.

I came to within four metres of the tree. Three. It may have been a slight scuffle that my boot made on a dry leaf. It may have been a sixth sense of danger. Whatever triggered her reflex, Inge suddenly leapt into view, going to my left with amazing agility. Already she was facing my way, and there was a pistol in her right hand.

Before she could bring it to bear, before I could raise my own rifle, a three-round burst hammered out behind me. The rounds cracked like thunderbolts as they passed my ear and put the woman flat on her back. For a moment she writhed about, struggling to get up, but the pistol had fallen from her hand and I could see she was dying.

I stood braced, with the rifle in my hands, finger on the trigger, ready for Muende to appear. When he didn't, I yelled, 'Come out!'

The trunk of the ebony was nearly a metre thick, and although I knew he was there, about ten feet from me, I couldn't see any part of him. Glancing at Inge, I saw she'd stopped moving.

I took a step to my right, then another. After the second, I could see boots – black, army-type boots with the heels together, toes pointing downwards. The guy was stretched out on his front, grovelling into the earth. Two more steps, and his whole body was in view. He was wearing pale-coloured, lightweight DPMs, and had his face pressed into a groove between two large roots, as though he was trying to shut out the danger. His forehead was against the base of the trunk, hands clasped on top of his head. There was a sub-machine gun lying on the ground beside him, but it was out of his reach.

I went forward and kicked him in the ribs. 'On your feet, cunt!' I shouted.

His eyes were rolling as he looked up at me. For a few seconds he seemed paralysed by fear. Then, slowly, he hauled himself up and stood shaking with his back against the tree.

'All right, Muende,' I went. 'You know who I am.'

He ran his tongue round his lips as he shook his head. 'No,' he said. 'I've never seen you in my life.'

'You fucking have. It was me you had beaten up the other night. The night you tortured my mate and ate his liver. You may have been pissed, but you can't have forgotten.'

As comprehension dawned, the guy's terror increased. He began to shake so violently that drops of sweat went flying in all directions off his forehead.

'What do you want?'

'The diamond. That's all.'

'What diamond?'

'The one you've just recovered from the plane.'

'Look,' he said, 'take it easy. There's some mistake here.'

He sounded pure American, and for a few moments his easy natural authority started to assert itself. But I wasn't in a mood to argue.

I drove the muzzle of the 203 hard into the top of his bulging stomach, stepped back, and said, 'You've got thirty seconds to produce it.'

He doubled forward with a gasp. As he straightened up again, his bloodshot eyes went from the barrel of the rifle to my face and back. Then, he said, 'You win.'

'Where is it?'

'On my belt.'

I looked at his midriff and saw a pouch of thick black canvas. It was too small to contain a pistol, the wrong shape for a knife.

'Okay,' I said. 'Take the belt off and throw it to me. Then get your hands above your head.'

He did as ordered. The belt landed at my feet. I picked it up and withdrew another pace. The pouch was modern, with a Velcro fastener on the flap. With one hand I ripped it open. Inside was a suede leather bag with something hard inside.

It needed teeth as well as fingers to pull out the string round the neck of the bag, but at last I got it open and looked down. There, in the nest of blue suede, sat a lump of what looked like brilliantly flashing glass. Forget pigeon's eggs, this thing was the size of a chicken's egg, for God's sake. The sight of it made my breath catch. I closed the bag by folding the long neck over and rolling it round, then stowed it in my right-hand belt pouch.

Muende's eyes had followed every movement of the stone, as if it were magnetic. Then, suddenly, he came away from the tree a couple of paces.

'Stop!' I yelled.

But he was only trying to buy time. He went down on his knees, with his hands together up in front of him, like he was praying in church.

'Look!' he cried, in a high, beseeching voice. 'You've got it! You're going to be rich for the rest of your life. You don't ever need to work again.'

I was too fired up to feel embarrassed at this grovelling. I just felt hatred, mixed with contempt. All I spat at him was, 'So?'

'Who gave you the diamond? *I* did! You don't need to shoot me. It won't get you anywhere.'

The guy was screaming pitifully. Still I just glared at him. Then, I said, 'Don't worry. I'm not going to shoot you.'

He didn't know what I meant. How could he? He couldn't see what I could see. Jason was silently creeping up on him from behind. But until the last second even I didn't realise what my trusty henchman was planning.

Suddenly, I saw that in his right hand he was holding aloft his fearsome machete. From a metre behind Muende, he sprang.

The blade flashed through dappled sunlight and buried itself – *thunk!* – in the right-hand side of its victim's neck. The blow was so violent that it almost severed the head. Blood spurted from the jugular, fountaining on to the ground at my feet. With half a groan the self-styled President of Free Kamanga toppled sideways to the ground. Before his limbs had stopped twitching, Jason swung in a back-handed second strike from the other side and cut through the rest of the neck. The next thing I knew, the head came rolling towards my feet with the eyes still opening and shutting.

I stood rooted, too shocked to speak. Jason was exactly the opposite. He went stomping off round the ebony glade, throwing back his head, letting off triumphant yells, leaping in the air, whirling his machete in fancy passes above his head. His wildness scared me shitless. What if he decided he wanted the diamond for himself?

The headless body kept quivering. I walked away from it and sat down heavily on a fallen log with my back to the scene of the massacre. The first thing I needed was a drink. My hands were shaking as I unscrewed the cap of the water-bottle. I took two big gulps, then steeled myself to save the rest.

It was several minutes before I'd chilled out enough to look at the diamond again, and when I got it in the palm of my hand I began to shake again, from wonder at the sheer size and brilliance of the stone. It didn't take an expert to see that this was one in a million, worth millions. I stared into its glittering depths half mesmerised. Here in my hand I held a secure future, not only for myself and Tim, but for all the survivors of the team. I thought of the night we'd sat round the fire with Rhino Bakunda, joking about what we'd do if we won the lottery. Well, now Pav would be able to hire Concorde and go screwing in the South Seas, Chalky could buy his yacht, Danny his arms business.

Or would any of that happen? Immediately, I began to think of problems. Number one: in the SAS you're supposed to hand in any booty that comes your way. Often, with minor gains, the lads ignore the rules, but what would I do with something of such value? Number two: the diamond would have to be cut before it was worth anything. How would I find a cutter or a dealer who could be relied on to keep quiet? Would I get landed with an asset I couldn't cash in?

Suddenly, a gust of wind got up. I heard it coming, a stir in the ebony grove. Leaves began to flutter, branches swung, and a cool blast of air came swirling past me from behind. In that stifling noonday heat any drop in temperature should have been welcome. But to me it was sinister and full of menace, because I instantly associated it with the night that Phil, Mart and I had stood in front of the witch doctor, when the child had died.

The breeze died away as quickly as it had come. All round me the leaves settled. Except for the go-away bird, which was still calling, stillness returned to the trees. I glanced across to see what Jason was doing. He'd gone down on his knees at the foot of a tree, and appeared to be praying, giving thanks.

I looked back at the great rock. Why had that wind come at the very moment I held it in my hand? Was it a natural phenomenon, caused by the hot air rising somewhere else, and the shape of the grove we were in? A couple of months before I'd have said it was. I'd have believed the timing of it was pure coincidence. Now I wasn't so sure. What I did know for certain was that I wanted nothing more to do with the diamond. No matter how many millions it might be worth, I knew it would only bring me bad luck. I didn't even want to look at it any more. Hurriedly, I fumbled it back into the blue bag and drew the neck strings together.

Jason was back on his feet and walking towards me with a big grin on his face. Skirting the bodies, I went to meet him. As we met he put up his right hand, palm forward, and I smacked mine against it – high fives, like footballers celebrating a goal.

'Fucking great!' I went. 'You got 'em.'

'Yassir! They don't make no more trouble.'

'Not for us,' I said. 'Not for anyone.'

Flies were already clustering on the fresh blood. Africa would deal with the bodies in short order.

'Jason,' I said, holding out the blue bag, 'you'd better have this.'

He took it in his long, elegant fingers and held it in both hands.

'Open it,' I told him. 'Have a look.'

Once again the diamond blazed in a shaft of sunlight, bright as a halogen lamp, *so* bright that I had to look away. Jason gave a whistle, and stared in astonishment.

'Ever seen one like that?' I asked.

He shook his head.

'Take it, anyway.'

'No, sah. It is for you, not me.' He held the damned thing out towards me.

'I don't want it.' I waved it away. 'I want you to have it. But be careful. Don't mention it to anyone. If somebody knows you've got it, they'll kill you for it. Take it to Mulongwe and sell it there, quickly. You'll be a rich man for the rest of your life – big house, car, television, everything.'

For what seemed a long time, he held it steadily in his fingers, gazing at it. Then he looked up at me, said, '*Zikomo*, sah,' very gracefully, and slipped it back into the bag.

As he stowed it in a belt-pouch I sensed immediate relief, as if a burden had been lifted from me. At the same time I felt entirely disorientated. I had to think hard to remember where the hell we were, and even harder to dream up some way of getting back to civilisation.

'So,' I began. 'The first thing is to head for the pinkie and mend that puncture. D'you know where it is?'

'Yassir.' He made one of his expansive gestures, flinging out a hand and pointing back up the hill. I'd been on the point of digging in my bergen for the GPS, but by then I trusted Jason's sense of direction implicitly, and was happy to walk on the line he gave.

I never went near the body of the German woman, or even took a close look at it. Like the diamond, she was already part of my past. We just pulled on our Bergens and left the ebony glade to the go-away bird who lived there.

Two hours later we were back at the pinkie. Jason helped

mend the punctures in both tyres, and as we worked he explained how, if I skirted the hills to the west, I would pick up another dirt road running northwards. With the wheels back in place, I emptied the last jerrican of diesel into the tank, and by 1500 I was ready to move.

Until the last moment, I assumed Jason was coming with me. He'd given no indication of having any other plan. But when I said, 'Right, all aboard,' he replied, 'I go this way,' and gestured to the east.

I was taken aback. For one thing, he was an extremely valuable escort. For another, I didn't like the thought of him alone, on foot, in that hostile environment. But when I asked, 'Are you sure?' he simply nodded, and I knew there was no point in arguing.

'Good luck, then. Got plenty of water?'

He nodded, patting the full bottles in his belt-kit.

'And thanks for all your help.' I grinned, holding out my hand.

He took it in a firm grip, and said, with a smile, '*Zikomo!*' and then '*Nayenda.*'

'What does that mean?'

'I am walking away.'

I banged him on his bony shoulder, climbed into the driving seat, started up and set off downhill. The last I saw of him, he was striding away over the big rocks.

Three or four hundred metres on, I came out on to a low ridge and stopped. Looking back, I had a long view of the mountainside behind. Jason should have been in sight. He couldn't have reached the far skyline already. Yet somehow he'd vanished. For three or four minutes I sat watching, expecting him to emerge from a gully or hollow. Yet in all that arid landscape, nothing moved. Africa seemed to have swallowed my faithful companion, and I drove on, knowing I would never see him again.

EIGHTEEN

Soon after Tim and I had eaten our packed lunch on the summit of Pen-y-Fan, the last of the clouds blew away and the band of rain gave way to a golden autumn afternoon. The sunshine, soft and gentle after the glare of Africa, encouraged me to keep talking and talking.

So did Tim. I didn't tell him all the gory details, of course: for instance, I only said that Whinger had been executed, and that at the end Jason had shot Muende. But I gave him a pretty good account of what had happened. Several times I sent him running off round some minor landmark, to keep his blood moving and give myself a break, and when he came back he was always full of questions. The longer we talked, the more I admired his intelligence, and his desire to get things straight.

He'd almost floored me, early on, when he said, 'If you die, Dad, what's going to happen to me?'

The question caught me below the belt, and I tried to turn it aside by saying jokily, 'Who said I'm going to die? I'm not planning on that yet.'

'No,' he persisted. 'But where will I live?'

I told him he could stay on with his gran and gramp, or with his cousins.

But there was something pathetic about his anxiety. I could see he felt thoroughly insecure, and whose fault was it that he had no proper home?

It was better when we kept to Africa.

'That scar on your cheek,' he said. 'How did you get that?'

'Somebody slammed me with a rifle butt. Mart wanted to put stitches in the cut, but we didn't have time.'

His next question was, 'How did you get out?'

'Luck, really,' I told him. 'I drove most of that first night. When it started to get light, I lay up again. I had food and water, remember. I was nearly out of fuel, so I was just planning to drive until the engine cut. But when I started again the next night, I came on a truck that had crashed into a ditch and been abandoned. Nobody had bothered to drain the tank, so I did it for them.'

'How d'you drain a tank?'

'With a piece of pipe. We'd been carrying one in the pinkie for that very purpose. You push one end down into the tank, and suck back until the fuel's almost at the top. Then you bend the tube down until your end's lower than the other one, and the petrol or diesel runs out into your can.'

Tim considered this, frowning, then said, 'But why does it run?'

'Gravity. Once you've got it going, it works fine. But you have to be careful not to suck too hard, or you get the stuff in your mouth, and it tastes horrible.' I glanced down at him, and went on, 'Anyway, then I had enough diesel to drive back to the place where we flew Andy's body out from. Remember - where we cleared a strip of road? Luckily, the coordinates for that were still in Stringer's GPS. With the satcom I got a message out to Hereford. They contacted the civilian pilot who air-lifted Andy's body, and he came and picked me up in his Cessna.'

'Then what?'

'I thought I might get arrested if anyone saw me in Mulongwe. So I got him to fly me to Harare, which is a bit friendlier.'

'Did you pay him?'

'I couldn't. I didn't have a single *kwatcha* on me.'

'What's a *kwatcha*?'

'Kamangan money. One *kwatcha* is worth about a hundredth of a penny.'

'Who did pay him, then?'

'The Regiment, I hope. I told him to e-mail a bill to Hereford.'

Tim scuffed his trainers together, and asked, 'How big was the diamond, exactly?'

'I can't say *exactly*. But about like this.' I held up finger and thumb. 'It must be one of the biggest ever found. Worth millions if it's sound. They have to cut tiny pieces off, to see if there are any flaws.'

'You ought to have kept it, then.'

'I told you, I had a feeling it would bring bad luck. I didn't *dare* keep it. Somehow the witch doctor had put a spell on it. Look what it did to Muende and the German woman.'

'What were *they* going to do with it?'

'Good question. Apparently they were planning to do a runner – leave the country altogether. Interpol – that's the police – found out they were going to do a bunk to Mexico. That shows you how powerful the diamond was. Is, I mean. For months Muende had been directing a civil war, trying to take over the country. He thought he was about to get his hands on nuclear weapons. If he'd managed that, he could have terrorised the north and taken charge of the whole of Kamanga. Then, suddenly, he had a fortune in his hands, and it went to his head. All at once politics didn't matter any more. He threw everything over, just for money.'

Tim thought for a while, then said, 'Were you going to kill them yourself?'

'I was planning on it. I was that angry. But, luckily, Jason did it for me. In the end I was glad I didn't have to.'

'Did the police interview you?'

'Of course.'

'What did you tell them about the diamond?'

'I said I threw it into a river because I knew it was unlucky.'

Another gap, and then, 'You should have gone back to the witch doctor and made him take the spell off it.'

'I thought of that. But in the end it didn't seem possible. If I'd shown him the rock, he'd have tried to claim it for himself. And if I'd reappeared in that village, where the boy died, I'd have been torn to pieces.'

'Were you scared of him?'

'Yes, I was. So was Phil. When that cold wind came, there was something going on we couldn't understand.'

'Will Jason be all right?'

'You mean medically? I don't know. I'm afraid he may have got a dose of radiation from being so close to the warheads. I hope not, but I can't be sure.'

'I really meant with the diamond.'

'Oh, I see. Well, he has magic spells of his own. All those medicines he was taking and giving other people. Who knows? Maybe one of them'll protect him.'

'How much will he get for it?'

'Only a fraction of what it's worth. He'll be cheated, for sure. But still he'll get enough to make him rich.'

Tim suddenly took off on another of his sprints, and when he came back, he panted, 'Genesis.'

'What about him?'

'You never went back.'

'Couldn't. Not a chance.'

'So he's still there.'

'Yes. He'll be there for ever, now.'

'Won't the animals dig him up?'

'I don't think they can. There was living rock under him, and we put all those stones on top.'

'He was a good man, though.'

'Yes. Sometimes he annoyed us, but he was one of the best.'

'Then why did he have to get killed?'

'I can't answer that. It's one of the mysteries of life – why good isn't always rewarded, why evil flourishes, why good people get diseases like cancer when they've done nothing to deserve it. Some people say God's fighting the Devil, but the Devil's pretty crafty and keeps hitting back.'

'You know when you got charged by the elephants?'

'Yes?'

'How many were killed?'

'People, or ellies?'

'Ellies.'

'Five or six, at least. There may have been more wounded

that went off and died somewhere else. That was horrible.'

'If you got swallowed by a crocodile, would you still be alive inside it?'

'Not for long. If you hadn't already been crunched, you'd suffocate from lack of air.'

The sun was nearly on the horizon. Time to go.

'We'd better be off,' I said.

'But, Dad, why did you bother to load up the shells, if you could have blown them up anyway?'

'I didn't know enough about it. I thought if we did that, we'd create a major hazard and put half of southern Africa at risk. As it is, there's widespread contamination of the area. The President's complained to the United Nations. He's suspended relations with Britain. It would have been better if we *could* have got them out.'

'What d'you think happened to the old man at the mine?'

'Boisset? No idea. I hope Joss didn't get suspicious of him as well, otherwise he'll have had him shot too.'

'Was it a failure, then?'

'What?'

'Your mission.'

'Our task. Well, we went out to train Alpha Commando, and we did that pretty well, for as long as they let us. But the civil war's still going on, and yes, the whole thing did go belly-up.'

'Was it your fault?'

'I don't think so. I made mistakes. Everyone makes mistakes at times. But the man who really wrecked everything was Joss. Then again, I blame the diamond. If it hadn't been for that, Joss might have stayed on-side.'

From behind us, a drift of cold evening air came blowing over the long, smooth slopes of the Beacons.

'Brrrrrrh!' I went, giving a violent shudder and jumping to my feet.

Tim stared at me in consternation. 'What's the matter, Dad?'

'That wind on the back of my neck. Like I said, ever since our session when the little kid died, it's given me the jankers.'

Still the boy was watching me. 'Dad,' he went. 'Are *you* dying?'

'What a question!' I forced myself to make a joke of it. But all I could say was, 'I don't know. I don't think so. But I'm not sure. The doctors don't know, either. I got myself a bad dose of radiation, right enough. But so far it hasn't done the damage they expected. They're giving me a fifty-fifty chance.'

'Was it that medicine Jason gave you?'

'That's going to save me? How do I know? Maybe it's helped.' I picked up my day-sack and slipped it on to my back. Long, purple shadows were stretching out over the folds in the mountains. Dusk was seeping into the valleys.

Looking down at the boy, I was disconcerted to see tears in his eyes.

'Come on,' I said, sweeping him up in my arms and sitting him on my left hip. 'On the way home we're going to drop in at Tesco's and get some things for a good fry-up, because I'm definitely not planning to snuff it today.'

'But Dad,' he persisted. 'Didn't you say the German woman was the ninth white person to die because of the spell?'

'If you leave out the two South Africans in the Beechcraft, yes.'

'Then I hope you're not going to be the tenth man down.'